The French Fantasy Treasury
Treasury
(Volume 1: The World's Edge)

IN THE SAME SERIES

The French Fantasy Treasury
(Volume 1: The World's Edge)

Texts by
**Mme d'Aulnoy, Chevalier de Béthune,
Chrétien de Troyes, Fénelon, Antoine
Galland, Mme Leprince de Beaumont,
Marie de France, Chevalier de Mouhy,
Rabelais, Marie-Anne de Roumier-Robert**
and **Tiphaigne de La Roche**

Selected by
Jean-Marc & Randy Lofficier

Translations by
**W.W. Comfort, Charles Lamb, Andrew Lang,
Eugene Mason, Peter Antony Motteux, Léonce
Rabillon, Michael Shreve, Brian Stableford** and
Sir Thomas Urquhart of Cromarty

Research by **Brian Stableford**

Cover by **Michel Borderie**

A Black Coat Press Book

Visit our website at www.blackcoatpress.com

ISBN 978-1-61227-544-4. First Printing. August 2016. Published by Black Coat Press, an imprint of Hollywood Comics.com, LLC, P.O. Box 17270, Encino, CA 91416. All rights reserved.

TABLE OF CONTENTS

Gargantua.

M. D. XXXVII.

Introduction

When embarking on a book of this kind, it is customary to start with a definition of its subject. So, what do we mean by *fantasy*? According to wikipedia, *fantasy* is

> ...*a genre of fiction that uses magic or other super-natural elements as a main plot element, theme, or setting. Many works within the genre take place in imaginary worlds where magic and magical creatures are common. Fantasy is generally distinguished from the genres of science fiction and horror by the expectation that it steers clear of scientific and macabre themes, respectively, though there is a great deal of overlap between the three, all of which are subgenres of speculative fiction.*

In French, the word *fantastique,* the nearest equivalent to *fantasy*, carries with it a much larger semantic field. According to writer Pierre Gripari (1925-1990), the simplest definition of the *fantastique* is "everything that is not rational." Within this definition, fantasy, as well as horror and science fiction, might all be viewed, as Belgian writer Jacques Sternberg (1923-2006) once put it, as mere *succursales*, or branches, of the *fantastique*.

However, while recognizing that Gripari has a point, we shall nevertheless treat *fantasy* as wikipedia suggrests, i.e. as a separate genre from the *fantastique*, and not as a mere subset. We do this because we believe that, from their very inceptions, the two reflected different literary objectives on the part of their writers, as well as filling the different literary needs of their readers.

For the purpose of this book, therefore, we shall construe *fantasy* as all of that which lies at the crossroad of the *merveilleux* and the fantastic, draws its inspiration from folklore, myths and legends and *"steers clear of scientific and macabre themes."* This approach received an official endorsement from the French Linguistic authorities who, in December 2006, finally recognized the word *fantasie* (not *fantaisie!*), as derived from the Greek *fantasia* (imagination), as an appropriate label for the genre in French.[1]

As we will see in this book, *fantasy*, whether expressed through drama, poetry or songs, first helped the medieval people illuminate the fearsome darkness in which they lived, before the Age of Enlightenment. Its lighter, more baroque side, mutated into the fairy tales of the 17th and 18th century, which eventually evolved into 19th century high fantasy, with all its romantic, symbolic and surrealistic variants, and eventually into modern-day forms.

Indeed, French fantasy has a noble and long history, quite distinct from the British and American models provided by such "founding fathers" as George MacDonald, William Morris, Lord Dunsany, Robert E. Howard and J.R.R. Tolkien—the primary reason being that none of these authors

---

[1] As Brian Stableford points out in his recent and essential work on the French *roman scientifique, The Plurality of Imaginary Worlds* (Black Coat Press, ISBN 978-1-61227-503-1): "Modern readers and critics of science fiction often try to draw a fundamental distinction between science fiction and fantasy on the ostensible grounds that marvels based in scientific speculation have a particular plausibility that marvels drawing upon the vocabulary of myth and magic do not, although the present pattern of book marketing, in which books labeled as science fiction and fantasy tend to be shelved in adjacent locations in bookshops, advertised in the same spaces and aimed at overlapping audiences strongly suggests that the distinction is largely illusory."

were translated into French until the second half of the 20th century.[2]

This first volume covers a period from the Middle Ages (c. 1100) to the French Revolution (1789). We have arranged the stories in both thematic and chronological order. Our second and third volumes will feature the rich tapestry of French Fantasy in the 19th century.

Jean-Marc & Randy Lofficier

---

[2] MacDonald's classic *Phantastes* remains untranslated today, and *The Princess and the Goblin* was first translated in 1990. Morris' *The Well at the World's End* was first translated in 2012. Dunsany's *The King of Elfland's Daugther* was first translated in 1976. Two volumes of Howard's *Conan* were first translated in 1972, but made no impact. It was only in 1980 that, helped by the release of the 1982 film, his works became best-sellers. Tolkien's *The Hobbit* was translated (but ignored) in 1969, and *The Lord of the Rings* in 1972. The fantasy works of Jack Vance were serialized in the French edition of *F&SF* in the early 1960s. Michael Moorcock's *Elric* was translated in 1969. Fritz Leiber's *Fafhrd and Gray Mouser* stories were translated in 1970.

SWORDS & SORCERY

French language, and therefore French literature, first took form in the Middle Ages. After the Roman Conquest, the Gaul dialects gave way to Latin, which evolved into a number of Romance languages, and eventually into something now called *Vieux Français*, or Old French.

It is worth noting that this development was not uniform. The language remained divided into the *langue d'oil*, employed in Northern France, and the *langue d'oc*, employed in Southern France.[3] As Northern France became politically dominant, so did the *langue d'oil*, even though the *langue d'oc* did not entirely disappear, and still survives today as Provençal and Occitan.

The first texts written in Old French that could be labeled as fantasy appeared during the reign of Emperor Charlemagne (742-814). It was under his rule that the feudal ideals of knightly behavior: courtesy, generosity, modesty, loyalty to one's liege, and consideration for the weak, first took root. Charlemagne was a great warrior-king, fighting for Christendom against the Saracens. His reign was a time of unique political stability and economic prosperity. He also encouraged scholars and writers. All these factors combined to foster a legend-making process which gave birth to French fantasy literature in the form of the Medieval Romance.

The word "romance" was derived from the Old French *romanz*, whose approximate meaning was "vernacular," and was initially used to refer to documents translated from Latin. By the twelfth century, however, the term and its evolving derivatives were more frequently and more particularly used

---

[3] These terms are derived from their respective expressions for *yes*.

11

with reference to a nascent genre of poetry and prose fiction that had moved on from translations of Latin epic poetry to prolific original composition. Just as the documents being translated had referred to what was by then a distant mythologized past, the imitations and pastiches also looked back nostalgically to a whole series of mythologized distant pasts.

This was a time when the supernatural was perceived as something to be preferably avoided, but still not outrageous or unbelievable. It was during the Middle Ages that the old Celtic, Frankish and Germanic myths were transformed from religion (implying serious belief *and* worship) into popular folklore (implying belief, but not worship).

The Catholic Church, as the dominant religion, made sure that the old myths, if they could not be eradicated, would remain just that: folklore, the latter being obviously less important than religion. In some cases, such as the Arthurian Romances, it even ensured that the myths were redressed in Christian trappings.

Finally, the Middle Ages were the period during which all the tales dealings with supernatural entities such as angels, demons, fairies, witches and warlocks, and characters familiar to modern-day fantasy readers, such as Melusine, Harlequin, Oberon, Morgan Le Fey, etc., were consolidated, unified and given modern form.

The first "sword & sorcery" epics were lengthy poetic sagas featuring knightly epics and courtly love that began as oral literature, that is to say, they were sung by wandering minstrels and troubadours. They were called *Chansons de geste*, or Songs of Deeds, and became an integral part of a vast oral tradition. Starting around the 12th century, they were eventually committed to paper by pious monks working in monastic libraries. About a hundred such *Chansons* are known to have existed.

Literary romance celebrated the kind of blending obtained by conquest and reorganization that was inherent in the actual history of feudalism, as well as the flattering ideological image that romancers tried to construct. Central to that process was the fundamental marriage of the Breton/Norman "chivalric romance," glorifying knightly prowess in combat, with the Provençal/Aquitanian "courtly romance," which offered idealized depictions of intimate relationships.

The writers were also willing, often enthusiastic allies, embracing other local folklores and superstitions, and gathering them into their melting-pot—always, of course, with the proviso that threats originating from such dubious imaginative apparatus could not withstand the ideological forces of Christian faith and knightly heroism.

It is against this background that the mythologies of Roland and Charlemagne's knights on the one hand, and later, of King Arthur and his knights on the other, were invented.

Although the legend of King Arthur was invented by Norman "historians" and developed in literary form by a French writer, it was not quintessentially French in the same way as the *Chanson de Roland* [The Song of Roland] (c. 1096). Therefore, it is not surprising that the latter remained much more to the forefront of the French imagination in later centuries, along with related *Chansons de geste* such as *Raoul de Cambrai* and, most importantly, *Renaud de Montauban*, also known as *Les Quatre Fils Aymon*.

The latter makes much of the hero's magical horse Bayard, later transferred to the ownership of Charlemagne. Like Roland, Renaud became an important character in imitative romances spun off from the Charlemagnian cycle in the Italian Renaissance, where he became Rinaldi or Rinaldo, as Roland became Orlando.

La Chanson de Roland tells of the desperate fight of Count Roland, Charlemagne's own son, against the Saracens, and his eventual doom in the Pyrenean mountain pass of Ronceval (or Roncevaux) on August 15, 778, after having been betrayed by the evil Ganelon. In reality, historical evidence would suggest that Roland was ambushed by Basque or Gascon brigands, but no minstrel ever let truth stand in the way of a great song! Charlemagne was returning from his expedition to Spain, and had left his rear-guard in command of Roland. His main army had passed unmolested; but at the moment when the rear-guard advanced into the pass, thousands of men fell upon the French army and slaughtered the whole guard to the last man.

From the moment of the defeat of Roncevaux, minstrels commenced their work to turn this heroic skirmish into a truly epic event which has found echoes throughout Europe. *La Chanson de Roland*, like most *Chansons de Geste*, contains the usual array of celestial phenomena, etc. However, it is memorable in that it features the first magical blade, Roland's sword, Durandal, as well as Roland's magical horn, Olifant.

The commentators generally agree in dating the composition of the poem before the first Crusade, in the year 1096. The author was likely Norman, as the dialect used by him is Norman throughout. According to some sources, his name might have been Turoldus, who is so credited in the last line of the poem, but this is subject to conflicting interpretations.

We have chosen to excerpt here the narrative of the battle itself when Olivier, Roland's trusted friend, first sees the Saracen army approaching and realizes they have been betrayed...

Anon.: *The Death of Roland*
(c. 1096) [4]

PRELUDE TO THE GREAT BATTLE

LXXXI.

Olivier from the summit of a hill / On his right hand looks o'er a grassy vale, / And viewed the Pagans' onward marching hordes; / Then straight he called his faithful friend Roland: "From Spain a distant rumbling noise I hear, / So many hauberks white and flashing helms / I see! This will inflame our French men's hearts. / The treason is the work of Ganelon / Who named us for this post before the King."/ "Hush! Olivier!" Count Roland replied, / "'Tis my stepfather, speak no other word."

LXXXII.

Count Olivier was posted on a hill / From whence Spain's Kingdom he descried, and all / The swarming host of Saracens; their helms / So bright bedecked with gold, and their great shields, / Their 'broidered hauberks, and their waving flags, / He couldn't count the squadrons; in such crowds / They came, his sight reached not unto their end. / Then all bewildered he descended the hill, / Rejoined the French, and all to them related.

LXXXIII.

---

[4] Excerpted from the seventh French edition of *La Chanson de Roland* (1872) prepared and adapted by Léon Gautier, translated into English in 1885 by Léonce Rabillon, introduced and annotated by Jean-Marc Lofficier.

Said Olivier: "I have seen Pagans more / Than eyes e'er saw upon the earth; at least / One hundred thousand warriors armed with shields, / In their white hauberks clad, with helmets laced, / Lances in rest, and burnished brazen spears. / Battle ye will have, such as ne'er was before. / French Lords, may God inspire you with his strength! / Stand firm your ground, that we may not succumb." / The French said: "Cursed be those who fly the field! / Ready to die, not one shall fail you here."

ROLAND'S PRIDE

LXXXIV.
Olivier said: "So strong the Pagan host; / Our French, methinks, in number are too few; / Companion Roland, sound your horn, that Carle[5] / May hear and send his army back to help." / Roland replied: "Great folly would be mine, / And all my glory in sweet France be lost. / No, I shall strike great blows with Durandal; / To the golden hilt the blade shall reek with blood. / In evil hour the felon Pagans came / Unto the Pass, for all are doomed to die!"

LXXXV.
"Roland, companion, sound your Olifant, / That Carle may hear and soon bring back the host. / With all his Baronage the king will give / Us help!" Replied Roland: "May God forefend / That for my cause my kindred e'er be blamed, / Or that dishonor fall upon sweet France. / Nay, I will deal hard blows with Durandal, / This my good sword now girt unto my side / Whose blade you'll see all reeking with red blood. / Those felon Pagans have for their ill fate / Together met; yea, death awaits them all."

---

[5] Charlemagne (Carolus Magnus).

LXXXVI.

"Companion Roland, sound your Olifant! / If Carle who passes through the mounts shall hear, / To you I pledge my word, the French return." / Answered Roland: "May God forbid! Ne'er be / It said by living man that Pagans could / Cause me to blow my horn, to bring disgrace / Upon my kin! When on the battle field, / I'll strike one thousand seven hundred blows, / And Durandal all bleeding shall you see. / The French are brave and bravely will they strike. / Those Spanish Moors are doomed to certain death."

LXXXVII.

Olivier said: "To me there seems no shame; / I have beheld the Moors of Spain; they swarm / O'er mountains, vales and lands, hide all the plains; / Great is this stranger host; our number small." / Roland replied: "The more my ardor grows. / God and his blessed angels grant that France / Lose naught of her renown through my default. / Better to die than in dishonor than live. / The more we strike, the more Carle's love we gain!"

LXXXVIII.

Roland was brave and Olivier was wise; / Both knights of wond'rous courage, and in arms / And mounted on their steeds, they both would die / Ere they would shun the fight. Good were the Counts / And proud their words. The Pagan felons rode / In fury on! "Roland," said Olivier, / "One moment, look! Our foes so close, and Carle / Afar from us! You have not deigned to blow / Your horn! If came the king, no hurt were ours. / Cast your eyes toward the great defiles of Aspre; / There see this most unhappy rear-guard. Those / Who here fight, ne'er shall fight on other fields." / Roland retorted: "Speak not such shameful words. / Woe unto him who bears a coward's heart / Within his breast. There firm shall we remain; / The combat and the blows from us shall come."

LXXXIX.

Now when Roland the battle saw at hand, / More than a leopard's or a lion's pride / He showed. He called the French and Olivier: / "Companion, friend, pray, speak of this no more. / The Emperor who left his French in trust / To us, has chosen those twenty thousand men. / Right well he knows none has a coward's soul. / A man should suffer hurt for his good lord, / Endure great cold or scorching heat, and give / Even to his flesh and blood! Strike with your lance, / And I with Durandal, my trusty sword, / Carle's gift. If here I die, may he who wins / It, say: "'Twas once the sword of a brave knight."

XC.

Turpin the Archbishop from another side, / Spurring his courser, mounted a hill and called / The French around. This sermon to them he spoke: / "Seigneurs Barons, Carle left us here: for him, / Our King, our duty is to die, to aid / In saving Christendom, the Faith of Christ / Uphold. There, battle will ye have, for there / Before your eyes behold the Saracens. / Confess your sins, and for God's mercy pray! / For your soul's cure I absolution give. / If you should die, as holy martyrs ye / Will fall, and places find in Paradise!" / The French alight'd and fell upon their knees; / The Godly Archbishop granted them benison, / Giving for penance his command to strike.

XCI.

The French arose. They stood assoiled and quit / Of all sins, blessed by Turpin in God's name. / On swift destriers [6] they mounted, armed cap-a-pie / As Knights arrayed for battle. Count Roland / Called Olivier: "Companion, sire, full well / You know, it is Count Ganelon who has / Betrayed us all, and guerdon [7] rich received / In gold and silver; well the Emperor

---

[6] Battlehorses.
[7] Reward.

should / Avenge us! King Marsile [8] a bargain made / Of us, but swords will make the reckoning good."

XCII.
Through the defiles of Spain hath passed Roland / Mounted on Veillantif, his charger swift / And strong, bearing his bright and glittering arms. / On goes the brave Roland, his lance borne up / Skyward, beneath its point a pennon bound, / Snow-white, whose fringes flap his hand. / Fair is his form, his visage bright with smiles./ Behind him followed Olivier his friend; / The French with joy, him as their champion, hailed. / He on the Heathens threw a haughty glance, / But cast a sweet and humble look upon / His French, and to them spoke with courteous tone: / "Seigneurs Barons, march steadily and close. / These Pagans hither came to find a grave; / We here shall conquer such great spoil to-day / As never yet was gained by Kings of France." / Even as he spoke the word, the armies met.

XCIII.
Said Olivier: "No care have I to speak, / Since you deigned not to blow your Olifant, / All hope of help from Carle for you is lost. / He knows no word of this; the fault lies not / In him, nor are yon Knights to blame—ride on / And gallop to the charge as best you can. / Seigneurs Barons, recoil not from the foe, / In God's name! bearing ever this in mind, / Hard blows to deal and hard blows to endure / Forget we not the war-cry of King Carle!" / At this word all the French together shouted. / Who then had heard the cry, "Montjoie!" had known / What courage is. Then all together rushed / Right onward; God! with what an onset fierce! / Deeply they spurred their steeds for greater speed; / They burned to fight. What else could they

---

[8] King of the Saracens. He first appears in Stanza 1, asking his barons for counsel because he is losing the war against Charlemagne.

desired? / The Saracens stood firm with no fear showing. / Behold the Franks and Pagans hand to hand...

THE MELEE.

XCIV.

The nephew of Marsile—his name Aëlroth, / Forwarded the first of all spurs on his horse / Against our French, hurling forth insulting words: / "Today, French villains, ye will joust with us; / Who was to guard you, has betrayed you; mad / Must be the King who left you in the pass. / So now the honor of sweet France is lost, / And Carle the great shall lose his right arm here." / Roland heard. God! What pain to him! He drove / His golden spurs into his courser's flanks, / And rushed at full speed against Aëlroth; / His shield he broke, dismailed the hauberk linked; / Cleaving his breast, he severed all the bones, / And from the spine the ribs disjointed. The lance / Forth from his body thrusted the Pagan's soul; / The Heathen's corpse reeled from his horse, fell down / Upon the earth, the neck cloven in two halves. / Roland still taunted him: "Go thou, wretch, and know / Carle was not mad. Ne'er did he treason love, / And he did well to leave us in the pass. / Today sweet France will not her honor lose! / Strike, Frenchmen, strike; the first sword-stroke is ours; / We have the right, these gluttons have the wrong!"

XCV.

Then came a Duke whose name was Falsarun; / He was the brother of the King Marsile. / The lands of Dathan and of Abirun / He held: no viler wretch lived under Heaven. / Vast was his forehead, and the space between / His deeply sunken eyes was half a foot. / Seeing his nephew dead, in grief he bounded / Forth from the serried ranks, and shouted aloud / The Pagan war-cry, furious against the French. "Today," he cried, "at last sweet France shall lose / Her fame!" When Olivier heard this, in wrath / He pricked with golden spurs his charger's flanks, / And, like true baron, lifted his arm to strike,

/ Shivered the Pagan's shield, his hauberk tore / Apart. The pennon's folds passed through his breast / As with the shaft he hurled him from the saddle, / A mangled corpse; here lie he on the ground. Unto the prostrate body Olivier / Said proudly: "Wretch, to me thy threats are vain! / Strike boldly, Franks! The victory shall be ours! / Montjoie!" he shouted, the battle-cry of Carle.

XCVI.
A king, named Corsablis, from Barbary, / A distant land, was there. The Pagan host / He called: "The field is ours with ease: the French / So few in numbers we may well disdain, / Nor Carle shall rescue one; all perish here. / Today, they all are doomed to death!" Turpin / The Archbishop heard him; lived no man on earth / He hated more than Corsablis; he pricked / His horse with both his spurs of purest gold, / And against him rushed with tremendous force. / The shield and hauberk split; and with a stroke / Of the long lance into his body driven, / Corsablis lifeless dropped across the path; / Him, though a corpse, Turpin addressed thus: / "Thou, coward Pagan, thou hast lied! Great Carl / My lord, was ever and will ever be / Our help; and Frenchmen know not how to fly. / As for thy fellows, we can keep them here; / I tell you, each this day shall die. Strike, Franks, / Yourselves forget not. This first blow, thank God, / Is ours! Montjoie!" cried he, to hold the field.

XCVII.
Gerin attacked Malprimis de Brigal / Whose good shield now was not a denier [9] worth: / The crystal boss all broken, and one half / Fall'n on the ground. Down to the flesh Gerin / His hauberk cleaved, and passed through his heart / The brazen point of a stout lance. Then fell / The Pagan chief and died by that good blow; / And Satanas bore off the wretched soul.

---

[9] a French coin, equal to one twelfth of a *sou*, which was withdrawn from use in the 19th century.

XCVIII.
Gerier, his comrade, struck the Amurafle, / Broke his good
shield, his hauberk white unmailed, / Planted in his heart a
spear's steel point with such / Good aim, one blow has pierced
the body through; / And his strong lance-thrust hurled him
dead to earth. / Said Olivier: "A noble combat ours!"

XCIX.
Duke Sansun rushed on the Almazour; / He split the shield
with painted flowers and gold / Embossed. The strong-mailed
hauberk sheltered not, / As he was pierced through liver, heart
and lungs. / For him may mourn who will—death-struck he
fell: / "That is a Baron's stroke!" the Archbishop cried.

C.
Anseïs gave his steed the rein, and charged / Fierce on Turgis
de Turteluse; beneath / The golden boss asunder broke the
shield, / Ripped up the hauberk double-linked; so true / The
thrust, that all the steel passed through his breast. / With this
one blow the shaft had struck him dead. / Roland exclaimed:
"The stroke is of a Knight!"

CI.
Then Engelier, the Gascon of Burdele,[10] / Spurred deep his
horse, and casting loose the rein, / Rushed upon Escremiz de
Valterne; /Broke down the buckler fastened to his throat / And
rended his gorget-mail; full in the breast. / The lance struck
deep and passed in between / The collar bones; dead from the
saddle struck / He fell.--And Turpin said: "Ye all are lost!"

CII.
Othon assailed a Pagan, Estorgant, / His thrust hit hard the
leather of the shield, / Effacing its bright colors red and white,
/ Broke in his hauberk's sides, and plunged deep / Within his
heart a strong and trenchant spear, / From off the flying steed

---

[10] Bordeaux.

striking him dead. / This done, he said: "No hope for you remains!"

CIII.
And Berengier smote now Estramaris, / Split down his shield, shivered his coat of mail / In shreds and through his bosom drove a lance. / Dead amidst one thousand Saracens he dropped. / Of their twelve Peers now ten have breathed their last: / Chernuble, Margariz, the Count, survived.

CIV.
Most valiant Knight was Margariz. 'Mid all / Beauteous, strong, slender, quick of hand. He spurred / His horse and charged Olivier; beneath / The boss of purest gold his shield broke down, / Then at his side a pointed lance he aimed; / But God protected him, for the blow ne'er reached / The flesh. The point grazed only, wounding not. / Then Margariz unhindered rode away / And sounded his horn to rally his own men.

CV.
The battle raged fierce. All men engaged. / Roland, the dauntless, combated with his lance / As long as held the shaft. Fifteen good blows / It dealt, then broke and fell; now his good sword, / Loved Durandal, he drew, spurred on his steed / Against Chernubles, split his bright helm adorned / With gems; one blow cleaved through mail-cap and skull, / Cutting both eyes and visage in two parts, / And the white hauberk with its close-linked mail; / Down to the body's fork, the saddle all / Of beaten gold, still deeper went the sword, / Cut through the courser's chine, nor sought the joint. / Upon the verdant grass fell dead both knight / And steed. And then he cried: "Wretch! ill inspired / To venture here! Mohammed helped thee not! / Wretches like you this battle shall not win."

CVI.
The Count Roland rode through the battlefield / And made, with Durandal's keen blade in hand, / A mighty carnage of the

Saracens. / Ah! had you then beheld the valiant Knight / Heap corpse on corpse; blood drenching all the ground; / His own arms, hauberk, all besmeared with gore, / And his good steed from neck to shoulder bleed! / Still Olivier halted not in his career. / Of the twelve Peers not one deserved reproach, / And all the French struck well and massacred / The foe. The Pagans dead or dying fell. / Cried the Archbishop: "Well done, Knights of France! / Montjoie! Montjoie! It is Carle's battle cry!"

CVII.
Olivier grasped the truncheon of his lance, / Spurred through the storm and fury of the fight, / And rushed on the Pagan Malsarun, / Broke down his shield with flowers and gold embossed, / Thrusted from their orbs his eyes; his brains dashed out / Were crushed and trampled 'neath the victor's feet; / With seven hundred men of theirs he fell. / The Count next slew Turgis and Estorgus; / But now the shaft broke short off by his hand. / Then said Roland: "What mean you, Companion? / In such a fight as this 'tis not a staff / We need, but steel and iron, as I deem. / Where now that sword called Halteclere, with hilt / Of gold and crystal pommel?" "I lack time / To draw it," valiant Olivier replied, / "So busy is my hand in dealing blows!"

CVIII.
Lord Olivier then his good sword unsheathed, / For which Roland entreated him so much, / And showed it to his friend with knightly pride; / Struck down a Pagan, Justin de Val-Ferrée, / Whose head is severed by the blow; cut through / The embroider'd hauberk, through the body, through / The saddle all with studs and gold embossed, / And through the backbone of the steed. Both man / And steed fell on the grass before him, dead. / Roland exclaimed: "Henceforth, you are indeed / My brother! These, the strokes loved by King Carle!" / And echoed round the cry: "Montjoie! Montjoie!"

CIX.

The Count Gerin sat on his horse, Sorel, / And his companion Gerier, on Passe-Cerf, / They loose the reins, and both spurred on against / A Pagan, Timozel. One struck the shield, / The other struck the hauberk; in his heart / The two spears met and hurled him lifeless down. / I never heard it said nor can I know / By which of them the swifter blow was struck. / Esperveris, son to Borel, was next / By Engelier de Burdele slain. Turpin / With his own hand gave death to Siglorel / The Enchanter who once entered hell, led there / By Jupiter's craft. Turpin said: "Forfeit paid / For crime!" "The wretch is vanquished," cried Roland, / "My brother Olivier, such blows I love!"

CX.

The combat paused not. Franks and Pagans vied / In dealing blows; attacking now, and now / Defending. Splintered spears, dripping with blood / So many; o'er the field such numbers strewn: / Of banners torn and shattered gonfalons! / So many valiant French mowed in their prime, / Whom mothers and sweet wives will never see / Again, nor those of France who in the Pass / Awaited them! Carle for these shall weep and mourn. / But what avails? Naught can he help them now. / Ill service rendered Ganelon to them / The day when he to Sarraguce [11] repaired / To sell his kin. Ere long for this he lost / Both limb and life, judged and condemned at Aix, / There to be hanged with thirty of his race / Who were not spared the punishment of death.

CXI.

The battle raged. Wonders all performed; / Roland and Olivier struck hard; Turpin / The Archbishop, dealt more than a thousand blows; / The twelve Peers dallied not upon the field, / While all the French together fought as if / One man. By hundreds and by thousands fell / The Pagans: none escaped death, save those who fled / Whether they willed or no, all lost their

---

[11] Zaragoza.

lives. / And yet the French had lost their strongest arms, / Their fathers and their kin they would ne'er see / Again, nor Carle who waited for them in the Pass.

Meantime in France an awful scourge prevailed: / Wind, storm, rain, hail and flashing lightning bolts / Conflicted confusedly, and naught more true, / The earth shook from Saint Michel-del-Peril / As far as to the Saints, from Besançon / Unto the sea-port of Guitzand;[12] no house / Whose walls unshaken stood; darkness at noon / Shrouded the sky. No beam of light above / Save when a flash ripped up the clouds. Dismayed / Beholders cried: "The world's last day has come, / The destined end of all things is at hand!" / Unwitting of the truth, their speech is vain.... / 'Tis dolor for the death of Count Roland!

CXII.
The French struck hard; they struck with all their force. / In multitudes, by thousands died their foes; / Not two out of one hundred thousand now / Survived. Turpin said: "Brave are all our men; / None braver under Heaven; In the Geste / Of France 'tis written true vassals have our Kings." / Seeking their friends, they overran the field. / Their eyes were filled with tenderness and tears / For their dear kindred they so fondly loved... / Now King Marsile with his great host appeared

CXIII.
Marsile advanced 'midst a valley deep, / Surrounded by the mighty host he brought, / In twenty squadrons mustered and arrayed. / Bright shone the helmets strewn with gold and gems, / And shields and hauberks graved. They sounded a charge / With seven hundred clarions sending forth / Loud blasts throughout the land; Thus said Roland: / "Companion Olivier, my brother, friend, / The traitor, Ganelon, has sworn our death... / His treason is too sure; the Emperor Carle / For

---

[12] Wissant, near Calais.

this vile crime will take a vengeance deep. / A long and cruel battle we shall have, / Ere this unknown to man. There, I will fight / With my good Durandal; you, friend, will strike / With Halteclere; Those noble swords we bore / Throughout so many lands; such combats won / By them, vile strains must never chant their deeds."

CXIV.
When the French saw the Pagan cohorts swarm / The country o'er, they called on Olivier, / Roland and the twelve Peers to guard their lives. / Unto them now the Archbishop spoke his mind: / "Barons, be not unworthy of yourselves! / Fly not the field, for God's sake, that brave men / Sing not ill songs of you! Far better die / In battle. Doomed, I know, we are to death, / And ere this day has passed, our lives are o'er. / But for one thing ye can believe my word: / For you God's Paradise stands open wide, / And seats await you 'mid the blessed Saints." / These words of comfort reassured the French; / All in one voice cried out: "Montjoie! Montjoie!"

CXV.
There was a Saracen from Sarraguce / Lord of one half the city, Climorin, / Unlike a Baron; he received the faith / Of Ganelon, and sealed the treacherous bond / By pressing on his lip a kiss; Besides / Unto him gave his sword and carbuncle. / "I will," said he, "put your great France to shame / And from the Emperor's head shake off the crown!" / Mounted on Barbamouche that faster flew / Than hawk or swallow on the wing, he spurred / His courser hard, and dropping on its neck / The rein, he struck Engelier de Gascogne; / Hauberk nor shield was for him a defense: / Deep in the core the Pagan thrusted his spear / So mightily, its point came out behind, / And with the shaft o'erturned him on the field / A corpse; he cried: "Fit for destruction these! / Strike, Pagans, strike, and let us break their lines!" / The French cried: "God! to lose so brave a Knight!"

CXVI.

The Count Roland called Olivier: "You know, / Companion, sire, Engelier is no more... / No better Knight had we." The Count replied: / "God grant that I avenge him well!" He drove / His golden spurs into his charger's flanks; / And waving Halteclere's blood dripping blade, / The Pagan he assailed, and dealt a blow... / O'erthrown was Climorin. The fiends of hell / Bore off his soul. The Knight then slayed the Duke / Alphaïen, beheaded Escababi, / Unhorsed seven Arabs with such skill / They rose no more to fight. Then said Roland: / "Wroth is my sire, and by my side achieves / Renown! by such good blows Carl's love is gained. / Strike, Chevaliers! strike on!" he cried aloud.

CXVII.

From otherwhere was Valdabrun who armed / Marsile a Knight; lord of four hundred ships./ There was no sailor but swore by his name; / 'Twas he by treason took Jerusalem, / Who there the shrine of Solomon profaned, / And slew before the Fonts the Patriarch; / 'Twas he, received Count Ganelon's vile oath / And gave him with his sword a thousand marks; / Faster than falcon in its flight his steed / Named Graminond. He sharply spurred his flanks / And rushed against the mighty Duke Sansun, / Broke down his shield—the hauberk rended, and thrust / Within his breast the pennon of the flag; / The shaft o'erthrew him from the saddle, dead. / "Strike Pagans! strike, for we shall conquer them!" / The French said: "God! what Baron true we lost!"

CXVIII.

When Count Roland saw Sansun lifeless fall, / You may well know what grief was his. He spurred / His horse down on the Pagan. Durandal / More worth than precious gold he lifted to strike / With all his might; gold studded helm, head, trunk, / Hauberk asunder cleaved; the blow, e'en through / The gold embossed saddle, struck the courser's back, / Killing both horse and man. Blame or approve / Who may. The Pagans

28

said: "Hard is this blow!" / Retorted Roland: "For yours no pity can / I feel! With you the vaunting and the wrong!"

CXIX.
An African fresh from the desert land / Was there; Malquidant, son of king Malcud; / His armor highly wrought in beaten gold / Outshone all others in the sun's bright rays. / Mounted upon his horse named Salt-Perdut, / He aimed a blow at Anseïs' shield, and cut / The azure and vermillion all away. / His hauberk rove asunder, side from side, / And through his body passed both point and shaft. / The Count was dead. His last breath spent and flown. / The French said: "Baron, such great woe for you!"

CXX.
The Archbishop Turpin rode across the fields; / No shaven priest sang ever mass so well / As he showed such prowess in his deeds. / He cried to the Pagan: "May God send all ills / To thee, who slew the knight my heart bewails!" / Turpin spurred hard his good steed against the wretch; / One blow struck down his strong Toledo shield: / The miscreant dead upon the green sward fell.

CXXI.
Elsewhere stood Grandomie who was the son / Of Capuel, king of Cappadoce. He sat / On a steed named Marmorie, than flying bird / More swift. Loosening the rein, and spurring deep, / To smite Gerin with all his force he rode; / Torn from the neck which bore it, shattered fell / The purple shield, through the rent mail he drove / The whole blue pennon in his breast. Gerin / Dropped lifeless by this blow, against a rock. / The Pagan also slew Gerier, his friend, / And Berengier, and Gui de Saint-Antoine; / Assailing then the noble Duke Austoire / Who held Valence and fiefs along the Rhone, / He struck him dead. The Saracens extolled / Their triumph, but how many fell of ours!

CXXII.

Hearing the Frenchmen's sobs, the Count Roland / Grasped in his hand his sword, all reeking blood. / His mighty heart nigh breaking with his grief, / Cried to the foe: "May God all evils send / On thee! him hast thou slain for whom thou shalt / Most dearly pay!" He spurred his flying steed... / Conquer who may—these two fight hand to hand.

CXXIII.

A wise and valiant knight was Grandonie, / Virtuous and fearless vassal. 'Mid his way / Encountering Count Roland, though never seen / Before, at once he knew 'twas he, as well / By his proud mien and noble beauty, as / By his fair countenance and lofty look. / Awe-struck, despite himself, he vainly tried / To fly, but rooted to the spot he stayed. / The Count Roland smote him so skillfully, / He split in two the nazal, helm, nose, mouth, / And teeth, the body and mailed-armor, then / Hewn through the golden saddle, both silver-flaps; / With a still deeper stroke the courser's back / Was gashed. So both were slain past remedy. / The men of Spain cried out all sorrowful; / But said the French: "Well our defender stuck."

CXXIV.

Marvelous the battle, and the tumult fierce; / The French of strength and fury full, raised high / Their swords: backs, ribs and wrists are slashed; the flesh / Cut through rent garments to the quick; along / The verdant soil the red blood ran in streams. / The Pagans cried "We cannot more endure! / Great land, Mohammed curse thee! More than all / This people bold." Not one who does not cry / "Marsile! ride on, O King, thy aid we need!"

CXXV.

A battle fierce and wonderful!—Hard struck / The French with glittering lance, and there you might / Have seen what miseries man can suffer: Mowed / And heaped in bloody mounds, all gasping out / Their lives, some on their backs, some on their teeth. / The Saracens gave way, willing or not; / By the French lances forced, they fled the field.

CXXVI.
Marsile his warriors massacred beheld, / And, bidding all his horns and trumpets blow, / Rode forward, and his whole van rode with him. / In the van rode a Saracen, Abisme, / The vilest wretch among his men, sunk deep / In crimes and shame, who had no faith in God, / Sainte Marie's son; as black as melted pitch / His face; more fond of blood and treason foul / Than of the gold of all Galice. None saw / Him laugh or play; for courage and rash deeds / He pleased the vile Marsile whose dragon flag / He bore. No pity could the Archbishop feel / For him, and at his sight he craved to try / His arm, all softly saying to himself: / "This Saracen is but a heretic; / Far better die than not to give him death. / Ne'er cowardice nor coward I endured!"

CXXVII.
The Archbishop gave the signal for the fight; / He rode the horse he captured from Grossaille, / A King he slew among the Danes: a horse / Of wondrous fleetness, light-hoofed, slender-limbed; / Thigh short; with broad and mighty haunch; the flanks / Were long, and very high his spine; pure white / His tail, and yellow is his mane; his ears / Were small; light brown his head. This paragon / Of all the beasts of earth had not his peer. / The Archbishop, baron-like, spurred on the horse, / Full bent upon the encounter with Abisme; / He gained his side and hard he struck his shield / Glittering with gems, topaz and amethyst, / Crystals and carbuncles, which to him gave / The Emir Galafés—a demon's gift / To this in Val-Metas. Him Turpin smote / Nor mercy showed; against such a blow availed / The shield but little; sheer from side to side / Passed the blade; dead on the place he fell. / At such exploit amazed, the French exclaimed: / "The archbishop's crosier in his hand is safe!"

31

CXXVIII.

The Count Roland called Olivier: "With me, / Companion, sire, confess that amongst brave knights / The archbishop upon earth or under Heav'n / Has not his peer in casting spear or lance." / Olivier answered: "To his rescue on!" / At this the French once more resumed the fight. / Hard were the blows, rough was the strife; Meantime / The Christian host in greatest sorrow mourned.

CXXIX.

Whoever could this fight describe? Roland / And Olivier vied with Turpin in skill / And glorious deeds; The slain can counted be; / In charts and briefs their numbers were enrolled: / More than four thousand fell, so says the Geste. / Four times the French arms were victorious, / But on the fifth, a cruel fate they met; / The knights of France found there a grave, except / Three more whose lives God saved; yet those brave knights, / Ere falling, their last breath would dearly sell.

THE HORN.

CXXX.

Seeing so many warriors fall'n around, / Roland unto his comrade Olivier / Spoke thus: "Companion fair and dear, for God / Whose blessing rest on you, those vassals true / And brave lie corpses on the battle-field: / Look! We must mourn for France so sweet and fair, / From henceforth widowed of such valiant knights. / Carle, would you were amongst us, King and friend! / What can we do, say, brother Olivier, / To bring him news of this sore strait of ours!" / Olivier answered: "I know not; but this / I know; for us is better death than shame."

CXXXI.

Roland said: "I will blow mine Olifant, / And Carle will hear it from the pass. I pledge / My word the French at once retrace their steps." / Said Olivier: "This a great shame would be, /

One which to all your kindred would bequeath / A lifetime's stain. When this I asked of you, / You answered nay, and would do naught. Well, now / With my consent you shall not; if you blow / Your horn, of valor true you show no proof. / Already, both your arms are drenched with blood." / Responded the Count: "These arms have nobly struck."

CXXXII.
"The strife is rude," Roland said. "I will blow / My horn, that Carle may hear." Replied Olivier: / "This would not courage be. What I desired, / Companion, you disdained. Were the king here, / Safe would we be, but yon brave men are not / To blame. By this my beard," said Olivier, / "I swear, if e'er I see again sweet Aude, / My sister, in her arms you ne'er shall lie."

CXXXIII.
Roland asked Olivier: "Why show to me / Your anger, friend!" "Companion, yours the fault; / True courage means not folly. Better far / Is prudence than your valiant rage. Our French / Their lives have lost, your rashness is the cause. / And now our arms can never more give Carle / Their service good. Had you believed your friend, / Amongst us would he be, and ours the field, / The King Marsile, a captive or a corpse. / Roland, your valor brought ill fortune, nor / Shall Carle the great e'er more our help receive, / A man unequaled till God's judgment-day. / Here you shall die, and dying, humble France, / This day our loyal friendship ends; 'ere falls / The Vesper-eve, dolorously we part!"

CXXXIV.
The Archbishop heard their strife. In haste he drove / Into his horse his spurred of purest gold, / And quick beside them rode. Then chiding them, / Said: "Sire Roland, and you, Sire Olivier, / In God's name be no feud between you two; / No more your horn shall save us; e'en if 'twere / Far better Carle should come and soon avenge / Our deaths. So joyous then these Spanish foes / Would not return. But as our Franks alight, /

Find us or slain or mangled on the field, / They will our bodies on their chargers' backs / Lift in their shrouds with grief and pity, all / In tears, and bury us in holy ground: / And neither wolves, nor swine, nor curs shall feed / On us." Replied Roland: "Well have you said."

CXXXV.
Roland raised to his lips the Olifant, / Drew a deep breath, and blew with all his force. / High are the mountains, and from peak to peak / The sound re-echoed; thirty leagues away / 'Twas heard by Carle and all his brave compeers. / Cried the king: "Our men make battle!" Ganelon / Retorted in haste: "If thus another dared / To speak, we should denounce it as a lie."

CXXXVI.
The Count Roland in his great anguish blew / His Olifant so mightily, with such / Despairing agony, his mouth poured forth / The crimson blood, and his swollen temples burst. / Yea, but so far the ringing blast resounded; / Carle heard it, marching through the pass; Duke Naimes hark; / The French all listened with attentive ear. / "That is Roland's horn!" Carle cried, "which ne'er yet / Was, save in battle, blown!" But Ganelon / Replied: "No fight is there! You, sire, are old, / Your hair and beard are all bestrewn with gray, / And as a child your speech. Well do you know / Roland's great pride. 'Tis marvelous God bore / With him so long. Already took he Noples / Without your leave. The Pagans left their walls / And fought Roland, your brave Knight, in the field; / With his good blade he slew them all, and then / Washed all the plain with water, that no trace / Of blood was left; yea, oftentimes he runs / After a hare all day and blows his horn. / Doubtless he takes his sport now with his peers; / And who 'neath Heav'n would dare attack Roland? / None, as I deem. Nay, sire, ride on apace; / Why do you halt? Still far is the Great Land."

CXXXVII.

Roland with bleeding mouth and temples burst, / Still in his anguish, blew his Olifant; / Carle heard it, and his Franks. The king exclaimed: / "That horn has a long breath!" Duke Naimes replied: / "Roland it is, and in a sore distress, / Upon my faith, a battle rages there! / A traitor he who would deceive you now. / To arms! Your war-cry shout, your kinsman save! / Plainly enough you hear his call for help."

CXXXVIII.

Carle ordered all the trumpeters to sound / The march. The French alighted. They armed themselves / With helmets, hauberks and gold hilted swords, / Bright bucklers, long sharp spears, with pennons white / And red and blue. The barons of the host / Leaped on their steeds, all spurring on; while through / The pass they marched, each to the other said: / "Could we but reach Roland before he dies, / What deadly blows, with his, our swords would strike!" / But what avails? Too late they will arrive.

CXXXIX.

The ev'n was clear, the sun its radiant beams / Reflected upon the marching legions. Spears, / Hauberks and helms, shields painted with bright flowers, / Gold pennons all ablaze with glitt'ring hues. / Burning with wrath the Emperor rode on; / The French with sad and angered looks. None there / But wept aloud. All trembled for Roland. / The King commanded Count Ganelon be seized / And given to the scullions of his house. / Their chief, named Bègue, he called and bid: "Guard well / This man as one who all my kin betrayed." / Him Bègue received, and set upon the Count / One hundred of his kitchen comrades; best / And worst; they plucked his beard on lip and cheek; / Each dealt him with his fist four blows, and fell / On him with lash and stick; they chained his neck / As they would chain a bear, and he was thrown / For more dishonor on a sumpter mule, / There guarded so until to Carle brought back.

CXL.

High were the mountains, gloomy, terrible, / The valleys deep, and swift the rushing streams. / In van, in rear, the brazen trumpets blew, / Answ'ring the Olifant. With angry look / Rode on the Emp'ror; filled with wrath and grief, / Followed the French, each sobbing, each in tears, / Praying that God may guard Roland, until / They reached the battlefield. With him what blew / Would they not strike? Alas! what booted it now? / Too late they were and could not come in time.

CXLI.

Carle in great anger rode; his snow-white beard / O'erspread his breast-plate. Hard the Barons spurred, / For never one but inwardly doth rage / That he was far from their great chief, Roland, / Who combats now the Saracens of Spain: / If wounded he, would one of his survive? / O God! What Knights those sixty left by him! / Nor King nor captain better ever had...

THE ROUT.

CXLII.

The Count Roland cast o'er the mounts and vales / A glance: French corpses strew the plains in heaps; / He for them mourned as gentle knight. / At such a sight the noble hero wept: / "Seigneurs, to you may God be merciful! / To all your souls may He grant Paradise, / And there may they on beds of heavenly flowers / Repose! No better vassals lived! so long / Have ye served me! So many lands for Carle / Ye won! The Emperor for this ill fate / Has nurtured you! O land of France, most sweet / Art thou, but now forsaken and a waste. / Barons of France, today I see you die / For me; nor can I save or e'en defend / Your lives. Be God your aid, who ne'er played false! / Olivier, brother, I must not fail thee! / If other death comes not, of grief I die. / Come, sire companion... come to fight again!"

CXLIII.
Soon to the field returned the Count Roland / With Durandal
in hand; as a true knight / He fought. Faldrun del Pin he
cleaved in half / With twenty-four among the bravest foes. /
Never was man so bent upon revenge. / As run wild deer before the chasing hounds, / Before Roland the Pagans fled.
"Well done!" / The Archbishop cried, "Such valor a true
Knight / Should have, when mounted, armed, on his good
steed! / Else, not four deniers is he worth: a monk / In cloister
should he be, and spend his life / In praying for our sins!"
"Strike," said Roland, / "No quarter!" At the word the French
renewed / The combat... yet the Christian loss was great.

CXLIV.
When soldiers on the battlefield expect / No quarter, desperate
they fight; and thus / The French, like lions, fiercely stood at
bay. / Like a true baron, King Marsile rode forth / Upon his
steed Gaignon, and spurred him on / Against Bevum, of Belne
and Digun lord, / His buckler cleaved, his hauberk with a blow
/ Shattered, and lay him dead upon the field. / Then fell beneath the Pagan King, Ivoire / And Ivun; then Gerard de
Roussillon. / The Count Roland was nigh and cried aloud: /
"God give damnation unto thee who thus / So foully slay'st
my friends! But 'ere we part, / Dearly shalt thou abye it[13], and
today / Shalt learn the name my good sword bears." He struck
/ The King a true Knight's stroke, and his right hand / Lopped
at the wrist; then Turfaleu the fair, / Marsile's own son, beheaded. The Pagans said: / "Aid us, Mahum! Avenge us, Gods
of ours, / On Carle, who brought such villains to our land, / As
rather than depart will die."And each / To each cried: "Let us
fly!" Upon the word, / A hundred thousand turned in sudden
flight. / Whoever called them, ne'er would they return.

---

[13] Pay a penalty.

CXLV.

Alas, it not avails! If Marsile fled, / His uncle Marganice un-
hurt remained. / 'Twas he who held Carthage, Alferne,
Garnaille, / And Ethiopia, a land accursed; / Chief of the
Blacks, a thick-nosed, large-eared race. / Of these he more
than fifty thousand led, / Who rode on proudly, full of wrath,
and shouted / The Pagan war-cry. "Here," said Count Roland,
/ "Here shall we fall as martyrs. Well I know / Our end is nigh;
but dastard I count him / Who sells not dear his life. Barons,
strike well, / Strike with your burnished swords, and set such
price / On death and life, that naught of shame shall fall / On
our sweet France. When Carle, my lord, shall come / Upon
this field, and see such slaughter here / Of Saracens, fifteen to
one of ours, / Then will he breathe a blessing on his Knights."

OLIVIER'S DEATH.

CXLVI.

When saw Roland this tribe accursed, more black / Than ink,
with glist'ning teeth, their only gleam / Of white, he said:
"Truly I know today / We die! Strike, Frenchmen, that is my
command." / And Olivier, "Woe to the laggards," cried. / These words the French hearts fired to meet the fray.

CXLVII.

The Pagans, when they mark how few the French, / Were
filled with pride and comfort, and they said / One to the other:
"Their King Carle is wrong!" / Upon his sorrel steed sat
Marganice; / Urging him hard with pricking spurs of gold, /
Encountered Olivier, struck him behind, / Drove his white
hauberk-links into his heart, / And through in front came forth
the pointed lance. / The Kalif cried: "That blow struck home!
Carlemagne, / For thy mishap, left you to guard the Pass! /
That he has wronged us, little may he boast. / Your death
alone for us a vengeance full!"

CXLVIII.
Olivier knew his death-wound. In his hand / He grasped
Halteclere's bright steel, and struck a blow / Well aimed upon
the Kalif's pointed helm; / He scattered golden flowers and
gems in dust. / His head the trenchant blade cleaved to the
teeth, / And dead the Kalif fell. "Pagan accursed," / He cried,
"not here shalt thou say Carle lost aught; / To wife nor lady
shalt thou ever boast / In thine own land, that thou hast reft
from Carle / One denier's worth, or me or others harmed!" /
And then he called Roland unto his aid.

CXLIX.
Olivier felt that he was hurt to death. / No vengeance could
suffice him; Baron-like / He struck amid the press, cut shields
embossed / And ashen shafts, and spears, feet, shoulders,
wrists / And breasts of horsemen. He who saw him thus /
Dismember Saracens, corpse over corpse / Heap on the
ground, would of a vassal true / Remembrance keep. Nor did
he now forget / The rallying cry of Carle: "Montjoie!" he cried
/ Loudly and clear; then called Roland, his friend / And com-
peer: "Sire companion, stand by me! / This day our breaking
hearts forever part!"

CL.
Roland looked Olivier full in the face; / Pale, livid, colorless;
pure crimson blood / Dripped from his body, and streamed on
the earth. / "God!" cried Roland, "I know not what to do, /
Companion, friend, thy courage was betrayed / Today; nor
will such courage e'er be seen / In human heart. Sweet France,
oh! how shalt thou, / As widow, wail thy vassals true and
brave, / Humbled and wrecked! The great heart of King Carle
/ Will break!" He spoke and on his saddle swooned.

CLI.
Behold Roland, there, fainting on his steed, / While Olivier
stood wounded to the death. / So great the loss of blood, his
troubled eyes / See naught afar or near, nor mortal man /

Could recognize. Encountering there Roland, / Upon his golden-studded helm he struck / A dreadful blow, which to the nose-plate cleft, / And split the crest in twain, but left the head / Untouched. Roland at this, upon him looked, / And softly, sweetly asked: :"Sire companion! / Was that blow meant for me? I am Roland / By whom you are beloved so well; to me / Could you by any chance, defiance give?" / Said Olivier: "I hear your speech, but see / You now no more. May God behold you, friend! / I struck the blow; beseech you, pardon me." / Roland responded: "I am not wounded; here / And before God I pardon you." At this, / Each to the other bent in courtesy. / With such great tenderness and love they part.

CLII.
Olivier felt the agony of death; / His vacant eyes rolled wildly in his head, / And all his hearing and his sight were lost. / Dismounting, on the ground he lie, and smote / His breast, aloud confessing all his sins; / With joined hands toward Heaven lifted up / He prayed to God to give him Paradise, / To bless Carlemagne, sweet France, and far beyond / All other men, Roland, his companion. / His heart failed; forward drooped his helmet; prone / Upon the earth he lie; 'tis over now... / The Count was dead. Roland, the Baron, mourned / And weeps as never mortal mourned before.

CLIII.
When saw the Count Roland the breath of life / Gone from his friend, his body stretched on earth, / His face low in the dust, his tears gush out / With heavy sobs. Then tenderly he spoke: / "Alas! for all thy valor, comrade dear! / Year after year, day after day, a life / Of love we led; ne'er didst thou wrong to me, / Nor I to thee. If death takes thee away, / My life is but a pain." While speaking thus, / The Marchis fainted on Veillantif, his steed. / But still firm in his stirrups of pure gold: / Where'er Roland may ride, he could not fall.

CLIV.

Scarce hath the Count recovered from his swoon, / When all the great disaster met his sight; / The French lie on the field; all lost to him / Save the Archbishop and Gualtier de l'Hum, / Who had descended from the mountain height / Where he the men of Spain all day withstood / Till all his own fell 'neath the Pagan swords. / Willed he or not, he fled into the vale, / And now upon Roland he called for aid: / "Most gentle Count, most valiant, where art thou? / Ne'er had I fear where'er thou wert! 'tis I, / Gualtier, who conquered Maëlgut, who am / Old gray-haired Droün's nephew; till this day / My courage won thy love. So well I fought / Against the Saracens, my spear was broken, / My shield was pierced, my hauberk torn and wrung, / And in my body eight steel darts I bear. / Done are my days, but dear the last I sold!" / The words of that brave knight Roland heard, / Spurred on his steed and galloped to his help.

CLV.

With grief and rage Roland's great heart was full; / Amidst the thick ranks of a swarming foe / He rode. He fought; and twenty Pagans fall / Slain by his hand; by Gualtier's six, and five / By the Archbishop's. Loud the Pagans cried: / "Vile wretches these! Let none escape alive! / Eternal shame to them who dare not make / Attack; foul recreants those who let their flight / Avail." Renewing then their hues and cries, / The Pagans rushed from all parts against the knights.

CHARLEMAGNE APPROACHES.

CLVI.

The Count Roland was ever great in war; / Most valiant was Gualtier de l'Hum; Turpin / The Archbishop, of a valor proved: each left / The other naught to do, and 'mid the throng / Struck Pagans down, who though one thousand foot / And forty thousand horsemen mustering, yet / Dared not approach, forsooth; but from afar / Against them hurled their javelins, spears and darts, / Their lances and winged arrows. First of all / Was slain Gualtier; Turpin de Reins' good shield / Was pierced, his helmet broken, and his head / Wounded, his hauberk shattered and dislinked; / Four spears pierced his body; his good steed / Died under him. Alas! the Archbishop fell.

CLVII.
Hardly had Turpin fallen on the earth, / By four spear-shafts transfixed, when the brave knight / Sprang quickly to his feet once more. His look / Sought for Roland to whom he ran in haste. / One word he said: "Unconquered yet am I! / While life doth last, a true knight yields it not!" / He drew Almace, his sword of burnished steel, / And rushing 'mid the throng, one thousand blows / And more he dealt, Carle said in after days, / Turpin spared none, as dead upon the field / He saw four hundred men, some cut in twain, / Some with lopped heads: so says the Geste of France, / And one who saw the field, the brave Saint-Gille / For whom God showed his might; who in the cloister / Of Loüm wrote the record of these deeds. / Who knows not this, he knows not anything.

CLVIII.
As hero fought the Count Roland; but all / His body burned with heat and dripped with sweat; / His head was torn by pain; his temple burst / By that strong blast he gave the Olifant. / Still would he know if Carle returned; once more / He blew his horn; Alas, with feeble blast. / Carle caught the distant sound, and, list'ning, waited: / "Seigneurs," cried he, "great evils fall apace; / I hear his dying blast upon his horn. / If we would find him yet alive, we need / Urge on our steeds. Let all our trumpets blow!" / Then sixty thousand trumps rang forth their peals; / The hills reechoed, and the vales responded. / The Pagans heard; and stayed their gabbling mirth. / One to the other said: "'Tis Carle who comes!"

CLIX.

The Pagans said: "The Emperor returns; / These are the clarions of the French we hear. / If Carle should come, 'twill be our doom; if lives / Roland, the war begins anew, and Spain / Our land is lost to us for evermore." / Four hundred warriors well armed cap-a-pie, / The bravest of the host, then closed their ranks / And dashed in fierce attack against Roland. / Mighty the deeds the Count must now achieve!

CLX.

As they drew near, Roland called up his pride / And summoned all his strength to meet the charge. / No foot of ground he yielded while life remained. / Firm on his courser Veillantif he sat / And gored his flanks with spurs of purest gold. / Into the thickest ranks he and Turpin / The Archbishop rushed. And now the Pagans all / Unto each other cried: "Hence, friends, away! / The horns of those of France we now have heard, / Carlemagne the mighty Emperor returns!"

CLXI.

Ne'er could the Count Roland a coward love, / Nor proud, nor wicked men, nor faithless knights. / He called to the Archbishop: "You, on foot, / And I on horseback, sire! For love of you / I by your side will stand; together we / Will share or good or ill; I leave you not / For aught of human mold. This day we shall / Hurl back the Pagan charge, and Durandal / Shall deal his mightiest blows!" To this replied / The Archbishop: "Traitor he who strikes not well! / King Carle returns; Great shall his vengeance be!"

CLXII.

The Pagans said: "For such ill were we born! / What fatal morn this day for us has ris'n! / Dead lie our lords and Peers! With his great host / King Carle returns, the mighty Baron— Hark! / His clarions sound, and loud the cry 'Montjoie;' / Roland has so great pride, no man of flesh / Can make him yield, or vanquished fall. 'Twere best / We pierced him from afar, and left him lying / Upon the field!" 'Twas done: darts, lances, spears, / Javelins, winged arrows flew so thick, / That his good shield was pierced, his hauberk rent / And torn apart—his body yet unharmed. / Veillantif, pierced with thirty wounds, fell dead / Beneath the Count. The affrighted Pagans fled. / The Count Roland stood on the field, alone.

THE LAST BENEDICTION OF THE ARCHBISHOP.

CLXIII.
Raging in wrath the Pagans fled, and toward / The land of Spain they hasted. The Count Roland / Pursued them not, for Veillantif lie dead. / On foot he stood whether he will or not. / To help Turpin, the Archbishop, fast he ran, / His helm unclasped, removed the hauberk white / And light, then ripped the sides of his blialt [14] / To find his gaping wounds; then tenderly / Pressing him in his arms, on the green sward / He laid him gently down, and fondly prayed: / "O noble man, grant me your leave in this; / Our brave compeers, so dear to us, have breathed / Their last; we should not leave them on the field; / I will their bodies seek and gather here, / To lay them out before you." "Go, and soon / Return," the Archbishop said; "the field is yours / And also mine, thanks to Almighty God!"

CLXIV.
Alone the Count Roland retraced his steps / Throughout the field. Vales, mounts, he searched, and found / Gerin and his companion Gerier, then / Berengier and Otun; here Anseïs, / There Sansun, then beyond, Gerard the old / De Roussillon he found—one after one / He bore each knight within his arms, and placed / Them gently, side by side, before the knees / Of Turpin who could not restrain his tears; / With lifted hands he

---

[14] A sort of undergarment made of gold and silk brocade worn in time of war under the coat of mail, and in time of peace under the mantle of fur. In the latter case it was of silk.

blessed them and said: / "Most hapless Knights! May God the Glorious / Receive your souls, and in his Paradise / 'Mid holy flowers place them! In this hour / Of death, my deepest grief is that no more / The mighty Emperor I shall behold!"

CLXV.
Roland turned back, and searching through the field, / Found, alas! his comrade Olivier. / He pressed him against his bosom tenderly, / And, as he could, returning to Turpin, / Stretched on a shield he lay him down among / The other knights. The Archbishop then assoiled / And signed him with the holy cross. The grief / And pity were more sore than heart could bear... / Then said Roland: "Fair comrade Olivier, / Son of the good Count Renier, he who held / The marches to the distant shores of Gennes; / To break a lance, to pierce a shield, the brave / To counsel, traitors to dismay and foil, / No land e'er saw a better knight."

CLXVI.
 When Count Roland beheld his Peers lie dead, / And Olivier, that friend so tenderly / Beloved, his soul by pity was o'erflowed; / Tears from his eyes gushed out, his countenance / Turned pale; distressed, he could no longer stand. / Would he or not, he swooned and fell to earth. / The Archbishop said: "Baron, what woe is yours!"

CLXVII.
The Archbishop, when he saw Count Roland swoon, / Felt keener grief than e'er he felt before; / Stretched forth his hand, and took the Olifant. / In Ronceval there was a running stream; / Thence will he water bring to Count Roland. / Staggering, with feeble steps, thither he went, / But loss of blood had made him all too weak: / Ere he had gone an acre's length, his heart / Failed, and he sank in mortal agony.

CLXVIII.

Meantime the Count Roland revived. Erect / He stood, but with great pain; then downward looked / And upward. Then he saw the noble lord / The Archbishop, holy minister of God, / Beyond his comrades lying on the sward / Stretched out. He lifted his eyes to Heav'n, recalled / His sins, and raising both his joined hands, / He prayed Our God to grant him paradise. / Turpin, Carle's Knight, was dead, who all his life, / With doughty blows and sermons erudite, / Ne'er ceased to fight the Pagans. May the Lord / Grant him His holy blessing evermore!

CLXIX.

The Count Roland saw lifeless on the field / The Archbishop lie; gush from the gaping wounds / His entrails in the dust, and through his skull / The oozing brain poured o'er his brow. In form / Of holy Cross upon his breast Roland / Disposed both his hands so fair and white, / And mourned him in the fashion of his land: / "O noble man! O knight of lineage pure! / To the Glorious One of Heav'n I thee commend; / For ne'er was man who Him more truly served, / Nor since the Apostles' days, such prophet, strong, / To keep God's law and draw the hearts of men. / From ev'ry pain your soul be freed, and wide / Before it open the Gates of Paradise!"

ROLAND'S DEATH.

CLXX.

Roland now felt his death was drawing nigh: / From both his ears the brain was oozing fast. / For all his peers he prayed that God may call / Their souls to Him; to the Angel Gabriel / He recommended his spirit. In one hand / He took the Olifant, that no reproach / May rest upon him; in the other grasped / Durandal, his good sword. Forward he went, / Far as an arblast [15] sends a shaft, across / A new-tilled ground and toward the

---

[15] Crossbow.

land of Spain. / Upon a hill, beneath two lofty trees, / Four terraces of marble spread: he fell / Prone fainting on the green, for death drew near.

CLXXI.
High were the mounts, and lofty were the trees. / Four terraces were there, of marble bright: / There Count Roland lie senseless on the grass. / Him at this moment spied a Saracen / Who lie among the corpses, feigning death, / His face and body all besmeared with blood. / Sudden he rose to his feet, and bounded / Upon the Baron. Handsome, brave and strong / He was, but from his pride sprang mortal rage. / He seized the body of Roland, and grasped / His arms, exclaiming thus: "Here vanquished Carle's / Great nephew lies! This sword to Araby / I'll bear." He drew it; this aroused the Count.
'

CLXXII.
Roland perceived an alien hand would rob / Him of his sword; his eyes he opened; one word / He spoke: "I trow,[16] not one of us art thou!" / Then with his Olifant from which he parted / Never, he smote the golden studded helm, / Crushing the steel, the head, the bones; both eyes / Were from their sockets beaten out; o'erthrown / Dead at the Baron's feet he fell: "O wretch," / He cried, "how durst thou, or for good or ill, / Lay hands upon Roland? Who hears of this / Will call thee fool. Mine Olifant is cleft, / Its gems and gold all scattered by the blow."

CLXXIII.
Now felt Roland that death was near at hand / And struggled up with all his force; his face / Grew livid; Durandal, his naked sword / He held; beside him rose a gray rock / On which he struck ten mighty blows through grief / And rage; The steel but ground; it broke not, nor / Was it notched; then cried the Count: "Saint Mary, help! / O Durandal! Good sword! ill

---

[16] Believe.

starred art thou! / Though we two part, I care not less for thee. / What victories together thou and I, / Have gained, what kingdoms conquered, which now holds / White-bearded Carle! No coward's hand shall grasp / Thy hilt; a valiant knight has borne thee long, / Such as none shall e'er bear in France the Free!"

CLXXIV.
Roland smote hard the rock of Sardonix; / The steel but ground, it broke not, nor grew blunt; / Then seeing that he could not break his sword, / Thus to himself he mourned for Durandal: / "O good my sword, how bright and pure! Against / The sun what flashing light thy blade reflects! / When Carle passed through the valley of Moriane, / The God of Heaven by his Angel sent / Command that he should give thee to a Count, / A valiant captain; it was then the great / And gentle King did gird thee to my side. / With thee I won for him Anjou, Bretagne; / For him with thee I won Poitou, Maine / And Normandie the free; I won Provence / And Aquitaine, and Lumbardie, and all / The Romanie; I won for him Bavière, / All Flandre; Buguerie; all Puillanie, / Constantinople which allegiance paid, / And Saxonie submitted to his power; / For him I won Ecosse and Galle, Irlande / And Angleterre he made his royal seat; / With thee I conquered all the lands and realms / Which Carle, the hoary-bearded monarch, rules. / Now for this sword I mourn... Far better die / Than in the hands of Pagans let it fall! / May God, Our Father, save sweet France this shame!"

CLXXV.
Upon the grey rock mightily he smote, / Shattering it more than I can tell; the sword / But ground. It broke not, nor received a notch, / And upwards sprang more dazzling in the air. / When saw the Count Roland his sword could never break, / Softly within himself its fate he mourned: / "O Durandal, how fair and holy thou! / In thy gold hilt are relics rare; a tooth / Of great Saint Pierre; some blood of Saint Basile, / A lock of hair

of Monseigneur Saint Denis, / A fragment of the robe of Sainte-Marie. / It is not right that Pagans should own thee; / By Christian hand alone be held. Vast realms / I shall have conquered once that now are ruled / By Carle, the King with beard all blossom-white, / And by them made great emperor and Lord. / May thou ne'er fall into a cowardly hand."

CLXXVI.
The Count Roland felt through his limbs the grasp / Of death, and from his head ev'n to his heart / A mortal chill descended. Unto a pine / He hastened, and fell stretched upon the grass. / Beneath him lie his sword and Olifant, / And toward the Heathen land he turned his head, / That Carle and all his knightly host may say: / "The gentle Count a conqueror has died..." / Then asking pardon for his sins, or great / Or small, he offered up his glove to God.

CLXXVII.
The Count Roland felt now his end approach. / Against a pointed rock, and facing Spain, / He lie. Three times he beat his breast, and said: / "Mea culpa! Oh, my God, may through thy grace, / Be pardoned all my sins, or great or small, / Until this hour committed since my birth!" / Then his right glove he offered up to God, / And toward him angels from high Heav'n descend.

By the 12th century, as Old French came into being, formally educated poets started expanding their repertoire by using dramas drawn either from Roman or Greek sources, but also from Celtic or Germanic legends, imported into France by other scholars. (The fact that Latin was still the *lingua franca* of the literary elite greatly facilitated international communication.) In these new *Chansons*, Christian Miracles were replaced with pagan ones.

One such epic was the popular *Le Roman de Tristan et Iseult* [The Novel of Tristan and Ysolde], which made its first appearance c. 1170 and became an overnight success. Another popular epic was the heavily fictionalized lifestory of King Arthur of Britain, adapted from Geoffrey of Monmouth's 1136 historical tome *History of the Kings of Britain* and Wace's *Roman de Brut*.

The most important French poet of the times was Chrétien de Troyes, who became the virtual founder of Arthurian romance. Born around 1135 and died between 1181 and 1191, Chrétien is considered the founder of Arthurian literature and one of the first authors of chivalric romances. He spent time at the Court of Champagne, serving Count Henri 1st and his wife, Marie de France. He had already produced a number of more classic works, such as *Erec et Enide, Cligès* (which reused the *Tristan and Ysolde* motif), before he began to tackle Arthurian romances.

Chrétien became the most popular of the late 12th-century writers of romance, and was also the most inventive. He was the great pioneer of romances featuring the Court of King Arthur, including *Le Chevalier de la Charrette*, also known as *Lancelot*, which tells the story of the conflict generated by the knight's deeply problematic love for Arthur's wife, Guinevere.

In it, Guinevere is abducted by Meleagant; Lancelot, one of King Arthur's best knights, rushes to her rescue but before reaching the villain's castle, he has to pass several tests, including that of perilous bed and the bridge of the sword. When Lancelot accepts to be led by a herdsman in a cart reserved for criminals, he dishonors himself, but it enables him to rescue the queen he loves and eventually kill Meleagant. The choice to sacrifice one's honor to win one's love is typical of courtly romances...

Chrétien de Troyes: *Lancelot and the Damsel*
(c. 1177)[17]

Upon a certain Ascension Day, King Arthur had come from Caerleon,[18] and had held a very magnificent court at Camelot as was fitting on such a day. After the feast the King did not quit his noble companions, of whom there were many in the hall. The Queen was present, too, and with her many a courteous lady able to converse in French. And Kay, who had furnished the meal, was eating with the others who had served the food.

While Kay was sitting there at meat, behold there came to court a knight, well equipped and fully armed, and thus the knight appeared before the King as he sat among his lords. He gave him no greeting, but spoke out thus:

"King Arthur, I hold in captivity knights, ladies, and damsels who belong to thy dominion and household; but it is not because of any intention to restore them to thee that I make reference to them here; rather do I wish to proclaim and serve thee notice that thou hast not the strength or the resources to enable thee to secure them again. And be assured that thou shalt die before thou canst ever succor them."

The King replied that he must endure what he has not the power to change; nevertheless, he was filled with grief. Then the knight made as if to go away, and turned about, without tarrying longer before the King; but after reaching the door of

---

[17] Excerpted from *Lancelot, ou Le Chevalier de la Charrette* by Chrétien de Troyes, translated into English in 1914 by W.W. Comfort, introduced and annotated by Jean-Marc Lofficier.

[18] Today, a suburban community located in the northern outskirts of Newport, Wales.

the hall, he did not go down the stairs, but stopped and spoke from there these words:

"King, if in thy court there is a single knight in whom thou hast such confidence that thou wouldst dare to entrust to him the Queen that he might escort her after me out into the woods whither I am going, I will promise to await him there, and will surrender to thee all the prisoners whom I hold in exile in my country if he is able to defend the Queen and if he succeeds in bringing her back again."

Many who were in the palace heard this challenge, and the whole court was in an uproar. Kay, too, heard the news as he sat at meat with those who served. Leaving the table, he came straight to the King, and as if greatly enraged, he began to say:

"O King, I have served thee long, faithfully, and loyally; now I take my leave, and shall go away, having no desire to serve thee more."

The King was grieved at what he heard, and as soon as he could, he thus replied to him:

"Is this serious, or a joke?"

And Kay replied:

"O King, fair sire, I have no desire to jest, and I take my leave quite seriously. No other reward or wages do I wish in return for the service I have given you. My mind is quite made up to go away immediately."

"Is it in anger or in spite that you wish to go?" the King inquired; "seneschal, remain at court, as you have done hitherto, and be assured that I have nothing in the world which I would not give you at once in return for your consent to stay."

"Sire," said Kay, "no need of that. I would not accept for each day's pay a measure of fine pure gold."

Thereupon, the King in great dismay went off to seek the Queen.

"My lady," he said, "you do not know the demand that the seneschal makes of me. He asks me for leave to go away, and says he will no longer stay at court; the reason of this I do not know. But he will do at your request what he will not do for me. Go to him now, my lady dear. Since he will not consent to stay for my sake, pray him to remain on your account, and if need be, fall at his feet, for I should never again be happy if I should lose his company."[19]

The King sent the Queen to the seneschal, and she went to him. Finding him with the rest, she went up to him, and said:

"Kay, you may be very sure that I am greatly troubled by the news I have heard of you. I am grieved to say that I have been told it is your intention to leave the King. How does this come about? What motive have you in your mind? I cannot think that you are so sensible or courteous as usual. I want to ask you to remain: stay with us here, and grant my prayer."

"Lady," he said, "I give you thanks; nevertheless, I shall not remain."

The Queen again made her request, and was joined by all the other knights. And Kay informed her that he was growing tired of a service which was unprofitable. Then the Queen prostrated herself at full length before his feet. Kay beseeched her to rise, but she said that she would never do so until he granted her request. Then Kay promised her to remain, provided the King and she would grant in advance a favor he was about to ask.

"Kay," she said, "he will grant it, whatever it may be. Come now, and we shall tell him that upon this condition you will remain."

So Kay went away with the Queen to the King's presence. The Queen said:

"I have had hard work to detain Kay; but I have brought him here to you with the understanding that you will do what he is going to ask."

The King sighed with satisfaction, and said that he would perform whatever request he might make.

---

[19] The high value here set upon Kay by King Arthur is worth noting in view of the unfavorable light in which Chrétien usually portrayed him.

"Sire," said Kay, "hear now what I desire, and what is the gift you have promised me. I esteem myself very fortunate to gain such a boon with your consent. Sire, you have pledged your word that you would entrust to me my lady here, and that we should go after the knight who awaits us in the forest."

Though the King was grieved, he trusted him with the charge, for he never went back upon his word. But it made him so ill-humored and displeased that it plainly showed in his countenance. The Queen, for her part, was sorry too, and all those of the household say that Kay had made a proud, outrageous, and mad request. Then the King took the Queen by the hand, and said:

"My lady, you must accompany Kay without making objection."

And Kay said:

"Hand her over to me now, and have no fear, for I shall bring her back perfectly happy and safe."

The King gave her into his charge, and he took her off. After them all the rest went out, and there was not one who is not sad. You must know that the seneschal was fully armed, and his horse was led into the middle of the courtyard, together with a palfrey, as was fitting for the Queen.

The Queen walked up to the palfrey, which was neither restive nor hard-mouthed. Grieving and sad, with a sigh the Queen mounted, saying to herself in a low voice, so that no one could hear:

"Alas, alas, if you only knew it, I am sure you would never allow me without interference to be led away a step."[20]

She thought she had spoken in a very low tone; but Count Guinable heard her, who was standing by when she mounted. When they started away, as great a lament was made by all the men and women present as if she already lay dead upon a bier. They did not believe that she would ever in her life come back.

---

[20] This remark is addressed to the absent Lancelot, who is Guinevere's secret lover.

The seneschal in his impudence took her where that other knight was awaiting her. But no one was so much concerned as to undertake to follow him; until at last my lord Gawain thus addressed the King his uncle:

"Sire," he said, "you have done a very foolish thing, which causes me great surprise; but if you will take my advice, while they are still nearby, I and you will ride after them, and all those who wish to accompany us. For my part, I cannot restrain myself from going in pursuit of them at once. It would not be proper for us not to go after them, at least far enough to learn what is to become of the Queen, and how Kay is going to comport himself."

"Ah, fair nephew," the King replied, "you have spoken courteously. And since you have undertaken the affair, order our horses to be led out bridled and saddled that there may be no delay in setting out."

The horses were at once brought out, all ready and with the saddles on. First the King mounted, then my lord Gawain, and all the others rapidly. Each one, wishing to be of the party, followed his own will and started away. Some were armed, but there were not a few without their arms. My lord Gawain was armed, and he bade two squires lead by the bridle two extra steeds.

And as they thus approached the forest, they saw Kay's horse running out; and they recognized him, and saw that both reins of the bridle were broken. The horse was running wild, the stirrup-straps all stained with blood, and the saddle-bow was broken and damaged.

Everyone was chagrined at this, and they nudged each other and shook their heads. My lord Gawain was riding far in advance of the rest of the party, and it was not long before he saw coming slowly a knight on a horse that was sore, painfully tired, and covered with sweat.

The knight first saluted my lord Gawain, and his greeting my lord Gawain returned. Then the knight, recognizing my lord Gawain, stopped and thus spoke to him:

"You see, sir, my horse is in a sweat and in such case as to be no longer serviceable. I suppose that those two horses belong to you now, with the understanding that I shall return the service and the favor, I beg you to let me have one or the other of them, either as a loan or outright as a gift."

And Gawain answered him:

"Choose whichever you prefer."

Then he who was in dire distress did not try to select the better or the fairer or the larger of the horses, but leaped quickly upon the one which was nearer to him, and rode him off. Then the one he had just left fell dead, for he had ridden him hard that day, so that he was used up and overworked.

The knight without delay went pricking through the forest, and my lord Gawain followed in pursuit of him with all speed, until he reached the bottom of a hill. And when he had gone some distance, he found the horse dead which he had given to the knight, and noticed that the ground had been trampled by horses, and that broken shields and lances lay strewn about, so that it seemed that there had been a great combat between several knights, and he was very sorry and grieved not to have been there.

However, he did not stay there long, but rapidly passed on until he saw again by chance the knight all alone on foot, completely armed, with helmet laced, shield hanging from his neck, and with his sword girt on. He had overtaken a cart. In those days, such a cart served the same purpose as does a pillory now; and in each good town where there were more than three thousand such carts nowadays, in those times there was only one, and this, like our pillories, had to do service for all those who commit murder or treason, and those who were guilty of any delinquency, and for thieves who had stolen others' property or had forcibly seized it on the roads. Whoever was convicted of any crime was placed upon a cart and dragged through all the streets, and he lost henceforth all his legal rights, and was never afterward heard, honored, or welcomed in any court. The carts were so dreadful in those days that the saying was then first used: "When thou dost see and meet a cart, cross thyself and call upon God, that no evil may befall thee."

The knight on foot, and without a lance, walked behind the cart, and saw a dwarf sitting on the shafts, who held, as a driver does, a long goad in his hand. Then he cried out:

"Dwarf, for God's sake, tell me now if thou hast seen my lady, the Queen, pass by here."

The miserable, low-born dwarf would not give him any news of her, but replied:

"If thou wilt get up into the cart I am driving thou shalt hear tomorrow what has happened to the Queen."

Then he kept on his way without giving further heed. The knight hesitated only for a couple of steps before getting in. Yet, it was unlucky for him that he shrank from the disgrace, and did not jump in at once; for he would later rue his delay. But common sense, which is inconsistent with love's dictates, bid him refrain from getting in, warning him and counseling him to do and undertake nothing for which he might reap shame and disgrace. Reason, which dared thus speak to him, reached only his lips, but not his heart; but love was enclosed within his heart, bidding him and urging him to mount at once upon the cart.

So he jumped in, since love would have it so, feeling no concern about the shame, since he was prompted by love's commands. And my lord Gawain pressed on in haste after the cart, and when he found the knight sitting in it, his surprise was great.

"Tell me," he shouted to the dwarf, "if thou knowest anything of the Queen."

And the dwarf replied:

"If thou art so much thy own enemy as is this knight who is sitting here, get in with him, if it be thy pleasure, and I will drive thee along with him."

When my lord Gawain heard that, he considered it great foolishness, and said that he would not get in, for it would be dishonorable to exchange a horse for a cart:

"Go on, and wherever thy journey lies, I will follow after thee."

Thereupon they started ahead, one mounted on his horse, the other two riding in the cart, and thus they proceeded in company.

Late in the afternoon they arrived at a town, which, you must know, was very rich and beautiful. All three entered through the gate; the people were greatly amazed to see a knight borne upon the cart, and they took no pains to conceal their feelings, but small and great and old and young shouted taunts at him in the streets, so that the knight heard many vile and scornful words at his expense. They all inquired:

"To what punishment is this knight to be consigned? Is he to be rayed, or hanged, or drowned, or burned upon a fire of thorns? Tell us, thou dwarf, who art driving him, in what crime was he caught? Is he convicted of robbery? Is he a murderer, or a criminal?"

And to all this the dwarf made no response, vouchsafing to them no reply. He conducted the knight to a lodging-place; and Gawain followed the dwarf closely to a tower, which stood on the same level over against the town. Beyond there stretched a meadow, and the tower was built close by, up on a lofty eminence of rock, whose face formed a sharp precipice.

Following the horse and cart, Gawain entered the tower. In the hall they met a damsel elegantly attired, than whom there was none fairer in the land, and with her they saw coming two fair and charming maidens. As soon as they saw my lord Gawain, they received him joyously and saluted him, and then asked news about the other knight:

"Dwarf, of what crime is this knight guilty, whom thou dost drive like a lame man?"

He would not answer her question, but he made the knight get out of the cart, and then he withdrew, without their knowing whither he went. Then my lord Gawain dismounted, and valets came forward to relieve the two knights of their armor. The damsel ordered two green mantles to be brought,

which they put on. When the hour for supper came, a sumptu-
ous repast was set. The damsel sat at table beside my lord
Gawain. They would not have changed their lodging-place to
seek any other, for all that evening the damsel showed them
great honor, and provided them with fair and pleasant company.

When they had sat up long enough, two long, high beds
were prepared in the middle of the hall; and there was another
bed alongside, fairer and more splendid than the rest; for, as
the story testifies, it possessed all the excellence that one could
think of in a bed.

When the time came to retire, the damsel took both the
guests to whom she had offered her hospitality; she showed
them the two fine, long, wide beds, and said:

"These two beds are set up here for the accommodation
of your bodies; but in that one yonder no one ever lay who did
not merit it: it was not set up to be used by you."

The knight who came riding on the cart replied at once:

"Tell me," he said, "for what cause this bed is inaccessible."

Being thoroughly informed of this, she answered unhesi-
tatingly:

"It is not your place to ask or make such an inquiry. Any
knight is disgraced in the land after being in a cart, and it is
not fitting that he should concern himself with the matter upon
which you have questioned me; and most of all it is not right
that he should lie upon the bed, for he would soon pay dearly
for his act. So rich a couch has not been prepared for you, and
you would pay dearly for ever harboring such a thought."

He replied:

"You will see about that presently."

"Am I to see it?"

"Yes. It will soon appear."

"By my head," the knight replied, "I know not who is to
pay the penalty. But whoever may object or disapprove, I intend to lie upon this bed and repose there at my ease."

Then he at once disrobed in the bed, which was long and raised half an ell above the other two, and was covered with a yellow cloth of silk and a coverlet with gilded stars. The furs were not of skinned vair but of sable; the covering he had on him would have been fitting for a king. The mattress was not made of straw or rushes or of old mats.

At midnight there descended from the rafters suddenly a lance, as with the intention of pinning the knight through the flanks to the coverlet and the white sheets where he lay. To the lance there was attached a pennon all ablaze. The coverlet, the bedclothes, and the bed itself all caught fire at once. And the tip of the lance passed so close to the knight's side that it cut the skin a little, without seriously wounding him. Then the knight got up, put out the fire and, taking the lance, swung it in the middle of the hall, all this without leaving his bed; rather did he lie down again and slept as securely as at first.

In the morning, at daybreak, the damsel of the tower had Mass celebrated on their account, and had them rise and dress. When Mass had been celebrated for them, the knight who had ridden in the cart sat down pensively at a window, which looked out upon the meadow, and he gazed upon the fields below. The damsel came to another window close by, and there my lord Gawain conversed with her privately for a while about something, I know not what. I do not know what words were uttered, but while they were leaning on the window-sill they saw carried along the river through the fields a bier, upon which there lay a knight,[21] and alongside three damsels walked, mourning bitterly.

Behind the bier they saw a crowd approaching, with a tall knight in front, leading a fair lady by the horse's rein. The knight at the window knew that it was the Queen. He continued to gaze at her attentively and with delight as long as she was visible. And when he could no longer see her, he was minded to throw himself out and break his body down below.

---

[21] The defeated seneschal.

And he would have let himself fall out had not my lord Gawain seen him, and drawn him back, saying:

"I beg you, sire, be quiet now. For God's sake, never think again of committing such a mad deed. It is wrong for you to despise your life."

"He is perfectly right," the damsel said; "for will not the news of his disgrace be known everywhere? Since he has been upon the cart, he has good reason to wish to die, for he would be better dead than alive. His life henceforth is sure to be one of shame, vexation, and unhappiness."

Then the knights asked for their armor, and armed themselves, the damsel treating them courteously, with distinction and generosity; for when she had joked with the knight and ridiculed him enough, she presented him with a horse and lance as a token of her goodwill.

The knights then courteously and politely took leave of the damsel, first saluting her, and then going off in the direction taken by the crowd they had seen. Thus they rode out from the town without addressing them. They proceeded quickly in the direction they had seen taken by the Queen, but they did not overtake the procession, which had advanced rapidly. After leaving the fields, the knights entered an enclosed place, and found a beaten road. They advanced through the woods until it might be six o'clock, and then at a crossroads they met a damsel, whom they both saluted, each asking and requesting her to tell them, if she knew, whither the Queen has been taken. Replying intelligently, she said to them:

"If you would pledge me your word, I could set you on the right road and path, and I would tell you the name of the country and of the knight who is conducting her; but whoever would essay to enter that country must endure sore trials, for before he could reach there he must suffer much."

Then my lord Gawain replied:

"Damsel, so help me God, I promise to place all my strength at your disposal and service, whenever you please, if you will tell me now the truth."

And he who had been on the cart did not say that he would pledge her all his strength; but he proclaimed, like one whom love makes rich, powerful and bold for any enterprise, that at once and without hesitation he would promise her anything she desired, and he put himself altogether at her disposal.

"Then I will tell you the truth," said she.

Then the damsel related to them the following story:

"In truth, my lords, Meleagant, a tall and powerful knight, son of the King of Gorre, has taken her off into the kingdom whence no foreigner returns, but where he must perforce remain in servitude and banishment."

Then they asked her:

"Damsel, where is this country? Where can we find the way thither?"

She replied:

"That you shall quickly learn; but you may be sure that you will meet with many obstacles and difficult passages, for it is not easy to enter there except with the permission of the king, whose name is Bademagu; however, it is possible to enter by two very perilous paths and by two very difficult passage ways. One is called the water-bridge, because the bridge is under water, and there is the same amount of water beneath it as above it, so that the bridge is exactly in the middle; and it is only a foot and a half in width and in thickness. This choice is certainly to be avoided, and yet it is the less dangerous of the two. In addition there are a number of other obstacles of which I will say nothing.

"The other bridge is still more impracticable and much more perilous, never having been crossed by man. It is just like a sharp sword, and therefore all the people call it 'the sword-bridge.' Now I have told you all the truth I know."

But they asked of her once again:

"Damsel, deign to show us these two passages."

To which the damsel made reply:

"This road here is the most direct to the water-bridge, and that one yonder leads straight to the sword-bridge."

Then the knight, who had been on the cart, said:

"Sire, I am ready to share with you without prejudice: take one of these two routes, and leave the other one to me; take whichever you prefer."

"In truth," my lord Gawain replied, "both of them are hard and dangerous: I am not skilled in making such a choice, and hardly know which of them to take; but it is not right for me to hesitate when you have left the choice to me: I will choose the water-bridge."

The other answered:

"Then I must go uncomplainingly to the sword-bridge, which I agree to do."

Thereupon, they all three parted, each one commending the others very courteously to God. And when she saw them departing, the damsel said:

"Each one of you owes me a favor of my choosing, whenever I may choose to ask it. Take care not to forget that."

"We shall surely not forget it, sweet friend," both the knights called out.

Then each one went his own way, and he of the cart was occupied with deep reflections, like one who has no strength or defense against love which holds him in its sway. His thoughts were such that he totally forgot himself, and he knew not whether he was alive or dead, forgetting even his own name, not knowing whether he was armed or not, or whither he was going or whence he came. Only one creature he had in mind, and for her his thought was so occupied that he neither saw nor heard aught else.

And his horse bore him along rapidly, following no crooked road, but the best and the most direct; and thus proceeding unguided, he brought him into an open plain. In this plain there was a ford, on the other side of which a knight stood armed, who guarded it, and in his company there was a damsel who had come on a palfrey.

By this time the afternoon was well advanced, and yet the knight, unchanged and unwearied, pursued his thoughts. The horse, being very thirsty, saw clearly the ford, and as soon as he saw it, hastened toward it. Then he on the other side cried out:

"Knight, I am guarding the ford, and forbid you to cross."

He neither gave him heed, nor heard his words, being still deep in thought. In the meantime, his horse advanced rapidly toward the water. The knight called out to him that he would do wisely to keep at a distance from the ford, for there was no passage that way; and he swore by the heart within his breast that he would smite him if he entered the water. But his threats were not heard, and he called out to him a third time:

"Knight, do not enter the ford against my will and prohibition; for, by my head, I shall strike you as soon as I see you in the ford."

But the knight was so deep in thought that he did not hear him. And the horse, quickly leaving the bank, leaped into the ford and greedily began to drink. And the knight said he shall pay for this, that his shield and the hauberk he wore upon his back shall afford him no protection. First, he put his horse at a gallop, and from a gallop he urged him to a run, and he struck the knight so hard that he knocked him down flat in the ford which he had forbidden him to cross.

His lance flew from his hand and the shield from his neck. When he felt the water, he shivered, and though stunned, he jumped to his feet, like one aroused from sleep, listening and looking about him with astonishment, to see who it could be who had struck him. Then face to face with the other knight, he said:

"Vassal, tell me why you have struck me, when I was not aware of your presence, and when I had done you no harm."

"Upon my word, you had wronged me," the other said: "did you not treat me disdainfully when I forbade you three times to cross the ford, shouting at you as loudly as I could? You surely heard me challenge you at least two or three times, and you entered in spite of me, though I told you I should strike you as soon as I saw you in the ford."

Then the knight replied to him:

"Whoever heard you or saw you, let him be damned, so far as I am concerned. I was probably deep in thought when you forbade me to cross the ford. But be assured that I would make you reset it, if I could just lay one of my hands on your bridle."

And the other replied:

"Why, what of that? If you dare, you may seize my bridle here and now. I do not esteem your proud threats so much as a handful of ashes."

And he replied:

"That suits me perfectly. However the affair may turn out, I should like to lay my hands on you."

Then the other knight advanced to the middle of the ford, where the other lay his left hand upon his bridle, and his right hand upon his leg, pulling, dragging, and pressing him so roughly that he remonstrated, thinking that he would pull his leg out of his body. Then he begged him to let go, saying:

"Knight, if it please thee to fight me on even terms, take thy shield and horse and lance, and joust with me."

The other answered:

"That will I not do, upon my word; for I suppose thou wouldst run away as soon as thou hadst escaped my grip."

Hearing this, he was much ashamed, and said:

"Knight, mount thy horse, in confidence for I will pledge thee loyally my word that I shall not flinch or run away."

Then once again he answered him:

"First, thou wilt have to swear to that, and I insist upon receiving thy oath that thou wilt neither run away nor flinch, nor touch me, nor come near me until thou shalt see me on my horse; I shall be treating thee very generously, if, when thou art in my hands, I let thee go."

He could do nothing but give his oath; and when the other heard him swear, he gathered up his shield and lance which were floating in the ford and by this time had drifted well down-stream; then he returned and took his horse. After catching and mounting him, he seized the shield by the shoulder-straps and lay his lance in rest. Then each spurred toward the other as fast as their horses could carry them. And he who had to defend the ford first attacked the other, striking him so hard that his lance was completely splintered. The other struck him in return so that he threw him prostrate into the ford, and the water closed over him.

Having accomplished that, he drew back and dismounted, thinking he could drive and chase away a hundred such. While he drew from the scabbard his sword of steel, the other jumped up and drew his excellent flashing blade. Then they clashed again, advancing and covering themselves with the shields which gleamed with gold. Ceaselessly and without repose, they wielded their swords; they had the courage to deal so many blows that the battle finally was so protracted that the Knight of the Cart was greatly ashamed in his heart, thinking that he was making a sorry start in the way he had undertaken, when he had spent so much time in defeating a single knight. If he had met yesterday a hundred such, he did not think or believe that they could have withstood him; so now he was much grieved and wroth to be in such an exhausted state that he was missing his strokes and losing time. Then he ran at him and pressed him so hard that the other knight gave way and fled.

However reluctant he may be, he left the ford and crossing free. But the other followed him in pursuit until he fell forward upon his hands; then he of the cart ran up to him, swearing by all he saw that he should rue the day when he upset him in the ford and disturbed his reverie.

The damsel, whom the knight had with him, upon hearing the threats, was in great fear, and begged him for her sake to forbear from killing him; but he told her that he must do so, and could show him no mercy for her sake, in view of the shameful wrong that he had done him. Then, with sword drawn, he approached the knight who cried in sore dismay:

"For God's sake and for my own, show me the mercy I ask of you."

And he replied:

"As God may save me, no one ever sinned so against me that I would not show him mercy once, for God's sake as is right, if he asked it of me in God's name. And so on thee I will have mercy; for I ought not to refuse thee when thou hast besought me. But first, thou shalt give me thy word to constitute thyself my prisoner whenever I may wish to summon thee."

Though it was hard to do so, he promised him. At once the damsel said:

"O knight, since thou hast granted the mercy he asked of thee, if ever thou hast broken any bonds, for my sake now be merciful and release this prisoner from his parole. Set him free at my request, upon condition that when the time comes, I shall do my utmost to repay thee in any way that thou shalt choose."

Then he declared himself satisfied with the promise she had made, and set the knight at liberty. Then she was ashamed and anxious, thinking that he would recognize her, which she did not wish. But he went away at once, the knight and the damsel commending him to God, and taking leave of him. He granted them leave to go, while he himself pursued his way, until late in the afternoon he met a damsel coming, who was very fair and charming, well attired and richly dressed. The damsel greets him prudently and courteously, and he replied:

"Damsel, God grant you health and happiness."

Then the damsel said to him:

"Sire, my house is prepared for you, if you will accept my hospitality, but you shall find shelter there only on condition that you will lie with me; upon these terms I propose and make the offer."

Not a few there were who would have thanked her five hundred times for such a gift; but he was much displeased, and made a very different answer:

"Damsel, I thank you for the offer of your house, and esteem it highly, but, if you please, I should be very sorry to lie with you."

"By my eyes," the damsel said, "then I retract my offer."

And he, since it was unavoidable, let her have her way, though his heart grieved to give consent. He felt only reluctance now; but greater distress would be his when it was time to go to bed. The damsel, too, who led him away, would pass through sorrow and heaviness. For it was possible that she would love him so that she would not wish to part with him.

As soon as he had granted her wish and desire, she escorted him to a fortified place, than which there was none fairer in Thessaly; for it was entirely enclosed by a high wall and a deep moat, and there was no man within except him whom she brought with her.

Here she had constructed for her residence a quantity of handsome rooms, and a large and roomy hall. Riding along a river bank, they approached their lodging-place, and a drawbridge was lowered to allow them to pass. Crossing the bridge, they entered in, and found the hall open with its roof of tiles. Through the open door they passed, and saw a table laid with a broad white cloth, upon which the dishes were set, and the candles burning in their stands, and the gilded silver drinking-cups, and two pots of wine, one red and one white.

Standing beside the table, at the end of a bench, they found two basins of warm water in which to wash their hands, with a richly embroidered towel, all white and clean, with which to dry their hands. No valets, servants, or squires were to be found or seen.

The knight, removing his shield from about his neck, hung it upon a hook, and, taking his lance, lay it above upon a rack. Then he dismounted from his horse, as did the damsel from hers. The knight, for his part, was pleased that she did not care to wait for him to help her to dismount. Having dismounted, she ran directly to a room and brought him a short mantle of scarlet cloth which she put on him. The hall was by no means dark; for beside the light from the stars, there were many large twisted candles lighted there, so that the illumination was very bright. When she had thrown the mantle about his shoulders, she said to him:

"Friend, here is the water and the towel; there is no one to present or offer it to you except me whom you see. Wash your hands, and then sit down, when you feel like doing so. The hour and the meal, as you can see, demand that you should do so."

He washed, and then gladly and readily took his seat, and she sat down beside him, and they are and drank together, until the time came to leave the table.

When they had risen from the table, the damsel said to the knight:

"Sire, if you do not object, go outside and amuse yourself; but, if you please, do not stay after you think I must be in bed. Feel no concern or embarrassment; for then you may come to me at once, if you will keep the promise you have made."

And he replied:

"I will keep my word, and will return when I think the time has come."

Then he went out, and stayed in the courtyard until he thought it was time to return and keep the promise he had made. Going back into the hall, he saw nothing of her who would be his mistress; for she was not there. Not finding or seeing her, he said:

"Wherever she may be, I shall look for her until I find her."

He made no delay in his search, being bound by the promise he had made her. Entering one of the rooms, he heard a damsel cry aloud, and it was the very one with whom he was about to lie. At the same time, he saw the door of another room standing open, and stepping toward it, he saw right before his eyes a knight who had thrown her down, and was holding her naked and prostrate upon the bed. She, thinking that he had come of course to help her, cried aloud:

"Help, help, thou knight, who art my guest. If thou dost not take this man away from me, I shall find no one to do so; if thou dost not succor me speedily, he will wrong me before thy eyes. Thou art the one to lie with me, in accordance with thy promise; and shall this man by force accomplish his wish before thy eyes? Gentle knight, exert thyself, and make haste to bear me aid."

He saw that the other man held the damsel brutally uncovered to the waist, and he was ashamed and angered to see him assault her so; yet it was not jealousy he felt, nor would he be made a cuckold by him. At the door there stood as guards two knights completely armed and with swords drawn. Behind them there stood four men-at-arms, each armed with an axe the sort with which you could split a cow down the back as easily as a root of juniper or broom. The knight hesitated at the door, and thought:

"God, what can I do? I am engaged in no less an affair than the quest of Queen Guinevere. I ought not to have the heart of a hare, when for her sake I have engaged in such a quest. If cowardice puts its heart in me, and if I follow its dictates, I shall never attain what I seek. I am disgraced, if I stand here; indeed, I am ashamed even to have thought of holding back. My heart is very sad and oppressed: now I am so ashamed and distressed that I would gladly die for having hesitated here so long. I say it not in pride: but may God have mercy on me if I do not prefer to die honorably rather than live a life of shame! If my path were unobstructed, and if these men gave me leave to pass through without restraint, what honor would I gain? Truly, in that case the greatest coward alive would pass through; and all the while I hear this poor creature calling for help constantly, and reminding me of my promise, and reproaching me with bitter taunts."

Then he stepped to the door, thrusting in his head and shoulders; glancing up, he saw two swords descending. He drew back, and the knights could not check their strokes: they had wielded them with such force that the swords struck the floor, and both were broken in pieces. When he saw that the swords were broken, he paid less attention to the axes, fearing and dreading them much less. Rushing in among them, he struck first one guard in the side and then another. The two who were nearest him he jostled and thrust aside, throwing them both down flat; the third missed his stroke at him, but the fourth, who attacked him, struck him so that he cut his mantle and shirt, and sliced the white flesh on his shoulder so that the blood trickled down from the wound. But he, without delay, and without complaining of his wound, pressed on more rapidly, until he struck between the temples him who was assaulting his hostess.

Before he departed, he would try to keep his pledge to her. He made him stand up reluctantly. Meanwhile, he who had missed striking him came at him as fast as he could and, raising his arm again, expected to split his head to the teeth with the axe. But the other, alert to defend himself, thrust the knight toward him in such a way that he received the axe just where the shoulder joins the neck, so that they were cleaved apart. Then the knight seized the axe, wresting it quickly from him who held it; then he let go the knight whom he still held, and looked to his own defense; for the knights from the door, and the three men with axes were all attacking him fiercely. So he leaped quickly between the bed and the wall, and called to them:

"Come on now, all of you. If there were thirty-seven of you, you would have all the fight you wish, with me so favorably placed; I shall never be overcome by you."

And the damsel watching him, exclaimed:

"By my eyes, you need have no thought of that henceforth where I am."

Then at once she dismissed the knights and the men-at-arms, who retired from there at once, without delay or objection. And the damsel continued:

"Sire you have well defended me against the men of my household. Come now, and I'll lead you on."

Hand in hand they entered the hall, but he was not at all pleased, and would have willingly dispensed with her.

In the midst of the hall a bed had been set up, the sheets of which were by no means soiled, but were white and wide and well spread out. The bed was not of shredded straw or of coarse spreads. But a covering of two silk cloths had been laid upon the couch.

The damsel lay down first, but without removing her chemise. He had great trouble in removing his hose and in untying the knots. He sweated with the trouble of it all; yet, in the midst of all the trouble, his promise impelled and drove him on. Was this then an actual force? Yes, virtually so; for he felt that he was in duty bound to take his place by the damsel's side. It was his promise that urged him and dictated his act.

So he lied down at once, but like her, he did not remove his shirt. He took good care not to touch her; and when he was in bed, he turned away from her as far as possible, and spoke not a word to her, like a monk to whom speech is forbidden. Not once did he look at her, nor show her any courtesy. Why not? Because his heart did not go out to her. She was certainly very fair and winsome, but not everyone is pleased and touched by what is fair and winsome. The knight had only one heart, and this one was really no longer his, but had been entrusted to someone else, so that he could not bestow it elsewhere. Love, which holds all hearts beneath its sway, requires it to be lodged in a single place. All hearts? No, only those which it esteems. And he whom love deigns to control ought to prize himself the more. Love prized his heart so highly that it constrained it in a special manner, and made him so proud of this distinction that I am not inclined to find fault with him, if he lets alone what love forbids, and remains fixed where it desires.

The maiden clearly saw and knew that he disliked her company and would gladly dispense with it, and that, having no desire to win her love, he would not attempt to woo her. So she said:

"My lord, if you will not feel hurt, I will leave and return to bed in my own room, and you will be more comfortable. I do not believe that you are pleased with my company and society. Do not esteem me less if I tell you what I think. Now take your rest all night, for you have so well kept your promise that I have no right to make further request of you. So I commend you to God; and shall go away."

Thereupon she arose; the knight did not object, but rather gladly let her go, like one who is the devoted lover of someone else; the damsel clearly perceived this, and went to her room, where she undressed completely and retired, saying to herself:

"Of all the knights I have ever known, I never knew a single knight whom I would value the third part of an angevin in comparison with this one. As I understand the case, he has on hand a more perilous and grave affair than any ever undertaken by a knight; and may God grant that he succeed in it."

Then she fell asleep, and remained in bed until the next day's dawn appeared.

At daybreak she awoke and got up. The knight awoke too, dressing, and putting on his arms, without waiting for any help. Then the damsel came and saw that he was already dressed. Upon seeing him, she said:

"May this day be a happy one for you."

"And may it be the same to you, damsel," the knight replied, adding that he was waiting anxiously for someone to bring out his horse.

The maiden had someone fetch the horse, and said:

"Sire, I should like to accompany you for some distance along the road, if you would agree to escort and conduct me according to the customs and practices which were observed before we were made captive in the kingdom of Logres."

In those days the customs and privileges were such that, if a knight found a damsel or lorn maid alone, and if he cared for his fair name, he would no more treat her with dishonor than he would cut his own throat. And if he assaulted her, he would be disgraced forever in every court. But if, while she was under his escort, she should be won at arms by another who engaged him in battle, then this other knight might do with her what he pleased without receiving shame or blame. This is why the damsel said she would go with him, if he had the courage and willingness to safe guard her in his company, so that no one should do her any harm. And he said to her:

"No one shall harm you, I promise you, unless he harm me first."

"Then," she replied, "I will go with you."

She ordered her palfrey to be saddled, and her command was obeyed at once. Her palfrey was brought together with the knight's horse. Without the aid of any squire, they both mounted, and rapidly rode away.

She talked to him, but not caring for her words, he paid no attention to what she said. He liked to think, but disliked to talk. Love very often inflicted afresh the wound it had given him. Yet, he applied no poultice to the wound to cure it and make it comfortable, having no intention or desire to secure a poultice or to seek a physician, unless the wound becomes more painful. Yet, there was one whose remedy he would gladly seek...[22]

They followed the roads and paths in the right direction until they came to a spring, situated in the middle of a field, and bordered by a stone basin. Someone had forgotten upon the stone a comb of gilded ivory. Never since ancient times had wise man or fool seen such a comb. In its teeth there was almost a handful of hair belonging to her who had used the comb.

When the damsel noticed the spring, and saw the stone, she did not wish her companion to see it; so she turned off in another direction. And he, agreeably occupied with his own thoughts, did not at once remark that she was leading him aside; but when at last he noticed it, he was afraid of being beguiled, thinking that she was yielding and was going out of the way in order to avoid some danger.

"See here, damsel," he cried, "you are not going right; come this way! No one, I think, ever went straight who left this road."

---

[22] Guinevere.

"Sire, this is a better way for us," the damsel said, "I am sure of it."

Then he replied to her:

"I don't know, damsel, what you think; but you can plainly see that the beaten path lies this way; and since I have started to follow it, I shall not turn aside. So come now, if you will, for I shall continue along this way."

Then they went forward until they came near the stone basin and saw the comb. The knight said:

"I surely never remember to have seen so beautiful a comb as this."

"Let me have it," the damsel said.

"Willingly, damsel," he replied.

Then he stooped over and picked it up. While holding it, he looked at it steadfastly, gazing at the hair until the damsel began to laugh. When he saw her doing so, he begged her to tell him why she laughed. And she said:

"Never mind, for I will never tell you."

"Why not?" he asked.

"Because I don't wish to do so."

And when he heard that, he implored her like one who held that lovers ought to keep faith mutually:

"Damsel, if you love anything passionately, by that I implore and conjure and beg you not to conceal from me the reason why you laugh."

"Your appeal is so strong," she said, "that I will tell you and keep nothing back. I am sure, as I am of anything, that this comb belonged to the Queen. And you may take my word that those are strands of the Queen's hair which you see to be so fair and light and radiant, and which are clinging in the teeth of the comb; they surely never grew anywhere else."

Then the knight replied:

"Upon my word, there are plenty of queens and kings; what queen do you mean?"

And she answered:

"In truth, fair sire, it is of King Arthur's wife I speak."

When he heard that, he had not strength to keep from bowing his head over his saddle-bow. And when the damsel saw him thus, she was amazed and terrified, thinking he was about to fall. Do not blame her for her fear, for she thought him in a faint. He might as well have swooned, so near was he to doing so; for in his heart, he felt such grief that for a long time he lost his color and power of speech.

And the damsel dismounted, and ran as quickly as possible to support and succor him; for she would not have wished for anything to see him fall. When he saw her, he felt ashamed, and said:

"Why do you need to bear me aid?"

You must not suppose that the damsel told him why; for he would have been ashamed and distressed, and it would have annoyed and troubled him, if she had confessed to him the truth. So she took good care not to tell the truth, but tactfully answered him:

"Sire, I dismounted to get the comb; for I was so anxious to hold it in my hand that I could no longer wait."

Willing that she should have the comb, he gave it to her, first pulling out the hair so carefully that he tore none of it. Never would the eye of man see anything receive such honor as when he began to adore these tresses. A hundred thousand times he raised them to his eyes and mouth, to his forehead and face: he manifested his joy in every way, considering himself rich and happy now. He laid them in his bosom near his heart, between the shirt and the flesh. He would not exchange them for a cartload of emeralds and carbuncles, nor did he think that any sore or illness could afflict him now; he held in contempt essence of pearl, treacle, and the cure for pleurisy;[23] even for St. Martin and St. James he had no need; for he had such confidence in this hair that he required no other aid.

But what was this hair like? If I tell the truth about it, you will think I am a mad teller of lies. When the mart is full

---

[23] Medieval remedies of dubious efficacy.

at the yearly fair of St. Denis,[24] and when the goods are most abundantly displayed, even then the knight would not take all this wealth, unless he had found these tresses too. And if you wish to know the truth, gold a hundred thousand times refined, and melted down as many times, would be darker than is night compared with the brightest summer day we have had this year, if one were to see the gold and set it beside this hair. But why should I make a long story of it? The damsel mounted again with the comb in her possession; while he reveled and delighted in the tresses in his bosom.

---

[24] A great annual fair at Paris marked the festival, on June 11, of St. Denis, the patron saint of the city.

Although the particular popularity of Chrétien de Troyes' works was undoubtedly a major factor in establishing Arthuriana as a core topic of the evolving genre of prose Romance, contemporary politics also played a leading part, many of the key events of the period being the slowly-unfolding consequences of the event that subsequently made 1066 the best-known date in British history, when William I defeated his Saxon rival for the English throne, Harold, at the Battle of Hastings. The wealthiest and most powerful woman in Western Europe throughout the latter half of the 12th century was Eleanor of Aquitaine, who first married Louis VI of France, but almost immediately, after the annulment of that marriage in 1152, married Henry, Duke of Normandy; the latter became Henry II of England two years later, and the sons she bore him included the future kings Richard Coeur-de-Lion and John, both of whom became key figures in English legend.

Eleanor's court was undoubtedly an important source of patronage for writers and performers of romances, especially the epic-imitating *Chansons de geste*, and her concerns undoubtedly help to shape the substance of the genre. Some subsequent historians credited her with the importation of an important element of southern "troubadour culture" into the chivalric romances of Northern France, hence generating the stories of problematic infatuation that played a central role in the genre, from *Tristan and Ysolde* onwards. Although her personal role might have been exaggerated, the effective fusion of the Duchy of Aquitaine with Normandy undoubtedly formed the practical background to the amalgamation, as well as assisting its symbolization. The confusion of influences, however, extended much further than the central marriage of Eleanor and Henry.

The conquering Normans, who had originated as invaders from Scandinavia, were pillars of the feudal political system, glorified in romance by the retrospective extrapolation of the contemporary hierarchy of kings, barons and knights into imaginary pasts, where it could be more easily credited with imaginary virtues. Much of that mythology was borrowed

79

from the Normans' neighbors in northern France, the Bretons, who were already taking a nostalgic delight in the 12th century in looking back to lost glory days of heroic *preux chevaliers* [gallant knights]. Meanwhile, the rulers of large parts of both France and England had long been descended from invaders—the Franks and the Saxons—who had partly displaced and partly absorbed previous cultures, loosely describable as Gauls and Celts, which had been previously conquered, at least briefly, by the Roman Empire. In consequence, the legendary pasts cooked up in France and England in the 12th century were blessed with a rich complexity and confusion of inherited and improvised materials.

Chrétien's romances reflect the political and cultural ideals of the times. They stage an aristocratic ideal blending the chivalrous adventure, courtly love and religious aspirations that symbolizes the spirit of crusade. In its introduction, Chrétien reported that the subject matter of *Lancelot* had been suggested to him by Mary de Champagne.

Chrétien's completed works in that subgenre were, however, eventually outshone—at least in terms of modern pseudoscholarship—by his unfinished allegory *Le Conte du Graal*, also known as *Perceval*, whose incompleteness left it with an intriguing aspect of mystery.

In *Perceval*, Chrétien's eponymous hero is a brave but innocent knight, who discovers the accursed land of the Fisher King, who is the guardian of the Holy Grail, but who suffers from a mysterious wound that does not heal. Perceval could heal the King and become the Grail's guardian, but misses his opportunity. In its original version, *Perceval* was not a Christian work. The Grail was not yet "holy," and bore no relation to the latter version of the cup being used by Joseph of Arimathea to collect Christ's blood. Instead, the early version of *Perceval* drew on a variety of pagan myths and symbols. Some were clearly Celtic in nature and echoed druidic ceremonies; others were more obscure, possibly incorporating elements drawn of the Greek "Mysteries" of Eleusis and the cult of Mithra.

In 1215, the Roman Catholic Church held the Council of Lateran, which formally established the dogma of the Eucharist—Christ's flesh and blood being mystically present in the wafer host and wine taken during the Holy Communion. It certainly was no coincidence that, at the same time, Robert de Boron,[25] one of Chrétien's continuators, tied together the Arthurian legends of Lancelot and Perceval and placed them firmly within a Christian context. It was de Boron, and not Chrétien, who established the now well-known origins of the Holy Grail, with Joseph of Arimathea and the blood of Christ. He also added the characters of Lancelot, King Arthur, Merlin, Morgan Le Fey, and, more generally, gave the saga the form that we know today.

Between 1215 and 1235, de Boron published five books: *Histoire du Saint-Graal* [The Tale of the Holy Grail], *Histoire de Merlin* [The Tale of Merlin], *Le Livre de Lancelot du Lac* [The Book of Lancelot of the Lake], *La Quête du Saint-Graal* [The Quest for the Holy Grail] and *La Mort du Roi Arthur* [The Death of King Arthur]. These books formed the basis for all subsequent Arthurian legends, including the later retelling by Sir Thomas Malory.

Among other *Chansons de Geste* told and/or written during the 13th century, there were three which included strong fantasy elements and which deserve to be mentioned here because of the archetypes they virtually established for later works of fantasy:

The first was *Huon de Bordeaux*, an anonymous epic in which Huon, one of Charlemagne's proud knights, meets the fairy king Aubéron, whom Shakespeare would later turn into Oberon for *A Midsummer Night's Dream*, and who is described there as the son of Julius Cesar and Morgane Le Fey. Cesar was, clearly, a great, almost magical emperor from a long-buried past. As for Morgane, she was originally a fairy queen named Morgue, whose origins predated that of the Ar-

---

[25] Late 12th-early 13th centuries. Little is known about him outside of the poems he allegedly wrote.

thurian legends. Aubéron gives Huon a magic ring and a magic horn which enable him to summon the legions of fairyland. He then goes on to fight an evil Saracen sorcerer-king, and eventually frees and marries the beautiful Esclarmonde.

Amadas et Ydoine, another anonymous epic, is a tale of thwarted love between Ydoine, betrothed to the Count of Nevers, and her brave lover, Amadas. It features witches and sorcery aplenty, as well as the mysterious character of the Maufé, who is either the Devil himself, or one of his demons. The Maufé (a deformation of the French *mauvais* meaning evil) is not like the crude and grotesque devil depicted in the Religious Dramas of the times; he is, on the contrary, a seductive, clever, charismatic character, imbued with evil supernatural powers, but bound by certain rules. The Maufé became the template for all subsequent "Prince of Darkness," from Faust's Mephistopheles to the Devil played by Jules Berry in the classic film *Les Visiteurs du Soir*.

Le Paradis de la Reine Sybille [Queen Sybil's Paradise] (c. 1200), credited to Antoine de la Salle (1386-1462), tells the story of a brave knight who discovers a hidden fairyland, ruled by the beautiful queen Sybil. The Queen and her maidens are succubae—they occasionally turn into snakes—and, as was often the case in such legends, the Knight can only leave the kingdom on certain days. Eventually, he does escape, but the memories of the sexual delights he experienced prove too great a temptation, and he chooses to return to Queen Sybil's Paradise, thereby losing his eternal soul. *Le Paradis de la Reine Sybille* became the template for numerous, similar tales, including Richard Wagner's *Tannhauser*. It also, clearly and emphatically, condemned the pleasures of the flesh, more evidence of the Christianization of the old legends.

Other similar works worthy of mention here include *Méliador*, by the famous historian Jean Froissart (1337-1405), *Méraugis de Portlesguez* by Raoul de Houdenc, *La Demoiselle à la Mule* [The Lady of the Mule] by Païen de Maisières, *Perlesvaus, Le Livre de Caradoc* [The Book of Caradoc], *Le Chevalier à l'Épée* [The Knight of the Sword], *Hunbaut,*

L'Atre Périlleux [The Perilous Hearth], *Gliglois*, *Le Roman de Jaufré* [The Book of Jaufre], *Blandin de Cornouaille* [Blandin of Cornwall], *Les Merveilles de Rigomer* [The Wonders of Rigomer], and *Le Chevalier au Papegau* [The Knight of the Papegau].

HIGH FANTASY

French medieval poetry was lyrical, elegant and full of allegorical meanings. As such, it often employed fantasy concepts as literary artifices. The famous *Le Roman de la Rose* [The Romance of the Rose] (c. 1230), by Guillaume de Lorris (1200-1238),[26] celebrates courtly love by showing two young lovers venturing into a dream-like world where the plucking of a rose symbolizes an amorous victory.

Le Jeu de la Feuillée [The Game of the Leaves] (c. 1275) by Adam de la Halle (1220-1288) is another epic poem which features fairy creatures and introduces the character of King Hellequin, patterned after a Germanic storm god. Hellequin is the Lord of the Wild Hunt, the Master of Spells. In the 14th century, Dante took this character and renamed him Harlequin. In the original poem, Hellequin is madly in love with Morgue the fairy, Morgan Le Fey or Fata Morgana in later incarnations.

In the anonymous *Le Livre de la Fontaine Périlleuse* [The Book of the Perilous Fountain] (c. 1425), a young man seeks the Fountain of Life. When he peers into its waters, an arm made of fire comes out and stabs him. In order to be cured, he then has to undergo a series of mystic tests. The poem can be read as an allegory of the alchemical *Grand Oeuvre,* and its young hero eventually finds enlightenment when he discovers the "hermetic sun." This was one of the first literary works in which the frontier between the occult and fantasy was crossed.

---

[26] *The Romance of the Rose,* left unfinished, was completed by Jean de Meun (1250-1305) in the 14th century.

The famous fairy queen *Mélusine* (also known as Ondine) took modern form in Jehan d'Arras's [27] 1475 eponymous poem. One day a week, the lovely bride Mélusine seeks isolation in order to revert to her natural form. She begs her husband, Raimondin de Lusignan, not to try to discover her secret, which is that she is half-human, half-reptile. When he does (as they always do!), this costs poor Mélusine her soul. She is forced to turn back into a winged serpent and fly away.

The Celtic ballads of Marie de France were filled with fantasy: *Yonec* features a lover who turns into a bird; *Milon*, an enchanted ring; *Eliduc*, a magic potion, etc. Marie de France was the first author to have written about the doom of the magical city of Ys, a mythical town located off the coast of Brittany, which was reputed to have sunk in the 5th century.

The place and date of birth of Marie are unknown. Her poems are written in the French of northern France; but that does not prove her to be a French woman, since French was, at the time, the language of the English Court. Occasionally, Marie inserts English words to better convey her meaning; but it does not indicate that her "*Lays*" were composed in that language. There are no indications of her origins in her work beyond her name and the statement that she is from France. Scholars presume that Marie was a subject of the English Crown, possibly born in Pitre, near Rouen, in Normandy, based on the accurate description of that village in *The Lay of the Two Lovers*. Her Prologue contains a dedication to some unnamed King and her *Fables* are dedicated to a Count William. The King was long supposed to be Henry III of England (which would suggest that she lived in the 13th century) but Gaston Paris has argued that it might be Henry II and the Count William Longsword, Earl of Salisbury, which would place Marie in the second half of the 12th century. (Even though it is difficult to recognize in the King of the Prologue, "in whose heart all gracious things are rooted," the King who

---

[27] 15th-century Northern French poet about whom little is known.

murdered Becket; read books during Mass, and never confessed.)

Gaston Paris suggests 1175 as an approximate date for the composition of the *Lays* of Marie de France. One thing is certain: their success was immediate and unequivocal. We have proof of this in the testimony of Denis Pyramus, the author who wrote a Life of St. Edmund the King, early in the following century. He says, in that poem, "And also Dame Marie, who turned into rhyme and made verses of Lays which are not in the least true. For these she is much praised, and her rhyme is loved everywhere; for counts, barons, and knights greatly admire it, and hold it dear. And they love her writing so much, and take such pleasure in it, that they have it read, and often copied. These Lays are wont to please ladies, who listen to them with delight, for they are after their own hearts."

It is no wonder that the lords and ladies of the times were so enthralled by Marie's romances. Even after 700 years her style remain fresh, and if the tapestry is now a little worn and faded in places, we still follow with interest the movements of the figures wrought so graciously upon it. Marie's inspiration comes from Celtic and Breton sources, with their peculiar blend of dreaminess, magic and mystery. Her portrait of Guinevere in *The Lay of Sir Lanval* is of a character that one does not recall with pleasure. To see how Arthur's Queen might be treated differently, we need but to turn to Chrétien de Troyes' *Lancelot*. One might say that Marie's romances began farther back than any Breton or Celtic dream. They are of that stuff from which romance itself is shaped.

Marie de France: *The Lay of Sir Lanval*
(c. 1175)[28]

I will tell you the story of another Lay. It relates the adventures of a rich and mighty baron, and the Breton calls it, the Lay of Sir Lanval.

King Arthur—that fearless knight and courteous lord--removed to Wales, and lodged at Caerleon-on-Usk, since the Picts and Scots did much mischief in the land. For it was the wont of the wild people of the north to enter in the realm of Logres, and burn and damage at their will. At the time of Pentecost, the King cried a great feast. Thereat he gave many rich gifts to his counts and barons, and to the Knights of the Round Table. Never were such worship and bounty shown before at any feast, for Arthur bestowed honors and lands on all his servants--save only on one. This lord, who was forgotten and misliked of the King, was named Lanval. He was beloved by many of the Court, because of his beauty and prowess, for he was a worthy knight, open of heart and heavy of hand. These lords, to whom their comrade was dear, felt little joy to see so stout a knight misprized. Sir Lanval was son to a King of high descent, though his heritage was in a distant land. He was of the King's household, but since Arthur gave him naught, and he was of too proud a mind to pray for his due, he had spent all that he had. Right heavy was Sir Lanval, when he considered these things, for he knew himself taken in the toils. Gentles, marvel not overmuch hereat. Ever must the pilgrim go heavily in a strange land, where there is none to counsel and direct him in the path.

---

[28] Excerpted from *The Lays of Marie de France,* translated into English in 1911 by Eugene Mason, introduced and annotated by Jean-Marc Lofficier.

Now, on a day, Sir Lanval got him on his horse, that he might take his pleasure for a little. He came forth from the city, alone, attended by neither servant nor squire. He went his way through a green mead, till he stood by a river of clear running water. Sir Lanval would have crossed this stream, without thought of pass or ford, but he might not do so, for reason that his horse was all fearful and trembling. Seeing that he was hindered in this fashion, Lanval unbitted his steed, and let him pasture in that fair meadow, where they had come. Then he folded his cloak to serve him as a pillow, and lay upon the ground. Lanval lay in great unease, because of his heavy thoughts, and the discomfort of his bed. He turned from side to side, and might not sleep. Now as the knight looked towards the river he saw two damsels coming towards him; fairer maidens Lanval had never seen. These two maidens were richly dressed in kirtles closely laced and shapen to their persons and wore mantles of a goodly purple hue. Sweet and dainty were the damsels, alike in raiment and in face. The elder of these ladies carried in her hands a basin of pure gold, cunningly wrought by some crafty smith—very fair and precious was the cup; and the younger bore a towel of soft white linen. These maidens turned neither to the right hand nor to the left, but went directly to the place where Lanval lay. When Lanval saw that their business was with him, he stood upon his feet, like a discreet and courteous gentleman. After they had greeted the knight, one of the maidens delivered the message with which she was charged.

"Sir Lanval, my demoiselle, as gracious as she is fair, prays that you will follow us, her messengers, as she has a certain word to speak with you. We will lead you swiftly to her pavilion, for our lady is very near at hand. If you but lift your eyes you may see where her tent is spread."

Right glad was the knight to do the bidding of the maidens. He gave no heed to his horse, but left him at his provand[29] in the meadow. All his desire was to go with the damsels, to

[29] Food, provisions.

that pavilion of silk and divers colors, pitched in so fair a place. Certainly neither Semiramis in the days of her most wanton power, nor Octavian, the Emperor of all the West, had so gracious a covering from sun and rain. Above the tent was set an eagle of gold, so rich and precious, that none might count the cost. The cords and fringes thereof were of silken thread, and the lances which bore aloft the pavilion were of refined gold. No King on earth might have so sweet a shelter, not though he gave in fee the value of his realm. Within this pavilion Lanval came upon the Maiden. Whiter she was than any altar lily, and more sweetly flushed than the new born rose in time of summer heat. She lay upon a bed with napery and coverlet of richer worth than could be furnished by a castle's spoil. Very fresh and slender showed the lady in her vesture of spotless linen. About her person she had drawn a mantle of ermine, edged with purple dye from the vats of Alexandria. By reason of the heat her raiment was unfastened for a little, and her throat and the *rondeur* of her bosom showed whiter and more untouched than hawthorn in May. The knight came before the bed, and stood gazing on so sweet a sight. The Maiden beckoned him to draw near, and when he had seated himself at the foot of her couch, spoke her mind.

"Lanval," she said, "fair friend, it is for you that I have come from my own far land. I bring you my love. If you are prudent and discreet, as you are goodly to the view, there is no emperor nor count, nor king, whose day shall be so filled with riches and with mirth as yours."

When Lanval heard these words he rejoiced greatly, for his heart was litten by another's torch.

"Fair lady," he answered, "since it pleases you to be so gracious, and to dower so graceless a knight with your love, there is naught that you may bid me do--right or wrong, evil or good--that I will not do to the utmost of my power. I will observe your commandment, and serve in your quarrels. For you I renounce my father and my father's house. This only I pray, that I may dwell with you in your lodging, and that you will never send me from your side."

When the Maiden heard the words of him whom so fond-ly she desired to love, she was altogether moved, and granted him forthwith her heart and her tenderness. To her bounty she added another gift besides. Never might Lanval be desirous of aught, but he would have according to his wish. He might waste and spend at will and pleasure, but in his purse ever there was to spare. No more was Lanval sad. Right merry was the pilgrim, since one had set him on the way, with such a gift, that the more pennies he bestowed, the more silver and gold were in his pouch.

But the Maiden had yet a word to say.

"Friend," she said, "hearken to my counsel. I lay this charge upon you, and pray you urgently, that you tell not to any man the secret of our love. If you show this matter, you will lose your friend, for ever and a day. Never again may you see my face. Never again will you have seisin [30] of that body, which is now so tender in your eyes."

Lanval plighted faith, that right strictly he would observe this commandment. So the Maiden granted him her kiss and her embrace, and very sweetly in that fair lodging passed the day till evensong was come.

Right loath was Lanval to depart from the pavilion at the vesper hour, and gladly would he have stayed, had he been able, and his lady wished.

"Fair friend," said she, "rise up, for no longer may you tarry. The hour is come that we must part. But one thing I have to say before you go. When you would speak with me I shall hasten to come before your wish. Well I deem that you will only call your friend where she may be found without re-proach or shame of men. You may see me at your pleasure; my voice shall speak softly in your ear at will; but I must nev-er be known of your comrades, nor must they ever learn my speech."

Right joyous was Lanval to hear this thing. He sealed the covenant with a kiss, and stood upon his feet. Then there en-

---

[30] Possession.

91

tered the two maidens who had led him to the pavilion, bringing with them rich raiment, fitting for a knight's apparel. When Lanval had clothed himself therewith, there seemed no goodlier varlet under heaven, for certainly he was fair and true. After these maidens had refreshed him with clear water, and dried his hands upon the napkin, Lanval went to meat. His friend sat at table with him, and small will had he to refuse her courtesy. Very serviceably the damsels bore the meats, and Lanval and the Maiden ate and drank with mirth and content. But one dish was more to the knight's relish than any other. Sweeter than the dainties within his mouth, was the lady's kiss upon his lips.

When supper was ended, Lanval rose from table, for his horse stood waiting without the pavilion. The destrier was newly saddled and bridled, and showed proudly in his rich gay trappings. So Lanval kissed, and bade farewell, and went his way. He rode back towards the city at a slow pace. Often he checked his steed, and looked behind him, for he was filled with amazement, and all bemused concerning this adventure. In his heart he doubted that it was but a dream. He was altogether astonished, and knew not what to do. He feared that pavilion and Maiden alike were from the realm of faery.

Lanval returned to his lodging, and was greeted by servitors, clad no longer in ragged raiment. He fared richly, lay softly, and spent largely, but never knew how his purse was filled. There was no lord who had need of a lodging in the town, but Lanval brought him to his hall, for refreshment and delight. Lanval bestowed rich gifts. Lanval redeemed the poor captive. Lanval clothed in scarlet the minstrel. Lanval gave honor where honor was due. Stranger and friend alike he comforted at need. So, whether by night or by day, Lanval lived greatly at his ease. His lady, she came at will and pleasure, and, for the rest, all was added unto him.

Now it chanced, the same year, about the feast of St. John, a company of knights came, for their solace, to an orchard, beneath that tower where dwelt the Queen. Together with these lords went Gawain and his cousin, Yvain the fair. Then said Gawain, that goodly knight, beloved and dear to all,

"Lords, we do wrong to disport ourselves in this pleasance without our comrade Lanval. It is not well to slight a prince as brave as he is courteous, and of a lineage prouder than our own."

Then certain of the lords returned to the city, and finding Lanval within his hostel, entreated him to take his pastime with them in that fair meadow. The Queen looked out from a window in her tower, she and three ladies of her fellowship. They saw the lords at their pleasure, and Lanval also, whom well they knew. So the Queen chose of her Court thirty damsels--the sweetest of face and most dainty of fashion—and commanded that they should descend with her to take their delight in the garden. When the knights beheld this gay company of ladies come down the steps of the perron, they rejoiced beyond measure. They hastened before to lead them by the hand, and said such words in their ear as were seemly and pleasant to be spoken. Amongst these merry and courteous lords hasted not Sir Lanval. He drew apart from the throng, for with him time went heavily, till he might have clasp and greeting of his friend. The ladies of the Queen's fellowship seemed but kitchen wenches to his sight, in comparison with the loveliness of the maiden. When the Queen marked Lanval go aside, she went his way, and seating herself upon the herb, called the knight before her. Then she opened out her heart.

"Lanval, I have honored you for long as a worthy knight, and have praised and cherished you very dearly. You may receive a queen's whole love, if such be your care. Be content: he to whom my heart is given, has small reason to complain him of the alms."

"Lady," answered the knight, "grant me leave to go, for this grace is not for me. I am the King's man, and dare not break my troth. Not for the highest lady in the world, not even for her love, will I set this reproach upon my lord."

When the Queen heard this, she was full of wrath, and spoke many hot and bitter words.

"Lanval," she cried, "well I know that you think little of woman and her love. There are sins more black that a man may have upon his soul. Traitor you are, and false. Right evil counsel gave they to my lord, who prayed him to suffer you about his person. You remain only for his harm and loss."

Lanval was very dolent [31] to hear this thing. He was not slow to take up the Queen's glove, and in his haste spoke words that he repented long, and with tears.

"Lady," said he, "I am not of that guild of which you speak. Neither am I a despiser of woman, since I love, and am loved, of one who would bear the prize from all the ladies in the land. Dame, know now and be persuaded, that she, whom I serve, is so rich in state, that the very meanest of her maidens, excels you, Lady Queen, as much in clerkly skill and goodness, as in sweetness of body and face, and in every virtue."

The Queen rose straightway to her feet, and fled to her chamber, weeping. Right wrathful and heavy was she, because of the words that had besmirched her. She lay sick upon her bed, from which, she said, she would never rise, till the King had done her justice, and righted this bitter wrong. Now the King that day had taken his pleasure within the woods. He returned from the chase towards evening, and sought the chamber of the Queen. When the lady saw him, she sprang from her bed, and kneeling at his feet, pleaded for grace and pity. Lanval--she said--had shamed her, since he required her love. When she had put him by, very foully had he reviled her, boasting that his love was already set on a lady, so proud and noble, that her meanest wench went more richly, and smiled more sweetly, than the Queen. Thereat the King waxed marvelously wrathful, and swore a great oath that he would set Lanval within a fire, or hang him from a tree, if he could not deny this thing, before his peers.

Arthur came forth from the Queen's chamber, and called to him three of his lords. These he sent to seek the knight who so evilly had entreated the Queen. Lanval, for his part, had

---

[31] Sorrowful.

returned to his lodging, in a sad and sorrowful case. He saw very clearly that he had lost his friend, since he had declared their love to men. Lanval sat within his chamber, sick and heavy of thought. Often he called upon his friend, but the lady would not hear his voice. He bewailed his evil lot, with tears; for grief he came nigh to swoon; a hundred times he implored the Maiden that she would deign to speak with her knight. Then, since the lady yet refrained from speech, Lanval cursed his hot and unruly tongue. Very near he came to ending all this trouble with his knife. Naught he found to do but to wring his hands, and call upon the Maiden, begging her to forgive his trespass, and to talk with him again, as friend to friend.

But little peace is there for him who is harassed by a King. There came presently to Lanval's hostel those three barons from the Court. These bade the knight forthwith to go with them to Arthur's presence, to acquit him of this wrong against the Queen. Lanval went forth, to his own deep sorrow. Had any man slain him on the road, he would have counted him his friend. He stood before the King, downcast and speechless, being dumb by reason of that great grief, of which he showed the picture and image.

Arthur looked upon his captive very evilly.

"Vassal," said he, harshly, "you have done me a bitter wrong. It was a foul deed to seek to shame me in this ugly fashion, and to smirch the honor of the Queen. Is it folly or lightness which leads you to boast of that lady, the least of whose maidens is fairer, and goes more richly, than the Queen?"

Lanval protested that never had he set such shame upon his lord. Word by word he told the tale of how he denied the Queen, within the orchard. But concerning that which he had spoken of the lady, he owned the truth, and his folly. The love of which he bragged was now lost to him, by his own exceeding fault. He cared little for his life, and was content to obey the judgment of the Court.

Right wrathful was the King at Lanval's words. He conjured his barons to give him such wise counsel herein, that

95

wrong might be done to none. The lords did the King's bidding, whether good came of the matter, or evil. They gathered themselves together, and appointed a certain day that Lanval should abide the judgment of his peers. For his part Lanval must give pledge and surety to his lord, that he would come before this judgment in his own body. If he might not give such surety then he should be held captive till the appointed day. When the lords of the King's household returned to tell him of their counsel, Arthur demanded that Lanval should put such pledge in his hand, as they had said. Lanval was altogether mazed and bewildered at this judgment, for he had neither friend nor kindred in the land. He would have been set in prison, but Gawain came first to offer himself as his surety, and with him, all the knights of his fellowship. These gave into the King's hand as pledge, the fiefs and lands that they held of his Crown. The King having taken pledges from the sureties, Lanval returned to his lodging, and with him certain knights of his company. They blamed him greatly because of his foolish love, and chastened him grievously by reason of the sorrow he made before men. Every day they came to his chamber, to know of his meat and drink, for much they feared that presently he would become mad.

The lords of the household came together on the day appointed for this judgment. The King was on his chair, with the Queen sitting at his side. The sureties brought Lanval within the hall, and rendered him into the hands of his peers. Right sorrowful were they because of his plight. A great company of his fellowship did all that they were able to acquit him of this charge. When all was set out, the King demanded the judgment of the Court, according to the accusation and the answer. The barons went forth in much trouble and thought to consider this matter. Many amongst them grieved for the peril of a good knight in a strange land; others held that it were well for Lanval to suffer, because of the wish and malice of their lord. Whilst they were thus perplexed, the Duke of Cornwall rose in the council, and said,

"Lords, the King pursues Lanval as a traitor, and would slay him with the sword, by reason that he bragged of the beauty of his maiden, and roused the jealousy of the Queen. By the faith that I owe this company, none complains of Lanval, save only the King. For our part we would know the truth of this business, and do justice between the King and his man. We would also show proper reverence to our own liege lord. Now, if it be according to Arthur's will, let us take oath of Lanval, that he seek this lady, who has put such strife between him and the Queen. If her beauty be such as he has told us, the Queen will have no cause for wrath. She must pardon Lanval for his rudeness, since it will be plain that he did not speak out of a malicious heart. Should Lanval fail his word, and not return with the lady, or should her fairness fall beneath his boast, then let him be cast off from our fellowship, and be sent forth from the service of the King."

This counsel seemed good to the lords of the household. They sent certain of his friends to Lanval, to acquaint him with their judgment, bidding him to pray his damsel to the Court, that he might be acquitted of this blame. The knight made answer that in no wise could he do this thing. So the sureties returned before the judges, saying that Lanval hoped neither for refuge nor for succor from the lady, and Arthur urged them to a speedy ending, because of the prompting of the Queen.

The judges were about to give sentence upon Lanval, when they saw two maidens come riding towards the palace, upon two white ambling palfreys. Very sweet and dainty were these maidens, and richly clothed in garments of crimson sendal,[32] closely girt and fashioned to their bodies. All men, old and young, looked willingly upon them, for fair they were to see. Gawain, and three knights of his company, went straight to Lanval, and showed him these maidens, praying him to say which of them was his friend. But he answered never a word. The maidens dismounted from their palfreys,

[32] A silk fabric in use during the Middle Ages.

and coming before the dais where the King was seated, spake him fairly, as they were fair.

"Sire, prepare now a chamber, hung with silken cloths, where it is seemly for my lady to dwell; for she would lodge with you awhile."

This gift the King granted gladly. He called to him two knights of his household, and bade them bestow the maidens in such chambers as were fitting to their degree. The maidens being gone, the King required of his barons to proceed with their judgment, saying that he had sore displeasure at the slowness of the cause.

"Sire," replied the barons, "we rose from Council, because of the damsels who entered in the hall. We will at once resume the sitting, and give our judgment without more delay."

The barons again were gathered together, in much thought and trouble, to consider this matter. There was great strife and dissension amongst them, for they knew not what to do. In the midst of all this noise and tumult, there came two other damsels riding to the hall on two Spanish mules. Very richly arrayed were these damsels in raiment of fine needle-work, and their kirtles were covered by fresh fair mantles, embroidered with gold. Great joy had Lanval's comrades when they marked these ladies. They said between themselves that doubtless they came for the succor of the good knight. Gawain, and certain of his company, made haste to Lanval, and said, "Sir, be not cast down. Two ladies are near at hand, right dainty of dress, and gracious of person. Tell us truly, for the love of God, is one of these your friend?"

But Lanval answered very simply that never before had he seen these damsels with his eyes, nor known and loved them in his heart.

The maidens dismounted from their mules, and stood before Arthur, in the sight of all. Greatly were they praised of many, because of their beauty, and of the color of their face and hair. Some there were who deemed already that the Queen was overborne.

The elder of the damsels carried herself modestly and well, and sweetly told over the message wherewith she was charged.

"Sire, make ready for us chambers, where we may abide with our lady, for even now she comes to speak with thee."

The King commanded that the ladies should be led to their companions, and bestowed in the same honorable fashion as they. Then he bade the lords of his household to consider their judgment, since he would endure no further respite. The Court already had given too much time to the business, and the Queen was growing wrathful, because of the blame that was hers. Now the judges were about to proclaim their sentence, when, amidst the tumult of the town, there came riding to the palace the flower of all the ladies of the world. She came mounted upon a palfrey, white as snow, which carried her softly, as though she loved her burthen. Beneath the sky was no goodlier steed, nor one more gentle to the hand. The harness of the palfrey was so rich, that no king on earth might hope to buy trappings so precious, unless he sold or set his realm in pledge. The Maiden herself showed such as I will tell you. Passing slim was the lady, sweet of bodice and slender of girdle. Her throat was whiter than snow on branch, and her eyes were like flowers in the pallor of her face. She had a witching mouth, a dainty nose, and an open brow. Her eyebrows were brown, and her golden hair parted in two soft waves upon her head. She was clad in a shift of spotless linen, and above her snowy kirtle was set a mantle of royal purple, clasped upon her breast. She carried a hooded falcon upon her glove, and a greyhound followed closely after. As the Maiden rode at a slow pace through the streets of the city, there was none, neither great nor small, youth nor sergeant, but ran forth from his house, that he might content his heart with so great beauty. Every man that saw her with his eyes, marveled at a fairness beyond that of any earthly woman. Little he cared for any mortal maiden, after he had seen this sight. The friends of Sir Lanval hastened to the knight, to tell him of his lady's succor, if so it were according to God's will.

"Sir comrade, truly is not this your friend? This lady is neither black nor golden, mean nor tall. She is only the most lovely thing in all the world."

When Lanval heard this, he sighed, for by their words he knew again his friend. He raised his head, and as the blood rushed to his face, speech flowed from his lips.

"By my faith," cried he, "yes, she is indeed my friend. It is a small matter now whether men slay me, or set me free; for I am made whole of my hurt just by looking on her face."

The Maiden entered in the palace--where none so fair had come before--and stood before the King, in the presence of his household. She loosed the clasp of her mantle, so that men might the more easily perceive the grace of her person. The courteous King advanced to meet her, and all the Court got them on their feet, and pained themselves in her service. When the lords had gazed upon her for a space, and praised the sum of her beauty, the lady spoke to Arthur in this fashion, for she was anxious to be gone.

"Sire, I have loved one of thy vassals,--the knight who stands in bonds, Sir Lanval. He was always misprized in thy Court, and his every action turned to blame. What he said, that thou knowest; for over hasty was his tongue before the Queen. But he never craved her in love, however loud his boasting. I cannot choose that he should come to hurt or harm by me. In the hope of freeing Lanval from his bonds, I have obeyed thy summons. Let now thy barons look boldly upon my face, and deal justly in this quarrel between the Queen and me."

The King commanded that this should be done, and looking upon her eyes, not one of the judges but was persuaded that her favor exceeded that of the Queen.

Since then Lanval had not spoken in malice against his lady, the lords of the household gave him again his sword. When the trial had come thus to an end the Maiden took her leave of the King, and made her ready to depart. Gladly would Arthur have had her lodge with him for a little, and many a lord would have rejoiced in her service, but she might not tarry. Now without the hall stood a great stone of dull marble, where it was the wont of lords, departing from the Court, to climb into the saddle, and Lanval by the stone. The Maiden came forth from the doors of the palace, and mounting on the stone, seated herself on the palfrey, behind her friend. Then they rode across the plain together, and were no more seen.

The Bretons tell that the knight was ravished by his lady to an island, very dim and very fair, known as Avalon. But none has had speech with Lanval and his faery love since then, and for my part I can tell you no more of the matter.

From 1550 until 1650, a strange, almost schizophrenic, literary cohabitation existed between humanist philosophy, devoted to the material universe, and *fantasy*; between pagan influences, harking back to the Greeks, and Christian faith.

The great 16th century French poet Ronsard (1524-1585), founder of the literary group *La Pleïade* (called thus as an homage to a group of seven 3rd century BC Alexandrian poets who had placed themselves under the protection of this constellation), drew heavily on the superstitions of his native Vendômois country, writing about witches and witchcraft. At the peak of his literary fame, he devoted several of his famous *Hymnes* (1552) to supernatural subjects.

In a poem entitled *Les Sepmaines* (1578), Guillaume de Salluste du Bartas (1544-1590) described the creation of the world by God, including scenes of battles with monsters in the Garden of Eden.

The ensuing Baroque period continued to rely heavily on warlocks and witches, often drawn from Antiquity, such as Medea, Circe, and the Witches of Thessalia, for dramatic purposes, in an imitation of the increasingly successful pastoral literature from Italy and Spain, in which Greek-Roman myths still played a strong role.

The classic novel *L'Astrée* (1607-27) by Honoré d'Urfé (1568-1625), with its druid Climante, its magic mirror and its Fountain of Truth, was inspired by the prose romance of chivalry *Amadis of Gaul*, a neo-*Chanson de Geste* which had been circulating in various forms since the late 13th century, and had reached its pinnacle of fame when retold by Spanish writer Garcia Rodriguez Montalvo (c. 1450-1504). *Amadis of Gaul* was originally based on myths derived from the Celtic Arthurian legends, but in its 16th century form, came to embody all the ideals of the now-vanished Age of Chivalry: a virtually invincible, handsome Christian knight who was totally loyal to his God-anointed King and terribly courtly and chaste towards his princess love. With *L'Astrée*, what had once been fiery, mystic, sword & sorcery had become high fantasy, filled with artificially contrived romance.

Raymond Lebègue in his article "*Le Merveilleux Magique en France dans le Théâtre Baroque*" [Magical Marvelous In France In Baroque Theater][33] lists no less than seventy-five plays where magicians playe a major part, often the same character appearing in several plays, written by different authors. For example, Ismen the Magician, created by Le Tasse, appears in Chrétien des Croix's *Les Amantes* [The Lovers] (1613). In *La Bague d'Oubli* [The Ring of Oblivion] (1628), Jean de Rotrou (1609-1650) introduces Alcandre the Sorcerer, who then goes on to star in Bazire's *Arlette* (1638).

Similar themes, often borrowed from classic Greco-Roman sources, became fodder for numerous operas which handily reused mythology, folk tales and legends, often bastardized and exacerbated romantic forms, being the precursors of today's modern big budget heroic-fantasy films.

---

[33] in *Revue d'Histoire du Théâtre*, Jan-Mar., 1963.

AT THE EDGE OF THE WORLD

By contrast with what came before, 16th century French literature was marked by the emergence of new ideas and trends, as a reaction against what was perceived to be the "obscurantism" of the Middle Ages.

The discoveries of new continents by Christopher Columbus (1451-1506), Vasco da Gama (1460-1524), Magellan (1480-1521), Verrazano (1485-1528) and Jacques Cartier (1491-1557) offered new imaginary vistas in which to locate fantasy stories; and Gutenberg's (?-1468) discovery of the printing press c. 1450 made the greater circulation of such literary works possible.

The Renaissance bloomed in France during the reign of king François 1st (1494-1547). As Charlemagne had done before, the new king created a favorable environment for the development of letters, arts and sciences. He founded several scientific colleges, attracted foreign artists, such as Leonardo da Vinci (1452-1519), to the French Court and, more generally, allowed official tolerance towards the publication of the new philosophy.

It was during the French Renaissance that traditional fantasy derived from myths and folklore, and incorporating the High Fantasy poetic traditions of the Middle Ages, eventually evolved into the *Contes de Fées*, or Fairy Tales.

It was also during the Renaissance that the thirst for learning combined with a natural sense of optimism, science and progress, to produce the Utopias, which often took the form of amazing journeys into mythical lands, to rival those imagined by William Morris and Lord Dunsany; and even, in some cases, planetary fantasies, not unlike E. R. Eddison's *Zimiamvian Trilogy*.

The invention of the first Utopia is to be credited to Sir Thomas More (1478-1535) who, inspired by Erasmus (1466-1536), wrote *The Utopia* in 1516 in Latin. Even though More's book was translated into French only in 1550 (and in English in 1551!), it inspired French writer François Rabelais (1494-1553) who, in a case of literary crossover, chose to locate several of his stories on the same island.

Rabelais was a scholar, a humanist, a physician and a writer. His works constituted an extraordinary blend of political and sociological satire, extraordinary voyages, pre-Utopia utopias, and fantasy quests. His larger-than-life, colorful characters with "gargantuan" appetites were also literary archetypes that have spawned many imitations. Rabelais, a former monk who had studied medicine, strongly believed that Man's body and spirit should be freed from medieval restrictions. He trusted nature and progress, and saw unlimited horizons ahead for Mankind. This, combined with his vivid imagination and prodigious sense of satire, led him to create an array of imaginary lands and societies which remains, today, among one of the most complex ever devised in fantasy literature.

In the 1540s, the faculty of the Sorbonne, reacting to the inexorable spread of literacy among the laity, based on the increasing availability of printed books, issued a list of books that were to be suppressed by all practical means. A licensing system by which legally-printed books required a royal warrant was already in existence, but was not yet protected with any great fervor, and the Sorbonne's list included, in any case, several works that had actually received a royal warrant. High on the list, and key targets for clerical ire and persecution on the grounds of their anti-religious inclinations, were Rabelais' two hectic ribald comedies featuring two giant kings: *Pantagruel* (c 1532, anagrammatically signed "Alcofribas Nasier") and *Gargantua* (1534)—Gargantua being King of the Dipsodes and Pantagruel's father.

The adventures of the giants in question were further elaborated in *Le Tiers livre des faits et dicts héroïques du bon Pantagruel* [The Third Book of the Adventures and Heroic

Deeds of Pantagruel] (1546), which introduced the character of the knavish and licentious Panurge, and then by a *Quart livre* [Fourth Book] (1552) and a *Cinquième et dernier livre* [Fifth and Last Book] (1564) of dubious authenticity, all five of which volumes were subsequently combined into an omnibus usually known as *Gargantua* et *Pantagruel*.

Rabelais' fantastic worlds were not places serving only satirical or comparative purposes, i.e.: designed to be contrasted by the reader with the real society of the time. Having served terms as a monk with both the Franciscans and Benedictines, Rabelais was in a unique position not merely to assault the tradition of monachism satirically, in his classic depiction of the Abbey of Thélème, a haven of gluttony and debauchery in which the presiding rule is "Do As Thou Wilt," and to lampoon the Sorbonne itself, but also to excite the particular resentment occasioned by perceived renegades.

The fight to suppress Rabelais begun by the Church—which could not be won and ultimately produced the opposite effect—and the manner in which Rabelais had cloaked his serious humanist ideas in broad humor, both became key exemplars for Voltaire and his contemporaries, even providing a veneer of justification for the writers of such scabrous works as *Thérèse Philosophe*, in which libidinous Churchmen play an exceedingly prominent part.

Although Rabelais, too, went through a period of relative disrepute when his humor came to seem a little too coarse for delicate minds—which only enhanced his stature in the eyes of the philosophers—he was read widely in the sixteenth and seventeenth centuries, throughout Europe, and his works became established as important landmarks and reference points in French literature. Rabelais' fantastic worlds are not places serving only satirical or comparative purposes, i.e.: designed to be contrasted by the reader with the real society of his time; they also contain some fantastic speculations. They include a journey to the Moon, deep sea diving, and miniaturization.

With the Reformation and its ensuing series of civil wars, including the infamous massacre of St. Bartholomew's day in 1572, the political climate changed during the second half of the 16th century; religious and political intolerance gained new ground, and Rabelais' works were forbidden. Even though his Third, Fourth and Fifth Books were much safer politically, they nevertheless caused their author many problems, even forcing him into internal exile for a while. In them, Rabelais developed the literary device of the "Extraordinary Journey" to a heretofore unprecedented extent.

Borrowing from a tradition going back to Homer's *Odyssey*, and inspired by the real-life journey of explorer Jacques Cartier, Rabelais described how French travelers to India used the then-legendary North-West passage and come across twenty-one islands, each one with its own strange society: one where people feed on wind, one where sound can be frozen and unfrozen at will, one where the king uses magnetic force, etc. In these books, Rabelais gave form to a genre which was later exploited by such writers as Cyrano de Bergerac, Jonathan Swift, and all great fantasy authors who followed.

The following excerpt is taken from Book II and tells of a mighty fight between Pantagruel and a Barbarian Warlord, followed by an amazing journey within Pantagruel's own body...

Rabelais: *Pantagruel's War Against the Dipsodes* (c. 1532)[34]

Chapter XXVIII.
How Pantagruel got the victory very strangely over the Dipsodes[35] and the Giants.

After all this talk, Pantagruel took the prisoner to him and sent him away, saying:

"Go thou unto thy king in his camp, and tell him tidings of what thou hast seen, and let him resolve to feast me tomorrow about noon; for, as soon as my galleys shall come, which will be tomorrow at furthest, I will prove unto him by eighteen hundred thousand fighting-men and seven thousand giants, all of them greater than I am, that he hath done foolishly and against reason thus to invade my country."

Wherein Pantagruel feigned that he had an army at sea. But the prisoner answered that he would yield himself to be his slave, and that he was content never to return to his own people, but rather with Pantagruel to fight against them, and for God's sake besought him that he might be permitted so to do.

Whereunto Pantagruel would not give consent, but commanded him to depart thence speedily and begone as he

---

[34] Excerpted from *La Vie de Gargantua et Pantagruel* (Livre II) by François Rabelais, translated into English in 1653 by Sir Thomas Urquhart of Cromarty & Peter Antony Motteux, introduced and annotated by Jean-Marc Lofficier.

[35] The name "Dipsodes" comes from the Greek "dipsôdês" meaning thirsty. (Dipsomania in English hares the same roots: "dipso," drink, and "mania" madness).

had told him, and to that effect gave him a boxful of euphorbium, together with some grains of the black chameleon thistle,[36] steeped into *aqua vitae*,[37] and made up into a jam, commanding him to carry it to his king, and to say unto him, that if he were able to eat one ounce of that without drinking after it, he might then be able to resist him without any fear or apprehension of danger.

The prisoner then besought him with joined hands that in the hour of the battle he would have compassion upon him. Whereat Pantagruel said unto him:

"After that thou hast delivered all unto the king, put thy whole confidence in God, and he will not forsake thee; because, although for my part I be mighty, as thou mayst see, and have an infinite number of men in arms, I do nevertheless trust neither in my force nor in mine industry, but all my confidence is in God my protector, who doth never forsake those that in him do put their trust and confidence."

This done, the prisoner requested him that he would afford him some reasonable composition for his ransom. To which Pantagruel answered, that his end was not to rob nor ransom men, but to enrich them and reduce them to total liberty:

"Go thy way," said he, "in the peace of the living God, and never follow evil company, lest some mischief befall thee."

The prisoner being gone, Pantagruel said to his men:

"Gentlemen, I have made this prisoner believe that we have an army at sea; as also that we will not assault them till tomorrow at noon, to the end that they, doubting of the great arrival of our men, may spend this night in providing and strengthening themselves, but in the meantime my intention is that we charge them about the hour of the first sleep."

---

[36] Today better known as Sichuan pepper.
[37] Concentrated aqueous solution of ethanol.

Let us leave Pantagruel here with his apostles, and speak of King Anarchus and his army. When the prisoner was come, he went unto the king and told him how there was a great giant come, called Pantagruel, who had overthrown and made to be cruelly roasted all the six hundred and nine and fifty horsemen, and he alone escaped to bring the news.

Besides that, he was charged by the said giant to tell him that the next day, about noon, he must make a dinner ready for him, for at that hour he was resolved to set upon him. Then did he give him that box wherein were those jams. But as soon as he had swallowed down one spoonful of them, he was taken with such a heat in the throat, together with an ulceration in the flap of the top of the windpipe, that his tongue peeled with it in such sort that, for all they could do unto him, he found no ease at all but by drinking only without cessation; for as soon as ever he took the goblet from his head, his tongue was on a fire, and therefore they did nothing but still pour in wine into his throat with a funnel.

Which when his captains, bashaws,[38] and guard of his body did see, they tasted of the same drugs to try whether they were so thirst-procuring and alterative or no. But it so befell them as it had done their king, and they plied the flagon so well that the noise ran throughout all the camp, how the prisoner was returned; that the next day they were to have an assault; that the king and his captains did already prepare themselves for it, together with his guards, and that with carousing lustily and quaffing as hard as they could. Every man, therefore, in the army began to tipple, ply the pot, swill and guzzle it as fast as they could. In sum, they drunk so much, and so long, that they fell asleep like pigs, all out of order throughout the whole camp.

Let us now return to the good Pantagruel, and relate how he carried himself in this business. Departing from the place of the trophies, he took the mast of their ship in his hand like a

---

[38] Another term for pasha.

pilgrim's staff, and put within the top of it two hundred and seven and thirty puncheons of white wine of Anjou, the rest was of Rouen, and tied up to his girdle the bark all full of salt, as easily as the lansquenets carry their little panniers, and so set onward on his way with his fellow-soldiers. When he was come near to the enemy's camp, Panurge[39] said unto him:

"Sir, if you would do well, let down this white wine of Anjou from the scuttle of the mast of the ship, that we may all drink thereof, like Bretons."

Hereunto Pantagruel very willingly consented, and they drank so neat that there was not so much as one poor drop left of two hundred and seven and thirty puncheons, except one flask or leathern bottle of Tours which Panurge filled for himself, for he called that his *vademecum*,[40] and some scurvy lees of wine in the bottom, which served him instead of vinegar.

After they had whittled and curried the can pretty handsomely, Panurge gave Pantagruel to eat some devilish drugs compounded of lithotripton, which is a stone-dissolving ingredient, nephrocatarticon, that purgeth the reins, the marmalade of quinces, called *codiniac*, a confection of cantharides, which are green flies breeding on the tops of olive-trees, and other kinds of diuretic or piss-procuring simples. This done, Pantagruel said to Carpalin:

"Go into the city, scrambling like a cat against the wall, as you can well do, and tell them that now presently they come out and charge their enemies as rudely as they can, and having said so, come down, taking a lighted torch with you, wherewith you shall set on fire all the tents and pavilions in the camp; then cry as loud as you are able with your great voice, and then come away from thence."

"Yea, but," said Carpalin, "were it not good to cloy all their ordnance?"

---

[39] A crafty knave, libertine and coward who is Pantagruel's sidekick.

[40] Something intended to be carried on one person at all times.

"No, no," said Pantagruel, "only blow up all their powder."

Carpalin, obeying him, departed suddenly and did as he was appointed by Pantagruel, and all the combatants came forth that were in the city, and when he had set fire in the tents and pavilions, he passed so lightly through them, and so highly and profoundly did they snort and sleep, that they never perceived him.

He came to the place where their artillery was, and set their munitions on fire. But here was the danger. The fire was so sudden that poor Carpalin had almost been burnt. And had it not been for his wonderful agility he had been fried like a roasting pig. But he departed away so speedily that a bolt or arrow out of a crossbow could not have had a swifter motion.

When he was clear of their trenches, he shouted aloud, and cried out so dreadfully, and with such amazement to the hearers, that it seemed all the devils of hell had been let loose. At which noise the enemies awaked, but can you tell how? Even no less astonished than are monks at the ringing of the first peal to matins, which in Lusonnois [41] is called rubbollock.

In the meantime, Pantagruel began to sow the salt that he had in his bark, and because they slept with an open gaping mouth, he filled all their throats with it, so that those poor wretches were by it made to cough like foxes, shouting:

"Ha, Pantagruel, how thou addest greater heat to the firebrand that is in us!"

Suddenly Pantagruel had will to piss, by means of the drugs which Panurge had given him, and pissed amidst the camp so well and so copiously that he drowned them all, and there was a particular deluge ten leagues round about, of such considerable depth that the history saith, if his father's great mare had been there, and pissed likewise, it would undoubtedly have been a more enormous deluge than that of Deucalion;

---

[41] Region located in the Vendée department in the Pays de la Loire in western France.

for she did never piss but she made a river greater than is either the Rhone or the Danube.

Which those that were come out of the city seeing, said:

"They are all cruelly slain; see how the blood runs along."

But they were deceived in thinking Pantagruel's urine had been the blood of their enemies, for they could not see but by the light of the fire of the pavilions and some small light of the moon.

The enemies, after that they were awaked, seeing on one side the fire in the camp, and on the other the inundation of the urinal deluge, could not tell what to say nor what to think. Some said that it was the end of the world and the final judgment, which ought to be by fire. Others again thought that the sea-gods, Neptune, Proteus, Triton, and the rest of them, did persecute them, for that indeed they found it to be like sea-water and salt.

O who were able now condignly to relate how Pantagruel did demean himself against the three hundred giants! O my Muse, my Calliope, my Thalia, inspire me at this time, restore unto me my spirits; for this is the logical bridge of asses! Here is the pitfall, here is the difficulty, to have ability enough to express the horrible battle that was fought. Ah, would to God that I had now a bottle of the best wine that ever those drank who shall read this so veridical history!

Chapter XXIX.
How Pantagruel discomfited the three hundred giants armed with free-stone, and Loupgarou[42] their captain.

The giants, seeing all their camp drowned, carried away their king Anarchus upon their backs as well as they could out of the fort, as Aeneas did to his father Anchises, in the time of

---

[42] The name means Werewolf.

the conflagration of Troy.[43] When Panurge perceived them, he said to Pantagruel:

"Sir, yonder are the giants coming forth against you; lay on them with your mast gallantly, like an old fencer; for now is the time that you must show yourself a brave man and an honest. And for our part we will not fail you. I myself will kill to you a good many boldly enough; for why, David killed Goliath very easily; and then this great lecher, Eusthenes, who is stronger than four oxen, will not spare himself. Be of good courage, therefore, and valiant; charge amongst them with point and edge, and by all manner of means."

"Well," said Pantagruel, "of courage I have more than for fifty francs, but let us be wise, for Hercules first never undertook against two."

"That is well cacked, well scummered," said Panurge; "do you compare yourself with Hercules? You have, by God, more strength in your teeth, and more scent in your bum, than ever Hercules had in all his body and soul. So much is a man worth as he esteems himself."

Whilst they spake those words, behold! Loupgarou was come with all his giants, who, seeing Pantagruel in a manner alone, was carried away with temerity and presumption, for hopes that he had to kill the good man. Whereupon he said to his companions the giants:

"You wenchers of the low country, by Mahom![44] If any of you undertake to fight against these men here, I will put you

---

[43] After the defeat of Troy in the Trojan War, the elderly Anchises was carried from the burning city by his son Aeneas, accompanied by Aeneas' wife Creusa, who died in the escape attempt, and small son Ascanius (the subject is depicted in several paintings, including a famous version by Federico Barocci in the Galleria Borghese in Rome. The rescue is also mentioned in a speech in Shakespeare's Julius Caesar when Cassius attempts to persuade Brutus to murder Caesar).

[44] Muhammad.

cruelly to death. It is my will that you let me fight single. In the meantime you shall have good sport to look upon us."

Then all the other giants retired with their king to the place where the flagons stood, and Panurge and his comrades with them, who counterfeited those that have had the pox, for he wreathed about his mouth, shrunk up his fingers, and with a harsh and hoarse voice said unto them:

"I forsake God, fellow-soldiers, if I would have it to be believed that we make any war at all. Give us somewhat to eat with you whilst our masters fight against one another."

To this the king and giants jointly condescended, and accordingly made them to banquet with them. In the meantime Panurge told them the legends of Turpin, the examples of St. Nicholas, and the Tale of the Stork.[45]

Loupgarou then set forward towards Pantagruel, with a mace all of steel, and that of the best sort, from Chalybes,[46] weighing nine thousand seven hundred quintals and two quarters, at the end whereof were thirteen pointed diamonds, the least whereof was as big as the greatest bell of Our Lady's Church at Paris—there might want perhaps the thickness of a nail, or at most, that I may not lie, of the back of those knives which they call cutlugs or earcutters, but for a little off or on, more or less, it is no matter--and it was enchanted in such sort that it could never break, but, contrarily, all that it did touch did break immediately.

Thus, then, as he approached with great fierceness and pride of heart, Pantagruel, casting up his eyes to heaven, recommended himself to God with all his soul, making such a vow as followeth"

"O thou Lord God, who hast always been my protector and my savior! thou seest the distress wherein I am at this time. Nothing brings me hither but a natural zeal, which thou hast permitted unto mortals, to keep and defend themselves, their wives and children, country and family, in case thy own

---

[45] Popular folktales of the period.

[46] Pontus and Cappadocia.

proper cause were not in question, which is the faith; for in such a business thou wilt have no coadjutors, only a catholic confession and service of thy word, and hast forbidden us all arming and defense. For thou art the Almighty, who in thine own cause, and where thine own business is taken to heart, canst defend it far beyond all that we can conceive, thou who hast thousand thousands of hundreds of millions of legions of angels, the least of which is able to kill all mortal men, and turn about the heavens and earth at his pleasure, as heretofore it very plainly appeared in the army of Sennacherib. If it may please thee, therefore, at this time to assist me, as my whole trust and confidence is in thee alone, I vow unto thee, that in all countries whatsoever wherein I shall have any power or authority, whether in this of Utopia or elsewhere, I will cause thy holy gospel to be purely, simply, and entirely preached, so that the abuses of a rabble of hypocrites and false prophets, who by human constitutions and depraved inventions have empoisoned all the world, shall be quite exterminated from about me."

This vow was no sooner made, but there was heard a voice from heaven saying:

"*Hoc fac et vinces*;" that is to say: "Do this, and thou shalt overcome."

Then Pantagruel, seeing that Loupgarou with his mouth wide open was drawing near to him, went against him boldly, and cried out as loud as he was able:

"Thou diest, villain, thou diest!" purposing by his horrible cry to make him afraid, according to the discipline of the Lacedaemonians.[47]

Withal, he immediately cast at him out of his bark, which he wore at his girdle, eighteen kegs and four bushels of salt, wherewith he filled both his mouth, throat, nose, and eyes.

At this Loupgarou was so highly incensed that, most fiercely setting upon him, he thought even then with a blow of his mace to have beat out his brains. But Pantagruel was very

---

[47] Spartans.

117

nimble, and had always a quick foot and a quick eye, and therefore with his left foot did he step back one pace, yet not so nimbly but that the blow, falling upon the bark, broke it in four thousand four score and six pieces, and threw all the rest of the salt about the ground.

Pantagruel, seeing that, most gallantly displayed the vigor of his arms, and, according to the art of the axe, gave him with the great end of his mast a homethrust a little above the breast; then, bringing along the blow to the left side, with a slash struck him between the neck and shoulders. After that, advancing his right foot, he gave him a push upon the couillons[48] with the upper end of his said mast, wherewith breaking the scuttle on the top thereof, he spilt three or four puncheons of wine that were left therein.

Upon that Loupgarou thought that he had pierced his bladder, and that the wine that came forth had been his urine. Pantagruel, being not content with this, would have doubled it by a side-blow; but Loupgarou, lifting up his mace, advanced one step upon him, and with all his force would have dashed it upon Pantagruel, wherein, to speak the truth, he so sprightfully carried himself, that, if God had not succored the good Pantagruel, he had been cloven from the top of his head to the bottom of his milt. But the blow glanced to the right side by the brisk nimbleness of Pantagruel, and his mace sank into the ground above threescore and thirteen foot, through a huge rock, out of which the fire did issue greater than nine thousand and six tons.

Pantagruel, seeing him busy about plucking out his mace, which stuck in the ground between the rocks, ran upon him, and would have clean cut off his head, if by mischance his mast had not touched a little against the stock of Loupgarou's mace, which was enchanted, as we have said before. By this means his mast broke off about three handfuls above his hand, whereat he stood amazed like a bell-founder, and cried out:

---

[48] Testicles.

"Ah, Panurge, where art thou?"

Panurge, seeing that, said to the king and the giants:

"By God, they will hurt one another if they be not parted."

But the giants were as merry as if they had been at a wedding. Then Carpalin would have risen from thence to help his master; but one of the giants said unto him:

"By Golfarin,[49] the nephew of Mahom, if thou stir hence I will put thee in the bottom of my breeches instead of a suppository, which cannot choose but do me good. For in my belly I am very costive, and cannot well shit without gnashing my teeth and making many filthy faces."

Then Pantagruel, thus destitute of a staff, took up the end of his mast, striking athwart and alongst upon the giant, but he did him no more hurt than you would do with a fillip upon a smith's anvil.

In the meantime Loupgarou was drawing his mace out of the ground, and, having already plucked it out, was ready therewith to have struck Pantagruel, who, being very quick in turning, avoided all his blows in taking only the defensive part in hand, until on a sudden he saw that Loupgarou did threaten him with these words, saying:

"Now, villain, will not I fail to chop thee as small as minced meat, and keep thee henceforth from ever making any more poor men athirst!"

For then, without any more ado, Pantagruel struck him such a blow with his foot against the belly that he made him fall backwards, his heels over his head, and dragged him thus along at flay-buttock above a flight-shot.

Then Loupgarou cried out, bleeding at the throat:

"Mahom, Mahom, Mahom!"

At which noise all the giants arose to succor him. But Panurge said unto them:

---

[49] Muhammad's "nephew," depicted in French legends as a deadly enchanter.

119

"Gentlemen, do not go, if will believe me, for our master is mad, and strikes athwart and alongst, he cares not where; he will do you a mischief."

But the giants made no account of it, seeing that Pantagruel had never a staff. And when Pantagruel saw those giants approach very near unto him, he took Loupgarou by the two feet, and lift up his body like a pike in the air, wherewith, it being harnessed with anvils, he laid such heavy load amongst those giants armed with free-stone, that, striking them down as a mason doth little knobs of stones, there was not one of them that stood before him whom he threw not flat to the ground. And by the breaking of this stony armor there was made such a horrible rumble as put me in mind of the fall of the butter-tower of St. Stephen's at Bourges when it melted before the sun.[50]

Panurge, with Carpalin and Eusthenes, did cut in the mean time the throats of those that were struck down, in such sort that there escaped not one. Pantagruel to any man's sight was like a mower, who with his scythe, which was Loupgarou, cut down the meadow grass, to wit, the giants; but with this fencing of Pantagruel's Loupgarou lost his head, which happened when Pantagruel struck down one whose name was Riflandouille, or Pudding-plunderer, who was armed cap-a-pie with Grison stones, one chip whereof splintering abroad cut off Epistemon's neck clean and fair. For otherwise the most part of them were but lightly armed with a kind of sandy brittle stone, and the rest with slates.

At last, when he saw that they were all dead, he threw the body of Loupgarou as hard as he could against the city, where falling like a frog upon his belly in the great Piazza

---

[50] Roman Catholic cathedral, dedicated to Saint Stephen, located in Bourges, France. It has been nicknamed the "Butter Tower" because of a popular belief that it was partly financed by the sums paid by the faithful in exchange for the permission to eat butter during Lent.

thereof, he with the said fall killed a singed he-cat, a wet she-cat, a farting duck, and a bridled goose.

Chapter XXXI

How Pantagruel entered into the city of the Amaurots,[51] and how Panurge married King Anarchus to an old lantern-carrying hag, and made him a crier of green sauce.

After this wonderful victory, Pantagruel sent Carpalin unto the city of the Amaurots to declare and signify unto them how the King Anarchus was taken prisoner and all the enemies of the city overthrown. Which news when they heard all the inhabitants of the city came forth to meet him in good order, and with a great triumphant pomp, conducting him with a heavenly joy into the city, where innumerable bonfires were set on through all the parts thereof, and fair round tables, which were furnished with store of good victuals, set out in the middle of the streets. This was a renewing of the golden age in the time of Saturn, so good was the cheer which then they made.

But Pantagruel, having assembled the whole senate and common councilmen of the town, said:

"My masters, we must now strike the iron whilst it is hot. It is therefore my will that, before we frolic it any longer, we advise how to assault and take the whole kingdom of the Dipsodes. To which effect let those that will go with me provide themselves against tomorrow after drinking, for then will I begin to march. Not that I need any more men than I have to help me to conquer it, for I could make it as sure that way as if I had it already; but I see this city is so full of inhabitants that they scarce can turn in the streets. I will, therefore, carry them as a colony into Dipsody, and will give them all that country,

---

[51] The name comes from the Greek word for the blind.

which is fair, wealthy, fruitful, and pleasant, above all other countries in the world, as many of you can tell who have been there heretofore. Everyone of you, therefore, that will go along, let him provide himself as I have said."

This counsel and resolution being published in the city, the next morning there assembled in the piazza before the palace to the number of eighteen hundred fifty-six thousand and eleven, besides women and little children. Thus began they to march straight into Dipsody, in such good order as did the people of Israel when they departed out of Egypt to pass over the Red Sea.

[...]

Chapter XXXII
How Pantagruel with his tongue covered a whole army, and what the author saw in his mouth.

Thus, as Pantagruel with all his army had entered into the country of the Dipsodes, everyone was glad of it, and incontinently rendered themselves unto him, bringing him out of their own good wills the keys of all the cities where he went, the Almirods only excepted, who, being resolved to hold out against him, made answer to his heralds that they would not yield but upon very honorable and good conditions.

"What!" said Pantagruel, do they ask any better terms than the hand at the pot and the glass in their fist? Come, let us go sack them, and put them all to the sword."

Then did they put themselves in good order, as being fully determined to give an assault, but by the way, passing through a large field, they were overtaken with a great shower of rain, whereat they began to shiver and tremble, to crowd, press, and thrust close to one another.

When Pantagruel saw that, he made their captains tell them that it was nothing, and that he saw well above the clouds that it would be nothing but a little dew; but, howsoever, that they should put themselves in order, and he would cover them. Then did they put themselves in a close order, and stood as near to each other as they could, and Pantagruel drew out his tongue only half-way and covered them all, as a hen doth her chickens.

In the meantime, I, who relate to you these so veritable stories, hid myself under a burdock-leaf, which was not much less in largeness than the arch of the bridge of Montrible,[52] but when I saw them thus covered, I went towards them to shelter myself likewise; which I could not do, for that they were so, as the saying is, At the yard's end there is no cloth left. Then, as well as I could, I got upon it, and went along full two leagues upon his tongue, and so long marched that at last I came into his mouth. But, O gods and goddesses! What did I see there? Jupiter confound me with his three-pronged lightning if I lie! I walked there as they do in Sophia at Constantinople, and saw there great rocks, like the mountains in Denmark—I believe that those were his teeth. I saw also fair meadows, large forests, great and strong cities not a jot less than Lyons or Poitiers.

The first man I met with there was a good honest fellow planting coleworts,[53] whereat being very much amazed, I asked him:

"My friend, what dost thou make here?"

"I plant coleworts," said he.

"But how, and wherewith?" said I.

"Ha, sir, said he, everyone cannot have his bollocks as heavy as a mortar, neither can we be all rich. Thus do I get my

---

[52] The Bridge of Mantible is a ruined bridge located near Logroño, Spain. It crosses the Ebro river between La Rioja and the Basque Country. It is featured in the Tale of Fierabras (from French: *fier à bras*, brave/formidable arm), a fictional Saracen knight of gigantic stature who appears in several *chansons de geste*. Fierabras is the son of Balan, King of Spain, and is frequently shown in conflict with Roland and Oliver. He eventually converts to Christianity and fights for Charlemagne.

[53] Primitive cultivated cabbage of the Middle Ages.

poor living, and carry them to the market to sell in the city which is here behind."

"Jesus!" said I, "is there here a new world?"

"Sure," said he, "it is never a jot new, but it is commonly reported that, without this, there is an earth, whereof the inhabitants enjoy the light of a sun and a moon, and that it is full of and replenished with very good commodities; but yet this is more ancient than that."

"Yea but," said I, "my friend, what is the name of that city whither thou carriest thy coleworts to sell?"

"It is called Aspharage,"[54] said he, "and all the indwellers are Christians, very honest men, and will make you good cheer."

To be brief, I resolved to go thither. Now, in my way, I met with a fellow that was lying in wait to catch pigeons, of whom I asked:

"My friend, from whence come these pigeons?"

"Sir," said he, "they come from the other world."

Then I thought that, when Pantagruel yawned, the pigeons went into his mouth in whole flocks, thinking that it had been a pigeon-house.

Then I went into the city, which I found fair, very strong, and seated in a good air; but at my entry the guard demanded of me my pass or ticket. Whereat I was much astonished, and asked them:

"My masters, is there any danger of the plague here?"

"O Lord!" said they, "they die hard by here so fast that the cart runs about the streets."

"Good God!" said I, "and where?"

Whereunto they answered that it was in Larynx and Pharynx, which are two great cities such as Rouen and Nantes, rich and of great trading. And the cause of the plague was by a stinking and infectious exhalation which lately vapored out of the abysms, whereof there have died above two and twenty hundred and threescore thousand and sixteen persons within

---

[54] From the Greek word for gullet.

this seven night. Then I considered, calculated, and found that it was a rank and unsavory breathing which came out of Pantagruel's stomach when he did eat so much garlic, as we have aforesaid.

Parting from thence, I passed amongst the rocks, which were his teeth, and never left walking till I got up on one of them; and there I found the pleasantest places in the world, great large tennis-courts, fair galleries, sweet meadows, store of vines, and an infinite number of banqueting summer out-houses in the fields, after the Italian fashion, full of pleasure and delight, where I stayed full four months, and never made better cheer in my life as then.

After that, I went down by the hinder teeth to come to the chaps. But in the way, I was robbed by thieves in a great forest that is in the territory towards the ears. Then, after a little further travelling, I fell upon a pretty petty village—truly I have forgot the name of it—where I was yet merrier than ever, and got some certain money to live by. Can you tell how? By sleeping. For there, they hire men by the day to sleep, and they get by it sixpence a day, but they that can snort hard get at least nine pence.

How I had been robbed in the valley, I informed the senators, who told me that, in very truth, the people of that side were bad livers and naturally thievish, whereby I perceived well that, as we have with us the countries Cisalpine and Transalpine, that is, behither and beyond the mountains, so have they there the countries Cidentine and Tradentine,[55] that is, behither and beyond the teeth. But it is far better living on this side, and the air is purer. Then I began to think that it is very true which is commonly said, that the one half of the world knoweth not how the other half liveth; seeing none before myself had ever written of that country, wherein are above five-and-twenty kingdoms inhabited, besides deserts, and a great arm of the sea. Concerning which purpose I have

[55] Before and Beyond the Teeth; names coined by the translator.

125

composed a great book, entitled, *The History of the Throatias*, because they dwell in the throat of my master Pantagruel.

At last, I was willing to return, and, passing by his beard, I cast myself upon his shoulders, and from thence slid down to the ground, and fell before him. As soon as I was perceived by him, he asked me:

"Whence comest thou, Alcofribas?"[56]

I answered him:

"Out of your mouth, my lord."

"And how long hast thou been there?" said he.

"Since the time," said I, "that you went against the Almirods."

"That is about six months ago," said he. "And wherewith didst thou live?"

"What didst thou drink? I answered. "My lord, of the same that you did, and of the daintiest morsels that passed through your throat I took toll."

"Yea but," said he, "where didst thou shite?"

"In your throat, my lord," said I.

"Ha, ha! thou art a merry fellow," said he. "We have with the help of God conquered all the land of the Dipsodes; I will give thee the *Chatellenie*, or Lordship, of Salmigondin."[57]

"*Grand merci*, my lord," said I, "you gratify me beyond all that I have deserved of you."

---

[56] Anagrammatic surname of the narrator, i.e.: Rabelais.

[57] Potluck, hodgepodge.

The 18th century was known to French historians as the *Siècle des Lumières* [Century of Lights], or The Enlightenment. Starting with the accession to the throne in 1643 of the Sun King Louis XIV (1638-1715), France entered a period of political, artistic and scientific grandeur, before settling into the decadent reigns of Louis XV (1710-1774) and, finally, Louis XVI (1754-1793). Religious persecution and witch hunts finally stopped in 1670, after the personal intervention of Louis XIV, who overruled the local Parliament of the city of Rouen, in an affair where five hundred persons were under suspicion of witchcraft.

Enlightenment could be said to have started with René Descartes (1596-1650) in 1637 with his *Le Discours de la Méthode*, or in 1687 when Isaac Newton (1643-1727) published his *Mathematical Principles of Natural Philosophy*, the basis for a comprehensive, mathematical description of the Universe, which demonstrated the power of science over the material world.

In fantasy literature, the baroque was replaced by classicism during the reign of the Sun King, with its roster of great playwrights: Corneille, Racine and Molière. The so-called "Quarrel of the Ancients and the Moderns" (c. 1690) freed French writers from the need to imitate the literature of antiquity. Finally, the passion for new philosophical ideas, incarnated by the great Voltaire, and the spread of cosmopolitan influences, such as those of Spinoza (1632-1677) and Newton, fostered a climate of debate that would eventually produce the blueprints for a new, modern society.

One of the oldest types of fantasy tales is the Imaginary Journey, for if wonders are to be encountered, they cannot plausibly be encountered at home, and the further from home a traveler has been, the less implausible it will seem to his readers when he tells his story of finding things different and strange.

The temptation to make a journey and its spectacles more dramatic in the retelling is undoubtedly forceful, and perhaps irresistible, further boosted by the occasional requirement to explain and excuse an absence, as Odysseus had to do when he made up the *Odyssey* to explain to poor Penelope why he was so late in returning from the Trojan War, thus providing an archetype for future tales of extraordinary adventure.

Following in the footsteps of Rabelais, Roger Bacon (1214-1292) (whose *New Atlantis* was published in 1629), Tommaso Campanella (1568-1639) (whose *City of the Sun* was published in 1637), and Francis Godwin (1562-1633) (whose *The Man in the Moone* was published in 1638), a number of French authors penned their own tales of Imaginary Journeys. We shall, however, distinguish between those with pure utopian elements, the purpose of which was social satire and philosophical discourse, and those fantasy elements which aimed to entertain and dazzle the reader.

Denis Vairasse d'Allais, a.k.a. Denis Veiras (1637-1683) penned a four-volume *Histoire des Sévarambes* [The History of the Sevarambi] (1675), about a fictional people inhabiting the "Austral Land." The story deals with the attempts by survivors of a shipwreck to establish a new society until they discover the city of Sporounde, whose exotic sexual mores seem attractive to the male castaways. Sporounde is, however, a vassal state of the empire of the Severambes, who trace their ancestry back to a second Eden created by God after the Flood, in which a new primordial couple became the ancestors of their alternative human race. They are sun-worshipers, who pride themselves on the rationality of their society, which maintains its purity by exiling deviants of all kinds. They are more advanced technologically than European societies, although the advancement is partially secured by espionage that allows them to appropriate useful inventions made elsewhere in the world. They live in orderly cities whose vast buildings each contain a thousand inhabitants, and their economy has no need of money. Their food supply is guaranteed by agricultural methods that take advantage of ingenious soil technology and elaborate systems of land-irrigation. They can also cure diseases. They are, however, exceptional, all the other inhabitants of the austral continent remaining primitive.

In 1676, Gabriel de Foigny (c. 1630-1692) published *La Terre Australe Connue* [The Known Austral Land], reissued in 1693 as *Les Aventures de Jacques Sadeur dans la Découverte et le Voyage de la Terre Australe* [The Adventures of Jacques Sadeur in the Discovery and the Exploration of the Austral Land], an elaborate novel about yet another enlightened Antipodean race. Sadeur explains how he overcame the stigma of being born a hermaphrodite to become an adventurer and explorer, initially in Africa, before being cast away in Terra Australis, where he is rescued from giant carnivorous birds by natives, who turn out to be representatives of an entire race of hermaphrodites. By virtue of that condition, which permits a perfect equality impossible in a sexually differentiated society, the "Australians" have been able to establish a truly egalitarian society with an economic organization that we would now call communist, although Foigny does not, the word not having yet been invented. The very perfection of their way of life, however, causes the Australians to feel *ennui*, apathy and suicide, the latter facilitated by a powerful narcotic.

François de Salignac de la Mothe-Fénelon (1651-1715), generally known simply as Fénelon, was a Catholic clergyman whose reputation as an orator resulted in his being commissioned, when Louis XIV revoked the Edict of Nantes—originally issued in 1598 by Henri IV to guarantee legal tolerance to French Protestants—to undertake missionary work to persuade the Protestants of France to convert to Catholicism, henceforth restored as the official State Religion.

Given that the alternatives to conversion were exile and, increasingly, "dragooning"—the forced confiscation of children from Protestant families, in order that they could be indoctrinated, by means of violence administered, often murderously, by soldiers—Fénelon's mission seemed simple enough, but did not prove so in practice, and he found it extremely distasteful to his conscience. Subsequently, however, he found an employment much more to his liking when he was appointed the tutor of the Dauphin's eldest son, Louis, Duc de Bourgogne, the second in line to the throne—although, like his father, he died before Louis XIV. His former friend and then rival, Jacques-Bénigne Bossuet, had served as the Dauphin's tutor, and had written a book fervently defending the divine right of kings; Fénelon decided to write a book of his own promoting his own reformist ideas about constitutional monarchy, but he decided to make it more child-friendly, for the sake of his pupil, by casting it as an adventure story, a sequel to Homer's *Odyssey*: *Suite du quatrième livre de l'Odysée d'Homère ou les aventures de Télémaque, fils d'Ulysse* [Sequel to the Fourth Book of Homer's Odyssey; or, The Adventures of Telemachus, son of Ulysses] (1699). The book was an immense bestseller, and added a new concept to several European languages in the name of its hero, Mentor, who serves as the tutor who guides the young Télémaque around the various quasi-utopian realms of the Mediterranean, some borrowing the names of real places, such as Tyr and Egypte, some mythological realms like Arcadie and others frankly allegorical, such as Bétique, all serving as preludes to the description of the supposedly authentic ideal state of Salente.

Prior to this, Fénelon had written several fables in prose, for the education of the Duke of Burgundy. These were not collected or published; and it was only after Fénelon's death that his nephew, and his friend, Mr. Ramsay, collected with dedicated care these scattered compositions, and issued, in 1718, the first authentic edition under the title *Fables et Opuscules pédagogiques* [Fables and educational pamphlets]. The tale excerpted below is a reworking of the story of the Ring of Gyges, a mythical magical artifact mentioned by Plato in Book II of his *Republic*, which granted its owner the power to become invisible at will.

Fénelon: *The Enchanted Ring*
(c. 1690)[58]

Once upon a time there lived a young man named Rosimond, who was as good and handsome as his elder brother Bramintho was ugly and wicked. Their mother detested her eldest son, and had only eyes for the youngest. This excited Bramintho's jealousy and he invented a horrible story in order to ruin his brother. He told his father that Rosimond was in the habit of visiting a neighbor who was an enemy of the family, and betraying to him all that went on in the house, and was plotting with him to poison their father.

The father flew into a rage, and flogged his son till the blood came. Then he threw him into prison and kept him for three days without food, and after that he turned him out of the house, and threatened to kill him if he ever came back. The mother was miserable, and did nothing but weep, but she dared not say anything.

The youth left his home with tears in his eyes, not knowing where to go, and wandered about for many hours till he came to a thick wood. Night overtook him at the foot of a great rock, and he fell asleep on a bank of moss, lulled by the music of a little brook.

It was dawn when he woke, and he saw before him a beautiful woman seated on a grey horse, with trappings of gold, who looked as if she were preparing for the hunt.

"Have you seen a stag and some deerhounds go by?" she asked.

---

[58] Excerpted from *Fables et Opuscules Pédagogiques* by François de Salignac de la Mothe-Fénelon, translated into English in 1892 by Andrew Lang, introduced and annotated by Jean-Marc Lofficier.

"No, madam," he replied.

Then she added, "You look unhappy; is there anything the matter? Take this ring, which will make you the happiest and most powerful of men, provided you never make a bad use of it. If you turn the diamond inside, you will become invisible. If you turn it outside, you will become visible again. If you place it on your little finger, you will take the shape of the King's son, followed by a splendid court. If you put it on your fourth finger, you will take your own shape."

Then the young man understood that it was a Fairy who was speaking to him, and when she had finished she plunged into the woods. The youth was very impatient to try the ring, and returned home immediately. He found that the Fairy had spoken the truth, and that he could see and hear everything, while he himself was unseen. It lay with him to revenge himself, if he chose, on his brother, without the slightest danger to himself, and he told no one but his mother of all the strange things that had befallen him. He afterwards put the enchanted ring on his little finger, and appeared as the King's son, followed by a hundred fine horses and a guard of officers all richly dressed.

His father was much surprised to see the King's son in his quiet little house, and he felt rather embarrassed, not knowing what was the proper way to behave on such a grand occasion. Then Rosimond asked him how many sons he had.

"Two," replied he.

"I wish to see them," said Rosimond. "Send for them at once. I desire to take them both to Court, in order to make their fortunes."

The father hesitated, then answered: "Here is the eldest, whom I have the honor to present to your Highness."

"But where is the youngest? I wish to see him too," persisted Rosimond.

"He is not here," said the father. "I had to punish him for a fault, and he has run away."

Then Rosimond replied, "You should have shown him what was right, but not have punished him. However, let the elder come with me, and as for you, follow these two guards, who will escort you to a place that I will point out to them."

Then the two guards led off the father, and the Fairy of whom you have heard found him in the forest, and beat him with a golden birch rod, and cast him into a cave that was very deep and dark, where he lay enchanted.

"Lie there," she said, "till your son comes to take you out again."

Meanwhile the son went to the King's palace, and arrived just when the real prince was absent. He had sailed away to make war on a distant island, but the winds had been contrary, and he had been shipwrecked on unknown shores, and taken captive by a savage people. Rosimond made his appearance at Court in the character of the Prince, whom everyone wept for as lost, and told them that he had been rescued when at the point of death by some merchants. His return was the signal for great public rejoicings, and the King was so overcome that he became quite speechless, and did nothing but embrace his son. The Queen was even more delighted, and fetes were ordered over the whole kingdom.

One day, the false Prince said to his real brother, "Bramintho, you know that I brought you here from your native village in order to make your fortune; but I have found out that you are a liar, and that by your deceit you have been the cause of all the troubles of your brother Rosimond. He is in hiding here, and I desire that you shall speak to him, and listen to his reproaches."

Bramintho trembled at these words, and, flinging himself at the Prince's feet, confessed his crime.

"That is not enough," said Rosimond. "It is to your brother that you must confess, and I desire that you shall ask his forgiveness. He will be very generous if he grants it, and it will be more than you deserve. He is in my ante-room, where you shall see him at once. I myself will retire into another apartment, so as to leave you alone with him."

Bramintho entered, as he was told, into the anteroom. Then Rosimond changed the ring, and passed into the room by another door.

Bramintho was filled with shame as soon as he saw his brother's face. He implored his pardon, and promised to atone for all his faults. Rosimond embraced him with tears, and at once forgave him, adding, "I am in great favor with the King. It rests with me to have your head cut off, or to condemn you to pass the remainder of your life in prison; but I desire to be as good to you as you have been wicked to me."

Bramintho, confused and ashamed, listened to his words without daring to lift his eyes or to remind Rosimond that he was his brother. After this, Rosimond gave out that he was going to make a secret voyage, to marry a Princess who lived in a neighboring kingdom; but in reality he only went to see his mother, whom he told all that had happened at the Court, giving her at the same time some money that she needed, for the King allowed him to take exactly what he liked, though he was always careful not to abuse this permission.

Just then a furious war broke out between the King his master and the Sovereign of the adjoining country, who was a bad man and one that never kept his word. Rosimond went straight to the palace of the wicked King, and by means of his ring was able to be present at all the councils, and learnt all their schemes, so that he was able to forestall them and bring them to naught. He took the command of the army which was brought against the wicked King, and defeated him in a glorious battle, so that peace was at once concluded on conditions that were just to everyone.

Henceforth the King's one idea was to marry the young man to a Princess who was the heiress to a neighboring kingdom, and, besides that, was as lovely as the day. But one morning, while Rosimond was hunting in the forest where for the first time he had seen the Fairy, his benefactress suddenly appeared before him.

"Take heed," she said to him in severe tones, "that you do not marry anybody who believes you to be a Prince. You must never deceive anyone. The real Prince, whom the whole nation thinks you are, will have to succeed his father, for that is just and right. Go and seek him in some distant island, and I will send winds that will swell your sails and bring you to him. Hasten to render this service to your master, although it is against your own ambition, and prepare, like an honest man, to return to your natural state. If you do not do this, you will become wicked and unhappy, and I will abandon you to all your former troubles."

Rosimond took these wise counsels to heart. He gave out that he had undertaken a secret mission to a neighboring state, and embarked on board a vessel, the winds carrying him straight to the island where the Fairy had told him he would find the real Prince. This unfortunate youth had been taken captive by a savage people, who had kept him to guard their sheep. Rosimond, becoming invisible, went to seek him amongst the pastures, where he kept his flock, and, covering him with his mantle, he delivered him out of the hands of his cruel masters, and bore him back to the ship. Other winds sent by the Fairy swelled the sails, and together the two young men entered the King's presence.

Rosimond spoke first and said, "You have believed me to be your son. I am not he, but I have brought him back to you."

The King, filled with astonishment, turned to his real son and asked, "Was it not you, my son, who conquered my enemies and won such a glorious peace? Or is it true that you have been shipwrecked and taken captive, and that Rosimond has set you free?"

"Yes, my father," replied the Prince. "It is he who sought me out in my captivity and set me free, and to him I owe the happiness of seeing you once more. It was he, not I, who gained the victory."

The King could hardly believe his ears; but Rosimond, turning the ring, appeared before him in the likeness of the Prince, and the King gazed distractedly at the two youths who seemed both to be his son. Then he offered Rosimond immense rewards for his services, which were refused, and the only favor the young man would accept was that one of his posts at Court should be conferred on his brother Bramintho. For he feared for himself the changes of fortune, the envy of mankind and his own weakness. His desire was to go back to his mother and his native village, and to spend his time in cultivating the land.

One day, when he was wandering through the woods, he met the Fairy, who showed him the cavern where his father was imprisoned, and told him what words he must use in order to set him free. He repeated them joyfully, for he had always longed to bring the old man back and to make his last days happy. Rosimond thus became the benefactor of all his family, and had the pleasure of doing good to those who had wished to do him evil. As for the Court, to whom he had rendered such services, all he asked was the freedom to live far from its corruption; and, to crown all, fearing that if he kept the ring he might be tempted to use it in order to regain his lost place in the world, he made up his mind to restore it to the Fairy. For many days he sought her up and down the woods and at last he found her.

"I want to give you back," he said, holding out the ring, "a gift as dangerous as it is powerful, and which I fear to use wrongfully. I shall never feel safe till I have made it impossible for me to leave my solitude and to satisfy my passions."

While Rosimond was seeking to give back the ring to the Fairy, Bramintho, who had failed to learn any lessons from experience, gave way to all his desires, and tried to persuade the Prince, lately become King, to ill-treat Rosimond. But the Fairy, who knew all about everything, said to Rosimond, when he was imploring her to accept the ring:

"Your wicked brother is doing his best to poison the mind of the King towards you, and to ruin you. He deserves to be punished, and he must die; and in order that he may destroy himself, I shall give the ring to him."

Rosimond wept at these words, and then asked:

"What do you mean by giving him the ring as a punishment? He will only use it to persecute everyone, and to become master."

"The same things," answered the Fairy, "are often a healing medicine to one person and a deadly poison to another. Prosperity is the source of all evil to a naturally wicked man. If you wish to punish a scoundrel, the first thing to do is to give him power. You will see that with this rope he will soon hang himself."

Having said this, she disappeared, and went straight to the Palace, where she showed herself to Bramintho under the disguise of an old woman covered with rags. She at once addressed him in these words:

"I have taken this ring from the hands of your brother, to whom I had lent it, and by its help he covered himself with glory. I now give it to you, and be careful what you do with it."

Bramintho replied with a laugh:

"I shall certainly not imitate my brother, who was foolish enough to bring back the Prince instead of reigning in his place," and he was as good as his word. The only use he made of the ring was to find out family secrets and betray them, to commit murders and every sort of wickedness, and to gain wealth for himself unlawfully. All these crimes, which could be traced to nobody, filled the people with astonishment.

The King, seeing so many affairs, public and private, exposed, was at first as puzzled as anyone, till Bramintho's wonderful prosperity and amazing insolence made him suspect that the enchanted ring had become his property. In order to find out the truth he bribed a stranger just arrived at Court, one of a nation with whom the King was always at war, and arranged that he was to steal in the night to Bramintho and to offer him untold honors and rewards if he would betray the State secrets.

Bramintho promised everything, and accepted at once the first payment of his crime, boasting that he had a ring which rendered him invisible, and that by means of it he could penetrate into the most private places. But his triumph was short. Next day he was seized by order of the King, and his ring was taken from him. He was searched, and on him were found papers which proved his crimes; and, though Rosimond himself came back to the Court to entreat his pardon, it was refused. So Bramintho was put to death, and the ring had been even more fatal to him than it had been useful in the hands of his brother.

To console Rosimond for the fate of Bramintho, the King gave him back the enchanted ring, as a pearl without price. The unhappy Rosimond did not look upon it in the same light, and the first thing he did on his return home was to seek the Fairy in the woods.

"Here," he said, "is your ring. My brother's experience has made me understand many things that I did not know before. Keep it, it has only led to his destruction. Ah! without it he would be alive now, and my father and mother would not in their old age be bowed to the earth with shame and grief! Perhaps he might have been wise and happy if he had never had the chance of gratifying his wishes! Oh! how dangerous it is to have more power than the rest of the world! Take back your ring, and as ill fortune seems to follow all on whom you bestow it, I will implore you, as a favor to myself, that you will never give it to anyone who is dear to me."

Simon Tyssot de Patot (1655-1727) dispatched his hero Jacques Massé to another Terra Australis in *Voyages et Aventures de Jacques Massé* [Voyages and Adventures of Jacques Massé] (1710), arguably the first modern "Lost World" novel. Shipwrecked in the South Atlantic, Massé and his crew are stranded on a landmass near the Falklands. After a difficult journey, Massé and his companions discover strange specimens of unknown flora and fauna, and an enclosed valley that is home to a peaceful and orderly society. Massé begins educating their king in science, while becoming interested in the country's religious ideas and the mythology of its origins. He runs into trouble after manufacturing a watch, when one of the king's several wives, eager to acquire one like it, seduces Massé's companion with dangerous promises that she has no intention of fulfilling. The ensuing complications result in Massé escaping from the valley, and being pursued along an underground river that eventually leads him back to the outside world.

In Tyssot de Patot's 1720 novel, *La Vie, les Aventures et le Voyage de Groenland du Révérend Père Cordelier Pierre de Mésange* [The Life, Adventures & Trip to Greenland of the Rev. Father Pierre de Mesange], Pierre de Mésange discovers in the Arctic a monstrous fauna and a curious society, living underground during the winter night, but emerging to the surface in summer. They are the descendants of African colonists who left their homeland four thousand years earlier. This proto-Pellucidar underworld is lit by a mysterious fire ball and also inhabited by small man-bat creatures. [59]

In 1735-38, Charles de Fieux, Chevalier de Mouhy (1701-1784) wrote *Lamékis, ou Les Voyages Extraordinaires d'un Égyptien dans la Terre Intérieure avec la Découverte de l'Île des Sylphides* [Lamekis, or The Extraordinary Voyages of

---

[59] Both books are available in a single volume, *The Strange Voyages of Jacques Massé and Pierre de Mésange*, translated by Brian Stableford, Black Coat Press, ISBN 9768-1-61227-370-9.

an Egyptian inside the Inner Earth with The Discovery of the Sylphides' Island], [60] in which Lamekis, a priest of ancient Egypt, rescues Motacoa, son of a king, a blue-skinned man exiled with his mother to an underground land called Trifolday. The fugitive tells the priest how he fought against races of worm-men. Pierre Versins, in his *Encyclopédie de l'Utopie et de la Science-Fiction*, labels the work "a remote ancestor of Abraham Merritt—especially *The Moon Pool*—and H.P. Lovecraft." There is no real moral or didactic purpose to Lamekis, just an author reveling in his wild, explosive, frenetic imagination, perhaps too strange for his time and better understood from a modern point of view. De Mouhy plays with both narrative and typographical strangeness—the adjective "extraordinary" in the title is no empty promise. The different physical mazes of the Inner Earth mirror his labyrinthine story structure and state of mind. His use of an invented language, confused and unusual references, fake notes, parentheses, ellipses, etc. have fun with the literature of his age. The novel's most exotic episodes take place in subterranean caverns that are home to the loathsome worm-men, most of them in a convoluted story narrated to Lamekis by Motocoa. Giant birds sometimes provide a convenient means of travel between realms, and a super-powered dog also plays a crucial role in

---

[60] The first part of *Lamekis* was published in Paris in 1735 by Dupuis; the second part came out the following year. Parts 3 and 4 came out in 1737 in Paris, but were published by Poilly. The final four parts, 5-8, were all published in 1738 in The Hague, Netherlands, by Neaulme. In 1788, *Lamekis* was reprinted in Volumes 20-21 of Charles Georges Thomas Garnier's ground-breaking imprint, *Voyages imaginaires, songes et visions et romans cabalistiques*, Amsterdam—the reprint did not include de Mouhy's prefaces to parts 3, 5 and 8 from the original edition. No other editions of *Lamekis* have been published in France since then. The book is available in an English translation by Michael Shreve as *Lamekis*, Black Coat Press, ISBN 9768-1-61227-003-6.

the embedded narratives. Lamekis is perhaps best regarded as a remote ancestor of modern pulp fantasy, but if one sets aside literary disdain, that is not an unremarkable achievement.

Chevalier de Mouhy: *The Worm-Men*
(1737)[61]

The birth of Motacoa and the jealousy of the Houcaïs

I am the son of the Houcaïs[62] or King of the Abdalles.[63] His kingdom was founded by the great Vilkonhis,[64] whom you know as the Universal Being. The extent of his realm is vast: my father ruled all the people who lived between the rock that I showed you and the mountain Collira.[65] His power had no limits. My mother, who was white, had been brought from far-off lands and he fell so madly in love with her that he married her.

With this marriage love was coupled with intelligence. Their happiness was perfect. If they ever argued, it was only in their love for each other, fighting over who loved the other more. One day the Queen wanted to get the better of the King and said to him:

"Well, the fruit that I bear will decide the matter. If the token of our mutual love is blue, it is undeniable proof that I love you more; and if the child is my color, I will consent that your love is greater than mine."

The Houcaïs accepted the test and they waited impatiently for the moment that would decide the crucial issue.

---

[61] Excerpted from *Lamékis* by Charles de Fieux, Chevalier de Mouhy, translated into English in 2011 and annotated by Michael Shreve.

[62] This means *caliph* in the native language.

[63] Abdalles, the people near the zenith.

[64] The Abdalles recognized only the Universal Being, whom they called Vilkonhis or Father of Light.

[65] Of ice.

I was born white.

"How can that be?" I interrupted. "You are the same color as the people here."

You will see in time. I use a trick to be blue and it's only to protect your life that we have dyed you that color.

My mother was carried away with joy when she saw me. She was delighted to lose the challenge because of her excessive love for my father. But the King took it very differently. He became glum and gloomy. His jealousy invented all kinds of suspicions about my birth. For some time, he considered how to get revenge. From the fateful day that I came into the world, he stopped seeing the Queen, who dissolved in tears because she could not imagine how she had lost his love. Imagine her surprise when the head kirzif[66] came to her one day with the dreadful kirmec[67] in his hand.

"What's this I see?" the poor Princess screamed. "Is the grandeur of my love to be the height of my disgrace? Am I condemned to death?"

"Ah, Madame," the Kirzif cried, "I am so unhappy to be in this position! If only I could take your place in the dreadful pit of Houzaïl![68] The Houcaïs sentences you and your son, the Prince, to this dreadful punishment. He thinks you committed adultery and has sworn to Vilkonhis that he will henceforth kill all whites who fall into his hands, supposing that of all the

---

[66] Vizier.

[67] Sealed letter. They only gave it to proclaim death. It was a leaf from a tree that was guarded at the house of the minister or kirzif and was the image of his power. It was kept in a huge pot behind a strong, iron gate whose key the king wore around his neck. When he wanted to get rid of someone he went to the chief minister, opened the gate, tore off a leaf and pressed it against his face—it kept the imprint forever.

[68] The famous pit of Houzaïl is so deep that they never found the bottom. It seems that the author wanted to play with the gullibility of the people living around the pit who claim they descend from Motacoa and reel off the following tales.

people who die, one of them must be the suspected perpetrator of his shame and the father of the Prince."

"Oh Heavens!" Hildaë cried out (that's the name of my mother), "Oh height of despair! How much innocence and virtue must be sacrificed to so much ingratitude?"

Her pleas were useless. The Houcaïs had gained so much power and it was so absolute that he answered only to himself. There was no point in the people moaning and groaning about such an unfair arrest, it was done. They lowered the Queen and me down into the deadly pit in a basket. As was the custom they gave us food for eight days and instead of a thousand lengths of rope, which was usually used to lower the basket into the abyss, on behalf of the criminal's status they gave us three thousands, which had never been done before and which eventually saved our lives.

It took three days and nights to go down into the center of the Earth.[69] On the fourth day the basket came to a stop on the top of a mountain. The Queen, who was thinking we would die at any moment, felt us land, took me in her arms, quickly got out of the basket and ran, afraid that the rope, which they usually dropped at the end, would kill us. It seemed that the Heavens wanted to preserve us by a miracle. It was a worthwhile precaution—an hour later the rope rained down with an awful racket.

When Hildaë got over her first fear, she examined her surroundings. They were frightening. The ground was scattered with bones and skulls and the mountain looked like it was built of nothing but these poor bodies that had been thrown down there. It was a chilling sight for a woman in my mother's situation. She hurried down the mountain and saw new, funny objects as she went. The variegated ground was oily and soft and the light that broke through created a play of

---

[69] The reader should pay attention here that the author says it took three days for the basket to reach the bottom of Houzaïl and later that it only took one day for Motacoa and Lodaï to come back. It is an important slip that cannot be understood.

shadows that would have charmed a less intimidated mind. But Hildaë was scared of the fate pursuing her and was so worried that she did not take thirty steps before she went back to where she started.

"Oh gods!" she cried. "What is to become of me? Won't the grand Vilkonhis be swayed by my innocence and by some strange miracle save us from this fatal fall?"

This plea lifted her spirits and she looked more confidently at the wondrous things around her.

She was surprised to see an incredibly high vault overhead that was cut with sideways openings spaced unequally apart. Waterfalls came out of some, reflecting the light in a multitude of colors. Others meandered down fissures that they seemed unable to escape. In a farther place a torrent of what looked like heavy silver[70] flowed out of the vault. The liquid was so shiny that she could barely look at it. Hildaë enjoyed (if we can call it that) looking at these wonders for a little while, but many other things amazed her. Turning to the left she saw a sea of fire[71] with many waves; everything around it was covered by dark, purple smoke and the restless flames moved the ground. Closer to us she saw columns of transparent and less restless water,[72] some flowing down and others flowing up. All these miracles of nature were too strange for her to analyze in such a short time and her situation was too critical to ponder over them for long.

Besides, I was weak because I had not eaten in such a long time. My mother saw this and noticed too late that in her desire to save us from the deadly falling rope she had forgotten to take the few provisions that they usually put in the basket. She became desperate and screamed frantically. She tried in vain to remedy the situation by scrambling back up to where it had fallen, but her search was fruitless and her weak-

---

[70] Quicksilver or mercury.

[71] The central fire.

[72] The vegetal soul or spirits.

ness prevented her from continuing. She left the awful place wailing and was surprised to hear a distant voice in answer:

"Patience, I'll be with you right away."

She turned and saw a man on the other side of the stream coming quickly toward us. She jumped with joy.

"Oh Vilkonhis!" she cried. "You are coming to save me."

She went to meet him and as she got closer she could see that he looked like the people who had just banished her. *Ah, she told herself, it's some poor creature like me who miraculously escaped the harsh fate to which he was, maybe, unjustly condemned.* In the middle of this thought she found herself face to face with the stranger, who stepped back and said:

"Oh Heavens, what's this? The Queen! I don't believe it! What awful deed has thrown you down here?"

"Ah!" my mother replied, not remembering the stranger. "Who are you? And how is that I hear my name spoken in this disgraceful place that does not render me honor but rather that covers me in shame by recognizing me?"

"Princess," the stranger replied, "whatever the reason you are here, it can only be to your glory. The grand Vilkonhis does not protect criminals and does not perform miracles in vain. I was sentenced to the infamy of a sure death like you, but I escaped punishment. The Heavens saved me from the deadly fall and aided me in my helplessness. My virtue triumphed. My enemies believed they had destroyed me, but instead they gave me a life unbelievably more peaceful than the one they thought they were depriving me of. Come, Princess, put that precious package in my arms—why, it can only be the legitimate Prince, who is the unlucky partner of our misery."

He took me in his arms and bade my mother follow him, telling her how he survived in the unknown land.

For five years since injustice had cast him down there, he had discovered all the monstrous ins and outs of the inner world. His adventures alone would fill volumes. His name was Lodaï and he was a minister of the Houcaïs. Being favored

146

and fair had earned him enemies. His honesty and openness never made his master's subordinates love him; being firm in his interests attracted them to him. He was too smart not to notice that they were trying to destroy him, but he asked only for the uprightness and kindness of the King to prevail over their calumnies. The King stood up to them for a long time, but in the end he fell victim to the suspicions they sowed in his mind. No people were ever more jealous of his authority than the Houcaïs. They made him believe that Lodaï was scheming to usurp his throne by leading a conspiracy. The minister of this complicated plot suggested the likelihood of treason and it worked as they expected. There was a trial and in spite of his innocence the wicked, corrupt judges convinced the King of the crime of high treason and he was sentenced to the pit of Houzaïl. His luck, or better said, the Heavens made it so that when they let go of the rope, it got caught on a branch growing out of a crack in the rock, which stopped the basket's fall four feet above ground. It was easy to get out and jump onto the mountain. And by this unheard of miracle he was the first one up until then to live in the center of the Earth. He was the one who told us about the wonders that are so fascinating today and that I will tell about later.

After Lodaï told my mother all these things, he led her to the banks of the stream whose rose-colored water flowed onto pure golden sand. This part of the Inner Earth was lit perpendicularly and the ceiling was so high that we could barely see it. A mountain of minerals, mainly sulfur and bitumen, rose up next to the stream. Lodaï had built a nice, comfortable dwelling inside it and since he knew so much about the environment he was able to get everything needed to live. He led Hildaë into the refuge and when he had put her on a bed made of the very finest moss, he gave me some water that I swallowed, which stopped my crying, and then he spoke to my mother.

Lodaï's story

Here is the refuge, Oh great Princess, which I made with patience and skill and where I live infinitely happier than in the ranks I was in before. Here I am King. And from my studies since I was young I have knowledge of nature. When I saw that I was banished but safe, the desire to save my life, which the Heavens seemed to be protecting, compelled me to look for food. The few provisions they give to those they throw down here were barely enough to give me time to find something else. But can you die when the Heavens protect you?

The third day I was wandering in this place I stopped on the banks of this stream. I saw a kind of chicken come out of the water, followed by a few others. I was transfixed by how strange it looked and by the novelty of the thing. I kept watching it and it beat its wings and the air was filled with the sweet smell of the water. All of them romped about for a little while on the golden sand of this little river. Their feathers and heads were crimson and black; they had two beaks with the lower one curving down; they walked pretty much like a duck and soon wandered far away from me. I followed them to find out what they would do. They jumped into a hollowed out path lined with pebbles that looked like mother-of-pearl and after a quarter karie[73] they went into the trunk of a tree that six men holding hands would barely wrap around. The opening they entered was so small that they had to duck to get in. When I saw the chickens holed up in the tree I decided to try to catch one. I went up to the opening and looked inside. It was huge and completely hollow. By the light that entered in different places I could make out a large number of these animals each with their young and cooing like pigeons. After examining them for a while I closed the opening with some moss that covered the tree bark and thought about how I could catch one of them.

---

[73] A league of five thousand feet.

Looking up I was surprised how beautiful and how high the tree was. Its branches were four times longer than an alder and twice as thick. I had to use my knife to cut one of them off because there was no way I could snap it. Just look (Lodaï continued) at the clothes and furniture I made and you can see for yourself what can be done with it. The discovery pleased me greatly, but not as much as the fruit that hung from it. I had quite a bit of trouble getting some down because they were so high. I had to throw rocks to knock them down and I spent a long time trying to gather them up. They fell and bounced like handballs except that they bounced so high and so crazily that whenever I got my hand under one, it slipped away. When I finally got hold of one of these fruits, I scrutinized it carefully. It was light and as fat as an Indian melon. When I split it open, a clear liquid came out. I was so thirsty that I couldn't find enough of them to quench my thirst. I drank so much that I got kind of drunk and felt groggy. I stretched out at the foot of the tree and fell into a deep sleep.

I hadn't been long in my peaceful state when I woke up with a start at the sound of horrifying screams overhead. I opened my eyes and saw the tree covered with those chickens I was talking about. They were all hot and bothered, jumping from one branch to another. I watched their little game for a while and figured that when they found the hole plugged up they got out somewhere higher up in the tree. I opened it up to see if that would change anything, but they just went higher up. One of the little ones was lying in front of the opening, apparently killed in a fall. I picked it up and after examining it I was no longer surprised by the hubbub—it came from the fact that they could not fly. Their wings were really fins folded back on each other and could only be used to swim. Only their back was covered with feathers; their stomach was scaly like a fish. Judging by their claws and their soft skin I figured they would taste great and the experiment I made proved me right.

After this test I went back to the fruit. I was hungry and its liquid had piqued my appetite. I wanted to see if the fruit tasted as good as its color and juice suggested. I ate with de-

149

light and found it tasted like the sweetbread we make in our country. Imagine my joy, Queen, for what could be better than being able to save your life? Taking a half dozen of these fruits I was going to leave the wonderful tree to come back to this dwelling here that I had already picked out, but then I saw the chickens leaving the hole I had left open. I snuck up on them, but they did not seem scared. I picked one up easily and petted it; it was very soft. So, I went to the rock loaded with my rich booty and all kinds of encouraging thoughts about my findings.

What can I tell you, Princess? With time and labor I gradually got used to this subterranean home. I dried out the fruit and ground flour for bread. For the dark nights I discovered fire from the bitumen on the other side of the rock. It burned continually and gave me the means to build an oven to bake my bread and cook the excellent meat. It was also veined with a kind of pitch that was bright when lit up and had a nice smell that was good for the health.

I haven't been bored for a minute since I got here. My books now are the wonders and contents of this Inner Earth. When I have lived through the four ages of man, I will still find new things every day. Every time I go out I come back with more new marvels than I know what to do with, so I put them up in a deep closet that I carved out of the rock where I can relax and enjoy myself. I hope, Princess, that in your exile you will be as charmed and amused as I have been.

Forget about your rank, which in reality is only a pure illusion and gives only false pleasures, which you will clearly understand if you think about it. True happiness depends on the things around us. My experience proves it and I hope that you will agree before too long.

Motacoa is raised underground

Hildaë was comforted by Lodaï's wise words. What calmed her completely was how easily I got used to the new food he gave me. Not only did I like it, but it was also so good for me that I grew before their very eyes. 12 years passed in total calm, untroubled by the sicknesses or worries that constantly bother us in the world. I was raised by the wise Lodaï, who taught me what he knew and when I was old enough he told me about my birth. They were surprised at how strongly I reacted to the King's injustice against my mother. I was so angry that I sometimes disturbed our tranquility and whenever our conversations turned to the subject, they always ended with me swearing that if ever I saw the light of day again, I would spend my life putting my mother back on the throne where she deserved to be. Lodaï lectured me in vain that I should not dream of such things because it was impossible to return to Earth. I shook my head at his protests and kept saying that I had a hunch that it would happen. Events proved me right, that a secret intelligence was giving me a glimpse of the future.

As I got older, my thoughts about everything that Lodaï had taught me expanded and focused on everything I could see. He taught me philosophy, but natural philosophy, not with prickly words but with things that are clear and obvious and I was so preoccupied with the miracles that I saw everyday that I often forgot to take care of myself. The research I was doing sometimes took me 10 or 12 karies from our home and I got lost twice. My mother and Lodaï, who loved me tenderly and worried about me a lot, begged me badly to stop alarming them, so for a while I did not go far and I made sure I got home to sleep.

One day when I went into a crevasse in a rock on a wide, clear path I found a flowing vein of such beautiful, perfect liquid[74] that I wanted to find the source. It was thick and the color of gold, but what was really amazing was that instead of following the natural downward slope, it flowed steadily upward. I followed it for more than three karies and the farther I went into the heart of the mountain, with light slanting in, the wider and rougher the path became. I had to sit down to rest

---

[74] The author seems to be talking about gold.

and I looked around. Through a crack in the rock I saw something so bright that I jumped up and ran to it. As soon as I got up close to it, I heard an awful hiss and I shrank away. I had discovered a dreadful animal, crawling on its belly, folding and unfolding on itself like it was rolling. I started running at full speed up the mountain because the monstrous worm was behind me and seemed to be chasing me. I was sorry, then, that I had not followed Lodaï's sage advice and I made a resolution that if I escaped this hideous threat, I would never expose myself to danger again—the oath of young people in danger that they forget when it's all over.

I was out of breath and the enemy in pursuit was slowly gaining on me. I could hear the noise it made dragging itself along and the hissing got louder. I was at death's door when I saw four feet above me another strange looking, but very different animal. I screamed at the sight of it. Not knowing what else to do, I hid in a hole on my left. I was so scared that when I grazed myself with my own hands I thought the animal had seized me and I shivered. But my enemy had other things to worry about. It was attacked by a formidable athlete that stood up on its hind legs and found the right time to strike. I saw the snake or worm coil up and spring out at its adversary hard and fast. Its mouth was open and a tongue armed with three hooks shot out of the gaping chasm. The slightest touch could have felled its enemy. Falbao, the same dog as you see here, dodged his attacks like an agile fighter by jumping to the side whenever the worm uncoiled and by this tactic wore him down. The fight lasted for a while like this until Falbao suddenly jumped on his enemy and cut it in two with his lethal fangs. The two parts tried to come back together again, but in vain: the skillful victor took one and threw it 30 feet away. After this precaution, which was no doubt done instinctively, he came back to the battlefield and looked around. Finally seeing me he dropped the head of the terrible enemy at my feet. He lay down looking at it and looking at me with eyes that cheered his victory.

My mind was so confused that I did not know what to do. My nerves were numb from fear. Falbao and I sat there looking at each other for about an hour until the animal finally let up the tension; he got up, took three steps forward and came back. It looked like he was inviting me to follow him and his gentle eyes gave me confidence, but because of my fright I stayed back afraid of being eaten. I cannot say if sympathy was the reason he took care to reassure me, but whatever his reasons it worked wonders—he came up, wagged his tail and nuzzled against me. I ventured to stretch out my hand to touch him. He lowered his head and gave me all the signs of gentleness that he could, so I plucked up all my courage to leave. He walked ahead and I followed. After one karie I was so tired that I had to take a rest next to the vein of gold. Falbao did the same and lapped up the liquid. I saw him try to lick a wound on his back, but his neck was not flexible enough to reach it. Then his eyes seemed to beg me for help. I cupped some of the liquid gold in my hands and rubbed it into the wound. He stretched out and let me do it. There was also a wound on his back paw and I was surprised that as soon as I applied the liquid the wounds healed. I, too, had grazed myself, so I put some of this divine balm on it and was relieved right away.

After resting a little while in this place, Falbao got up and I followed him. After a few more karies, imagine my surprise, Lamekis, when I found myself on top of a mountain in mid-air, which convinced me that I was in the regions that my mother and Lodaï had talked so much about. I felt a secret joy, enchanted by the splendid sight of nature. I stood there without moving, dazed, in awe of the beauty of the bright day while my eyes wandered over the immensity of the sky. I spent two hours like that, unable to get over my astonishment and if a new adventure had not pulled me out of my lethargy, I might still be there.

I was sunk in this ecstasy when I felt someone touch me. It was a man the same color as Lodaï. At first I thought it was him and I reached out my arms, but they hung back down when I did not recognize his face.

"Ah, young man, what are you doing here?" the stranger asked. "Are you running away? Where are you going? To your sure ruin. Where do you come from? Don't you know that you are in the empire of the Houcaïs and he has ordered all whites to be arrested and brought to the capital to be sacrificed?"

Imagine the impression those words had on me, Lamekis, finding out that I was in the empire of my father whom I hated more than anything else in the world with a hatred born in childhood for the sake of my unjustly banished mother who was dearer to me than the fate that had torn me from her arms. The dangers I had just faced had lulled my thoughts, but the stranger's speech woke them up and I fully felt my loss.

"Oh Heavens," I cried, "where is this barbarous King you're talking about who covered my mother in shame and sacrificed her to his anger? Where can I find him? Ah! As young as I am, my hatred will give me enough strength to take his life...but what am I saying, good gods! He's my father. The Houcaïs gave me life..."

"What's this I hear?" the stranger cried out. "What are you saying? You, the son of the King of Abdalles! Obviously fear has made you crazy and wild! But I can see a resemblance in your face. And your color almost...I recognize...but no, it can't be. Hildaë died a miserable death in the depths of Houzaïl and her son shared her fate. But, listen mortal, whoever you are, flee! Go back to the cave you came out of! Someone less compassionate than me will arrest you. The order is for everyone, everywhere. Since the day our Queen Hildaë brought a white into the world, it's happened to many men of this color. All the King's subjects are spies and the punishment is so strict against anyone who disobeys that no one would dare break his inhuman laws; not only would it cost him his life, but also the loss of his goods and family."

I stood there without moving as he spoke. Many different thoughts passed through my worried mind. In spite of my prejudice an inner voice rose up for my father, but fear, which was inseparable from my looming fate, got the upper hand and I cried out:

"Whoever you are, protect the son of the great Queen whom Heavens' kindness saved from a more tragic fate. Vilkonhis saved her from death, but oh, how much bitterness does she suffer now? I was her consolation and she has lost me. She has shed so many tears already! Oh my mother! Will I ever see you again and calm your soul? O Lodaï!..."

"What are you saying?" the stranger interrupted. "What names are these? Hildaë is alive and you're her son? What proof can you give of these extraordinary things?"

"My story," I replied, "and Lodaï's, who is alive."

"Lodaï!" he interrupted again. "Surely you've lost your mind…"

"No," I continued impatiently, "it's easy to prove the truth. I can lead you through this cave to the center of the earth where the pit of Houzaïl is only one way in. There you will see the Queen and Lodaï."

The stranger cried out again at these last words. He cast everything into doubt when he happened to look at Falbao whose weird face made him shudder. The animal seemed to be listening to us and the stranger could not move an inch without the animal looking like he wanted to eat him. His foaming mouth was hanging open and his eyes were furious. I was so preoccupied with the stranger that I had not paid attention to him. I trembled, too, and got so scared that I fell backward. The animal ran to my feet and looked so gentle and humble that I trusted him again. The stranger's eyes were all agog and he wavered between fear and admiration. I reassured him and told him how the animal and I had become so close. The adventure impressed him.

"I'm starting to believe," he said, "that there's something extraordinary in your story. I'll even admit that I'm getting interested, though I can't imagine why. I'm curious to know more, but still it's too dangerous for you to stay here any longer. Follow me. My cabin is in the middle of the desert nearby where you will be safe from any fanatics. There we can get to the bottom of this and see if you can convince me that you are the son of the Houcaïs. If so, I won't disappoint you. Even though I'm by myself here, I can get things moving. I don't live alone by chance. I have my reasons that you will appreciate when you know why, but I would be a criminal if you really are who you say you are."

Saying this the stranger led me into the dark woods. After many twists and turns we came into a little valley watered by a river where his house was. Along the way he told me that his name was Boldeon, the first Prince of the Houcaïs' blood. After the disgrace of my mother the King married again, but had no children. He was so in love that he had this Princess' brother, Ruraos, recognized as his heir provided that he and his successors exterminate all the whites found in his and the neighboring realms. A few months later he retired into the royal cave [75] and Ruraos mounted the throne where he ruled as a tyrant who was so detestable that all the nobles of Abdalles preferred to flee into faraway provinces rather than obey the usurper.

When we got to Boldeon's house and washed up, he was eager to hear my story. I told it so naturally and sincerely that he could not help but believe me and he humbled himself as if I were his legitimate Prince. I kissed him and he recognized me as the Prince and swore to me that he would spill his blood to put me back on the usurped throne. Then he let me in on the plans he had made to get rid of the tyrant since the Houcaïs was cut off from everything, just like his contact with the nobles of Abdalles who would form such a formidable opposition that Ruraos would surely fall. Boldeon had pretended to travel to far-off lands to accomplish his plot without suspicion, so no one knew about his house, which was near the capital and also in range of the conspirators whom he could contact when the time came. He told me that he would not let them know about my arrival, but would keep it for the final blow to

---

[75] The royal cave where once the King enters, he never leaves.

incite the people in case the tyrant's power got the upper hand, but that it was absolutely necessary that I go back down into the depths of Houzaïl to get my mother and Lodaï to prove my bloodline. Not only did I agree with his plan, but I was elated by it and we resolved to carry it out. The next day I found where I had come out of the abyss and I hoped that I could find where I had grown up. But, I could count on faithful Falbao who was constantly showing me new signs of loyalty. I already knew his bravery and now with him and the weapons we could take, there was no danger we could not face. But, Lamekis, we did not figure that the depths of the earth were inhabited. We would soon find that out, too.

The Worm-Men

The evening star had just appeared on the horizon when we left Boldeon's cabin loaded with the supplies needed for a journey that might take very long if we got lost. When we got to where we had first met, it was not hard to find the cavern entrance and the mysterious vein was only a few feet inside. I pointed it out to Boldeon and told him about the miraculous effect it had on Falbao's wounds after the battle with the snake.

"Aha! Motacoa," he said. "It can't be! Wonder of wonders! How long have I been searching for this divine vein? Don't regret your bad luck because it has brought you this treasure. This alone is enough to make us the happiest of mortals. It's one of the greatest benefits we could hope for. This vein contains the universal remedy and whoever has it is guaranteed to live without sickness and be forever healthy unto the grave."

Saying this he cupped some in his hands and drank three times, inviting me to do the same. After doing this we sat on a big rock and ate a light meal while Falbao lay down nearby. The liquid worked its wonders and soon put us to pleasant sleep.

I had barely closed my eyes when a mysterious dream churned my senses. I thought I was somewhere in the Inner Earth where I used to go before I left. There was a rock of talc, shiny and strange, that was very precious to me. Inside it was a kind of natural crucible in which the wondrous water was constantly boiling. When the fiery heat poured it out, it congealed and took on the strangest forms that I examined for a long time.

Then I dreamed that I was in a cave where the back was laid up by an earthquake and revealed a bright corridor. The ceiling was dotted with different colored gems that sparkled so brightly that my eyes could barely stand the fire. I went in. It ended in a big room that was decorated with so much beautiful art that it looked like our most skillful workers had been there. In the middle of the room was a table made of a single opal with an exquisite mother-of-pearl armchair in front of it. On the table was an open book with gold letters. I went up to it and, being alone, I could not hold back my curiosity: I read a sentence that stood out. It said, "You, mortal, cannot ascend a throne that belongs to you unless the marriage with Ascalis[76] puts you there."

These words seemed so fitting to me that I cried out, "Oh Vilkonhis, let your will be done!" Hardly had I said this when two winged men appeared, like the ones we picture as Spilghis.[77] They held a finger to their mouths and motioned me to follow them. I obeyed. They led me into another room, paneled with gold and in the middle was a bed on which a radiantly beautiful woman was sleeping. Her skin was the color of rose and her features beyond compare. I knelt on the ground and contemplated the young beauty whom I had not noticed was stirring. She sighed in her troubled sleep. Without knowing why, I shared her troubles. One of the Spilghis tapped her with a crystal rod and she woke up screaming, which made the two celestial men vanish. The stranger's reac-

---

[76] The color of rose.
[77] Angels.

tion affected me. I opened my mouth to say something reassuring, but I felt myself rising up despite myself. She jumped out of bed and grabbed my arm to help me, but a zenghuis[78] struck the divine woman's hand and she collapsed on the ground. I wanted to avenge this treachery, so I turned around to see what barbarian had the gall to attack and I found myself staring into the ghastly face of a monster, holding me in its arms, and I got so scared that I woke up with a start.

Boldeon was waiting impatiently for me to wake up because he was upset by my restlessness. He urged me to tell him what was wrong. I was so disturbed that I did not answer for a long time, but I finally got hold of myself and told him about my dream.

"It's not for nothing," he said, "that Vilkonhis speaks and this new evidence is sure proof of your birth. It is said in one of the prophecies that a woman the color of Ascalis will give birth to a hero who will make the Abdalles happy and their most valuable goods will be due to him. Oh Motacoa, if the oracle speaks through you, I hope you will be happy and become beloved and honored! Let's move on under the auspices of this divine omen; the master of the sun guides us. Can we get lost when we are led by such a powerful hand?"

Talking together like that we went into the depths of the mountain. Soon we came upon the snake that Falbao had conquered. It was still alive and its dying eyes were dreadful. The dog looked away and seemed to want me to do the same. I followed my instinct, which was a good thing because the awful snake struck out when it saw us and its forked tongue broke off a piece of rock. We sped up and after three karies or so we got out of the cave.

---

[78] Mouhy at times waits for the second mention of something before he footnotes it. He also, at times, will repeat a footnote (such as defining a unit of measurement). This, for example, is the first mention of a zenghuis (sword), but the explanation footnote is found later.

I was going to take a path that I thought I recognized and that I believed would lead me to Lodaï's grotto, but when I turned around I could not see Falbao. A grave anxiety took hold of me. I had got used to the animal and I loved it. I yelled at the top of my lungs and cried while Boldeon ran around looking for him. I did the same and as night was falling we got lost. No matter how loudly I yelled, nothing answered.

"Oh Heavens, here I am fallen into bad luck again. Falbao! Falbao, whom the gods gave me for comfort. Oh, I will never see you again! And you, Boldeon, whom I led into this awful desert, what is going to become of you! Wandering around and worn out by remorse as much as by walking, I'm going to lay down under the weight of sorrow and close my frightened, troubled eyes."

Weariness and weeping was starting to make me drowsy when I heard a dull, terrible sound. I opened my eyes. "Oh Heavens! What is this I see in the light of the subterranean fires! What horrifying sight is this?"

A man (can I call it that?) was coming toward me. His head, arms and chest was like a man, but the rest of his body was like a worm, except that he was as big as the thing that Falbao had battled. He was huge and moved using his coils. Sometimes he dragged himself along with his hands and sometimes he stood up straight. His nose was very fat and flat and bent down into a point that almost covered his upper lip. His eyes were small and round and completely surrounded by thick eyebrows. His horrid face was marbled red and his beard and all the hair that covered his body grew together.

Barely looking at him I yelled and ran away as fast as I could, turning around now and again, knowing that sooner or later I was going to fall prey to the monster. Leaning on his hands he bounded forward so far that he almost caught me, but then against all hope I saw Falbao running to my rescue. What a relief! When the worm man saw him he turned tail and rushed away. Falbao followed him. I got worried and called out to him as loudly as I could because I needed him around and could not stand the idea of losing him a second time.

When he came back I petted him and the lovable animal answered in his way. He went ahead and I followed him confidently.

We had barely gone 30 feet and I heard horrible screams. I was ready to run away again, but I stopped when I heard my name called and recognized Boldeon's voice. He was begging for my help and in spite of the fright I had just experienced I had to run toward the cries. My dog, as if reading my mind, went first and was on the trail in no time. Imagine how I felt after rounding a corner and seeing Boldeon in front of me in the arms of one of those monsters running away with his prey at full speed. Falbao followed them, but the worm man thrust forward with so much energy that whenever the dog got near him he jumped forward in a single bound and was thirty feet farther on. During this awful chase I could do nothing but follow at a distance, but seeing my dog scare everything he saw gave me confidence. We ran for around an hour and I was starting to peter out when a cave suddenly appeared in front of the monster and he flung himself inside. Falbao chased him and since I was desperate and afraid of being alone again in such a scary place knowing what kind of creatures lived there, I followed them.

I entered a large opening lit up so brightly by bitumen that it was easy to make out the minutest details. I went trembling into this dreadful place and had not gone 60 feet when the road split into four parts. I was in a terrible quandary because they all seemed to go in different directions. Which one had Falbao taken? Three of them were lit by bitumen snaking through the rock, but the fourth was deadly dark and horrifying. I was not sure what to do, but then I saw a bunch of those monsters coming down the middle path straight in front of me, apparently trying to tell me something. I was so gripped by fear that my legs shook and had no strength to move. In vain I tried to get hold of myself; my nerves refused to obey. Meanwhile, all the hideous faces surrounded me, twanging awful flute-like sounds.

After huddling together, one of them grabbed me with his strong, sturdy hand and shrieked, shaking me with all his might. What could I do against the iron fists of a giant? The monster put me under his arm and hurried down the dark passage. He held me so tightly that I was about to faint and he noticed it. Afraid that I might die, he grabbed me by the feet and carried me like that. Around twenty constantly buzzing creatures followed us. After walking for an hour like that, which seemed like a century in my uncomfortable position, we came out of the rock. I was so shaken up by the bouncing monster that I passed out, but snapped out of it right away because of the new, painful way of carrying me—by the hair. I screamed in pain and they twanged fluty again. The result was to carry me by the neck. As uncomfortable as this was, it was gentle compared with the others.

After walking half a karie like this an odd building came into view. It seemed to touch the sky, which I could see here. Its foundation looked like four shapeless columns made of a strange material supporting the building that had a round door, a square façade and a statue of a worm man whose two tails and coils formed the entablature. The building extended on both sides and the back looked like it was attached to the mass of shiny rock. A great number of worm men were coming and going, or better said were bouncing around on the platform, and others were crawling either up or down the ramp that led to the door of the building, which was guarded by several of these monsters who stood out from the others by a kind of short cape made of those crimson feathers I mentioned before. They wore a cap that looked pretty much like a dried pumpkin decorated with gems and in their belts they carried zenghuis made of shiny metal. But the most terrifying of all were their ghastly faces.

When we got to the building the monster carrying me made a stupendous jump to the door, which was more than ten measures up. The guards surrounded him when they saw him loaded with me and one after another they brushed their hand over my face. After this ridiculous, annoying ceremony, we went through the door into a huge room where 100 guards were lined up, looking surprised to see me. Then, the one carrying me, who could obviously go no farther, gave me to the first guard and he gave me to the second who gave me to the third and on and on I went faster and faster from hand to hand across the grand hall and through others that I did not have time to examine. Finally I arrived at a large door decorated with the most precious things that were found in the center of the earth and they put me down. Everyone in this big room came up and stared at me as hard as they could. A minute later the door opened and a daffodil-colored face that looked like a woman popped up with a finger over its mouth. At this sign the usual buzzing stopped and the people stood still. Then the door closed again very softly. But what really struck me was that I distinctly heard yapping that sounded like Falbao. I listened more carefully and had no doubt that it was my faithful dog.

I was concentrating on this when the door flung open. I had never seen such a strange and beautiful sight: there were four rows of worm women marvelously dressed and covered in gems. They carried a six-branched candlestick with pieces of wood burning like candles that lit up the room furnished with the most wonderful things you could imagine. It was a square room that went back as far as the eye could see and ended in a colonnade of transparent stones with very high arches. The middle of it was covered with a dome encrusted with many shiny, precious minerals. Behind this arch, which you could call "de triomphe," was an elevated armchair. Sitting there was a woman whose beauty captured all my attention and kept me from looking at anything else. Because of the distance I could not see her face clearly, but I was moved and could tell that she was shaped like me. Little ribbons of those feathers I talked about girded her body, arms and legs, showing off her perfection. Her hair was the most beautiful black in the world, partly floating over her breasts and shoulders and partly fastened with a stick covered with diamonds that were no less beautiful for being uncut. I sighed seeing myself so far away from this charming beauty, but a piercing cry rang out from the foot of the throne and I quickly turned my head. How happy I was to see Falbao. He had seen me and whimpered loudly to come join me, but he struggled in vain against the collar around his neck and his sad cries testified to it.

In 1760, in *Giphantie*, Charles-François Tiphaigne de La Roche (1729-1774) sent his heroes to the secret land of Giphantie in Africa. After getting lost in a sandstorm, the narrator wakes up on the edge of a magical plain. A mysterious Voice explains that it is a land given to the elemental spirits before humans were created in Eden, and where the spirits that work hard on Earth, supervising the elements for the preservation of human life, take their vacations. The Voice explains the nature of that virtuous labor to the narrator, and shows him a Globe whose map of the world consists of countless channels of communication, by means of which the elementals can overhear everything happening elsewhere on the planet's surface. The Voice then provides him with a magic mirror that enables him to see as well as hear, and thus obtain a broad overview of the whole human race before reverting to exemplary visions on a smaller scale.[79] After using that device to view a synoptic history of France, the traveler's guided tour takes him to witness the vegetal productions of three pips salvaged by the elementals from the discarded fraction of Adam's fatal apple, and the compensations that they are able to offer to fallen humankind via the elementals. The produce of the third pip, the Fantastic Tree, offers prophetic leaves, which provide the narrator with the substance of an "Epistle to the Europeans" and various fantastic technologies, including a "thermometer" and "lenses" whose functions are more meta-

---

[79] It is while further sophisticating this process of eavesdropping that the text comes up with an original literary device. Requiring a synoptic view of human history, in order that the author can comment on its broad shape—in a vein closer to lamentation than satire—Tiphaigne hit on the idea of presenting a series of *tableaux* [pictures] "painted" by light itself, and offers a detailed description of a liquid substance that can be used to coat a mirror, so that if it is then placed in a dark room to dry out it will preserve the last image that formed on its surface: an "invention" that won him a place of honor in modern histories of photography.

phorical than literal, after which he returns by a subterranean route to the mundane world.

Tiphaigne was born in Montebourg in Normandy and completed his education at the University of Caen. His first book, published in 1747 was *L'Amour dévoilé, ou le système des sympathistes* [Love Unveiled; or, The Theory of Sympathism], the extended subtitle of which claims that it will explain the origin of "inclinations, sympathies, aversions, antipathies, etc." It belongs to the category of accidental scholarly fantasies, in that the author presumably intended his arguments seriously, although hindsight informs us that there is not an atom of truth to them. It was, however, a bold project for its time; Tiphaigne was writing in an era of severe censorship, when writing a book to which the political or religious authorities objected could be direly dangerous; a text attempting a scientific explanation of sexual attraction, despite such august predecessors as Plato's *Symposium*—Tiphaigne was a great admirer of Plato—had the potential to be seen as sailing a little close to the wind, even from a devoutly religious author who went on to be loudly outspoken in his condemnation of the licentiousness of much contemporary literature.

Tiphaigne did not sign the book, publishing it under the pseudonym "l'A. de P***," the first item of the signature (an abbreviation of Abbé) suggesting that it was by a Churchman. The P*** might not stand for anything at all—as will be seen in the following pages, Tiphaigne was a profligate inventor of meaningless names—but if it was imagined to stand for anything, the likeliest contender is Plato. As well as being one of the most important Greek thinkers, Plato was also one of the more playful—or at least, one of those whose playfulness shows through in his surviving works, albeit not always obviously in the eyes of his more humorless critics. In particular, Plato was one of the first manifest authors of *contes philosophiques*: fantastic stories improvised in order to dramatize a philosophical issue. The three most notable examples are Aristophanes' account of the androgyne in the *Symposium* (the only one of his dialogues in which all the participants are drunk) and the tales of *Gyges and Er* in the *Republic*. *Contes philosophiques* made a big comeback in France during Tiphaigne's lifetime, largely due to the efforts of Voltaire (1694-1778), whom Tiphaigne righteously loathed.

Tiphaigne undoubtedly read Voltaire's Swiftian satire *Micromégas*, which can be recognized in hindsight as the founding text of French scientific romance, and disapproved of it thoroughly, even though its unsigned first edition claimed to have been published in Berlin in 1750 (it was probably printed in London in 1752) in order to dodge the French censors. He would also have read the first of Voltaire's *contes philosophiques*, "*Le Monde comme il va; vision de Babouc*" (1748), which assaults many of the aspects of life in Paris—here disguised as "Persepolis"—that he was later to attack himself, in a not-dissimilar way, but from a radically opposed rhetorical stance. There is a sense in which Tiphaigne's works represent an attempt to reclaim the tradition of the *conte philosophique*, along with some of its modern apparatus, to serve what he considered be the right causes—as opposed to Voltaire's supposedly mistaken ones

Giphantie remains Tiphaigne's best known book and is far more coherent than its predecessor, *Amilec*—even though it is, like it, a patchwork that probably took aboard several previously written fragments—because its narrative frame is so much more robust. "Giphantie" is an anagram of Tiphaigne, and the imaginary landscape it presents is effectively a map of the author's ideas. The book was, however, unsigned even by a pseudonym, the only information on its bald title-page, save for the title itself, being a terse statement of a fictitious place of publication: "à Babylon" [in Babylon]. In the text, "Babylon" is clearly Paris, just as "Persepolis" was clearly Paris in "*Le Monde comme il va*," so the attribution of that place of publication has an element of double bluff about it.

Although *Giphantie* uses a similar literary device to *Amilec* to operate most of its fantastic levers, substituting "Elementary Sprits" for the "Genies" of the earlier work, it also contains an important literary device of a different sort, which

167

brings the text closer to the tradition of scientific romance whose foundations it helped to lay. Requiring a synoptic view of human history, in order that the author can comment on its broad shape—in a vein closer to lamentation than satire—Tiphaigne hit on the idea of presenting a series of tableaux [pictures] "painted" by light itself, offering a detailed description of a liquid substance that can be used to coat a mirror so that if it is then placed in a dark room to dry out it will preserve the last image that formed on the illuminated mirror: an "invention" that won him a place of honor in modern histories of photography. Overall, Tiphaigne seems to have intended *Giphantie* to be a more serious work than the fantastic elements of *Amilec* and its sequel, more allegory than satire, although his irrepressible sarcasm and scathing wit came continually to the fore regardless of any attempts he made to hold them in check.

Brief and restricted as it was by comparison with that of his multitalented bête noire Voltaire, however, Tiphaigne's career nevertheless deserves recognition for its breadth, its ambition and its wit. He was not sufficiently far ahead of his time to make a very substantial contribution to the birth of scientific romance, but he was sufficiently of that time to make an admirable contribution to the rebirth of the *conte philosophique*, and it is for that reason, as well as for the particular artistry of *Giphantie* that he serves to be remembered and still warrants reading.

Tiphaigne de la Roche: *Journey to Giphantie* (1760)[80]

II. The Storm

I was on the frontier of Guinea, on the edge of the desert that terminates it toward the north, and I was considering that vast solitude, the very sight of which alarms the strongest soul. Suddenly, I was gripped by the most ardent desire to go into that desert and discover the extent to which nature there refuses human habitation. Perhaps, I said to myself, there is some fertile enclave in the middle of that burning plain, unknown to the rest of the world. Perhaps I shall find humans there whom commerce with others has neither civilized nor corrupted.

I reminded myself of the dangers to which such an enterprise would expose me, and the almost certain death to which it would lead, but in vain; I could never get the idea out of my head. One day in winter—for that was the most propitious time—when the wind was blowing from the south-west, the sky was cloudy and the atmosphere temperate, I set out from the frontier of Guinea and advanced into the desert, provided with a few condensates to appease hunger and thirst, a glass mask to protect my eyes from sandstorms and a compass to guide me.

I walked for two whole days without seeing anything extraordinary. At the beginning of the third, I no longer perceived anything around me but a few stunted trees, almost

---

[80] Excerpted from *Giphantie* by Charles-François Tiphaigne de la Roche, translated into English in 2011, introduced and annotated by Brian Stableford. Both *Giphantie* and *Amilec* are available in a single volume entitled *Amilec*, Black Coat Press, ISBN 978-1-61227-033-3.

devoid of sap, and clumps of rushes, the majority of which were desiccated by the Sun's heat. They are the last produce that nature draws from those arid regions; that is where fecundity ends; life cannot extend any further in those frightful solitudes.

I continued on my way. I had only been walking for two hours over a sandy terrain in which the gaze finds nothing on which to rest but sparse rocks, when the wind, becoming stronger, began to agitate the surface of the sand. To begin with, the sands only played about the bases of the rocks, forming little waves that oscillated gently over the plain, in the same way that one sees waves arising and rolling smoothly over the surface of the waters when the sea begins to furrow as a storm approaches. Soon, however, those waves grew, collided with one another and became confused, and I endured the most terrible storm.

Whirlwinds often formed, which gathered up the sands, causing them to rotate rapidly, raising them high into the air, while whistling horribly. A moment later, the sands, abandoned to their own devices, fell down vertically and formed mountains. Clouds of dust mingled with the atmospheric clouds; the Earth and the Heavens seemed to be confused. Sometimes, the density of the whirlwinds hid the daylight entirely. At other times, red transparent sands burst forth in the distance; the air seemed enflamed and the sky seemed to dissolve into sparks.

Meanwhile, sometimes lifted into the air by a gust of wind and sometimes precipitated by my own weight, I sometimes found myself inside the dust-clouds, and sometimes in abysmal depths. At every moment I ought to have been buried or broken. You shall soon know what benevolent being was watching over my safety.

The terrible storm ended with the day; the night was calm and, weariness getting the upper hand over fear, I became drowsy.

III. A Beautiful Vision

The Sun had not yet risen when I woke up, but its first rays were blanching the orient, and it was beginning to be possible to discern objects. Sleep had restored my strength and calmed my mind; on awakening, anxiety returned to my heart and the image of death appeared once again to my alarmed consciousness.

I was on an elevated crag, from which I was able to observe my surroundings. Quivering, I darted a glance over that arid and sandy region, where I believed that I would find my tomb. How surprised I was when, in a northerly direction, I perceived a uniform, vast and fecund plain! In an instant I leapt over the interval, often so long, that separates the greatest suffering from the greatest joy. Nature took on a new face for me, and the frightful sight of so many rocks thrown confusedly into the sands, only served to render the sight of the delightful plain that I was about to enter all the more pleasant and poignant. How admirable your distributions are, O Nature, and how sagely managed are the varied scenes that you offer to us!

The plants growing on the edge of that plain are very small; the ground does not yet furnish sufficient moisture, but as one advances further, the vegetation become animated and acquires more volume and height. Soon, one encounters bushes under which one can walk in the shade, and one finally finds trees as ancient as the Earth, which raise their crowns all the way to the clouds. Thus is formed an immense amphitheater, which extends majestically before the traveler's eyes and announces to him that such an abode was not made for mortals.

Everything in that unknown land seemed unfamiliar to me; everything threw me into astonishment. Of the productions of nature that my eyes avidly scanned, none resembled those that on sees everywhere else. Trees, plants, insects, reptiles, fish, birds—everything had an extraordinary conformation, elegant and infinitely various at the same time. What

171

caused me the greatest admiration, however, was that a universal sensibility, manifest in all imaginable forms, vivified the bodies that seemed to be the least susceptible to it; everything, including the plants, displayed evidence of sentiment.

I advanced slowly into that enchanted abode. A delicate coolness held my senses open to sensuality; a sweet odor flowed into my blood with the air that I breathed; my heart beat with an unaccustomed forcefulness, and joy enlightened the darkest depths of my soul.

IV. The Voice

One thing surprised me: I did not see any inhabitants in those gardens of delight. I don't know how many ideas were agitating my mind on that subject when a voice struck my ears.

"Stop," it said to me. "Look straight ahead and see who it was that inspired the perilous journey that you have just undertaken."

Very excited, I looked for some time without seeing anything. Finally, I perceived a sort of patch, a sort of shadow stationary in the air a few paces away from me. Thus a troubled pool of water betrays the hope of a shepherd who comes to consult it, only rendering a confused image of his features.

I continued to gaze most attentively; I thought I could discern a human form, and recognize a physiognomy so gentle and kind that, far from frightening me, the encounter was a further cause of joy.

"I am the prefect of this island," the benevolent shadow continued. "Your penchant for philosophy has prejudiced me in your favor. I have followed you in the journey you have made; I protected you against the storm. Now I want you to see the rarities that are to be found here—after which, I shall ensure that you return to your homeland.

"This solitude that enchants you stands in the middle of a stormy sea of moving sands; it is an island surrounded by inaccessible deserts, which no mortal is able to cross without superhuman assistance. Its name is Giphantie. It was given to the elementary spirits at a time before the Garden of Eden was assigned to the father of the human race.

"Not that the spirits spend their time here in leisure and idleness. What would you do, feeble mortals, if, spread throughout the air, the water, entrails of the Earth and the sphere of fire, they were not ceaselessly watching over your safety? Without our care, the unchained elements would have wiped out the last vestiges of the human race a long time ago. If only we could preserve you entirely from their unruly efforts! Alas, are power does not extend so far; we cannot entirely shield you from the evils that surround you; we can only prevent them from overwhelming you.

"It is here that the elementary spirits come to rest when they are tired; it is here that they hold their assemblies and agree the most just measures for the administration of the elements."

V. The Misinterpretation

"Of all the countries in the world," the elementary spirit continued, "Giphantie is the only one where nature still retains its primitive energy. It works incessantly here to augment the numerous families of vegetables and animals, to produce new species. It organizes everything with an admirable intelligence, but does not always succeed in perpetuating everything. The mechanism of propagation is the masterpiece of its wisdom; sometimes it is lacking, and its productions return to oblivion forever. We husband, with all the precaution of which we are capable, those which are sufficiently well-organized to be able to reproduce, and thereafter, we take care to distribute them over the Earth.[81]

---

[81] In French, all nouns are gendered, so there is no option but to refer to nature as "*elle*." English nouns are not, so referring to nature as "she" rather than "it" represents a voluntary personalization. Such figurative personalization is, of course,

173

"Naturalists are sometimes astonished to discover natural organisms that no one else has ever noticed before; that it because we have introduced them to the Earth recently without their suspecting it.

"Sometimes, too, these expatriated organisms, not finding a climate that would suit them perfectly, perish gradually, and the species becomes extinct. Such are those productions of which the ancients speak and modern men complain of not being able to find anywhere.

"Occasionally, a species of plants survives but languishes for centuries, losing its qualities and deceiving physicians, who routinely fail to produce its result. The art is blamed; people do not realize that it is nature that is at fault.

"Presently, I have a collection of new simples of the greatest virtue; I would already have made humans aware of them, if powerful reasons had not led me to postpone the revelation.

"For example, I have a sovereign plant for fixing the human mind, which would give it constancy, even to Babylonians—but in the five hundred years that I have been carefully observing Babylon, I have not found a single moment at which the penchants, customs, mores were worth the trouble of fixing.

"I have another, admirable for suppressing the sometimes-excessive effusions of the spirit of invention, but you know how rare that excessiveness is today—never has there been such a dearth of imagination. One might think that everything had been said, and that nothing remains but to give it the style of the century and fashionable dress.

"I have one root that would infallibly soothe the bitterness of men of letters who criticize one another, but I observe that, without their determination to tear one another apart, no

---

commonplace—I make use of it myself when the occasion seems to warrant it—but in the present instance it seemed more appropriate to maintain a careful neutrality, in spite of the obvious maternal proclivity here credited to nature.

one would be interested in their disputes. People like to see them debasing literature and dishonoring one another. I leave it to the malignity of readers to compete with the malignity of writers.

"Furthermore, don't imagine that nature rests anywhere on Earth; it works hard even in the infinitely small places that no eye is able to reach. In Giphantie, it arranges matter in extraordinary schemes, and tends incessantly to produce novelty; everywhere, too, it passes over the same ground repeatedly and endlessly, always striving to bring its works to a pitch of perfection that it never attains. Those flowers, the sight of which gives you such pleasure, it is still in the process of making even more dazzling. Those animals that seem to you so clever, it is still in the process of rendering even more industrious. Even humankind, which seems to you to be so far above the rest, it is still in the process of improving—and that is where it is having the least success.

"One might think, in fact, that the human race is doing everything it can to remain well below the level to which nature wishes to elevate it, and the most generous dispositions it makes available to humans for good are almost always turned to evil. In Babylon, for example, nature has thrown an inexhaustible capital of pleasure into minds, with the manifest objective of forming the most amiable people on Earth. That was done to cheer up reason, to extirpate the thorns with which the approaches of science are bristling, to soften the austerity of wisdom and, if possible, to embellish virtue. You know the result: the favors that humans should have lavished upon those objects, they turned away from their destination and clothed them in frivolity and disordered.

"In the hands of Babylonians, vice loses its revolting aspect. See with what discretion it is unveiled in their manners, their speech, their writings; with what artistry it interests; with what skill it insinuates itself; you have not yet thought about it, and it is established in your heart. Even those whose job it is to raise their voices to combat it dare not show it in all its

175

deformity; they offer apologies for not painting it with more restraint.

"Nowhere, finally, does crime seem less criminal than in Babylon. Even in its labeling, everything is altered, everything is softened. Respectable people, honest people are nowadays fashionable people, whose exterior is entirely attractive and whose interior is utterly corrupt. Good company is not that in which one finds the most virtuous people, but that which excels in palliating vice. A person whom the vicissitudes of fortune cannot shake you call strong-minded, but you speak inappropriately; only a person who braves providence should be thus named. To the most complete irreligion the name of freedom of thought is given; to blasphemy, that of boldness; to the most shameful excess that of gallantry.

"Thus, with what was necessary to become a model for all nations, the Babylonians, not to put it too strongly, have become libertines of the most seductive and dangerous species."

VI. Apparitions

"I shall return to the elementary spirits," the prefect of Giphantie continued. "The continual residence that they take up in air, always charged with vapors and exhalations, in water, always charged with salts and solids, in fire, almost incessantly busy about a thousand heterogeneous substances, and in the Earth, into which all the other elements insinuate themselves, thus becoming confused with it, gradually degrades the pure essence of the spirits, whose primal nature—so far as their material substance is concerned—is to be all fire, or another element, without any admixture.

"This degradation has something gone so far that, by the mixing of different elements, the spirits have acquired sufficient consistency to be seen. Humans have seen them in fire and have called them salamanders or cyclopes; they have seen them in the air and have called them sylphs, zephyrs or aquilons; they have seen them in water and have called them

176

nymphs, naiads, nereids or tritons; they have seen them in caverns, solitudes and forests and have called them gnomes, sylvains, fauns, satyrs and so on.[82]

"By virtue of the astonishment that these apparitions cause them, humans have fallen into dread, and from dread into superstition. They have raised altars to these beings, created like themselves, that should only have been raised to the Creator. Soon, their imagination exaggerating what they had seen, they formed a hierarchy of chimerical divinities. The Sun seemed to them to be a luminous chariot, which Apollo steered across the celestial plains; lightning a fiery dart with which Jupiter threatened guilty heads; the sea a vast empire in which Neptune rebuked the waves; the entrails of the Earth a tenebrous abode in which Pluto imposed the rule of law upon pale and timid shades. In brief, they filled the world with gods and goddesses. The Earth itself became a divinity.

"As soon as the elemental spirits realized the extent to which their apparitions were capable of inducing error in humans, they took measures that prevented them from becoming visible from then on. The devised a kind of filter, a sort of catch-trap, in which they periodically deposited that which was foreign to their substance. Since then, no mortal eye has seen the slightest trace of the spirits in question."

VII. Surfaces

Meanwhile, the prefect of Giphantie moved off, and I followed him, extremely astonished and pensive.

---

[82] Most of the names attributed to elementals in this list are still familiar; the principal oddity is the identification of cyclopes as fire-spirits, given that Greek myth made them a race of giants whose most famous member featured in the *Odyssey*. They were, however, said to have been reduced in the end to assisting Vulcan in his subterranean forges. Aquilon was one of the names given by the Romans to the north wind.

On emerging from the dense wood, we found ourselves facing a small hill, at the foot of which a hollow column rose up, its breadth being in proportion to its height, which was more than a hundred feet. I saw vapors emerging from the top of the column similar to the exhalations that summer heat cause to rise from the Earth in such abundance that they become sensible. I saw human forms emerge from the same column and disperse into the air: simulacra even lighter than the vapors that carried them.

"This," said the prefect, "is the elementary spirits' catch-trap. That column is filled with four essences, each of which has been extracted from each element. The spirits plunge into it and, by virtue of a mechanism that would take too long to explain, deposit any foreign substance therein. Those simulacra you see emerging from the top of the column are nothing other than the pelts of spirits—which is to say, he very thin surfaces that surround them and tend to make them visible. These pelts reflect the different qualities of spirits that excel to various degrees in certain respects, just as physiognomies reflect the characters of infinitely various human beings. Thus, they are the simulacra or surfaces of science, erudition, prudence, wisdom and so on.

"Humans often put them on, like masks that make them appear other than they are—with the result that, at every step, you find the appearance of all good qualities, all talents, all virtues, although you very rarely find their foundations anywhere.

"In Babylon, especially, the simulacra are held in singular esteem; everyone there judges by appearances. A Babylonian would rather be nothing but appear to be everything than be everything but appear to be nothing. Thus, you see nothing but surfaces everywhere, of every sort:

"The surface of modesty, the only thing necessary to a Babylonian, which is called decency.

"The surface of amity, by means of which Babylon seems only to be inhabited by a single family. Amity is like a powerful cord formed by an assembly of exceedingly weak threads. A Babylonian is not bound to anyone by that cord, but he holds each of his fellow citizens in a net.

"The surface of piety, once powerful in operation and very influential, today totally discredited. They give people a certain Gothic air, utterly ridiculous to modern eyes. Only a small number of people can be found still faithful to old religious duties, among a social class that, by virtue of its estate, cannot entirely rid itself of them, even if it wishes.

"The surface of opulence, one of the most striking things in Babylon. See how prosperous people seem in the churches, the meeting-places and the streets: those well-dressed fathers of families, those bejeweled wives, those elegant and lively children who promise one day to be as frivolous as their fathers; follow them home: furniture in the best taste, comfortable apartments, houses reminiscent of petty palaces—everything continues to advertise opulence. But go no further; if you dig deeper, you will find families in distress and hearts full of anxiety.

"The surface of probity, for the use of politicians and those involved with governing others. Those great men cannot be as honest as ordinary people; there are certain maxims that they believe it essential never to set aside, not the least essential of which is that they must seem extremely distant.

"The surface of patriotism, the foundations of which vanished a long time ago. It is necessary to distinguish between theory and practice in the conduct of Babylonians. The theory revolves entirely around patriotism: the public good, the interests of the nation, the glory of the Babylonian name. The practice has personal interest as its axis. What is singular is that, in this regard, the Babylonians fooled one another for a long time. Everyone knew full well that the fatherland was irrelevant to him, but he heard talk of it so frequently and so affectionately that he was convinced that true patriots still existed. Now, their eyes are open, and they can see that everyone is doing the same."

VIII. The Globe

"Such is the lot of the elementary spirits," the prefect of Giphantie continued. "Scarcely have they emerged from the cleansing column where they are purified than they return to their everyday work. In order to see where their presence is most necessary, where humans have the greatest need of their help, when they emerge from the column they go up the hill. There, by means of a process for which all the intelligence of spirits is scarcely sufficient, they can see and hear what is happening in all the countries in the world. You can assure yourself of that personally."

On either side of the column there was a great staircase with more than two hundred steps, which led up to the crown of the hill. We went up; we were scarcely half way when my ears were struck by an unwelcome buzz, which grew louder as we advanced.

Having reached a platform on top of the hill, the first thing that attracted my eyes was a globe of considerable diameter. The noise I could hear was coming from that globe. From a distance, it was a buzz; at close range, it was a frightful din, formed by a confused aggregation of cries of joy, groans of despair, screams of fear, plaints, songs, murmurs, acclamations, laughter and moans—everything that advertises the immoderate dejection or crazed joy of human beings.

"Tiny imperceptible channels," the prefect went on, "extend from every point on the world's surface to terminate in this globe. Its interior is organized in such a manner that the movement of the air passing through the imperceptible tubes, weakening all the while, recovers its energy on entering the globe and becomes sensible again. Hence these noises, this racket, this chaos. But what would be the point of these confused sounds, if a means had not been found to discern then?

"Look at the image of the Earth painted on the globe: those islands, those continents, those seas that embrace, connect and separate everything. Do you recognize Europe, that part of the world that causes so much unhappiness in all the others? Burning Africa, where the arts and the needs that follow them have never penetrated? Asia, whose luxury, in passing to the European nations, has done so much good, according to some, and so much harm, according to others? America, still stained with the blood of its unfortunate inhabitants, whom the representatives of a religion full of gentleness came to convert and slaughter?

"Concentrate on whatever point of the globe you please; by placing the tip of the staff that I put into your hands thereon, and putting the other to your ear, you will hear distinctly what is being said at the corresponding location on the Earth."

IX. Speech

Surprised by this prodigy, I placed the point of the staff on Babylon. I applied my ear to it, and heard what follows.

"Since you have consulted me about this manuscript I ought to give you my opinion of it frankly. I find it sensible—far too sensible. What! Not a word against the government, against mores, against religion! Who would read it? If you knew how weary people are of history, morality, philosophy, poetry, prose—everything! Everyone has started to write, and it's easier to find an author than a reader. How can one penetrate the crowd? How can you attract attention, if not by launching attacks, whether merited or not, against well-known people, by that debauchery of the imagination calculated to reawaken the taste for pleasure that abuse has blunted, by those petty arguments which, shaped and reshaped in a thousand ways, always please because they attack the things we dread?

"That, in my opinion, is the only route open to a writer who has any pretentions to renown. Look at our philosophers: when they reflect on the nature of the soul, for example, they fall into a doubt from which all their reasoning cannot extract them. What do they do when they write? They cut through the difficulty, and the soul is mortal. If they say so, it's not because they are personally convinced, but because they want to write, and to write something that will be read. Then again, if you had a few partisans, if you belonged to one of those coteries in which the incense-burner is passed from hand to hand and where each member is an idol in his turn...but no, in the midst of literary cabals, you're like a theologian who claims to be neither a Jansenist nor a Molinist.[83] Who do you expect to support your interests? Who will praise you? Who will accustom our eyes to seeing your name among those we respect?"

I placed the tip of the staff a little lower down and I heard what was probably a partisan hurling his calculations at the people.

"Isn't it true," he said, "that, in the interests of the state, everyone ought to contribute a proportion to his wealth, a deduction applied to the expenditure he makes? Isn't it also true that a very small man spends less on clothes than a very tall one? Isn't it true, finally, that that difference in expenditure is quite considerable nowadays, since one requires summer clothes, winter clothes, spring clothes, autumn clothes, country clothes, hunting clothes and I don't know how many others? One also ought to have morning suits and evening suits, but mornings are unknown in Babylon.

"I should like, therefore, to measure the height of all His Majesty's subjects, and demand a contribution from each one in inverse proportion to his height...also taking into consideration his weight. There has been talk of putting a tax on bachelors, but that is a bad idea. It is among those wealthy enough to marry, and especially those who are rich enough to risk have children, that it is necessary to look for money. Thus, it is necessary to tax fathers of families on a sliding scale, according to the number of their children. I have any number of projects in my portfolio that are just as good as that one, and from

---

[83] Cornelius Jansen (1585-1638) was a Dutch theologian who took a notoriously strict line on the doctrine of predestination; Luis Molina (1535-1600) was a Spanish Jesuit who, in sharp contrast, attempted to reconcile the notion of free will with divine omniscience and grace.

which I expect the best possible outcomes. Everyone has his talent; that's mine—and everyone knows how it is prized nowadays."

A short distance away, a grammarian was making his observations.

"Three languages are spoken in Babylon," he said, "that of the common people; that of fops and that of honest people.

"The first serves to say revolting things in a disgusting manner. With all the discernment with which they flatter themselves, authors have written in that language; the Babylonians, with their delicacy, have read them avidly.

"The second is formed of certain tissues of words, imagined to substitute for things. You can speak that language for an entire day, and at the end of it, you will be found to have said nothing. To enter into the character of the idiom more fully, it is essential to be incessantly irrational, to get as far away as possible from common sense.

"The third lacks a certain precision, a certain force and a certain grace, but it is susceptible to elegance and a singular clarity. It will not furnish sufficient extravagance to a poet, nor passion to a musician, but it will lend itself with an admirable facility to all the ideas of a person who observes, compares, discusses and seeks he truth. Undoubtedly, it is the language most appropriate to talk rationally, and it is unfortunately the least employed for that purpose."

I thought I heard a woman a few paces away, and I moved the staff toward her.

"I confess," she said, "that I love the novel madly; it couldn't be better written. However, this Julie, who defends herself for three volumes and only yields at the end of the fourth, imports a little too much languor into the intrigue. Thus, the vicomte makes such little progress with his project that it's pitiful. He pays so much attention to the preliminaries, wastes so much time in protests, and conducts his conquest so carefully that I—who am not unusually flighty—became impatient a hundred times over. The author is certainly not sufficiently familiar with the mores of the nation."

X. Happiness

As chance would have it, the tip of my staff fell on a company whose members were talking about happiness. Each of them had his own opinion, and I collected the various voices.

"That superb colonnade has finally been unveiled," someone said. "That large and beautiful portal obscured by small and wretched houses has been liberated, and repentance made for having built underground to ornament a square. Taste is re-established; the fine arts will flourish; in no time at all Babylon will advertise the magnificence of its monarch, and the happiness of its people..."

"It's not a question of peristyles, beautiful squares and great cities; to render a people happy, it must be enriched. It's necessary to stimulate industry, encourage agricultural endeavor, increase manufacture and help commerce flourish— the rest is immaterial..."

"Nonsense! I've said it more than once and I'll say it again: if we want to be happy, we have to get back to simple nature, to spread out into the forests, to live in caves and rejoin our ancient allies and friends, the animals of the fields..."

"I don't know what constitutes the happiness of peoples, but I believe that the happiness of individuals consists in the health of the body and the tranquility of the mind..."

"No, certainly not. Health makes no marked impression and tranquility is boring. To be happy, it's necessary to enjoy great renown, for at every moment, your ear is tickled by eulogies..."

"Yes, but at every moment it's also rent by criticisms, for one can't please everyone. My opinion is that one is happy in proportion to one's authority and power, for one can satisfy oneself in the same proportion..."

"Yes, but then one lacks the urgency that gives value to things; it's sufficient to be able to do anything not to care about anything. Personally, I believe that to be happy, it's necessary to be scornful of everything—that's the means of avoiding any kind of chagrin whatsoever..."

"And I believe that it's necessary to be interested in everything; that's the means of partaking of every source of joy that there is..."

"And I think it's necessary to be indifferent to everything; that's the means of enjoying an unalterable well-being..."

"For myself, I think it's necessary to be wise; only wisdom can raise us above all events..."

"And I say that it's necessary to be mad; madness creates its own separate happiness independently of everything troublesome that is happening around it..."

"Wherever you stand, you're mistaken. One can't establish any general rule to determine individual happiness. People vary; one person wants happiness of one sort, another of another sort; one man asks for wealth, another is content with what he needs; one wants to love and be loved; another regards any inclination of the heart as a precipice for the soul. It's necessary for everyone to study himself and follow his own penchant..."

"Not at all; you're no more right than anyone else. In vain, I persuade myself that I would be happy if I possessed such and such a thing; as soon as I possess it, I feel that it's insufficient and want something else. Desire is incessant; it is never satisfied. A man is perpetually on a journey and always on foot; worn out by fatigue, he says: 'If I had a horse, I'd be content.' He gets one, but the rain, the cold and the Sun continue to inconvenience him. 'A horse is insufficient,' he says. 'Only a carriage can shelter me from the vagaries of the weather.' His fortune increases; he provides himself with a carriage. What happens? Until then, exercise and fatigue have sustained the health of our traveler; as soon as he lacks them, he gets gout and becomes infirm—and soon it's impossible for him to go abroad, either on foot, on horseback or in a carriage."

I no longer set the tip of the staff in a particular spot; I drew it from side to side at random, and heard nothing but fragmented speech, such as the following:

"One dreads war, taxes, poverty, but they're petty anxieties. Alas, I have another. I developed a theory of earthquakes and, having made the calculations, I found that a focal point is currently forming near the center of the globe that will upset everything. Another six months, and the Earth will explode like a bomb: all of nature..."

"Yes, all of nature has disappeared from my sight; you alone exist for me; extinguish, dear lover, the fire that you have ignited within me. What a moment! Voluptuousness absorbs all my senses; my soul, penetrated by delights, seems ready to quite my body; it palpitates, it quivers, it escapes: receive it, dear lover; I deliver I to you in its entirety. Oh! I can hear my husband coming. Run...!"

"Courage, brave soldiers: strike, avenge the nation; let blood flow and spare no one. Death to the Islanders; long live the Babylonians..."

"I maintain, personally, that of all peoples, there is none so cheerful as the Babylonians. They always look on the bright side of things. A day of prosperity makes them forget a year of misfortune. They sing about everything, even their own poverty, and an epigram avenges the losses caused by the greatest stupidities..."

"Oh, how great our little people are! And how wise our madmen are! I cannot get it out of my head that humankind is a failure. I can see efforts in nature that tend to our improvement, but I can also see that those efforts are fruitless. There's no stuffing in us. We have only two ages: that of the imbecility into which we're born and spend two third of life, and that of infancy, in which we grow old and die. I've heard mention of an age of reason, but I don't see any sign of it. In conclusion, therefore, I say..."

"Yes, Madame, transparent cotton. The discovery has recently been made in Australia. No more colds or pneumonia. Diaphanous handkerchiefs, gloves and stockings will protect you against the cold, and simultaneously allow us to perceive that admirable throat, those charming arms and that divine leg..."

"Doubts everywhere, certainty nowhere. How tired I am of hearing, reading, reflecting and learning nothing precise. Who can simply tell me what's what..."

"It's that countryman, Monsieur, who's left his plough and has come to talk to you about the matter of those poor orphans, which never ends. It's true but what do you expect? We're so overburdened. No matter; I want to put an end to it, settle the affair as cheaply as possible..."

"Ah, dear Monsieur, I'm glad to see you; truly, I must compliment you: the last wig you made me lasted ten years. Surely Monsieur doesn't think that I have such a stern physiognomy? Oh, you know, my dear Monsieur, it wouldn't take much more to cover me with ridicule and lose you your reputation..."

"Lord, grant me three weeks of westerly wind, so that my ship might go forth..."

"Lord, grant me three weeks of easterly wind, so that my ship might come back..."

"Dear God, give me children..."

"Dear God, inflict a malignant fever of the son who is dishonoring me..."

"Dear God, give me a husband...

"Dear God, get rid of mine..."

Perhaps all this rubbish will not be to the taste of the majority of my readers. I'd be annoyed by it. Anyway, what should one think of people who say such bizarre things, so lacking in sense and so contradictory?

XII. The Mirror

As I was amusing myself with all this talk, the prefect of Giphantie presented me with a mirror. "You can only divine things," he told me "but with your staff and this mirror, you can see and hear at the same time. Nothing will escape you; it will be as if you were present while everything is happening."

The elementary spirit continued: "At intervals, there are volumes of air in the atmosphere where the spirits are so disposed that they receive light-rays reflected from different places on the Earth, and send them to the mirror that you have before your eyes—in such a way that by tilting the glass in different directions, different parts of the Earth's surface can be seen in it. One can see all of them in succession, if one places the mirror successively at every possible angle. You're the master of parading your gaze over the habitations of human beings."

I seized that marvelous mirror hastily. In less than a quarter of an hour, I had passed the entire Earth in review.

I perceived much emptiness, even in the most populous lands, and yet I saw people crowding one another, bumping into one another and massacring one another as if they were short of space.

I searched for happiness for some time, but did not find it anywhere—not even in the realms we call flourishing. I only perceived a few traces of it in rural areas whose remoteness protected them from the contagion of cities.

I embraced at a glance the vast countries that nature had decided to separate by means of even vaster seas, and I saw humans covering those seas with ships, making them serve as links between the countries in question. *It is manifestly contrary to the intentions of nature*, I said to myself. *Such steps cannot be successful. Is it evident that Europe has been any happier since it has been linked, in a fashion, to America? I don't know that it doesn't have more to mourn.*

I saw prejudices varying like climates, and doing a great deal of good and evil everywhere.

I saw wise people rejoicing in the birth of their children, and lamenting the deaths of their friends and relatives. I saw others even wiser surrounding new-born babies and weeping bitterly, at the thought of the storms that they would have to endure in the journey they were about to undertake; they reserved their rejoicing for funeral processions, congratulating the dead on finally being safe from all the miseries of human life.

I saw the Earth covered with monuments of every sort, which weakness raises to the ambition of heroes. Even in the temples, the bronze and the marble that enclose the ashes of the dead offer images of war and respire the carnage; even the statues of those friends of humankind, those peaceful sovereigns whom the misfortunes of time involve in wars of short duration, are surrounded by bellicose ornaments and nations in chains, as if only laurels stained with blood were worthy of crowning kings.

I saw the most respectable of all the penchants born in the human heart carry people to the most extravagant excesses. Some addressed their prayers to the Sun, others implored the assistance of the Moon, and others bowed down before mountains; some trembled at the sight of Jupiter's thunderbolts, others bent their knee before an ape. Cattle, dogs, and cats had their altars. Incense burned even for plants: wheat, beans, onions had their cults and heir worshipers.

I saw the family of humankind divide into as many parties as religions, those parties stripping themselves of all humanity in order to dress themselves in fanaticism, and those fanatics fight one another like so many ferocious beasts.

I saw people who worshipped the same god, sacrificing on the same altar, who preached the spirit of peace and gentleness to peoples, and saw them pick quarrels over unintelligible questions, and soon grow to hate one another, persecute one another and doom themselves mutually.

O Lord, what will become of humans, if they cannot find in you any greater measure of generosity than they find of weakness and folly in themselves?

Finally, I saw different nations, various in a thousand ways, resemble one another in that none was better than another. All men are wicked: the Ultramontane by dint of method; the Iberian by dint of pride; the Bavarian by dint of self-interest; the German by dint of rudeness, the Islander by dint of temperament; the Babylonian by dint of caprice—and all of them by dint of a general corruption of the human heart.

One cannot complete this panorama of lands at the edge of the world without including *La Découverte Australe par un Homme Volant* [Discovery of the Austral Continent by a Flying Man], published in 1781 by Nicolas-Edmé Restif de la Bretonne (1734-1806),[84] a prolific author of semi-autobiographic and somewhat pornographic novels. In it, a young scientist invents a flying machine with wings and parachute which enabled him to reach speeds of over 100 miles per hour. He then goes on to create his own city-state, accessible only by air, and conquers the girl he loves. Later, he relocates to the southern ocean, where he visits islands inhabited by giants and other variant human species, including beast-men combining the features of humans and animals. His voyage ends in the great City of Sirap, another utopia located in "Megapatagonia."

---

[84] Available from Black Coat Press, ISBN 978-1-61227-512-3.

PLANETARY FANTASIES

From Imaginary Lands located at the Edge of the World to other planets entirely, was but a short step, and the first planetary fantasies, not unlike David Lindsay's *A Voyage to Arcturus* (1920) and E. R. Eddison's *The Worm Ouroboros* (1922), began in the 17th century and grew by leaps and bounds thereafter, eventually leaving the domains of fantasy to evolve into science fiction.

The founding father of this type of story was Hector Savinien de Cyrano de Bergerac (1619-1655), whose *Histoire Comique des Etats et Empires de la Lune* [Comical History of the States and Empires of the Moon] was published posthumously in 1657, soon followed by H*istoire Comique des Etats et Empires du Soleil* [Comical History of the States and Empires of the Sun] in 1662, both eventually collected as *L'Autre Monde* [Other Worlds].

Cyrano de Bergerac became famous as the hero of a superb 1898 play by Edmond Rostand (1868-1918), which made his swordsmanship and the size of his nose illustrious. But he was also a poet, soldier of fortune and distinguished man of letters, whose writings were published after his death in order to avoid persecution for heresy. He wrote two remarkable utopias-cum-social satires which were also noteworthy because of their author's attempts at devising various methods of space travel, some of them clearly fanciful (even at the time), others more scientifically inspired (such as rockets, parachutes, use of magnetism).

The first story, in the full version of the text, begins with the narrator being ridiculed for asserting that the moon is a world. He then finds a copy of a book by the mathematician Girolamo Cardano open on his desk at a page in which the writer describes a mysterious visit from two men claiming to be inhabitants of the moon. Taking this as a sign, the narrator attempts to reach the moon by filling bottles with dew, which lift him into the air under the effects of sunlight, but only contrives to get as far as Canada. Later, he builds a machine powered by rockets in which he eventually completes his planned voyage, and finds himself in the earthy paradise, having landed in the branches of the Tree of Life. There the narrator learns the "true" stories of Adam, Enoch and Noah's daughter Achab from Elijah, an earlier lunar voyager who explains his own magnetic method of arriving there. Unfortunately, the narrator cannot resist the temptation to make a joke, and is banished from paradise by Elijah for his irreverence. After eating an apple from the Tree of Knowledge he finds himself in a strange land to which all the now-mythical creatures of Earth have been banished, and where he is captured and enslaved. Eventually, because of his claim that the Moon is a satellite and the Earth a planet, rather than vice versa, he is put on trial and forced to recant his heresy. Further philosophical discussions follow regarding the mores of the lunarians, atomic theory, the immortality of animal souls and other topics, before the narrator contrives, unwittingly, to return to Earth.

The second volume of *L'Autre monde* picks up the story exactly where the first part left off. The narrator hastens to write an account of his lunar journey, which promptly leads him to be denounced as a sorcerer. He is then involved in a series of discussions with his hosts—who address him as Monsieur Dyrcona—about enigmatic but seemingly revelatory dreams they have had, before he ends up in prison. After further earthly tribulations, he contrives to build another flying machine and set off on his extraterrestrial travels again, heading for the Sun and discovering the moons of Venus and Mercury *en route*. He makes numerous deductions in passing as to why he no longer needs food, why the Sun's heat does not burn him and why all planets have satellites. After four months of travel, Dyrcona lands on a sunspot, imagined as a small world, and finds a dwarfish inhabitant who can give him information on various matters, including a rapid account of

194

cosmogony and the origins of planetary life. Then he sets off again, this time traveling so far that the Earth becomes lost to sight in the cosmic background. When he reaches the "firmament," he finds that it is not solid, although, when he passes through it, he and his vehicle become transparent. Having turned round, it takes him nearly two years to get back to the Sun, but he finally succeeds in landing upon it.

On the Sun, Dyrcona encounters sentient and articulate fruit and birds, and soon finds an informant able to give him an elaborate account of nature on that world of light, music and metamorphoses, where things work very different from earthly nature. The solar birds, far in advance of humans, initially regard Dyrcona as a mere ape, and subject him to a searching examination, which leads to a trial before the full Parliament of Birds, to determine the extent and culpability of his humanity. The judgment does not go well, but he is enabled to escape to a forest of sentient trees, who tell him stories about various earthly humans—characters appropriated from Classical mythology—who ate their magical fruits, and other strange metamorphic and magnetic effects of those fruits.

Unfortunately, the trees are interrupted when the forest is threatened by the "plague" of conflagration, and Dyrcona has to leave, but he is able to do so in the company of Campanella. Just as they catch up with Descartes, the narrative is abruptly cut off.

The success of Cyrano's works popularized the concept of planetary fantasies and spawned many imitators. One was the Chevalier de Béthune [85] with his *Relation du Monde de*

---

[85] The Bibliothèque Nationale catalog does not attribute any dates to the author, and previous writers citing the work, including Charles Garnier, have not been able to say anything at all about him. The resources of the world wide web provide considerable detail regarding the various branches of the prolific Béthune family, but none of the members cited in the various guides to the French aristocracy who used the title "Chevalier de Béthune" was alive in 1750. The most likely

Mercure [The World of Mercury] (1750 but likely written before 1715, i.e. before Louis XIV's passing), a colorful utopia about the immortal, winged beings inhabiting the planet Mercury. To the notion that God would not have made a universe full of stars and planets without populating all of them, Béthune adds an elaborate system of linkage involving a complex and highly ordered system of cosmic palingenesis, long before Charles Bonnet's *Palingénésie philosophique* [Philosophical Palingenesis] (1769) repeated the notion of a soul's possible serial reincarnation on different worlds, much more tentatively, in the interests of a gradual ascent of a scale of moral perfection, in a more earnest framework.

In developing the elaborate secondary creation of his world of Mercury, Béthune sets out to shape the kind of world that God might have built had he been somewhat more kindly inclined toward humans than the existential situation of Earthly humans suggests. His description of Mercury is very much a tongue-in-cheek exercise, with many elements of pure comedy, and his account of life there is far closer in spirit to the land of Cockayne than to any kind of political Utopia, but that certainly does not rob the thinking behind it of any ingenuity or zest—quite the contrary, in fact. In particular, the description of the aerial conflict between the defenders of Mercury's Great Mountain and the monstrous invaders from the "crust" expelled from the Sun is triumphantly eccentric, a match in its colorful extravagance for any space battle featured in the great tradition of 20th century space opera.

---

candidate to be the author of the text, if the author does appear in the genealogical lists, was one of the sons of Henri de Béthune, Comte de Selles, Marie-Henri de Béthune, who died in Paris on 3 May 1744 at the age of 78.

Chevalier de Béthune: *The War Between the Sun and Mercury*
(pub. 1750) [86]

The one that is so called is prodigious in height by comparison with others, of such a vast extent and more embellished by the gifts of nature than it is possible to describe. The foot of the mountain is surrounded by precipices, and one can only reach it by a narrow path, extremely fortified and guarded by the best troops on the Planet. It is on that mountain that the Sages of Mercury live, who are distributed throughout the universe; the much vaunted Rosicrucians, the Fays, the Mages, the Genii, the Sylphs, the Salamanders, the Gnomes, the Undines—in sum, all the beings that we regard as fabulous—hold their meetings on that Mountain. They regulate the affairs of Society there, communicate their knowledge to one another there, cultivate that which they have acquired, and sometimes live there for centuries without, any thought of leaving, so pleasant is that abode.

The people of Mercury, who love those species of demigods, from whom they receive a thousand benefits, sometimes come to visit them, with the Emperor's permission, and those visits, although rare, further augment the admiration of the people for the inhabitants of the Great Mountain; so they have no difficulty in risking their lives and enduring all kinds of fatigues when it is attacked, which often happens in the following manner.

---

[86] Excerpted from *Relation du monde de Mercure* by the Chevalier de Béthune, translated into English in 2015, introduced and annotated by Brian Stableford. Available from Black Coat Press, ISBN 978-1-61227-410-2.

What we call Sunspots are calcined rocks of an immense size, which the prodigious movement of the star launches to an incredible distance. As those burned rocks are light, they are sustained for many centuries before falling, and during that long interval of time, the ever productive and vivifying ardor of the great star forms animals and humans on those crusts. Beneficent as the nature of the Sun's light might be, however, the inhabitants of those arid burned lands always resent the place where they have been born. The animals there are large and cruel, the humans savage and ferocious, enemies of all equity, devoid of art, morals and discipline, and closely resemble in character the way that we depict Giants and Cyclopes.

These flying lands, if it is permissible to name them thus, do not follow a perfectly regular course around the Sun, but sometimes find themselves closer to Mercury and sometimes further away. It even happens that they sometimes almost touch the Great Mountain. Now, the peoples that inhabit those rocks see from their hideous dwellings the beauties of Mercury and the felicity of that Planet's inhabitants, which gives them an ardent desire to live there. There is nothing that they do not attempt in that design, and as they have wings, they fly from time to time in such great quantities on to the mountain that it is always to be feared that they might make themselves masters of it.

Those perverse humans bear a considerable resemblance to the Demons of which such ugly portraits have been made. It is probable that a few of the Sages who inhabit the Great Mountain and have traveled throughout the world have given us a description of them, and that is why Painters represent to us frightful human creatures with hideous features, bestial visages, horns, tails and trenchant claws, and the entire apparatus of deformity that are attributed to Infernal Angels. That accursed race is born fully armed, like lions, tigers and elephants.

In addition, they are prodigiously strong—but they lack industry, and although they have much more of it than our cleverest animals, it is constant that the people of Mercury, although much smaller and weaker, are their superiors. In any case, the latter are led by Sages, whom nature almost always obeys. It must be admitted, however that it is only with difficulty that they defend themselves against the irruptions of their enemies. I was a witness to the last war, and as I served in it with sufficient good fortune and distinction, I am better placed than anyone else to offer an accurate account of it.

The Sages of all the parts of the world had gone to Mercury for a general assembly; for a few days, already, they had been regulating the interests of Society in public conferences, and distributing the offices that are allocated every year, when, after an obscurity of several hours that descended upon the Mountain, enemy troops were distinctly perceived, which, having abandoned their lands, were flying at top speed to fall upon the Planet.

The assembly of the Sages immediately broke up, and each one went to occupy his post, for everything is regulated in case of an alarm.

As soon as the Sages saw the enemies approaching, they built by the force of their art—which we call magic—a prodigiously high wall of diamond around the Great Mountain, in order to separate it from the rest of the Planet. Troops were immediately assembled and divided into the corps, distinguished by the arms of which they made use.

Generally speaking, all the Warriors on Mercury are armed as we paint Amours; the Sages have also furnished us with that idea. Some carry bows and quivers full of arrows, but those arrows are shafts of light and flame rendered solid, which conserve their natural activity and there is nothing that they cannot penetrate; they traverse the hardened skin and large bones of enemies with as much facility as they pass through the air. Nothing resists them, and the troop that makes use of those weapons is the most considerable.

The members of the second corps carry lighted torches, the flames of which can never be extinguished and whose

199

power of ignition is so dangerous and so sudden that nothing in the world can ward of its effect. They shake these torches when they fight, and any spark, no matter how slight, that strikes penetrates into the depths of hearts and devours them, from which inevitable and prompt death ensues.

The third troop carries simple strips of cloth known as streamers, instruments that do not seem very redoubtable but are, in fact, more dangerous than the other weapons. The slightest touch of that magic fabric initially dazzles and blinds almost instantaneously, with the consequence that, unable to see, one can neither defend oneself not escape; thus, one remains at the mercy of a pitiless enemy, who often insults your defeat and renders your death as ignominious as it is cruel.

The report that the Ages have given us of the weapons of the inhabitants of Mercury have doubtless given rise to the Allegory that causes us to depict winged Amours armed with inevitable arrows, cruel fires, and wearing a blindfold—which we mistakenly put over their eyes, although it really serves to blind those that they wish to enslave.

Those troops, arranged in battalions over three lines, each have seven Sages at their head mounted on chariots. The first seven are pulled by twelve butterflies very neatly harnessed, the next seven by twelve honey-bees released from their labor and the last seven by twelve cockchafers selected from the Stables of Demogorgon, the permanent and irrevocable Doyen of the Rosicrucians.[87]

The Sages could have harnessed their chariots to eagles, vultures or others birds of that sort, but they wanted to show that veritable Wisdom has no need of aid, and that heroic valor is sufficient in itself.

---

[87] Demogorgon crops up in numerous 17th century literary works, usually in a demonic role, but this particular reference probably derives from Jean-Baptiste Lully's opera *Roland*, performed at Versailles in 1685, in which Demogorgon is the king of the fays and functions in the plot of the opera as a master of ceremonies.

That disposition having been made, and the enemy still approaching, the three troops, with their Leaders, rise up into the air with incredible rapidity; sunbeams are not as light and lightning not as prompt. The enemies are alerted by the sight of these Phalanges sustaining themselves in the air with their wings and hovering there, waiting for them, but they are broken and knocked over in an instant; the abrupt attack of our troops does not give them the leisure to prepare for battle. The Mercurians, who agility renders them almost impossible to attack, have penetrated their ranks and shattered their order before they could close ranks. The combat cannot be sustained for very long, in spite of the surprise.

The ferocity and the rage on one side balanced the agility, skill and veritable valor on the other, but one of the Sages—it was Trevisan[88]—having taken flight more rapidly, rose above the enemy with his troop, while the other two troops, more powerfully armed, took the underside.

The troop following Trevisan was armed with fires, and shook its brands over the cohorts; the penetrating sparks fell like a fiery rain, and while the two corps that had remained below pierced the enemy with their arrows or blinded them, the flying quadroon occupying the median region of the air inflicted inexpressible ravages.

The enemy, pressed from all sides and, so to speak, surrounded by a thousand unavoidable deaths, precipitated their flight toward the summit of the Mountain, and abandoned the air.

They were followed closely, but as a fleeing enemy requires a golden bridge, the Sages sounded the retreat, content to have carried off the honors of the day and to see the ground covered with their mortal enemies, biting the dust.

---

[88] A number of 16th century alchemical works were attributed to Bernard Trevisan, who was supposed to have been active in the 15th century. One of the works in question was "edited"—and presumably faked—by the Belgian alchemist Gerhard Dorn (1530-1584).

After that glorious success, the Sages, without losing a moment, garnished the battlements of the diamond wall with a large number of inhabitants of Mercury. As our soldiers were much lighter than the enemies, and had a much more elevated position, and the barbaric people had, in any case, refrained from quitting their retrenchments and the entrances to the Mountain of which they had taken possession, preparations were made to attack them the following day in a regulation fashion.

In addition to the weapons I have mentioned, the inhabitants of Mercury, when at war, carry long chains whose slenderness renders them imperceptible, and which it is impossible to break. During the night they covered the environs of the fort and the enemy's retreats with them. The next day, at dawn, they put on an appearance of wanting to attack on foot; the enemies, promising themselves an easy victory and emerging full of confidence and fury to meet our troops, almost delivered themselves into the trap. Only the last saved themselves, but it did them no good to have avoided it; thousands of arrows reached them as they fled, with the result that in those two days, the planet was liberated from the inundation of the barbarians, having suffered only minimal losses.

With regard to those who remained in the Mercurians' invisible traps, their lives were spared. The Sages had them take certain powders that softened their natural ferocity for a time; in consequence, they were allowed to spend a few days on the Great Mountain, and even to travel on the Planet.

As they never bring any women with them when they go to war, there is no danger that their numbers might increase on Mercury, since, by the foresight of Nature, they cannot have children with our women. Without that sage precaution, which renders those monstrous men sterile on our world, one might sometimes see pretty women with children six times as large as them.

In 1765-66, Marie-Anne de Roumier-Robert (1705-1771) wrote *Voyages de Milord Céton dans les sept planettes, ou Le Nouveau Mentor* [*The Voyages of Lord Seaton to the Seven Planets*], first published in four volumes, ostensibly in The Hague. The first volume belongs squarely to the tradition of lunar satires, containing echoes of Cyrano. Madame Robert's account of the far-ranging educational tour to which the *génie* Zachiel subjects his protégés Céton and Monime is to a large extent an homage, and echoes many of the criticisms that Fénelon made of the court culture of Louis XIV's reign, although it also rebukes the earlier Mentor for the implication of *lèse-majesté* contained in his more radical ideas about parliamentary government. The story represents the "seven planets"—the Moon, Mercury, Venus, Mars, the Sun, Jupiter and Saturn, explored in that order—as Earth-clone worlds, in each of which a single human penchant is exaggerated to become an overriding theme of existence, thus exposing it to analysis, criticism and sometimes to ridicule. Most of the targets addressed are familiar: the follies of social affectation prominent on the Moon, the viciousness of avarice dominant on Mercury, and the relentless pursuit of social status on Jupiter are all conventional issues conventionally tackled; but there is an insistent quirkiness in the accounts of Venus, the planet ruled by Amour, the war-torn Mars, and the Apollonian Sun. The account of the supposedly-ideal society of Saturn is heavily influenced by the glorification of the pastoral so frequent in eighteenth-century French fiction, more reminiscent of Honoré d'Urfé than Rousseau.

The novel does not conclude with the visit to Saturn, but continues back on Earth, where the somewhat tormented relationship between Céton and Monime eventually reaches its conclusion in the context of a strange variant history, which employs several actual historical individuals—the novel is set in the mid-seventeenth century, although some of the visits to other planets involve drastic chronological inconsistencies—but soon moves into a spectacularly counterfactual account of the history of Georgia. Although it is not really an "alternative

203

history" in the sense that the term was later attributed to a subgenre of fiction, its historical inventions are nevertheless interesting in that context. Madame Robert's narrative has some striking compensatory virtues. Not the least of those compensations is the sheer bizarrerie of certain parts of the narrative, both in terms of the intensely exotic imagery of its odder passages—the visit to a comet, during which Céton and Monime observe a necromancer at work in spectacular fashion, is a particularly striking example, although partly plagiarized from an obscure English text[89]—and in the reckless mingling and confusion of the literal and the metaphorical, especially in the elaborate ventures into mythological allegory in the sections set on Venus and the Sun.

The following excerpt is set on the planet Mars...

---

[89] This passage was taken from a story first published anonymously in English in an issue of the *Royal Lady's Magazine* from 1831 under the title "Passages from the Diary of a Late Lunatic." An abridged version was reprinted in William Mudford's anthology of *Tales and Trifles from Blackwod's and Other Popular Magazines* (1849), where Madame Robert might have found it.

Marie-Anne de Roumier Robert: *Mars, The Fourth Heaven*
(1765-66)[90]

I.

We arrived on the planet Mars at nightfall. Dusk had already dressed the landscape in somber livery; silence marched in its wake; the animals and the birds had taken refuge in their places of retreat, the only one that remained was the nightingale, which, accustomed to amorous wakefulness, spends entire nights singing. Hesperus, the conductor of starry bands, was shining at their head; the firmament was sparkling with bright sapphires. The Moon was rising with a nebulous majesty, unveiling her tender light with the bearing of a Queen, extending her silvery mantle over the obscurity. The genius, continuing his rapid flight, took us down into a sandy and arid plain.

Monime, gripped by fear and scarcely able to breathe, begged the genius insistently not to stop on that planet.

"I implore you, in the name of the amity that you have avowed for us, to take us to another world. The name of Mars alone frightens me; I imagine that it is filled by barbaric and ferocious citizens, that everything only breathes for combat, blood and carnage. What do you expect me to do on such a world? Is a woman made to confront its hazards?

---

[90] Excerpted from *The Voyages of Lord Seaton to the Seven Planets* by Marie-Anne de Roumier-Robert, translated into English in 2015, introduced and annotated by Brian Stableford. Available from Black Coat Press, ISBN 978-1-61227-410446-1.

"Rid yourself, dear Monime," the genius said, "of these puerile and frivolous fears; my design is not to expose you to the fury of combats. But my dear daughter, do you not want anything done in favor of Seaton? It is only here that he can make his apprenticeship in the métier of war; you're not unaware that a Lord like him cannot be occupied with any other employment, nor achieve any other than military rank. If you love him, you can never give him greater evidence of amity than by stimulating him yourself not to neglect any of the means that present themselves to make the most of his courage."

"Which means that today," said Monime, with a kind of chagrin and impatience, "you would like me to resemble those women who only find pleasure in the choice they make of a soldier for a husband, and of seeing him leave for the army without being obliged to go with him. Content to be distanced from him, they enjoy the satisfaction, or at least the hope, of believing him to be more than a hundred leagues away for a long time. If they were deprived of that time of liberty, of which they doubtless take advantage, a warrior, or anyone else, would then become indifferent to them.

"In any case," Monime added, sardonically, "the strongest Hercules can never hold firm before an Omphale; one of our gazes is sufficient to change their club into a distaff. Let us therefore allow them to ornament themselves occasionally with the name of hero; we render them effeminate often enough. Finally, my dear Zachiel, if you are absolutely insistent on forcing me to make a long sojourn on this planet, I want to disguise myself; I declare to you that I shall don the uniform, the sword, the plume, the high collar, and the spontoon; I shall buy a regiment and become a colonel at a stroke. Perhaps you will tell me that in that accoutrement, which will rejuvenate me even more, I shall appear to be no more than a child—fine reasoning; I'm sure that I shall see more than one in this world who, having reached a superior rank, doubtless thinks himself important and believes himself more skillful than the most experienced, although less expert and more infantile than me."

Monime persisted for longer in attempting to make the genius take another decision, but it was a waste of time; her representations were futile, and it was necessary to set forth. After Zachiel had dissipated some of her fears with stories that were as amusing as they were singular, the charming young woman saw that she was constrained to vanquish her repugnance, no longer daring to oppose the will of the genius openly.

Our voyage was very pleasant; the roads were full of post-chaises, carriages, heavy wagons and mule trains, but especially of people, who seemed to be the most content in the world.

One said: "This is a campaign that will advance me to the head of the regiment; and if I'm rendered justice, I'll have every reason to hope for a good pension and a government post at the end of the war."

"The country is rich," said another. "We'll be able to obtain fine booty there."

Several of them wanted to wager that the war would be concluded by that single campaign. "It isn't possible," they said, "that the enemy can hold out even for two months."

In sum, all of them were marching with great confidence; they only talked about places taken, victories won. To hear them, one might have thought that the cities would advance to meet them that that the armies would take flight merely at the news of their approach.

Obliged to quit that road to take another, we encountered a few battalions returning to the army. They did not seem nearly as content as the first; as much as the others seemed enthusiastic, these appeared discouraged and weary. Monime mistook them at first for poor cripples, who were begging for alms on the highways. Officers soldiers, servants and horses were all equally fearful and pitiable. Their speech corresponded to their faces.

"We were led to butchery," they said.

The general had lost his head; the cavalry had advanced ineptly; the infantry, poorly commanded, had not done its duty.

"Why, said one of them, "before exposing us, did they not sent scouts to reconnoiter the position? If the enemy had been closely watched, their maneuvers would not have been hidden. Our spies are poorly paid; that's why they neglected to inform us."

In sum, each of those military men was only content with himself, and all had a desire to utter a thousand maledictions against a state of affairs with which they seemed extremely disgusted.

That sad spectacle was not calculated to renew Monime's courage; her fear and dread increased. "Let's leave this vile Mars, she said to Zachiel. "Let's take another route; I feel myself oppressed by the air, which is assuredly too keen for the delicacy of my temperament; the vapors are already overwhelming me and my heart is palpitating as we advance further on the planet."

Deaf to Monime's complaints, the genius continued his route without deigning to respond. We soon discovered the most eminent and celebrated place on the entire planet, the famous Temple of Glory to which all the citizens of the world flock.

"The grave and serious expression you adopt will never deter me, my dear Zachiel," Monime continued. "I even dare ask you for a favor, before you go on into this frightful country. Begin, I beg you, by taking us to that magnificent temple. A noble presentiment informs me that a sojourn in that admirable place might calm my senses, reanimate my courage and reconcile me at the same time to the rest of the planet. Gods, what do I see? You're frowning! You're going to refuse me again; I shudder; don't pronounce sentence on me."

"What you're asking isn't reasonable," Zachiel said. "It's not by way of the Temple of Glory that one succeeds in the empire of Mars; on the contrary, one has to pass through the most difficult ordeals and along the thorniest roads to arrive at that temple. I can't change such a just law in your favor; Renown, to whom the guard of the temple is confided, would be bold enough to refuse us entry; she only opens up to those she knows, and whose name has already been transmitted throughout the world."

"Do you think, my dear Zachiel," said Monime, looking at him with an enchanting smile, "that there are not devious routes here, as there are everywhere, by which one can introduce oneself through some false door? Personally, I think that one can make heroes, like doctors, by the fireside. The Renown of whom you speak does not have a very sound reputation for accuracy, and if she doesn't look any more closely in order to open the door than to blow her trumpet, it must be admitted that people often get in with more facility than you imply."

The slightest things sometimes determine victory; that reflection gave all the advantage to Monime. Zachiel gave in, and the carriage that as carrying us became the chariot of triumph on which our amiable conqueress led us like captives to the Temple of Glory.

That admirable edifice is situated on the summit of the highest and steepest rock there ever was. Once, it was enclosed by high walls, very difficult to approach, but several roads have been flattened; nowadays more accessible, one can arrive there easily from several directions, on roads that appear newly traced.

The temple gains considerably from being seen from afar; its beauties are developed successively; the further they are from the center, the more brilliantly they shine; their gleam is proportional to that distance.

Scarcely had we arrived at the foot of the rock than it confronted us everywhere with nothing but frightful precipices, Zachiel having maliciously guided us to the least accessible place. No well-beaten road presented itself to make the ascent. It was then that our courage failed. I had initially joined in with the genius to combat Monime's fears, but I began to tremble like her; shame prevented me from adopting her language, but in the depths of my heart I shared her sentiments.

Another sight, even more forbidding than the rock, inspired further repugnance in us. It was a pile of horribly disfigured cadavers covering the floor of the valley. Gripped by astonishment and horror, Monime and I looked at Zachiel without having the strength to speak to him, but it was easy for him to read in our eyes what was passing in our soul.

Looking at us with a serene expression, he said: "Those corpses that you see do no merit your attention or your pity; they are here in ignominy and forgetfulness, because they were never more than failed heroes, and falsely brave; several of them came to break themselves against the spur of rock you see to your left, which is known as the False Point of Honor; they are people who, in order to avenge an imaginary insult, have dishonored themselves by a shameful death, who have perished, not in battle, which ought to be the bed of honor of the truly brave, but in duels that are only appropriate to vile gladiators. There are hired assassins who put all their honor into taking men's lives; people who make honor, virtue, vice, infamy, truth and lies depend on the outcome of a combat, who have no other rectitude, no other justice and no other reason than murder, as well as the strongest and most skillful, who believe themselves the most worthy of immortality, all their virtue being measured at swordspoint.

"Some of those you see on the other side had received the most fortunate dispositions from nature to become great men one day, but, by virtue of the abuse they made of them, they were only pernicious men and great scoundrels. Such, in particular, is the one you see near here suspended by the feet, head down, covered in blood that seems recently shed and whose stain will never be effaced. Do you know him, my dear Seaton? It's the author of all the misfortunes of your fatherland, as well as those of your family in particular: Cromwell. You shudder at that name; you're right, my dear; England would have been happy if it had not given birth to that monster, who ought to have been its glory but will forever be its opprobrium. He began by soiling it with the blackest of assaults against its king, and after having engaged it to condemn him to death of a scaffold, he ended up usurping the crown and becoming its tyrant.

"Look a little further on and you will see Totila, King of the Goths, who rendered himself frightful under the emperor Justinian I. That Prince fought numerous battles, as many at sea as on land, where he always had the advantage, and in spite of the resistance of Belisarius, whom the emperor sent against him, he besieged and took Rome, destroyed it almost entirely, burned the Capitol and toppled half the walls, ordered the citizens to abandon the city under pain of death, and treated those who did not profess his religion cruelly.

"That big pug-faced fellow you see over there is Attila, King of the Huns, the scythe of nations; he had a subtle intelligence, was ambitious, full of cunning, finesse and treasons, cruel, arrogant, rascally and reckless. The seat of his empire was in Sicambria, on the Danube. He was called to the aid of Genseric, King of the Vandals, against the Goths, and same with an army of five hundred thousand men, ravaged all the provinces of the Roman Empire and put all the places through which he passed in Germany and Italy to fire and the sword; but the run of his victories was finally stopped in Gaul by Aetius, the chief of the Romans and Merovech, the King of the Franks, who destroyed more than a third of his army in a single day and constrained him to flee to Hungary. The Prince, after having crushed a number of provinces, demolishing all their cities, attacked Aquileia, sacked Milan and Pavia, and finally died of a flux of blood that suffocated him, occasioned by his execrable debauches.

"There is Nicocles, tyrant of Sicyon in the Peloponnese, who was expelled from his states and died of hunger and cold. To the right you can see Hermias, son of Artane Donien,[91]

---

[91] This name is enigmatic, although the slightly-misrendered reference is obviously to Hermias of Atarneus, who was tor-

211

who fought a bloody war against Memnon—who, after having vanquished him, had him sown up in the skin of an ox to serve as a plaything, and made him suffer a thousand indignities.

"Look," Zachiel continued, "at those who men who seem to be tied together. They are Cassius and Brutus, two traitors who took up arms against the common father of the land—I mean Caesar. That Emperor was so fond of Brutus that he had named him as his heir, but the ingrate, believing that he would acquire immortal glory, took treason so far as to become the leader of a conspiracy, and although Caesar had received advice not to go to the Senate that day, Brutus took him there personally. As soon as the Emperor entered, sixty assassins surrounded him and struck him with their swords. Caesar defended himself courageously, but when Brutus had also struck him he ceased to defend himself. 'Oh, my son,' he said to him, 'in whom I have put all my confidence, is it necessary for you to give me death?' Caesar said no more, covered his head with his robe, and let himself fall against the statue of Pompey, pierced by twenty-three sword-thrusts, of which he died in the hall of the Senate. But Heaven avenged his death with that of all the conspirators, who are all buried here in the dust, and that same Brutus, after having lost a battle near the city of Philippi, fell on his own sword, and died instantly, killing himself with same blade that he had employed in the parricide that he had committed on Caesar's person.

"I would never finish," the genius added, "if I name for you all those you see here. It is true that some performed fine deeds, but they soiled them by actions even more barbaric; brigands rather than conquerors, it was their ferocity that animated them and not worth; they only sought to vanquish in order to massacre and pillage, and the name that they left after them is only immortal in the horror and execration of men, because they did not know the true path that leads to the Tem-

---

tured by Memnon of Rhodes. Ovid records that he was sewn up in an ox-hide, but not by Memnon.

ple of Glory and, although they took great steps in order to reach it, their faults and vices banished them from it forever."

"All these men horrify me," said Monime. "I find it repugnant to the society of reasonable beings that subjects dare to dictate the law to their masters and attribute to themselves to privilege of inflicting their punishments, since a sovereign is only accountable for the conduct to the tribunal of the divinity. However he disposes of our bodies and our wealth, one ought only to oppose to him submission and obedience; that has always been my way of thinking. I see it justified by the number of traitors, tyrants and the impious who, in seeking glory and immortality, have found nothing but opprobrium and scorn. One might think that tyranny is a species of rage, which is often pushed to the ultimate extremity. Oh, my dear Zachiel, let us flee, and no longer amuse ourselves with the contemplation of such monsters."

"I consent to that," said Zachiel, "but before going on, I want Seaton to look at this reef, which is scarcely confronted by except by those of his nation, and which is deadly to numerous Englishmen; its name is Suicide. Would you believe, my dear, that the greater number of all those you see are your compatriots who have been made enough to give themselves death? That kind of fury is regarded in England as a grandeur of the soul; it is a noble disdain for life, confusing despair with intrepidity, and that pusillanimity that allows itself to be felled by the slightest troublesome event, with the heroism that renders us superior to all the woes that surround us."

While Zachiel was making me that list, which I found very interesting, we saw a troop of individuals advancing toward us, very poorly clad and rather surly in appearance, who were holding large scrolls of paper, quills and writing desks. They saluted us in a pedantic fashion, and told us that they had come to offer us their services.

"I'm not dear," said one of them, who called himself a gazetteer. "For a small fee I promise to render you to the temple and sign you a distinguished place there."

Then a quantity of poets and historians presented themselves, to offer us immortality in verse and prose.

"Here, sirs," said one of the poets, "are poems that I have composed for the great conquerors, and here are some for great politicians; these are for the men of vast genius whose intelligence and enlightenment extend over all the sciences. I've left all the names blank; if you want to choose one, I'll immediately fill in yours, provided that you do me the kindness of making me a little present of a hundred guineas."

My curiosity excited by that singular compliment, I took one in order to examine it, but I only found it filled with enthusiasm and bloated verses; great words formed a complete collection of all the most anciently coupled rhymes: battles and chattels, sun and run, glory and victory, sublime and chime, hazard and Caesar, thunder and asunder, fights, mights, advantages, carnages, errors, terrors and many more. In the end, all those cadenced words, like a tune played on a pipe, which would be too long to reproduce here, appeared to me to signify very little. However, the poet offered nothing less than to put Monime at the rank of the goddess Pallas, and to make me occupy the place of the god Mars himself.

From the other side Monime was assailed by people presenting new pamphlets to her. "My Lady," said one of them, "this is new; if your grandeur will permit, I shall have the honor of dedicating this little work to you; it is bound in pink, which is the color in fashion."

"Take mine," said another, "it's in flax-gray, the delights of a tender soul."

"My Lady," said a third, "give preference to this collection; it's in green and yellow, to paint springtime; the book is sown with nothing but flowers and brilliant words; it's divine."

"Beautiful goddess," said a man with a languorous expression, "Allow me to present this elegy to you."

"And me these epistles, which are above those of Cicero."

Other brought odes, rondeaux and vaudevilles; those requested very little money. Afterwards however, came historians of great repute, who offered us the same services—which is to say, to have the most beautiful events in our lives inscribed in the book of bronze that is never erased. Oh, those were very dear!

I was tempted at first to place myself in that great book. The writer was already beginning to sharpen a fine quill, delicate and light, but when the hand posed on the paper, ready to trace my great deeds, he asked me under what title I wanted to announce myself. I confess that the question embarrassed me; I sensed internally that I did not merit any. After having thought for a moment, I said: "Give me whichever one you wish; perhaps hazard will enable you to encounter the right one, and if the zeal I feel to live up to it can substitute for merit, you won't be taking any risk."

II.

Zachiel, who was present at that conversation, warned me that it was only by heroic actions that one could acquire the glory of occupying a place in the great book, without which whatever vulgar writers attempted to inscribe therein was easily erased by envy or jealousy, which pardon nothing, but the darts of which are blunt and cannot tarnish the reputation of individuals whom Heaven has endowed with true merit and invincible courage.

"The rank or the place that great men merit," added the genius, "can only be decided after their death, because there are some who lose in the last moments of their life a part of the glory that they acquired over several years, and others who become even greater in dying than they were when they enjoyed perfect health.

"Scipio, the father-in-law of Pompey, redeemed at the moment of his death the poor opinion that people had had of him; he showed by his confidence and boldness that the people who have seemed the weakest can sometimes raise them-

215

selves to the grandeur of soul of heroes. Having been cast up on the shore of Africa by a horrible tempest, and his vessel captured by enemies, Scipio wanted to save in his person the glory of his name, and could not suffer seeing the Africans, being accustomed to see them vanquished, put him in chains. As great as the vanquisher of Carthage, he tamed the horrors of death, by plunging his sword into his bosom. That example, my dear Seaton, ought to suffice to inform you that he last moments of life ought to be regarded as the touchstone that distinguishes the heroes and the true philosophers from those who have only usurped the name."

We were interrupted by a man, who came running toward us with a whip in his hand, saying: "Sirs, I am the English postillion; I guarantee to take you from here to the temple without spilling you; would you like a coach, a post-chaise, a two-wheeler, a cabriolet? Choose—we have vehicles of every sort here."

"Stand aside," said another, "you're nothing but a chatterbox. These gentlemen merit going forth on Pegasus; he's ready saddled and bridled, only waiting for you to depart; he's the gentlest animal in the world, and allows himself be mounted easily. Take advantage of it, beautiful goddess; I promise you that you'll arrive at the temple in the blink of an eye."

A runner advancing with a proud and audacious attitude told us, in a methodical tone, that he was the forerunner, who ordinarily matched his pace to the gifts that were made to him. He was followed by a quantity of scholars, who, all for a price of silver, cane to offer us immortality.

Aggravated by all these offers and that crowd of merchants of reputation, whose number was increasing at every moment, we made the decision to get rid of them, but we could only do so by accepting large volumes of praise, which they gave us very cheaply and which put us at least at the level of the most famous heroes and heroines of antiquity.

Renown immediately announced herself with her hundred mouths and her hundred trumpets, with which she intoned our pretended great deeds; at the same time her horse was hitched to our chariot; in a trice we were borne up to the clouds, and, without having touched the rocks, we found ourselves in the great square of the temple.

"I would prefer not to advance any further," said Monime, "with making a halt here. We're hungry, and I feel too weak to go on."

"What are you saying?" said Zachiel, interrupting her abruptly. "Is this the place to talk about eating and drinking? Know, beautiful Monime, that in the abode of glory, one only feeds on wind and smoke; one only gets drunk on one's own merit. Sleeping in the shade of those laurels, receiving incense, throwing dust in the eyes—that's the life and the sole occupation of immortal heroes."

Monime did not appear to have any appetite for that diet of immortality; she was already preparing to dip into her bag of dried fruits when we were suddenly invested by a swirl of exceedingly odorous smoke, Then came a gust of wind, which seemed to reanimate volcanoes of sulfur and saltpeter, which spread more smoke throughout the square. Combining with the other, it seemed to intoxicate all the spectators. Unable to sustain the force of that wind, Zachiel took us into a vestibule.

"Here you are," he told us, "in the midst of the most vaunted heroes in the universe."

Our astonishment at the sight of that singular company is inexpressible. Scarred faces, punctured eyes, slashed craniums, sliced ears, arms in slings, wooden legs, bodies covered in wounds and plasters, and women, one of whose breasts had been hacked off: such were the frightful sights that presented themselves to our eyes.

"Great God, where are we?" exclaimed Monime, utterly bewildered. "Oh, wicked Zachiel, you've deceived us; what pleasure have you gained in thus taking us for fools? Why have you forced me to undertake this long voyage? Why excite my curiosity with stories that have no kind of connection with what I see? Why, finally, have you claimed to be introducing us into the sanctuary of immortality, when I can see

217

that all those magnificent promises have ended up bringing us to a hospital?"

The genius, smiling at her error, told her that he was sorry that these unfortunate officers had only excited her alarm, when they ought at least to inspire sentiments of admiration; and that it was only by way of such accidents that one could lay claim to glory."

"What!" said Monime. "You still expect to persuade me that we're in a temple here?"

"Assuredly," said Zachiel. "You're under one of its porticoes—but let's go into that vast colonnade on the left."

Frightened to see a large tower that was in the middle moving, Monime uttered a cry, dreading that it might fall on top of us. The tower, which machinery similar to our windmills was causing to rotate rapidly, showed us several figures that its movement appeared to animate. Monime's disturbance was augmented by that appearance, and in spite of the desire she had to discover what such an extraordinary decoration signified, I noticed that she would have liked to be much further away. However, Zachiel, attentive to all her movements, finally fixed her attention.

"Look at these different heroes," he said. The one that you see nonchalantly leaning on the arm of his squire is the great Cyrus, who transferred the empire of the Medes to the Persians, won an infinite number of battles and conquered entire provinces, who traversed Asia, Media, Hyrcania, Persia and, in sum, ravaged more than half of the world he inhabited."

"He was doubtless an ambitious Prince," said Monime, "who wanted all the earth to be submissive to him?"

"Not at all," Zachiel replied. "Amour alone prompted him to all that disorder. He only wanted to free the Princess

Mandana, with whom he was passionately in love; but that Princess was snatched away from him eight times."[92]

"There," I said, "is a beauty that passed all proofs."

"That's true—but all her abductors were illustrious scoundrels, who nevertheless had virtue enough to respect her; they never dared even to lay a finger on her, and if her square could talk, he would recount marvels.

"The other who is appearing is Romulus, the first King of the Romans, whom he citizens put to death, and afterwards affirmed that he had risen up to Heaven. That one is Codrus, the King of Athens, who devoted himself to death for the service of the fatherland."

"I'd be curious," I said, "to know who that beauty is who appears with such a proud attitude."

"That's Cloelia, the most illustrious of all Roman ladies; she swam the Tiber in order to escape from Lars Porsena's camp."

"That one," said Monime, "appears to me to be a heroine very heavily armed; is she not some Queen of the Amazons?"

"That's the Maid of Orléans," said Zachiel. "You can't be unaware that she was the one who liberated France from the English yoke. The one that you see in the alcove is Zenobia, Queen of Palmyra, who governed that realm with as much wisdom and mildness for more than thirty years, until the time when Aurelian came to declare war on her. That Prince, after having vanquished her, took her as a captive behind his chariot of triumph. He had her two sons, Hernianus and Timolaus, killed.[93] There's Elizabeth, Queen of England; her glory would have been perfect if it had not be tarnished by the death of the Earl of Essex and that of Mary Stuart, Queen of Scots. It is claimed that jealousy had a great deal to do with

---

[92] According to Herodotus, Mandana of Media was Cyrus the Great's mother, while his wife was Cassandane. How Madame Robert acquired this misconception is unclear.

[93] There appears to be no evidence of Zenobia having had sons with these names.

the reasons that determined the pronunciation of those two condemnations."

Then we heard something akin to a hurricane excited by several winds that were in conflict. The wind of glory and that of immortality appeared to be struggling against that of jealousy. Renown was blowing from the south. To the north, the winds of envy and calumny were making such a frightful racket, shaking the edifice with so much violence, that they were bringing down various figures from the paneling and the colonnades, which were still attracting out curiosity.

"There," said Zachiel, "is a King of Phrygia, who was the richest Prince of his time, and the one whose enlightenment, intelligence and politics were the most useful to his people, in enabling him to discover the secrets of his allies and the ruses of his enemies. That monarch profited so considerably from the gifts he had received from Heaven, in making them serve the glory of his realm, that he rendered his subjects perfectly happy. His name was Midas."

"What!" said Monime. "Is that the Midas who is depicted with asses' ears, and whom the indiscreet request he made of Bacchus to change everything he touched into gold caused him to die of starvation?"

"The same—which proves that posterity often spoils, by allegorical fables, the finest actions and embellishes pitiful ones; as witness the story of Lucretia, who has just fallen beside Midas; you're not unaware of the fashion in which her death was published; reading it ought to instruct you. Nothing, however, is as false as the story that is told of it; the truth is that Collatinus, her husband, having learned of her intrigues with the young Prince, stabbed her himself, and put about false rumors against the Tarquins, in order to take possession of the Republic conjointly with his colleague Brutus."[94]

---

[94] The historical accuracy of the story of Lucretia's rape, which allegedly sparked the revolution that established the Roman Republic, as told by Livy and Dionysius of Helicarnasus, was always regarded with some skepticism; that

"I suspected as much," I said. "Not that I presume that all women are coquettes, but that story of Lucretia always seemed to me to be a trifle apocryphal, in that it seems that it would have been more natural first to turn her weapon against the man who wanted to dishonor her, or at least not to wait until the crime had been committed to kill herself."

Aggravated by the fatigue of being obliged to struggle against the impetuosity of the winds that were blowing relentlessly, Monime asked the genius to take us into a building that was on the right.

The vault and pilasters of that building were made of glass; several columns of cardboard supported the edifice. On those columns, blackened by smoke and agitated by the winds, as in the other building, the great deeds of heroes—as many ancient as modern—were inscribed. It is true that when the gusts of wind became violent, some of those columns toppled, and although the poets and historian hired by the State to maintain the edifice applied an extreme attention to their reestablishment, it often happened, in the disorder, that they forgot a great many heroes, who, by virtue of that negligence, found themselves deprived of immortality in spite of the efforts they had made to merit it.

We saw several people walking there who seemed to us to be greatly predisposed in their favor. One of those men approached me and asked whether I was newly arrived, and what was being said about him on our world.

"When you've told me your name," I said, "perhaps I'll be able to reply to the question you've asked me."

"I am Mucius Scaevola, a noble Roman, whom seeing my city besieged by King Lars Porsena, took my leave of the Senate and went to his camp with the intention of killing him; but as I did not know the King I was deceived and mistook

---

did not prevent it becoming an oft-cited moral exemplar, employed by both St, Augustine and Dante, and a significant theme in Renaissance art and literature; English writers who employed it include Chaucer and Shakespeare.

one of his favorites for him, whose life I took. I was immediately arrested and taken before the King, but, without being
astonished by any of the threats he made against me for daring
to make an attempt on his life. I showed him how little I cared
about the cruelest torments by putting my right hand into an
ardent fire, and suffered the pain constantly until it was entirely burned. Lars Porsena, astonished by my firmness, could not
help admiring my great courage and sent me away without
doing me any harm. Scantly sensible to that generosity, I declared to him that I was not the only one that had conspired
against his person, and that there were another three hundred
Romans who had sworn his death. That was what determined
him to make an alliance with the Romans, fearing their intrepidity because of the example I had just shown him."

"You horrify me," I said. "How dare you boast of the
blackest of all attempted murders? Are those your fine exploits? What! After a cowardly homicide, you claim immortality? It isn't be treasons that one attempts to vanquish one's
enemy. The action from which you want derive vanity would
only be regarded today, in our world, as a model of rascality
and ferocity, and you would have no other glory at present
than being placed in the ranks of those bandits who hire themselves out as assassins and put a certain price on each murder
proportionate to the difficulties they encounter in committing
the crime. For myself, I do not see anything great in voluntary
homicide. The basis of all the virtues is humanity; it flows like
a pure and salutary stream that fertilizes everything it encounters; but you, vile assassin, if you have acquired any honors,
they are illegitimate."

Mucius, very discontented by my reception, shrugged his
shoulders and went away.

Soon afterwards I was surrounded by a large number of
people. One of them told me that he was Achilles, another
Caesar, and a third Alexander. I could not hear the names of a
great many of those heroes because they were all speaking at
the same time. As I saw that each of them was preparing to tell

me his story, I interrupted them to beg them to explain themselves one at a time.

"I am Childebren," said a fat, wheezy man. "I would like to know what is being said about me."

"What is said about you? I can assure you that I've never heard your name pronounced on any world."

"And me," said another, with an air of generosity. "I am Montezuma."

"Ha! You, I know; you're an honest man to whom the Spanish did great injustice. But you, who announce yourself to be a Caesar, tell me what country you come from, which world you inhabited and in which realm you were born?"

"The question is singular; has there ever been more than one Caesar? You are an imbecile who only has a human face, and have not the intelligence of a carp."

"I have not learned to reply to invective, but I can assure you that there are at present on our earth more than a million Caesars and at least as many Alexanders, since the least of our officers, and even our soldiers, regard themselves as such."

I had no sooner uttered those words, which they doubtless took for as many blasphemies, than the entire crowd of heroes disappeared, to the great contentment of Monime, who was beginning to fear their petulance.

Zachiel then took us through a large hall filled with heaps of silk and cotton of different colors. Three old women seemed to be continuously occupied in spinning them. Monime and I looked at them very intently, without being able to discover the mystery. This is how the genius explained it to us.

"The three old women you see are the Fates who spin the lives of mortals. Humans can only remain on earth for as long as they take to finish each mass. When they have completed a skein, Destiny attaches a little gold, silver or lead plaque to it, which defines the good or bad qualities of person whose thread has just been cut; his name is engraved on the plaque and his virtues or vices traced in indelible characters. Then an old man, whose rapid course can never be halted, fills the flaps of his robe with them and goes to throw them in the river of forgetfulness, which you can see in the distance on the left flank of that hill.

"The old man comes back continually to take more, untiringly, without ever being able to diminish their number; but when, with an air of chagrin, he has discharged his burden, two swans whiter than snow, which float incessantly on the river, take care to detach with their beaks the names of the most illustrious mortals and put them in the hands of a nymph of ravishing beauty, whose unique employment is to carry them to the Temple of Glory, in order to consecrate them to immortality there. There she attaches them, with great care, to a simulacrum placed on a column elevated in the middle of the temple."

"It's easy to deduce," said Monime, "that the old man you have depicted for us is Time; but what do the swans signify, which, careful to detach the names of heroes from those of vulgar humans, prevent them from being swallowed up by the river of forgetfulness?"

"They represent the great poets and the best historians," said the genius, "who both, by their late nights and assiduous labors, serve to immortalize monarchs, princes, great politicians and all those who have distinguished themselves in the course of their life by heroic actions. The nymph depicts History, who, under that figure, represents the candor, purity, simplicity and above all the verity that a historian ought to employ in the pictures that he gives us in tracing the lives of the heroes that he sets out to put before our eyes."

After leaving that hall the genius took us across a large courtyard. We noticed that the sun, by the heat of its rays, had concentrated the smoke in the entrails of the earth; all the winds had dissipated; the only one that remained was that of glory, which, like all zephyrs, was only blowing to render the air milder and more agreeable.

"We have finally arrived," Zachiel told us, "at the Temple of Immortal Glory."

That temple, the dome of which appeared by its elevation to pierce the clouds, immediately fixed our gaze; we were enchanted by the beauty and the regularity of its architecture. Monime and I, dazzled by its majesty, felt a faint terror take possession of our souls; we approached it with the respect that divinity inspires.

Under the steps of the temple is a profound lair, in which we saw Vulcan forging, on an anvil, the redoubtable thunderbolts of which the Marcians[95] make use to sustain their rights and ensure the destiny of States. To one side of the door of the sanctuary was the divine Urania, a compass in one hand and a map in the other, one which were traced realms, cities, citadels, lakes and sea. On the other side, Calliope was holding a history book, using her finger to point out the finest features. Further away were ranged Intrepid Valor, Vigilant Toil, Tranquil Composure, Hope, Cunning, Deflection, Disguise and Imagination, who seemed to be occupied with a thousand brilliant projects that they were presenting to the confidant of Mars, whom Zachiel identified to us as Impenetrable Secrecy. The temple is surrounded by laurels, with which Pallas herself forms the crowns that Mars subsequently presents to his favorites.

---

[95] The original text employs both *Marciens* and *Marsiens* to describe inhabitants of Mars, although the former is employed to refer to a regional population, contrasted with the Salians and Bellonians, and might be derived from the name of the Byzantine emperor known in French as Marcien rather than the name of the planet. When first introduced, the latter seems to be used in a more general sense, but is subsequently used in the limited one. In consequence, I have maintained the inconsistency, transcribing the two terms as Marcians and Marsians, rather than unifying them or substituting the now-standardized "Martians." Some early English scientific romances employed "Marsians" rather than the more familiar term.

III.

"You ought not to be proud," said Zachiel, "of the un-merited glory that you are receiving today in entering this temple. Covered by my wings, I shall render you invisible to the eyes of all these heroes, and those of Mars himself; I only want to excite in you the martial ardor and noble courage that animates and forms great captains in order to render you worthy of one day occupying a place beside these demigods."

Mars, seated in the middle of the temple on an elevated throne, sustained on the wings of the genius of war, appeared to be gazing at a hero placed beside him to his right, obligingly showing him several passages in a large book that Destiny was holding in front of him. I dared not ask questions of the genius for fear of being discovered, but he anticipated my desires and gave me an indescribable pleasure by telling me that the person who excited my curiosity by virtue of the preference he had obtained over the others was Henri IV, the good King of France, whom Mars was enabling to read, in the book of Destiny, the glory of his race and the striking actions that were to be accomplished by all his descendants.

"O gods!" said Monime, in a low voice, "What an amity I feel for that hero! He is the one, then, whose memory will be perpetuated eternally from race to race among the people as well as the great and sovereigns, who will always have the glory of being taken for a model throughout the universe? But tell me, my dear Zachiel—I'm curious to learn whether he knows how much his memory is revered in all the nations of Earth, and whether he enjoys here the renown that he so justly acquired."

"I give you my word," said Zachiel, "that what makes his recompense, and the proof that the divinity created him in an eminent degree of superiority of intelligence and talents in order to reign over all men, is that those who were most jealous of his glory are forced to admit today that he alone merits commanding the entire universe, since Henri IV has been placed above the greatest men that Rome produced in her greatest elevation.

"I hate flattery and false praise," the genius added, "and only ever applaud true merit. Scipio Africanus is, without contradiction, the greatest that Rome produced, but Henri IV required much more strength of genius, grandeur of soul, intrepidity and courage to reach the goal of becoming king of France than was necessary for what the Roman achieved.

"Scipio, supported by good troops, expelled Hannibal from Italy, reassured the Romans frightened by the loss of the battle of Cannes and carried to the Carthaginian lands the furies of a cruel war with which they had shortly before set all Italy ablaze; in sum, he liberated Rome from that proud and dangerous rival. But what puts the glory of Henri IV above that of the Roman is that, at the head of semi-naked soldiers, devoid of money and without any other aid than his courage and his right, he sets out to recover the crown; he is obliged to make the conquest of his own kingdom, usurped by the member of the Ligue, the Spaniards and others even more redoubtable. In spite of all his oppositions, Henri IV carried through his plans, and after having reestablished himself on the throne of his fathers he made those same Spaniards tremble who, a few years earlier, had combined scorn with presumption in merely referring to him as "the Béarnois."

"You see, my dear Seaton, the affairs of Henri IV were in much greater disorder on the death of his predecessor than those of the Romans after the battle of Cannes, since they at least had money and the means of reestablishing their army. Far from the king of France having the same assistance, I recall a letter that he wrote to one of his generals, in which he indicated that his finances were in a pitiful state, that his cooking pot had been empty for a week, that his suppliers had not had a penny, and that he was obliged to eat with the officers of his army."

I would have liked Zachiel to add to that account and summary of the lives of some of the heroes that I saw assembled in the temple, but Monime, who was beginning to weary

227

of such a long fast, assured us that she did not have enough strength to want to attempt to resemble those great individuals, and that being unable to imitate Henri IV in his great deeds, she would still find enough glory in resembling him in his humiliation by going to ask for supper from some officer whose turnspit was not dismantled. It was necessary to satisfy Monime.

When we emerged from the temple we encountered a large number of troops, whose officers, dressed in different colors, were carrying on their flags or ensigns the emblems of battles they had fought. On some the depiction of an honorable retreat was seen; others described an advantageous capitulation; this one showed the conquest of an entire province; that one the destruction of a well-fortified city filled with all sorts of munitions; that other a naval combat that represented an entire fleet that seemed to have been dissipated or sunk. Further away, the standard of victory shone, borne on a chariot followed by various other troops; in fact, I cannot describe or enumerate the prodigious quantity of ensigns hoisted by the multitude of claimants of immortal glory, for it is necessary not to think that only military men can make the claim; all estates have the same rights, and Renown blows her trumpet for the favorites of Apollo as well as those of Mars, thus forming a perpetual competition in the vicinity of the temple.

As we advanced into the country we discovered a manor house whose form and structure indicated that it had seen several centuries; Zachiel took us to it. The manor house was occupied by an old officer who gave us a good welcome, but during supper he began giving us a account of the battles in which he had been involved, the duels in which he had been employed, the wounds he had received, the injustices that had been done to him in gratifying men far inferior to him, and a thousand other things just as uninteresting for strangers. That conversation bored Monime so much that she had the vapors. We took our leave of our host in order to depart at dawn the next day.

Zachiel took us in the empire of the Salians, where the fire of war was ignited everywhere. As we approached one of their cities we were obliged to pass through the middle of a camp. The officers, helmets on their heads and fully armored, were preparing to leave; the movement of the soldiers was already producing a cloud of dust that was rising into the air and the trumpets, fifes and drums were already sounding the march, when a courier arrived, bringing a countermand that stopped them.

Monime, observing their movements, seemed disconcerted at first by the sight of the blades of their bristling pikes and the brilliant gleam of weapons, which dazzled the eyes. Gripped by fear and dread, she begged the genius in a tremulous voice to take us to some other world, unable to bear the sight of those men, who seemed to be respiring nothing but death, blood and carnage.

"I see that you are still prey to unworthy weaknesses," said Zachiel, in a severe tone. "Ought you to dread anything while I'm accompanying you? Is this the fruit that I must expect from my care and my complaisance? Rid yourself of these vain terrors if you want to merit the gifts that I intend to make you."

Monime blushed; ashamed and confused by having attracted the reproaches of the genius, she dared not reply, and was constrained to follow Zachiel, who took us through the camp in order to enter the city, where we obtained a room in a lodging-house. We spent the reminder of the day resting, while listening to the instructions of the genius.

"These people are very different from the Marcians. Among the latter, morality, candor and good faith form the most solid foundations of their empire, and among the Salians those virtues have long been banished. You will see nothing in this realm but a tissue of false pretexts, vain arguments, frivolous complaints, crude and borrowed colors, muted and hidden intrigues, and artifices suggested by individuals interested in finding means to continue the war in order to enrich themselves at the expense of the people."

"I find the condition of humans very deplorable," I said, "especially when they take their own passions or those of others as guides for their conduct. If war is proposed, the soldier, dazzled by the lure of pillage, delivers himself to it with enthusiasm, and the citizens, seduced by the false pretext of conserving the fatherland and their liberty, seem to animate the troops; the officer, guided by another interest, encourages them, while he often runs to his own doom."

"It's true," said Zachiel, "that nothing is more persuasive for the persons one wants to rally to one's party than setting an example; that is an inclination attached to nature; it seems that humans are only made to imitate one another; an entire province observes what its neighbors do; the fire spreads, is communicated, and soon becomes a general conflagration. It is from those kinds of muted mines that one often sees an evil spring gush forth, and the politics of those who foment them often employs al the artifices that it has put to work until the blood of the troops is shed. This realm has furnished a terrible example, since the war they have undertaken too lightly is reducing the State to cruel extremes. Imbecility, ignorance, corruption and debasement are the dominant vices of the Salians, the usual source of the poverty and misery of peoples; judge, my dear Seaton, whether they are to be pitied."

The next day we were visited by several officers. Monime's surprise was extreme when, instead of seeing robust men with martial features she only saw young Adonises, powdered, primped and perhaps painted, for they had complexions as fine as that of a woman who spends three-quarters of the day in her toilette. Those plumed demigods with red heels and doubly-ruffed sleeves did not have the slightest scent of gunpowder; ambered from head to toe they perfumed Monime's whole apartment. Those darlings of the god Mars doubtless made their principal occupation imitating him in his amours, leaving the care of their glory to hazard or fortune. They only talked to us about the favors they had received from their beauties, the feasts with which they had been regaled, and those they still proposed to give in the city, and invited Monime and me to take part in them.

That debut gave me a very poor idea of the prudence and talents of those young officers. However, curious to instruct myself regarding a profession of which I only knew the theory, which I soon hoped to put into practice, in order not to neglect anything, I asked them numerous questions about their manner of combat and certain rules that I thought necessary.

First I asked them whether they had a thorough knowledge of the map of the country into which they were about to go, and the character of the people they were going to attack, because I thought that knowledge very useful to facilitate the passage of their troops, taking precautions against enemy ruses and avoiding falling into the traps that might be extended for them. I added that I also thought that a good officer ought to know engineering, fortification, cartography and mathematics, especially the parts concerning the military art.

"Not a word of all that," replied one of the gentlemen, pirouetting on tiptoe. "Among us, courage and valor substitute for everything."

"But sir, valor that is not accompanied by prudence and composure becomes an impetuous courage that looks at danger from afar and wants to be at grips at the time when it is necessary to camp. Thus, I regard that valor as a false bravery or a blustering courage, instead of which a great soul, a penetrating genius and an intrepid heart sees peril at close range without being frightened by it."

"It appears to me," said the young officer, "that the men of your country are very phlegmatic; it's necessary to hope that a little of our way of operating can contribute to banishing useless reflections from your mind." Those words were pronounced in the most jovial tone, accompanied by a bow that announced their departure.

Surprised to see so much ignorance in an officer entrusted with an important position, I asked Zachiel whether the other officers were not more learned.

"It is necessary not to be astonished by the vivacity of the Salians," said the genius, "any more than that of all the peoples who inhabit this world. As this planet is much closer to the sun than the others, the influences that dominate them communicate the fire and petulance that often leads them to act without giving themselves time to reflect."

We spent a few days in that city, where we saw the most frenetic license reigning; pleasures—fine food, gambling, spectacles, concerts, balls and amorous assignations—were the sole occupations of a the officers; their tables, always served with profusion, represented nothing less than the calamities of war, always onerous for peoples. During those pleasures and that dissipation, however, the wretched soldiers who were camped in the vicinity of the city were exercising a thousand disorders therein, because of the poor discipline observed there.

Monime and I were invited to a great supper and to a masked ball that would be given thereafter by the steward of the province. That man, whom fortune had extracted from the most mediocre estate to raise him to the highest degree of favor, had rendered himself hateful throughout the city by the airs of grandeur that he effected with regard to the nobility and the scorn he displayed for the richest burgers. The women, piqued by the scant regard that he had for them, complained of it to the officers of the garrison, who promised to avenge them

The plan was to dress a dozen soldiers as women, magnificently dressed, who were to harass the steward all night long. The masque favoring that disguise, they had no fear of being recognized. We were only told about the comedy they intended to play two hours after the ball began. The pretended goddesses had already surrounded the steward, and were preparing to play a thousand pranks on him when a confused noise was heard of whinnying horses, men and women uttering frightful screams, and troops filing the air with bellicose roars. The alert was immediately sounded and the call to arms issued; the enemy had mounted a surprise attack on the city, and had entered through a passage that had not been guarded.

Then, all the young officers, without appearing to be frightened by the danger or the dolor of their beauties, calmly left them in order to run to give orders and assemble their troops. In spite of all their vivacity, however, and even though they deployed considerable bravery, their efforts were futile. The city was taken and put to contribution, in spite of all the efforts of the inhabitants, who defended themselves with courage and intrepidity.

Zachiel, who had anticipated that disorder, came to our rescue; he got us out of the city in order to take us to another province. I could not imagine that those pretty faces, which had been admiring themselves in all the mirrors a few hours before, had had the courage to precipitate themselves at the enemy squadrons; that appeared to me to smack of enchantment.

"After having thought about that event," I said to Zachiel, "I find the conduct of those men very imprudent. Since the guard of the city had been confided to them, why did they neglect to fortify the places at which it might be attacked?"

"It's because the enlightenment of those men is very limited," said the genius. "The majority have only one marked point of view, beyond which they cannot extend their penetration. They are, so to speak, enclosed in the darkness of human politics, which makes them blind to everything presented to them. They arm themselves with specious pretexts to embellish good or bad arguments in order to find the means of engaging their allies by motives of ambition or chimerical concessions, with which they are not miserly, but the ruses they employ often rebound on them."

During the journey the genius instructed us as to the religions and mores of the Marsians.

"Their way of thinking is free," he told us. "All the great men of this world prefer what they imagine to what they have seen or learned; all their sentiments belong to them; they think that in matters of opinions one should always follow the mild-

233

est and most moderate, and those which tend to conciliate minds and maintain social repose.

"There is nothing more absurd, say their pretended philosophers, than to try to subjugate beings who ought necessarily to be happy, in order to oblige them to regulate the celestial spheres and combine all the events that happen on earth in order to make gods of them susceptible to hatred and vengeance, who allow themselves to be moved by tears and prayers, and who can be offended by our disorders even though several among them furnish more than one pernicious example themselves; ought we, after that, to regard them as veritable gods? We ought, therefore to believe that if the world is submissive to the power of true gods, it would be much better guided, and that everything would happen in a manner worthy of those wise and enlightened gods who governed it. As we see the contrary every day, that is evident proof that hazard alone presides over everything that happens here.

"In spite of sentiments so contrary to their religion, one sees them regularly in the temple of Pallas in the position of supplicants, offering the goddess prayers and incense. As they relate everything back to union, they recommend to all the citizens to lend themselves to public ceremonies and the acts of religion that their mythologies impose, even when they are not penetrated by them to the depths of the heart, since persons of intelligence can scarcely be convinced of the verity of all the fabulous translations presented to them; but because the people believe them, and whom it is dangerous to disabuse, since they serve to maintain peace and mildness among them, the great are obliged to put at least their external appearance in uniformity with that of their compatriots.

"The most reasonable among their philosophers are convinced that good and evil are only vain or chimerical things that opinion has introduced. Good is, according to them, that which really augments the power one has to act, and that which can pass for a greater perfection; evil is the contrary and is that which weakens the same power.

"What, then, can nature offer more convenient to these different views than to attach them to pleasure? Is that not what inclines the soul toward good with all the more force because good is much more desirable than evil? When humans abuse pleasure and run after it blindly without any moderation, those are their crimes. But is nature not sufficiently avenged for that abuse by the sharp pains engendered thereby and remorse even more terrible than the pains? In general, one of the greatest obligations of humans is to watch incessantly over the safety and conservation of their being; that is a concern nature has engraved in every heart, even though they are persuaded that their days are numbered and that nothing can change their destiny.

"This world is divided, like all the others, into different sects. Some put their confidence in idols that they fabricate themselves; others address their prayers to divinities that the foolish imagination of their ancient mythologies have fabricated in order to trick the good faith of people who cannot be cured of their prejudices; but all the nobles and the majority of their scholars recognize no other divinity than Nature, which they regard as the invisible soul of the world; they say that she has a supernatural virtue, which produces, arranges and conserves all the parts of the universe.

"Those scholars distinguish two wills in Nature, one of which they suppose to be good and the other evil. They believe that there is a kind of equilibrium that enables everything to be balanced and remain in an equal proportion, and that it is absurd to think that a bountiful being created the world and that, able to fill it with all kinds of perfections, he set out to do precisely the opposite. But argue with those false scholars, ask them what that Nature is, of which the term seems so vague, and they will reply to you that it is an active principle, an economical entity that regulates all things with so much art that good does not surpass evil; it is, they say, a superb divinity, full of ostentation, powerful, which tries above all to hide its secrets in order not to be discovered."

235

"So, according to their system," I said to Zachiel, "Nature, fate and hazard are all the same thing?"

"You will see here," the genius went on, "almost all the great lords cultivating the sciences; they have books of morality, philosophy and history, which they conserve without any change or alteration; the foolish love of novelty does not impassion them, and what distinguishes them from other worlds is that the same language has been spoken here since their creation. That kind of immobility of language enables them to understand their most ancient authors, who are often not very reliable, whereas on your earth one sees the language of a people change entirely in less than a century; one might think that others come to establish themselves on the ruins of those that disappear.

"Music is regarded, throughout the extent of the planet, as a universal remedy capable of curing the worst diseases of the body and even of the mind; and the officers who command their armies draw infallible and incessantly present assistance from it, lifting the soul by means of noble chords in order to fortify courage and virtue, to govern and guide the passions at their will, to excite them and appease them at need. That is why all their exercises are preceded by agreeable and loud music that seems, in some way, to dispose the soul and render it bolder; for as the sound of the music penetrates it, they are transported, if one might put it like that, by a divine fervor, and believe that the god of war is entering via their ears to animate them to combat and better enable them to obey.

"The men who are born on this planet feel its influences very keenly; they are all bellicose, and when they are not making war on one another they compensate themselves by making it on animals; furthermore, their manners are always simple, frank and uniform in their societies. They guard their speech religiously, because lies are severely punished here. An officer who has broken his word cannot avoid the scorn of the entire nation; he will be stripped of his rank, expelled from his corps and forced to seek to hide his shame and humiliation abroad."

IV.

We finally arrived in the realm of Bellonia, then governed by a tyrant named Tracius. That Prince, of a cruel and ambitious spirit, did not take pleasure in anything but blood and carnage. He was only occupied in seeking new ways of invading neighboring states and employing them to carry out the most unjust vexations there, while the legitimate sovereign, exiled, expelled from his kingdom, obliged to wander hither and yon in various states, groaned at the evils he saw overwhelming his people, especially those of which he anticipated that his unfortunate family would be the target.

Having arrived in the vicinity of the capital city, we were obliged to traverse a great plain strewn with dead and dying. One young woman whose sighs and sobs made the grief she was suffering manifest excited our pity and our interest in knowing her.

Monime, always full of zeal for the unfortunate, had our carriage stop and asked her what had occasioned the distress of which she was giving evidence.

"Alas, my Lady, you're doubtless unaware that a bloody battle took place on this plain yesterday. You see in me a spouse in despair, who bears in her womb the innocent fruit of a sacred union. Since daybreak I have been roaming this plain in vain; in vain I have visited all the bodies massacred by enemy fire; nothing has been offered to my frantic gaze, no hope has presented itself to my soul; disastrous fate has doubtless cut short my husband's days."

The young woman's tears redoubled. After having employed the consolations dictated by the generosity of her soul, Monime, touched by her distress, succeeded in calming her dolor somewhat. She invited her to take a seat in our carriage to return to the city, where we put her back in the hands of her family.

On the road we encountered a host of inhabitants who had come out in the hope of finding those who loss was exciting their groans.

There was an old man weighed down by the burden of his years; his organs, enfeebled by age, no longer permitting him to distinguish the objects surrounding him, he addressed himself to all those he encountered, asking them for news of his son.

"Alas," he said to one, his eyes bathed with tears, "the support of my old age has doubtless perished in the battle; I could not disarm or weaken his proud courage, but I lacked the strength to go with him and die beside him."

After those few words, suffocated by grief, his knees buckled and he was ready to fall, but, reanimating himself with a final effort, he approached the next stranger, and sighed as he gripped his arm. "Convey to my son," he said to him, "this last embrace; tell him never to forget an unfortunate father who only lived in him, and whom his absence has reduced to despair."

In other places, friends were searching urgently to procure some assistance for their friends. Elsewhere, young women could be seen running with great strides toward the plain, in the hope of encountering the young warriors who had promised them his faith.

When we reached the city, we learned the details of the battle, in which more than thirty thousand men had perished. To that bad news was added that of a complete rout of its navy. So many combined calamities spread consternation through all hearts. It seemed that such reverses ought to have corrected Tracius, or at least moderated his ambition, but in spite of those scourges, the tyrant could not resolve himself to abandon his foolish enterprises. Insensible to the calamities of the State, barbaric toward the people, he hid from them with a cruel concern the greater part of the disgraces that fortune had inflicted, and in spite of the number of troops already sacrificed in several deadly encounters, and the exhaustion of men and finances to which he was reduced, nothing could stop him.

An old officer whose acquaintance we had made assured us that for a long time, every step he had taken had always been stained with blood, obliged to go in search of the enemy in arid lands devastated by the number of troops who had already passed through it, who were accustomed to pillage because of the poor discipline maintains in the companies.

"To those difficulties can be added the misery of our soldiers, poorly paid, poorly dressed, poorly maintained and poorly assisted in their maladies by the fraudulent conduct of our entrepreneurs; that is what causes the defections in our armies; the majority of the soldiers, and even the officers, are going over to the enemy and increasing their numbers even further. All those malcontents then find themselves motivated by their own vengeance."

Dissatisfied with what we had been told, we left the city in order to continue our observations. As we advanced through the land, we encountered a multitude of poor peasants forced to follow a soldier what had just enlisted them, by surprise or by authority. Those wretches, in despair at quitting their cottages, even though most of the time they lacked the bare necessities of life, appeared to be in the utmost consternation.

I noticed one in particular who touched me sensibly; I approached him in order to ask him what reason he had to be so afflicted by following a métier that would at least provide him with the means of subsistence.

"Alas, sir," the young man replied, sobbing, "the excess of my despair will not surprise you when you know that I was snatched from the arms of a mother charged with eight children, of whom the oldest that remains is barely ten years old. In the eighteen months since I lost my father, I have at last been able to allow them to subsist by my hard labor; what completes my woes in that in taking me away from my family they have been deprived of all help, and I can assure you that very little can be expected from me in a métier that I do not know and for which I have no appetite—because, sir, I do not even know how to load a rifle, the sight of a sword causes me to treble and almost too faint. All my comrades are no braver than me; judge from that what troops can be opposed to enemies long accustomed to vanquish."

I left the young soldier after giving him all the money I had on me.

"It appears to me," said Monime, "that that troop of soldiers has no ambition to obtain a place in the Temple of Glory. I'd rather confront the enemy with a cardboard army, like those employed in our theaters."

"Which is to say," said Zachiel, smiling, "that you're comparing the Marsians to swarms of flies that one can frighten by presenting them with grotesque figures. But do you know that the Marsians are the most prudent men on this planet, the most judicious and he most intrepid in case of danger. Such are, my dear Monime, the enemies of the Bellonians. It is to their army that I am taking Seaton; it is there that I want him to serve his apprenticeship in the métier of war, under Prince Aricdef, who is the general commanding the army sent to combat that of Tracius. I presume, given the elevation of your sentiment, that you will not raise any objection to the design that I've conceived in order to enable Seaton to profit from this voyages."

Far from opposing the views of the genius, Monime, who only intended to render me worthy of one day occupying the rank destined for me, appeared, on the contrary to be charmed by the opportunity that was offered to me to distinguish myself by some action that would merit Zachiel's approval.

During our journey I could not help sighing at the thought that I was going to be separated from Monime.

"Why that expression of sadness?" asked the genius. "Are you insensible to the pleasure that a great heart ought to feel when it's a matter of acquiring glory?"

"Pardon the sigh," I said. "It does not come from a pusillanimous heart that fears danger, but may I give nothing to the dolor of being separated from you and Monime?"

"I dare not tell you that I am sensible to that separation," said Monime with tears in her eyes, "since it is necessary to your advancement."

"Calm yourselves, both of you," said Zachiel. "The separation will not be long; it's necessary, my dear Seaton, to show more strength and accustom yourself gradually to my absence; you will not always have me. I am only taking you into the midst of dangers in order to teach you not to be prodigal in shedding blood. Heaven has given birth to you in order to command one day, so remember that a good general ought to be model of all his officers; it is his example that animates the army. You will learn under Prince Aricdef to merit the title of a great captain.

"Remember, my son, that valor is perhaps only a virtue when it is regulated by prudence and moderation., without which it is merely an insensate scorn for life or a brutal ardor that only leads to doom. A man who cannot retain his self-possession in danger is more reckless than brave, because it seems that he needs in order to be animated to put himself beyond the dread that he cannot overcome by the natural situation of his heart.

"Know that by delivering oneself recklessly to dangers, one can trouble the order and discipline of troops; by giving an example of temerity, one often exposes an entire army to great misfortunes; so refrain, my dear Seaton, from seeking glory with too much impatience; the true means of finding it is to wait tranquilly for favorable opportunities. Remember, too, not to attract the envy of anyone; do not be jealous of the success of others, never seek to diminish its value; on the contrary, be the first to give praise to those who merit it.

"Consult the oldest captains; ask the most skilful to instruct you; show them meekness and docility in listening to their advice. It is necessary nevertheless to be on your guard, to convince yourself that even the most enlightened cannot see everything, and that the wisest often make gave mistakes when they only follow their impulses or their prejudices. Above all, avoid revealing yourself to certain flatterers who take pleasure in sowing division among the officers in order indispose the chiefs and profit from the disorder they create."

I listened avidly to these lessons from the genius, which seemed to pass into my soul like a stream of pure fresh water that one sees flowing between flowers. My tender Monime also appeared to me to be penetrated by the keenest gratitude. Until then I had only filled my memory with great names and great events, without giving myself the time to make any judicious reflection. That conversation—or, to put it better, the instructions of the genius—gave birth within me to an ardent desire to take as a model of my conduct the actions of illustrious men, to profit from their virtues and to avoid falling into their vices.

On arriving among the Marsians, we learned that their general was to leave the following day in order to put himself at the head of his troops. Without losing any time, the genius introduced me that same day to the Prince, who received me with marks of generosity that immediately attached me to him. He promised Zachiel to watch over my conduct, and to take care of my advancement. In order to begin giving me immediate proof of his benevolence he ordered that an apartment should be prepared for me to spend the night in his house, in order that I would be able to leave with him.

The genius left me after giving me a few more items of advice, and the strongest assurances that he would not abandon Monime—which tranquilized me considerably.

The sun had risen and was already gilding the summits of the mountains when Prince Aricdef departed to rejoin the army. I was by his side in the capacity of an aide-de-camp. When we reached the rendezvous, the Prince gave orders for the encampment. I had the advantage of being employed on several occasions that attracted praise on his part, and procured me his confidence and amity. I had the good fortune to accompany him into various actions in which the Prince gave evidence of his intrepidity and the invincible courage that never abandoned him.

I could not weary of admiring the advantageous situations that he was always able to chose for the encampment of his troops, either because of the forage or the necessities of fighting. I also admired the order and discipline that reigned in his camp, the intelligence and impenetrable secrecy necessary to the success of an enterprise, the care that he took in visiting his camp personally, the attention he paid to the least of the soldiers, in order that anything that could be useful to them, either for clothing or for nourishment, would not be lacking, and, finally, the obedience that they showed to the slightest indication of his will.

That first campaign had nothing remarkable except the capture of a few places that we took from the Bellonians. The Prince distributed his winter quarters and we went back to the capital city with a young officer who had acquired a considerable reputation among the troops. His modesty, his candor and the purity of his morals, rare qualities in a young man, had attracted all my esteem and confidence. We were soon linked by an intimate amity; I invited him to spend his winter quarters with me. I introduced him to Zachiel and Monime, who both appeared to confirm the choice I had made by the eulogies that they gave him. It is true that it seemed that he carried with him a charm that drew all hearts in his favor.

Out walking one day with that amiable chevalier, after a few vague remarks, I said: "How fortunate you are to have commenced so young a métier that has so often procured you opportunities to distinguish yourself."

"It's true," said the other, "that I entered the service very early, but my dear Milord, what do you expect a man of condition to do whom of fortune has, if I might put it like that, adopted the task of humiliating in the most sensitive places? The next campaign promises us a decisive battle; if I can only have the opportunity to acquire some glory therein! But what am I saying? Is it for me, alas, to dare to flatter myself? No, however things turn out, I shall retire after that action, and no longer think about anything but trying to procure a repose for which I've been searching in vain for a long time; for it's necessary to agree, my dear, that unless one has a great employment in the army, it's a métier that's scarcely attractive to those who can do without it. I can only regard it as a resource

243

for poor gentlemen who have neither enough wealth nor enough authority to be considered, and the majority of whom don't know how to occupy themselves. It's assuredly the most honest profession that a man of condition can chose; I like it a great deal, and if it weren't for the annoyances I encounter at every step I'd have difficulty quitting it; pressing motives would already have forced me to make a different decision, if a secret penchant hadn't drawn me into Aricdef's army."

"You haven't always been with the Marsians?"

"No," said the chevalier, "I only arrived a short time before you did. I began serving with the Salians, but their service involved so many annoying things; one depends there on so many interested and ignorant people, incessantly the butt of brutes who are mostly scoundrels, debauchees, gamblers or drunks, that it became insupportable to me. In sum, those who have morals pass among them for pedants. Nothing compensates for the loss of one's wealth or repose. The injustices of the illicit favors are a more sensible aggravation. Among them, merit, great talent, prudence and valor count for nothing; all the positions are bought for money or by vile obligations—which means that in spite of the number of their troops and the superiority of their forces, it's often easy to defeat them, by virtue of the ignorance of their officers, who don't have enough prudence to be able to take full advantage of their strength. In any case, the alliance they've made with the Bellonians determined me entirely to go into the service of the Marsians.

"Don't believe, because of that, my dear Milord," the chevalier went on, "that the ambition or the desire to obtain a considerable post from the Prince attracted me to his army; I wasn't led there by any of those views, but only that of numbing myself to the misfortunes that had overwhelmed me. Yes, my dear, I want to try to vanquish the fortune that is the enemy of my happiness and my repose, which, in robbing me of the honors in which I was born, has been unable to change my heart. Powerful reasons don't permit me to tell you any more at present; let it suffice for you to know that it's neither the dangers nor the fatigues of war that have taken away my taste for it. I'm a man of sound constitution; I get by easily on very little; but I dread dependency and would greatly prefer death to renouncing my liberty."

"I feel sorry for you, my dear sir, and dare not enquire as to the reasons that occasion your distaste for military service; however, I find that war, in spite of the aggravations you've just represented, has many advantages that ought to counterbalance them; all the vices that you believe to be inseparably attached to it, are not innate, since there are laws that punish them severely, and you'll agree that the Prince who commands us is not stained by the vices that you say are commonplace in the officers at the head of the armies of the Salians and the Bellonians.

"What idea ought we to have of Prince Aricdef? Without pausing at that which only ought to dazzle vulgar minds, you can't disagree that one can't help admiring in him the true virtues that form heroes. It's not his invincible courage that charms me, not his scorn for death and danger that I admire; it's his presence of mind, that intrepidity, that coolness in the disorder of the most furious combats, the indefatigable activity that is the true character of a conqueror; the unexpected rapidity with which he falls on the enemy army and carries off a signal victory when he's believed to be dead or cut off in a gorge, or his entire army seems defeated.

"We've both witnessed in the last campaign that with a handful of men he rendered all the strength of the Salians futile and took from the Bellonians several well-fortified places. In sum, he has always denied his enemies the means to attack him. One can therefore say that it's by virtue of his talents and rare qualities that he has acquired the love and confidence of his troops. It's certain that the soldier who loves and can count on his general is invincible; instead of which, those who are commanded by cowardly courtiers that they cannot hold in high esteem, allow themselves to be defeated easily. It's only necessary to wait for the opportunity of some court intrigue, which sows division among their troops; then, when one has good spies that keep you informed, one can take advantage of their dysfunction. I've heard it said that Prince Aricdef never lets one of those advantages escape.

"One can also add to all his qualities his incorruptible probity, his love of justice, his liberality, his clemency, his inviolable attachment to his work, his good faith, his mild and amiable manners, his attention for the officers and his generosity to the soldiers. One cannot, therefore, without injustice refuse him the titles of great warrior, redoubtable captain, good politician and sage philosopher, since he's an honest and honest man and loyal to his friends. We see that he even cultivates with care those who are beneath him."

"I confess," said the chevalier, "that all these qualities are Aricdef's prerogatives, that he justly merits the praise and admiration of all men; the renown that has published them all over the world gave birth in me to the desire to come and participate in his glory; without that desire, my dear Milord, perhaps I would never have had the advantage of knowing you."

A sigh accompanied those last words, which, combined with those that had preceded it, appeared to me to enclose an impenetrable mystery. I dared not ask the chevalier the reason for it. Remarking a good deal of trouble and agitation in his eyes, I was anxious; in order to distract him from his melancholy I proposed that we should go to see Monime.

We were staying in the same house, and the chevalier rarely spent a day without seeing Monime; I even believed that I could perceive the pleasure he felt in her company, given the urgency that he showed to be near her. Monime also showed him a distinguished complaisance, which was only in accord with his true merit. The chevalier's character, mild without being insipid, attentive without any baseness, was combined with all the gifts he had received from nature and those that depended on a noble education; he possessed all sorts of talents, but he was naturally borne to melancholy. Zachiel, who was doubtless able to penetrate the reasons for his sadness, attempted, out of condescension for the chevalier and Monime, to give birth every day to new opportunities for amusement and dissipation.

We were scarcely approaching the welcome return of the season of flowers when Prince Aricdef was already preparing to reassemble his troops. I was ordered to join him near a frontier city belonging to the Bellonians, to which he intended to lay siege.

Engineers are surveying all the surroundings, drawing up plans; trenches are being dug and covered ways formed, and the Prince, always active, is supervising the work. He sees defects, he corrects them, doing everything that is to his advantage, following them and animating them in their labor, pressing the siege of the city with ardor, animating all his troops by distributing liquor to them, which he sometimes drinks with them, with the familiar air that, better than speeches and recompenses, often passes into the soldier's soul the noble ardor that animates the hero, who seems to be rendering himself their companion.

The enemy was unable to hold out against the valor and vigilance of Aricdef; the city was taken and he entered it in triumph at the head of his troops, received the oath of fidelity from the burgers, fortified the place, and, after having reestablished abundance and tranquility there, we emerged therefrom to follow the Prince, who went to take possession of an advantageous position in order to observe the enemy.

Surprised not to see the chevalier arrive, I began to fear that the secret chagrin I had remarked in him might have constrained him to withdraw. I was preparing to write to him when I received a letter from Monime which told me that he had been retained by a bad fever. Anxiety about my friend's illness, combined with the urgency I felt to see Monime, caused me to ask for a week's leave. I had difficulty obtaining it, at the commencement of a campaign in which our army, already victorious, was only waiting for a movement on the enemy's part to direct its march, pursue it or disrupt its projects, but I could not refuse myself the pleasure of seeing Monime again.

Her eyes, I said to myself, *will animate my courage; a word from her adorable mouth will fortify my virtue; Zachiel, by his sage advice, will contribute to enabling me to acquire glory; perhaps, too, I shall bring back the chevalier, who, I feel sure, is burning with desire to find a decisive action.*

I obtained relay horses, which I sent forth, and then presented myself to the Prince in order to receive his orders.

"I've just learned," he told me, "that the Bellonians are advancing, with the intention of forcing us back to our retrenchments. My duty is to anticipate them, and I presume that the battle will be bloody, so I believe there's no need to recommend you not to let any opportunity escape to signal your courage. I permit you to go where your affairs summon you, provided that you return by the time we set forth, in order to fulfill the duties of your employment."

After leaving the Prince I climbed into my chaise and traveled all night, in order to bring forward the moments of happiness that I anticipated. What sweeter charm is there in the world than that of the union of hearts?

Oh, dear Monime, you combine virtue and innocence with amity; no dread or shame troubles your felicity. I am sure of being loved without division by a sister, the most perfect of all women.

Those reflections enabled me to enjoy in advance the pleasure of surprising her.

I finally arrived at ten o'clock in the morning. I flew to Monime's apartment, where I thought I had been petrified. Great God, what do I see? The chevalier in her arms; she is holding him tightly, and seems to be reassuring him with regard to ill-founded dreads. She kisses him; I believe I can see their sighs confounded.

"Oh, perfidy!" I cry. "By what charm have you been able to seduce her? Your blood will wash away the shame I feel."

Those words, pronounced with vehemence, cause them to turn their heads. Surprised to see me, they both blush; I want to flee; the chevalier stops me without being able to pronounce a single word. Monime, trembling and bewildered, falls unconscious.

"I perceive only too well," I said to the chevalier, pushing him away with eyes full of the anger that is animating me, "by the disorder and trouble I am causing, that you have completed your treasons."

"No, my dear Milord," said the chevalier, in an emotional voice that was almost extinct. "In spite of appearances, refrain from daring to suspect two people who are equally attached to you. I shall leave instantly, and will tell you at the camp everything that is the cause of your surprise today. I shall wait for you there to give you the satisfactions you demand. Begin by helping Monime."

Zachiel, who appeared at that moment, followed by one of Monime's maids, extracted me with a single word from the new anxieties that that speech had just plunged me.

"No, my Lady," he said, stopping the chevalier, "you shall not leave. It's no longer in the danger of combats that you ought to seek glory; you've disguised yourself for too long; it's necessary to resume the clothing appropriate to your sex. Follow my advice and allow Zerbine to accompany you into this dressing room."

"Oh, my dear Zachiel," I exclaimed, "with what concerns are you occupying yourself? Alas, Monime is dying."

The genius went to her and made her swallow a spoonful of universal elixir. I was at her feet; I held one of her hands, which I moistened with my tears. She finally opened her eyes; her first gaze was for me; it was tender; its languor passed into my soul. I felt annihilated by the reproaches that she seemed to be making for my outburst.

"Is it really true, my Lord," said Monime, in a voice that was still ill-assured, "that you were able to suspect me? Alas, my heart is not yet known to you? But where is the Princess? She is the one who must justify me."

"You have no need of her, my adorable Monime; a single word from Zachiel has done that. But who will justify me to you for my unjust suspicions? Will you pardon me for an initial impulse of which I was not the master? It is honor that was responsible or my crime; that is what will judge me."

"Well," said Monime, "get up, amity pardons you."

"Oh, that admission restores calm to my soul," I said, kissing the hand that I had not released, delightedly.

"I agree," Monime went on, "that appearances must have alarmed you, not being disabused as to the sex of the pretended chevalier, whom you have always regarded s a man; so can I not support the idea of the suspicions that I perceive the situation in which you found us presented to our mind?"

We were interrupted by Princess Marsine, who came back in after having put on garments appropriate to her sex.

"You're doubtless surprised, Milord, only to rediscover in me an unfortunate woman, from whom fate has stolen everything. You have seen me fight in several encounters with some considerable advantage, which have attracted your esteem and amity to me. Do not reproach me for not having accorded you all my confidence at first; I know that you merit every regard, not only by your virtues but also by the thousand services that I have received from you on various occasions; be persuaded that I have always distinguished you from all the other officers. Had I told you about my birth and sex, however, it would have been necessary to explain my misfortunes to you, in order to justify in some measure the disguise that the austere wisdom that you profess might perhaps have disapproved. Besides which, I had promised myself never to reveal my secret to anyone.

"When the Prince's orders recalled you to him I was counting on joining you soon; stopped by a bad fever, I could not carry out my project. I owe the reestablishment of my health to the charming Monime; her kindness, her care and assiduous attentions, and that charm which enables the union of souls, finally extracted from me that which I believed was in my interest to bury eternally in a profound silence. She has repaid my confidence with a sincere attachment and the confession of the sentiments of esteem that link you to one another.

"Dispense me, Milord, from telling you the story of my adventures; I have hidden nothing from the beautiful Monime; I permit her to make you party to my secrets; the interest she has taken in my misfortunes, and the graces she puts into everything she says, will render them more touching, so I dare flatter myself that her account will reestablish me in your opinion."

Princess Marsine left without waiting for my response, leaving me at liberty to talk to Monime. After we had said all the most tender things that our two truly touched hearts could imagine, I begged her to acquaint me with the reasons that had engaged Marsine to maintain her disguise for such a long time.

This chapter would not be complete without a mention of editor-publisher Charles-Georges-Thomas Garnier, who in 1787 launched a 36-volume specialized collection—perhaps the first dedicated imprint ever—entitled *Voyages Imaginaires, Songes, Visions et Romans Cabalistiques* [Imaginary Journeys, Dreams, Visions and Occult Novels]. During the two years of its existence, *Voyages Imaginaires* reprinted and popularized works by French authors such as Cyrano de Bergerac, Chevalier Mouhy, Gabriel de Foigny, Denis Veiras, Voltaire, Louis-Sébastien Mercier, Jacques Cazotte, etc.

FAIRY TALES

Baroque (whether in forms of novels, theater or even operas) was the link between the *Merveilleux* of the Renaissance and the more formalized *Contes de Fées*, or *Féeries*, of the Enlightenment period. The undeniable popularity of the genre was, in great part, attributable to the fact that *Féeries* were safe; they did not imperil the soul—a serious concern for a nation which had just come out of an era of great religious persecution—and they appropriately reflected the grandeur of the Sun King's reign.

The precursor in the genre was Marie-Catherine Le Jumel de Barneville, Baroness d'Aulnoy (a.k.a. Madame d'Aulnoy) (1651-1705) who, in 1690, introduced in her rambling novel *Histoire d'Hyppolite, Comte de Douglas* [Story of Hippolyte, Count of Douglas] a fairy tale entitled *L'Île de la Félicité* [The Island of Happiness].

D'Aulnoy was born in Barneville-la-Bertran, Calvados, as a member of the noble family of Le Jumel de Barneville. In 1666, at the age of fifteen, she was given in an arranged marriage to a Parisian thirty years older—François de la Motte, Baron d'Aulnoy, of the household of the duc de Vendôme. The baron was a freethinker and a known gambler. Over the next three years, the couple had three children. In 1669, the Baron d'Aulnoy was accused of treason, but the accusations, in which Mme d'Aulnoy appeared to be involved, proved to be false, and two men implicated in the accusation were executed. Mme d'Aulnoy had three more children and discontinued involvement in the Paris social scene for twenty years. During this period, she later said that she had traveled to Spain, with her mother, who remained in Madrid, and England (the latter voyage cannot be confirmed). Much of this time, however, was also spent writing stories inspired by these destinations; these stories later became her most popular works.

Madame d'Aulnoy was again a permanent resident of Paris by 1690, where her salon was frequented by leading aristocrats and princes, including her close friend, Saint-Evremond. Over the next thirteen years she published twelve books, including three pseudo-memoirs, two fairy tale collections and three historical novels. Gaining a reputation as a historian and recorder of tales from outside France, and elected as a member of Paduan Accademia dei Ricovatri, she was called by the name of the muse of history, Clio. However, at this time the idea of history was a much looser term, which included her fictional accounts. In 150 years, the more strictly documented form of the term led to her accounts being declared fraudulent. However, in France and England at the time her works were considered as mere entertainment, a sentiment reflected in the reviews of the period. Her truly accurate attempts at historical accounts telling of the Dutch wars of Louis XIV were less successful.

Her most popular works were her fairy tales and adventure stories as told in *Les Contes des Fees* [Tales of fairies],[96] (1697) and *Contes Nouveaux, ou Les Fées à la Mode* (1698). Unlike the folk tales of the Grimm Brothers, who were born some 135 years later than d'Aulnoy, she told her stories in a more conversational style, as they might be told in salons. These stories were far from suitable for children and many English adaptations are very dissimilar to the original. Madame d'Aulnoy deliberately reconfigured folk tales with a modern spirit of irony and satire, and sometimes with sophisticated eroticism, as well as adapting them for the purpose of "civilizing" children. Eclectic in her plundering of sources, while proudly advertising her willingness to draw on humble

---

[96] The title of Madame d'Aulnoy's collection was translated into English as "fairy tales," thus foisting that label on an entire genre, most of whose included stories do not, in fact, feature "fairies."

folk tales, she was also happy to draw, alternatively or simultaneously, on the more venerable resources of legends and myths.

It was also in 1697 that the true genius of the *Féerie* appeared. Charles Perrault (1628-1703), until then a renowned literary figure, a man who was a champion of science, the author of a decisive article in the so-called "Quarrel of the Ancients and Moderns"—on the side of the latter—released under his son's name[97] *Histoires ou Contes du Temps Passé* [Histories or Tales of Past Times] a.k.a. *Contes de ma Mère l'Oie* [Tales of Mother Goose]. In it, Perrault had carefully collected a number of popular folk tales and legends, such as *Cinderella, Sleeping Beauty, Donkey Skin, Little Red Riding Hood, Blue Beard, Puss in Boots,* etc. The book proved incredibly successful and immediately spawned many imitators. However, it was worth noting that, unlike some of these, Perrault had not softened or prettified his fairy tales. His yarns preserved the cruelty, some would say savagery, and goriness of the original medieval tales. In his stories, sorcery was still very real. A number of his literary successors, on the other hand, chose to emphasize nicer sentiments and tinseltown-like magic.

Unlike Perrault, Madame d'Aulnoy used her tales for satirical purposes, deliberately aiming them at a more adult readership. As a result, her tales were a little more complex and sophisticated, and perhaps unfairly, did not survive the test of time as well. Her best-remembered stories are *L'Oiseau Bleu* [The Blue Bird], which introduced one of the very first "Prince Charmings" in the world of fairy tales, and the lesser-known *Le Nain Jaune* [The Yellow Dwarf], which spawned a popular board-and-card game.

Together, Perrault and Madame d'Aulnoy virtually defined the first boundaries of modern fantasy. After them, magicians, ogres, dragons, dwarves and fairies were definitely integrated into the realms of fantasy.

---

[97] Pierre Perrault Darmancourt (1678-1700), also a folklorist.

Madame d'Aulnoy: *The Yellow Dwarf*
(1698)[98]

There was once a queen who had lost all her children except one daughter, who was all the world to her. But, being a
widow, and loving the young princess as the dearest thing on
earth, she was so fearful of losing her that she never corrected
her faults. Thus the maiden, whose beauty was extraordinary
and divine rather than mortal, and who was destined to wear a
crown one day, became so headstrong and so vain of her bud-
ding charms that she looked down on everybody.

Her mother, by her caresses and indulgence, encouraged
her in the belief that there was nobody worthy of her. She was
nearly always dressed as Pallas or Diana, attended by the
greatest ladies of the court attired as nymphs. And, to put the
finishing stroke to her vanity, the queen called her
Toutebelle,[99] and having had her picture painted by the most
skilled artists, sent it to several kings with whom she kept up a
close friendship. When they gazed on the picture, not one of
them was proof against the irresistible power of her charms.
Some fell ill, others went out of their mind, and the more fortunate who reached her side in good health, no sooner set eyes
on her than they became her slaves.

Never was there such gallantry and courtesy at any court.
Twenty kings vied with each other to please her; and, after
spending three and four hundred millions on a single fête, they
thought themselves only too well recompensed if they ob-

---

[98] *Le Nain Jaune*, excerpted from *Contes nouveaux ou Les
Fées à la mode* by Madame d'Aulnoy, translated into English
in 1889 by Andrew Lang, introduced and annotated by Jean-
Marc Lofficier.
[99] All beautiful.

tained from her a word, such as "How pretty!" Their adoration delighted the queen. Not a day passed but there came to her court seven or eight thousand sonnets, and as many elegies, madrigals, and songs, sent by all the poets of the universe. Toutebelle was the one and only subject of the prose and verse of the authors of the time. Yet these poems served for nothing but lighting bonfires, and they sparkled and burned better than any kind of fuel.

The princess was fifteen years old, but no one dared aspire to the honor of becoming her husband; and yet there was no one who did not desire to be the happy man. But how were they to touch a heart like hers? They would have thought little of being hanged five or six times a-day just to please her, but she would have regarded it as a mere trifle. Her lovers murmured loudly against her cruelty, and the queen, who wished her to marry, did not know how to persuade her to make up her mind.

"Will you not," she used sometimes to say, "lay aside a little of the intolerable pride that causes you to look with contempt on all the kings who come to our court? I want you to marry one of them. You have no desire to please me."

"I am so happy," replied Toutebelle. "Allow me, madam, to remain as I am, calm and indifferent. If I once lost my peace of mind you would be sorry."

"Yes," replied the queen; "I should be sorry if you loved someone beneath you; but consider those who ask you, and learn that nowhere are others to be found like them."

That was true; but the princess's idea of her own merits was such that she thought herself worth something better still; and by degrees her obstinacy in remaining single began deeply to grieve her mother, who repented, but too late, of having been so indulgent.

Uncertain what she ought to do, she determined to go all by herself to see a celebrated fairy called the Fairy of the Desert. But it was no easy matter to get at her, for she was guarded by lions. The queen would have found it impossible had she not long since learnt that you had to throw them a cake made of millet seed, sugar candy, and crocodiles' eggs. She kneaded the cake herself, and put it in a little basket which she carried on her arm. Unaccustomed to so much walking, she became tired, and lay down at the foot of a tree to take some rest. Before she was aware of it she had fallen asleep, and on awaking found that the cake was no longer in the basket; and, to complete her misfortune, she heard the lions approaching. They had scented her, and were making a great noise.

"Alas!" she cried, sorrowfully, "what will become of me? I shall be eaten up."

She wept, and, having no strength to run away, remained by the tree where she had slept. At the same time she heard a sound like "Chet! Chet! Hem! Hem!" Raising her eyes, she looked all round her, and saw on the tree a little man no bigger than your arm, eating oranges.

"Oh! queen," he said to her, "I know you well, and I know the fright you are in lest the lions should eat you up; and you have every reason to be afraid, for they have eaten many others. To add to your misfortune, you have no cake."

"I must make up my mind to die," said the queen, sighing. "Alas, I should be less distressed if my dear daughter were married!"

"What? You have a daughter!" cried the yellow dwarf, who was so called from the color of his complexion and the orange tree in which he lived. "Truly, I rejoice, for I have been seeking a wife over sea and land. Come now, if you promise to give her to me I will undertake to protect you from lions, tigers, and bears."

The queen looked at him, and was scarcely less afraid of his hideous little face than of the lions. She seemed to be pondering, and she answered not a word.

"What! You hesitate, madam?" he cried. "Then you do not care much for your life?"

At the same moment the queen saw the lions on the top of a hill running towards her. They had each two heads, eight feet, four rows of teeth, and their skin was as hard as shell, and as red as morocco leather. At that sight the poor queen, more fearful than a dove at the sight of a kite, exclaimed with all her might:

"Sir Dwarf! Toutebelle is yours".

"Oh!" he said, with a contemptuous air, "Toutebelle is too beautiful; I don't want her; keep her."

"Ah, sir," continued the distressed queen, "do not refuse her. She is the most charming princess in the world."

"Well," he replied, "I will take her out of charity; but remember the gift you make me."

The orange tree immediately opened; the queen rushed headlong inside. It closed again, and the lions caught nothing. The queen was so upset that she did not notice a door which had been contrived in this tree. At last, she saw it, and opened it. It looked on a field of nettles and thistles, and was surrounded by a muddy ditch, while a little further off was a low thatched hut, out of which came the yellow dwarf with a sprightly air. He wore wooden shoes and a yellow frieze jacket. He had no hair on his head, big ears, and looked a perfect little villain.

"I am delighted, mother-in-law," he said to the queen, "for you to see the little castle in which your Toutebelle will live with me. With the nettles and thistles she can feed an ass to ride on. Under this rustic roof she will be protected from stress of weather. She will drink of this water and feed on the fat frogs that live in it; and then she will have me beside her day and night, handsome, lively, and gallant as you see me; for I should be sorry if her shadow were a closer companion to her than I."

The unhappy queen, suddenly realizing the miserable existence the dwarf promised her beloved daughter, and unable to endure so terrible a thought, fell prostrate on the floor, unconscious and without strength enough to utter a single word. While in this condition, she was put to bed with the greatest care, and in the finest night-cap, trimmed with the prettiest ribbon knots she had ever worn in her life.

The queen, when she awoke, remembered what had happened, but she thought it must have been a delusion, for, finding herself in her palace in the midst of her ladies with her daughter by her side, there seemed no evidence of her having been in the desert, of her having encountered such great danger, nor of the dwarf having saved her on the hard condition of Toutebelle's hand in marriage. And yet this night-cap of valuable lace and the knot of ribbons were quite as surprising as the dream she thought she had dreamt. These things preyed on her mind to such an extent that she could scarcely speak, eat, or sleep for the extraordinary melancholy that took possession of her.

The princess, who loved her with all her heart, was exceedingly uneasy, and entreated her over and over again to tell her what was the matter. But the queen would put her off by telling her sometimes that it was caused by her bad health, sometimes that one of her neighbors was threatening her with a great war.

Toutebelle saw that these replies were plausible enough, but that there was something more behind which the queen was trying to hide from her. Unable to endure her anxiety any longer, she determined to seek the celebrated Fairy of the Desert, whose wisdom was known far and wide. She was also desirous of asking her advice as to whether she should remain single or marry; for everybody was strongly urging her to choose a husband. She took care to knead with her own hands the cake which was to appease the fury of the lions; and, pretending to go to bed early in the evening, she went out by a little secret stair-case, her face covered with a long white veil that reached to her feet; and thus, alone, she took her way towards the grotto where the wise fairy lived.

But reaching the fateful orange tree, of which I have already spoken, she saw that it was full of fruit and flowers, and was seized with a longing to pluck some. Placing her basket on the ground, she gathered and ate a few oranges. But when she wished to pick up her basket and her cake it was no longer there. As she stood there uneasy and unhappy at her loss, she suddenly saw in front of her the hideous little dwarf I mentioned before.

"What is the matter with you, my fine maiden? Why do you weep?" said he.

"Alas! Who would not weep?" she replied. "I've lost my basket and my cake, and I can never reach the Fairy of the Desert safely without them."

"Well, and what do you want with her, pretty maid?" said the ugly little man. "I am her relative, her friend, and, to say the least, as clever as she is."

"The queen, my mother," replied the princess, "has for some time been so terribly melancholy that I fear for her life. I cannot help thinking that I am perhaps the cause, for she wants me to marry. I confess to you that as yet I have found no one worthy of me. All these reasons make me desirous of speaking with the fairy."

"Don't take the trouble, princess," said the dwarf; "I am better able than she to explain these matters to you. The queen is in trouble because she has promised you in marriage."

"The queen has promised me!" she said, interrupting him. "Ah, doubtless you are mistaken; she would have told me, and I have too much interest in the matter for her to have pledged me without my consent."

"Beautiful princess," said the dwarf, suddenly falling on his knees, "I flatter myself that this choice will not be displeasing to you when I tell you that it is I who am destined to such happiness."

"My mother wishes you to be her son-in-law!" exclaimed Toutebelle, falling back a step or two; "was ever any one so mad as you?"

"I care very little for the honor," said the dwarf, testily. "Here come the lions. In three bites they will avenge me for your unjust contempt."

At the same moment the princess heard them coming with loud roars.

"What is to become of me?" she exclaimed. "Am I thus to end my fair days?"

The wicked dwarf looked at her, and smiled contemptuously.

"You will at least have the satisfaction of dying unmarried," said he, "and of not allying your shining merit with a miserable dwarf like myself."

"Do not be angry, I beg of you," said the princess, clasping her beautiful hands. "I would rather marry all the dwarfs in the world than perish in this frightful way."

"Look at me well, princess, before pledging your word," he replied, "for I have no desire to entrap you."

"I have looked at you enough and to spare. The lions are on me; my terror grows. Save me! Save me! Or I shall die of fear."

Indeed, scarcely had she uttered these words before she swooned; and, without knowing how, she found herself in her own bed in the most beautiful night gown trimmed with the prettiest ribbons, and a little ring made of a single red hair which clung so closely that it would have been easier to have torn off her skin than to have removed the ring from her finger.

When the princess saw these things and remembered what had happened in the night, she fell into a melancholy that surprised and alarmed the whole court. The queen was the most distressed of all, and asked her hundreds and hundreds of times what was the matter. But she persisted in concealing her adventure.

At length the estates of the realm, impatient to see their princess married, after holding a council, came to the queen begging her to choose a husband. She said that was exactly what she wished to do, but that her daughter showed so much repugnance that she advised them to go and talk to her themselves. They did so without delay. Since her adventure with the yellow dwarf, Toutebelle's pride had been greatly humbled, and she could conceive no better way of getting out of the difficulty than by marrying some great king, with whom the ugly little man would be in no position to dispute so glorious a prize. Thus she replied more favorably than could have been expected, that, although she should have considered herself happy in remaining single all her life, she consented to marry the King of the Gold Mines. He was a powerful, handsome prince, who had loved her with the utmost passion for some years, and who, so far, had had no reason to flatter himself that his love was returned.

When he learned the delightful news his supreme joy can be easily imagined, arid also the rage of all his rivals at losing forever the hope that fed their passion. But Toutebelle could not marry twenty kings; it had given her trouble enough to choose one, for her vanity did not fail her, and she was entirely persuaded that no one in the world could be compared with her.

Everything necessary for the greatest fête imaginable was prepared. The King of the Gold Mines sent such enormous sums that the whole sea was covered with the ships that brought them. He sent to the most elegant and brilliant courts, and especially to that of France, to procure the most valuable things to adorn the princess, although her beauty was so perfect that she had little need of ornaments to set it off. The King of the Gold Mines, seeing himself on the point of becoming happy, never left the side of the charming princess.

It was to her interest to know him well, and, studying him with care, she discovered in him so much merit and intelligence, such lively and delicate feelings--in short, so beautiful a soul in so perfect a body—that she began to feel for him something of what he felt for her. These were happy times for both, when, in the loveliest gardens in the world, they were free to speak to each other all their passion. Those delights were often accompanied by music. The king, always gallant and loving, made poems and songs for the princess. Here is one which pleased her very much:

> "*These woods and meadows don their gayest dress,*
> "*Shine out their best to greet your loveliness;*
> "*And west winds blow and fairest flowers up-spring,*
> "*While loving birds their sweetest roundels sing.*
> "*All nature hastes, in humor gay,*
> "*Homage to love's own queen to pay.*"

They were at the height of their joy. The king's rivals, disconsolate at his good fortune, returned to their homes overwhelmed with the keenest sorrow, Unable to be present at Toutebelle's wedding. They bade her farewell in so touching a manner that she could not but pity them.

"Ah, madam," said the King of the Gold Mines, "of what are you robbing me? You grant your pity to lovers who are only too well paid for their distresses by a single one of your glances."

"I should be sorry," replied Toutebelle, "if you had not observed the compassion I show these princes, who are losing me forever; it is a proof of your delicacy which I prize. But, sir, their condition is so different from yours. You have so much reason to be pleased with me, and they have so little, that you should not carry your jealousy further."

The King of the Gold Mines, ashamed at the kindly way in which the princess took a thing that might have annoyed her, threw himself at her feet, and, kissing her hands, asked her pardon a thousand times.

At last the long-expected and much-desired day arrived: when everything was ready for Toutebelle's wedding, musical instruments and trumpets announced the great fête through the city. The streets were laid with red cloth, strewn with flowers, and the people rushed in crowds to the great courtyard of the palace. The queen was so excited that she had scarcely been to bed at all; and she rose before the dawn to give the necessary instructions and to choose the precious stones with which the princess was to be decked. She was covered with diamonds to her very shoes, which were made of them. Her gown of silver brocade was trimmed with a dozen sunbeams, of countless price indeed; but there! what could have been more brilliant?—only the beauty of the princess herself. A magnificent crown adorned her head; her hair hung down to her feet; and her dignified bearing marked her out from all the ladies attending her.

The King of the Gold Mines was no less perfectly appointed and magnificent. His joy appeared in his countenance and in all his actions. No one went to greet him without returning loaded with gifts; for round his banqueting hall he had had placed a thousand casks filled with gold, and big velvet bags embroidered with pearls filled with gold pieces. Each one held a hundred thousand. They were given indiscriminately to all who came for them; so that this little ceremony, which was not the least useful and pleasant part of the wedding, attracted many persons who would scarcely have appreciated the other entertainments.

As the queen and the princess were on their way to join the king, they saw two big turkey cocks, dragging a very ill-made box, enter the long gallery where they were. Behind them came a tall old woman, whose advanced age and decrepitude were not less surprising than her exceeding ugliness. She leaned on a crutch, and wore a black silk ruff, a red velvet hood, and a ragged farthingale. She went three times round with the turkey cocks without saying a word; then, stopping in the middle of the gallery and brandishing her crutch in a threatening manner:

"Ho! ho queen!- Ho! ho! princess!" she shouted. "You think you can break with impunity the promise you gave m friend the yellow dwarf! I am the Fairy of the Desert. Without him, without his orange tree, do you not know my big lions would have eaten you up? Such insults are not endured in Fairyland. Consider quickly what you intend to do; for I swear by the cap on my head that you shall marry him or I will burn my crutch."

"Ah! princess," said the queen, in tears, "do I hear? What have you promised?"

"Ah! mother," replied Toutebelle, sorrowfully, "what did you promise yourself?"

The King of the Gold Mines, angry at what was going on and because the wicked old woman had come in the way of his happiness, approached her, sword in hand, pointing it at her throat.

"Wretched woman," he said, "depart from this place for ever, or your life shall pay for your wickedness."

He had scarcely spoken these words when the lid of the box jumped right up to the ceiling with a fearful noise, and out came the yellow dwarf, mounted on a big Spanish cat. He placed himself between the Fairy of the Desert and the King of the Gold Mines.

"Rash youth," he said, "do not seek to injure this most distinguished fairy. It is with me that you have to reckon. I am your rival; I am your enemy. The faithless princess who intends to marry you has given me her promise, and accepted mine. Look if she has not a ring made of one of my hairs. Try to take it from her, and even by that slight test you will see that your power is less than mine."

"Wretched monster," said the king, "you are actually bold enough to call yourself the adorer of this divine princess, and to lay claim to so splendid a possession? Consider, you are an ugly little imp, whose hideous face hurts one's eyes. I should have already taken your life had you been worthy of so glorious a death."

The yellow dwarf, mortally offended, struck his spurs into the cat, which set up a horrible mewing, and, jumping first to one side and then to the other, frightened everyone except the brave king. He was grappling with the dwarf when the creature drew a large cutlass with which he was armed, and, challenging the king to a combat, with a strange noise rushed down into the courtyard of the palace.

With hasty strides the wrathful king followed him. Hardly were they face to face, and the whole court on the balconies, than the sun growing suddenly red as if stained with blood, darkness came on so that they could scarcely distinguish each other. Thunder and lightning seemed bent on the destruction of the world; and the two turkey cocks looked by the side of the wicked dwarf like two giants, taller than the mountains, casting forth fire from their mouths and eyes in such quantities that you might have taken them for a fiery furnace.

All these things would not have terrified the brave heart of the young monarch. The boldness of his look and actions reassured all who were anxious for his preservation, and even, perhaps, somewhat troubled the yellow dwarf. But his courage was not equal to seeing the condition to which his beloved princess was reduced. The Fairy of the Desert, like Tisiphone[100] her head covered with long snakes, was mounted on a winged griffin and armed with a spear, with which she struck the princess such cruel blows that she fell into the queen's arms bathed in blood. The tender mother, more hurt by the blow than her daughter, uttered the most piteous cries and laments. At this the king lo his courage and his presence of mind, and, giving up the combat, ran to help the princess, and to die with her. But the yellow dwarf did not give him time to reach her. With his Spanish cat he sprang on to the balcony where she was tore her from the hands of the queen and of all her ladies, and, jumping on to the roof of the palace, disappeared with his prey.

The king, stupefied and motionless was regarding with the uttermost despair so extraordinary an event, and one in which he had the misfortune to be quite powerless when, to add to his ill-luck, he felt a veil come over his eyes, which deprived him of all sense of sight; while someone with re-markable strength carried him away into the Vast region of air. What a tale of misfortunes! Love, cruel love! Is it thus you treat those who own you for their conqueror?

The wicked Fairy of the Desert, who had come to help the yellow dwarf to carry off the princess, had scarcely looked at the King of the Gold Mines when, her savage heart feeling the worth of the young prince, she wished to make him her prey. So she carried him to the depths of a horrible cave and loaded him with chains which she had fastened to a rock, hop-ing that the fear of a speedy death would make him forget Toutebelle, and induce him to do whatever she wished.

---

[100] One of the Erinyes or Furies, and sister of Alecto and Megaera. She was the one who punished crimes of murder.

As soon as they arrived she restored his sight without giving him his liberty, and, borrowing from the fairies' art the grace and charm nature had denied her, she appeared before him as a lovely nymph whom chance had led to that spot.

"Whom do I see here?" she cried. "What! It is you, charming prince? What ill fortune has come upon you and keeps you in so sorry an abode?"

The king, deceived by these false appearances, replied:

"Alas, lovely nymph, I have no idea what the fiendish fury who brought me here wants of me. Although she deprived me of the use of my eyes when she carried me off and has not appeared since, I did not fail to recognize, by the Sound of her voice, that she was the Fairy of the Desert."

"Ah, sir," cried the pretended nymph, "if you are in the power of that woman you will not get free until she has married you. She has played this trick on more than one hero, and she is the least manageable person in the world with regard to her infatuations."

While she was pretending to sympathize with the king's distress, he looked at the nymph's feet, and saw that they resembled those of a griffin. The fairy, in her various metamorphoses, might always be recognized by these; for she was unable to change that part of her griffin nature. The king took no notice, and went on speaking in a confidential tone:

"I have no aversion," he said, "for the Fairy of the Desert, but I cannot brook that she should protect the yellow dwarf from me and keep me chained like a criminal. What have I done to her? I loved a charming princess; but, if she restores me my liberty, I feel that gratitude would oblige me to love only her."

"Are you speaking sincerely?" asked the deluded nymph.

"Do not doubt it," replied the king; "the art of feigning is unknown to me, and I confess that the idea of a fairy flatters my vanity more than a mere princess; but, even were I dying of love for her, I should always show her nothing but hatred until I was set free."

The Fairy of the Desert, deceived by these words, resolved to carry the king away to a place as delightful as the present solitude was horrible. Forcing him to get into her chariot, to which she had yoked swans instead of the bats that usually drew her, she flew from one end of the earth to the other.

But what were the prince's feelings when, traversing the vast region of air, he saw his beloved princess in a castle of steel, whose walls, struck by the sun's rays, formed glowing mirrors that burned all who attempted to approach them!

She was in a grove, lying by the side of a stream. One of her hands supported her head, while with the other she seemed to be wiping away her tears. As she lifted her eyes to heaven, as if to ask its aid, she saw the king pass with the Fairy of the Desert, who, employing the fairy art in which she was skilled to appear beautiful in the eyes of the young monarch, seemed, in fact, in those of the princess the most wondrously fair lady in the world.

"What!" she exclaimed, "am I not wretched enough in this inaccessible castle to which the horrible yellow dwarf has brought me? To add to my misfortunes, must I be persecuted by the demon of jealousy? By so strange an adventure must I learn the faithlessness of the King of the Gold Mines? He thought in losing sight of me that he was freed from all the oaths he made me. But who is this formidable rival, whose fatal beauty surpasses mine?"

While she was speaking thus the amorous king felt sick at heart at flying with such speed from the beloved object of his vows. If he had had less know ledge of the fairy's power he would have tried everything to get away from her, either by killing her, or by any other means his love and courage might have suggested. But what could he do against so powerful a personage? Only time and cunning could free him from her clutches.

The fairy had seen Toutebelle, and sought to discover in the king's eyes the effect of the sight on his heart.

"I am better able than any one," he said, "to tell you what you desire to know. The unexpected meeting with an un fortunate princess, to whom I was attached before I knew you, has somewhat moved me, but you rank so far above her in my heart that rather than be faith less to you I would die."

"Ah, prince," she said, "may I flatter myself that I have inspired in you such a strong affection?"

"Time will convince you, madam," he said; "but, if you wish to prove to me that I have found favor with you, do not refuse me your assistance for Toutebelle."

"Think what you are asking," said the fairy, frowning and looking askance at him. "You wish me to use my skill against the yellow dwarf, who is my best friend, and take out of his hands a haughty princess, whom I cannot but regard as my rival?"

The king sighed, and answered never a word. What could he have replied to this keen-sighted person?

They reached a vast meadow brilliant with a thousand different flowers. A deep river surrounded it, and many a rivulet flowed gently under the thick- spreading trees, in whose shade it was always cool. In the distance rose a magnificent palace, the walls of which were of transparent emerald. Immediately the swans that drew the fairy alighted under a portico with a pavement of diamonds and a roof of rubies. Then appeared on all sides a thousand beautiful ladies, who received her with great shouts of joy, singing these words:

> "*When love would fain subdue a heart*
> "*Resistance but augments the smart:*
> "*The warrior, most famed in fight,*
> "*Must soonest yield to Cupid's might.*"

The Fairy of the Desert was charmed to hear them sing the story of her love. She led the king into the most magnificent chamber ever seen within the memory of fairy; and, that he should not think himself absolutely a prisoner, left him there a few minutes. He felt pretty certain that she was not far off, and that, hidden in some place, she was watching what he did. So he went up to a large mirror, and, addressing it, said:

"Faithful counselor, show me what I can do to make myself agreeable to the charming Fairy of the Desert, for the desire to please her is never out of my mind.".

Then he combed and powdered his hair, put on a patch, and, seeing on a table a coat more splendid than his own, hastily put it on. The fairy entered, so carried away by her joy, that she was unable to restrain it.

"I see," she said, "the care you take to please me; without any effort you have discovered the secret; judge then, sir, if, when you wish it, it will be difficult."

The king, who had his reasons for saying pretty things to the old fairy, was not sparing of them, and, little by little, gained permission to walk along the sea-shore. By her art she had made the sea so terrible and stormy that there were no pilots bold enough to sail it. Thus she had nothing to fear from the indulgence she showed her prisoner; and he found some consolation for his troubles in being able to dream in solitude, without the interruptions of his wicked gaoler.

After walking for some time on the sand, he bent down and wrote these lines with a stick he carried in his hand:

"*Here am I free*
"*To ease my grief with pouring out my tears,*
"*For that my loved one never more appears.*
"*O wind-toss'd sea! That scal'st heaven's height,*
"*Searchest Hell's night,*
"*Driving poor mortals from this churlish shore!*
"*The winds torment thee with an endless strife,*
"*Yet my heart struggleth more.*
"*O cruel fate, that bore Toutebelle away,*
"*O Heaven, that said my loved one might not stay,*
"*Wilt thou not take my life?*
"*Fair goddess of the wave,*
"*If that thou ever yet hast felt love's power,*
"*Come from thy deepest cave,*
"*And help the lover in his darkest hour!*"

While he was writing he heard a voice, which, in spite of himself, attracted his whole attention, and, seeing that the waves began to swell, he looked all around, and saw a woman of extraordinary beauty. Her only covering was her long hair, which, gently stirred by zephyrs, floated on the water. She held a mirror in one hand and a comb in the other. Her body ended in a long fish's tail with fins.

The king was very much surprised at so strange an encounter. As soon as she was within speaking distance, she said to him:

"I know the sad plight to which you are reduced by the loss of your princess, and by the strange passion the Fairy of the Desert has for you. If you like, I will take you away from this fatal place, where, it may be, you will languish for more than thirty years."

The king did not know what reply to make to the proposal, not from any lack of desire for his liberty, but because he feared the Fairy of the Desert had only borrowed this shape to deceive him. As he hesitated the mermaid, who divined his thoughts, said:

"Do not think I am setting a trap for you; I am too sincere to wish to serve your enemies. The doings of the Fairy of the Desert and of the yellow dwarf have incensed me against them. I see your beautiful princess every day. Her beauty and merit alike make me Pity her. I again repeat that, if you have Confidence in me, I will save you."

"I trust you so entirely," cried the king, "that I will do everything you command, but, since you have seen my princess, give me news of her."

"We should lose too much time talking," said she. "Come with me; I will take you to the castle of steel, and leave on this shore a figure so nearly resembling you that the fairy will be deceived."

She then cut some sea rushes, made a big bundle of them, and, breathing on them three times, said:

"Sea rushes, my friends, I command you to remain stretched out on the sand, without moving, until the Fairy of the Desert con to carry you off."

The sea rushes had all the appearance of being covered with skin, and were so like the King of the Gold Mines that nothing more wonderful was ever seen. They were dressed in a coat like his, and were pale and feeble to look like the drowned king. Then the good mermaid made the king seat himself on her big fish tail, and both, equally pleased, sailed out to sea.

"I will now tell you," said she, "that when the wicked yellow dwarf carried off Toutebelle, notwithstanding the wound the Fairy of the Desert had inflicted on her, he put her behind him on his terrible Spanish cat. She lost so much blood and was so disturbed by the adventure that her strength failed, and she remained in a Swoon the whole way. But the yellow dwarf would not stop to restore her to consciousness until he was safely arrived in his terrible castle of steel. There he was received by the most beautiful ladies in the world, whom he had stolen away. Each vied with the other in her eagerness to serve the princess. She was placed in a bed made of cloth of gold, embroidered with pearls bigger than nuts."

"Ah," exclaimed the King of the Gold Mines, interrupting the mermaid. "He has married her. I am faint; I shall die."

"No, sir," said she, "make yourself easy; Toutebelle's firmness preserved her from the violence of the horrid dwarf."

"Go on, I beg of you," said the king.

"What more have I to tell you?" replied the mermaid. "She was in the wood when you passed. She saw you with the Fairy of the Desert, who was so disguised that she seemed her superior in beauty. Her despair cannot be imagined; she thinks you love the fairy."

"She thinks I love her Oh, ye gods "cried the king, "into how fatal an error has she fallen! and how shall I undeceive her?"

"Consult your heart," replied the mermaid, with a charming smile. "When a man is so passionately in love he has no need of advice."

By this time they had reached the castle of steel. The side looking seawards was the only part that the yellow dwarf had not fortified with the formidable walls that burned up everybody.

"I know," said the mermaid to the king, "that Toutebelle is by the side of the same stream where you saw her when you passed; but, since you will have foes to vanquish before reaching her, here is a sword with which, provided you do not let it fall, you can undertake anything and brave the greatest dangers. Farewell; I shall betake myself to the shade of the rock you see there. If you have need of me to help you further with your beloved princess, I shall not fail you; for the queen is my best friend, and it was to serve her that I came to your aid."

So saying, she gave the king a sword made of a single diamond, brighter than the sun's rays. He well understood its use; and, unable to find words strong enough to express his gratitude, he begged her to supply those that would describe what a grateful heart is capable of feeling for such good service.

We must now tell something of what has been happening to the Fairy of the Desert. Since her charming lover did not return, she hastened in search of him, betaking herself to the shore with a hundred damsels of her suite, all bearing magnificent presents for him. Some carried large baskets filled with diamonds, others golden vases wonderfully wrought, several containing ambergris, coral, and pearls. Others bore on their heads bales of stuffs of inconceivable richness; others, again, fruits, flowers and even birds.

But what were the feelings of the fairy, who was following this fine and numerous company, when she saw the sea rushes so like the King of the Gold Mines that no difference could be discovered? At the sight, struck with astonishment and the keenest sorrow, she uttered a terrible cry, which pierced the heavens and made the mountains tremble and re-echo even to the depths of hell. The faces of the furies, Megara, Alecto, and Tisiphone themselves, could not have been more terrible to look on than hers. Throwing herself on the king's body, she wept, she howled, she tore in pieces fifty of the most beautiful damsels who had ac companied her, sacrificing them to the spirit of her dead lover.

Afterwards she summoned eleven of her sisters, fairies like herself begging them to aid her building a magnificent mausoleum for the young hero. There was not one who was not deceived by the sea rushes. This may seem surprising, for the fairies knew everything; but the clever mermaid knew even more than they did.

While they were providing the porphyry, the jasper, the agate, and the marble, the statues, the inscriptions the gold, and the bronze to immortalize the memory of the king whom they thought dead, he was thanking the good mermaid and imploring her to grant him her protection. She promised with the best grace in the world, and vanished from his sight. Nothing remained but to advance towards the castle of steel.

So, guided by his love, he walked with great strides, looking about eagerly for his adored princess. But he was not long without occupation. Four terrible sphinxes surrounded him, and, sticking their sharp claws into him, would have torn him in pieces, had not the diamond sword been as useful as the mermaid had foretold. It scarcely glittered in the eyes of the monsters before they fell helpless at his feet.

Giving each a mortal wound, he advanced further and saw six dragons covered with scales harder to pierce than iron. However alarming the encounter was he did not lose heart, and, making use of his formidable sword, cut each one of them in half. He hoped he had now overcome the greatest difficulties; but there still remained an embarrassing one. He met four-and-twenty nymphs, beautiful and charming, holding long wreaths of flowers, and by their means barring his passage.

"Where do you wish to go, sir?" said they. "We are the guardians of this place; if we let you pass endless disasters will happen to you and to us. We entreat you not to persist. Would you stain your victorious hand with the blood of four innocent damsels who have never done you any harm?"

At this sight the king remained dumbfounded and undecided, not knowing what to do. He, who professed to respect the fair sex and to be their knight to the death, must, on this occasion, destroy them. But a voice that he heard suddenly gave him strength:

"Strike! strike! spare no one," said the voice, "or you will lose the princess forever!"

Then, without answering the nymphs, he rushed into their midst, broke their wreaths, attacked them without quarter, and scattered them in a moment, it was one of the last obstacles he was to find, and he at length entered the little wood where he had seen

Toutebelle she was beside the stream, pale and languishing. He approached her trembling, and would have thrown himself at her feet, but she drew back as quickly as if he had been the yellow dwarf.

"Do not condemn me unheard, madam," he said. "I am neither faithless nor guilty; I am unfortunate enough to have displeased you without intending it."

"Ah! cruel one!" she exclaimed, "I saw you ride through the air with a woman of extra ordinary beauty. Did you set out on that journey against your will?"

"Yes, princess," he replied, "it was against my will. The wicked Fairy of the Desert, not satisfied with chaining me to a rock, carried me off in a chariot to one of the ends of the earth, where, if it had not been for the unexpected aid of a good mermaid who brought me here, I should be languishing now. I come, princess, to snatch you from the hand that keeps you captive. Do not refuse the help of the most faithful of all lovers."

He threw himself at her feet, but in laying hold of her gown unfortunately dropped his famous sword. The yellow dwarf, who was hidden under a lettuce, no sooner saw it out of the king's hands than, knowing its power, he threw himself upon it and seized it.

The princess uttered a heartrending cry on seeing the dwarf; hut her lamentations only served to exasperate the little monster. Uttering two words in his own jargon, two giants appeared, who loaded the king with chains and irons.

"Now," said the dwarf to the princess, "I am master of my rival's destiny; but I will grant him his life and permission to leave this place, if you will agree to marry me without delay."

"Ah! Let me rather die a thousand deaths!" said the love-stricken king.

"Alas!" cried the princess. "What more terrible than that you should die?"

"And what more frightful," replied the king, "than that you should become the victim of this monster?"

"Let us then die together," continued she.

"Let me, my princess, have the consolation of dying for you."

"Nay, rather do I consent," she said to the dwarf, "to your wishes."

"In my sight," replied the king; "in my sight, you would take him for your husband, cruel princess? Life would be hateful to me."

"No," said the yellow dwarf. "The betrothal will not take place in your presence; I dread too much a favored rival."

At these words, in spite of the tears and cries of Toutebelle, he stabbed the king to the heart and stretched him at his feet. The princess, who could not live after her lover's death, fell on his body, and it was not long before her soul joined his. Thus perished the unhappy prince and princess; and the mermaid could give them no help, for all the power of her magic lay in the diamond sword.

The wicked dwarf was better pleased to see the princess dead than in the arms of another; and the Fairy of the Desert, having heard what had happened destroyed the mausoleum she had built, conceiving for the memory of the King of the

Gold Mines as great a hatred as she had felt affection for his person before. The only favor the good mermaid, in despair at the ill-fortune, could obtain from Destiny was to change the lovers into palm trees. The two perfect bodies became two beautiful trees, bearing ever a faithful love one to the other, embracing each other with their intertwined branches, and in this tender union immortalizing their loves.

Mme Jeanne-Marie Leprince de Beaumont (1711-1780) authored forty collections of tales (dubbed "*Magasins*" or Stores), published in London between 1750 and 1780. Her classic story, *La Belle et la Bête* [Beauty and the Beast] (1756) was based on an earlier fairy tale originally published by Mme Gabrielle-Suzanne Barbot de Villeneuve (c. 1695-1755) in 1740 in *La Jeune Américaine et les contes marins*. Her lengthy version was then abridged, rewritten in order to aim it at "well-bred young ladies" and republished in *Le Magasin des enfants*, resulting in the version we know today.

Mme de Villeneuve belonged to a new, more sophisticated generation of French fairy tale writers following in the footsteps of Madame d'Aulnoy, Charles Perrault, and others. Her version owed as much to Classic Greek authors—the tale of Cupid and Psyche in Apuleius' Golden Ass in which Psyche weds a flying serpent who is really Cupid, under a spell. By night, a man makes love to her but she is forbidden to look at him. She breaks this taboo, and is punished by losing her beloved husband and she must complete a series of arduous tasks to win him back. It also contained a further allegorical layer that criticized women's lack of social status, in particular being treated like chattel and married against their wills—often at a young age—to unsuitable husbands. It is not hard to read the story as a thinly-veiled parable describing the fears of women facing an unwanted marriage to a man—or a monster.

Mme de Villeneuve's tale is about a hundred pages long and was clearly intended for adult readers. It was reprinted in translation in Andrew Lang's celebrated *Blue Fairy Book* (1889). The starting point is similar: Beauty's father gives her over to the Beast to save his own life. The Beast is a savage monster, seeking to regain his lost humanity. The tale shows us how he achieves this goal through the redeeming effects of Beauty's civility, kindness, and, ultimately, love. Madame de Villeneuve's tale takes great pains to show that the Beast's transformation occurs only after Beauty has married him (read: has had intercourse) and she wakes up in her bed to finally discover a human prince lying beside her.

Mme Leprince de Beaumont was born to a poor family named Leprince in Rouen and several of her siblings had to be sent away for adoption. She lost her mother when she was only eleven, but as she had suffered terribly at not being able to maintain contact with her children or even find out what had become of them, her death was likely a blessing. At age 20, she began teaching young children, first at Ernemont, near Rouen, then ten years later, as a singing teacher at the Court of the Duke of Lorraine at Lunéville. Her first marriage to M. de Beaumont in 1743 was disastrous and was annulled two years later. The Duke of Lorraine had personally paid her dowry, a huge sum, so that she could marry well, but her husband used it to pay off his debts, then used the rest to buy a hotel. There, he held wild parties and entertained disreputable characters. After her husband contracted a communicable disease as a result of his lifestyle, she was able to obtain an annulment but she retained her husband's name.

In 1746, Mme Leprince de Beaumont left France to become a governess in London, where she wrote the moralistic novel *The Triumph of Truth* (1748) and other fairy tales for children. After a successful publishing career, she remarried, bore many children, and eventually left England to live the rest of her life in Savoy. She continued her literary career by publishing schoolbooks and collections of educational and moral stories and poems for children.

Mme Leprince de Beaumont's version of Beauty and the Beast not only tones down the implied sex and scathing criticism of forced marriage, but also eliminates several subplots. The backstory of both characters was pared down to the minimum. In Mme de Villeneuve's tale, the Beast was a prince who lost his father at a young age, and whose mother had to wage war to defend his kingdom. The queen left him in the care of an evil fairy who tried to seduce him when he became an adult; when he refused her advances, she transformed him into a beast. Beauty's story reveals that she is not really a merchant's daughter, but the offspring of a king and a good fairy. The wicked fairy had tried to murder Beauty so she could marry her father the king, and Beauty was put in the place of the merchant's dead daughter to protect her. Mme de Villeneuve also gave the castle elaborate magic, which obscured the more vital pieces of it. Mme Leprince de Beaumont did away with all but the archetypal elements, but, more importantly, she shifted the focus from the Beast to Beauty. The spotlight is now not on the man's need to change, but on the girl having to adapt to her husband and help him recognize the good inside of him.

Eventually Mme Leprince de Beaumont's version became the dominant version of the tale in the 19th century, being widely disseminated in cheap editions, often without any credit. However, Jean Cocteau's wonderful 1946 film adaptation reincorporated many of the elements discarded by Mme Leprince de Beaumont: from the magical elements of the Beast's castle to the sexual subtext of the original. Beauty's nightly refusal of the Beast and the slow awakening of both her attraction to him and her sexuality are contrasted with the Beast's struggles to contain his own animalistic nature...

Jeanne-Marie Leprince de Beaumont: *Beauty and the Beast*
(1756)[101]

There was once a very rich merchant, who had six children, three sons, and three daughters; being a man of sense, he spared no cost for their education, but gave them all kinds of masters. His daughters were extremely handsome, especially the youngest; when she was little, everybody admired her, and called her *The little Beauty*; so that, as she grew up, she still went by the name of *Beauty*, which made her sisters very jealous.

The youngest, as she was handsome, was also better than her sisters. The two eldest had a great deal of pride, because they were rich. They gave themselves ridiculous airs, and would not visit other merchants' daughters, nor keep company with any but persons of quality. They went out every day upon parties of pleasure, balls, plays, concerts, etc. and laughed at their youngest sister, because she spent the greatest part of her time in reading good books. As it was known that they were to have great fortunes, several eminent merchants made their addresses to them; but the two eldest said they would never marry, unless they could meet with a Duke, or an Earl at least. Beauty very civilly thanked them that courted her, and told them she was too young yet to marry, but chose to stay with her father a few years longer.

All at once the merchant lost his whole fortune, excepting a small country-house at a great distance from town, and

---

[101] *La Belle et la Bête*, excerpted from *Le Magasin des Enfants* by Jeanne-Marie-Leprince de Beaumont, translated into English in 1843 by Charles Lamb, introduced and annotated by Jean-Marc Lofficier.

told his children, with tears in his eyes, they most go there and work for their living. The two eldest answered, that they would not leave the town, for they had several lovers, who they were sure would be glad to have them, though they had no fortune; but in this they were mistaken, for their lovers slighted and forsook them in their poverty. As they were not beloved on account of their pride, everybody said:

"They do not deserve to be pitied, we are glad to see their pride humbled, let them go and give themselves quality airs in milking the cows and minding their dairy. But," added they, "we are extremely concerned for Beauty, she was such a charming, sweet-tempered creature, spoke so kindly to poor people, and was of such an affable, obliging disposition."

Nay, several gentlemen would have married her, though they knew she had not a penny; but she told them she could not think of leaving her poor father in his misfortunes, but was determined to go along with him into the country to comfort and attend him. Poor Beauty at first was sadly grieved at the loss of her fortune; "but," she said to herself, "were I to cry ever so much, that would not make things better, I must try to make myself happy without a fortune."

When they came to their country-house, the merchant and his three sons applied themselves to husbandry and tillage; and Beauty rose at four in the morning, and made haste to have the house clean, and breakfast ready for the family. In the beginning she found it very difficult, for she had not been used to work as a servant; but in less than two months she grew stronger and healthier than ever. After she had done her work, she read, played on the harpsichord, or else sung whilst she spun. On the contrary, her two sisters did not know how to spend their time; they got up at ten, and did nothing but saunter about the whole day, lamenting the loss of their fine clothes and acquaintance.

"Do but see our youngest sister," said they one to the other, "what a poor, stupid mean-spirited creature she is, to be contented with such an unhappy situation."

The good merchant was of a quite different opinion; he knew very well that Beauty out-shone her sisters, in her person as well as her mind, and admired her humility, industry, and patience; for her sisters not only left her all the work of the house to do, but insulted her every moment.

The family had lived about a year in this retirement, when the merchant received a letter, with an account that a vessel, on board of which he had effects, was safely arrived. This news had liked to have turned the heads of the two eldest daughters, who immediately flattered themselves with the hopes of returning to town; for they were quite weary of a country life; and when they saw their father ready to set out, they begged of him to buy them new gowns, caps, rings, and all manner of trifles; but Beauty asked for nothing, for she thought to herself, that all the money her father was going to receive would scarce be sufficient to purchase everything her sisters wanted.

"What will you have, Beauty?" said her father.

"Since you are so kind as to think of me," answered she, "be so kind as to bring me a rose, for as none grow hereabouts, they are a kind of rarity."

Not that Beauty cared for a rose, but she asked for something, lest she should seem by her example to condemn her sisters' conduct, who would have said she did it only to look particular.

The good man went on his journey; but when he came there, they went to law with him about the merchandize, and after a great deal of trouble and pains to no purpose, he came back as poor as before.

He was within thirty miles of his own house, thinking on the pleasure he should have in seeing his children again, when going through a large forest he lost himself. It rained and snowed terribly, besides, the wind was so high, that it threw him twice off his horse; and night coming on, he began to apprehend being either starved to death with cold and hunger, or else devoured by the wolves, whom he heard howling all around him, when, on a sudden, looking through a long walk of trees, he saw a light at some distance, and going on a little farther, perceived it came from a palace illuminated from top to bottom.

The merchant returned God thanks for this happy discovery, and hasted to the palace; but was greatly surprised at not meeting with anyone in the out-courts. His horse followed him, and seeing a large stable open, went in, and finding both hay and oats, the poor beast, who was almost famished, fell to eating very heartily. The merchant tied him up to the manger, and walked towards the house, where he saw no one, but entering into a large hall, he found a good fire, and a table plentifully set out, with but one cover laid. As he was wet quite through with the rain and snow, he drew near the fire to dry himself.

"I hope," said he, "the master of the house, or his servants, will excuse the liberty I take; I suppose it will not be long before some of them appear."

He waited a considerable time, till it struck eleven, and still nobody came: at last he was so hungry that he could stay no longer, but took a chicken and ate it in two mouthfuls, trembling all the while. After this, he drank a few glasses of wine, and growing more courageous, he went out of the hall, and crossed through several grand apartments with magnificent furniture, till he came into a chamber, which had an exceeding good bed in it, and as he was very much fatigued, and it was past midnight, he concluded it was best to shut the door, and go to bed.

It was ten the next morning before the merchant waked, and as he was going to rise, he was astonished to see a good suit of clothes in the room of his own, which were quite spoiled.

"Certainly," said he, "this palace belongs to some kind fairy, who has seen and pitied my distress."

He looked through a window, but instead of snow saw the most delightful arbors, interwoven with the most beautiful flowers that ever were beheld. He then returned to the great hall, where he had supped the night before, and found some chocolate ready made on a little table.

"Thank you, good Madam Fairy," said he aloud, "for being so careful as to provide me a breakfast; I am extremely obliged to you for all your favors."

The good man drank his chocolate, and then went to look for his horse; but passing through an arbor of roses, he remembered Beauty's request to him, and gathered a branch on which were several; immediately he heard a great noise, and saw such a frightful beast coming towards him, that he was ready to faint away.

"You are very ungrateful," said the beast to him, in a terrible voice. "I have saved your life by receiving you into my castle, and, in return, you steal my roses, which I value beyond anything in the universe; but you shall die for it; I give you but a quarter of an hour to prepare yourself, to say your prayers."

The merchant fell on his knees, and lifted up both his hands:

"My Lord," said he, "I beseech you to forgive me, indeed I had no intention to offend in gathering a rose for one of my daughters, who desired me to bring her one."

"My name is not 'My Lord,'" replied the monster, "but Beast; I don't love compliments, not I; I like people should speak as they think; and so do not imagine I am to be moved by any of your flattering speeches; but you say you have got daughters; I will forgive you, on condition that one of them come willingly, and suffer for you. Let me have no words, but go about your business, and swear that if your daughter refuse to die in your stead, you will return within three months."

The merchant had no mind to sacrifice his daughters to the ugly monster, but he thought, in obtaining this respite, he should have the satisfaction of seeing them once more; so he promised upon oath, he would return, and the Beast told him he might set out when he pleased; "but," added he, "you shall not depart empty handed; go back to the room where you lay, and you will see a great empty chest; fill it with whatever you like best, and I will send it to your home," and at the same time Beast withdrew.

"Well," said the good man to himself, "if I must die, I shall have the comfort, at least, of leaving something to my poor children."

He returned to the bed-chamber, and finding a great quantity of broad pieces of gold, he filled the great chest the Beast had mentioned, locked it, and afterwards took his horse out of the stable, leaving the palace with as much grief as he had entered it with joy. The horse, of his own accord, took one of the roads of the forest; and in a few hours the good man was at home. His children came around him, but, instead of receiving their embraces with pleasure, he looked on them, and, holding up the branch he had in his hands, he burst into tears.

"Here, Beauty," said he, "take these roses; but little do you think how dear they are like to cost your unhappy father;" and then related his fatal adventure: immediately the two eldest set up lamentable outcries, and said all manner of ill-natured things to Beauty, who did not cry at all.

"Do but see the pride of that little wretch," said they. "She would not ask for fine clothes, as we did; but no, truly, Miss wanted to distinguish herself; so now she will be the death of our poor father, and yet she does not so much as shed a tear."

"Why should I," answered Beauty, "it would be very needless, for my father shall not suffer upon my account, since the monster will accept of one of his daughters, I will deliver myself up to all his fury, and I am very happy in thinking that my death will save my father's life, and be a proof of my tender love for him."

"No, sister," said her three brothers, "that shall not be, we will go find the monster, and either kill him, or perish in the attempt."

"Do not imagine any such thing, my sons," said the merchant. "Beast's power is so great, that I have no hopes of your overcoming him; I am charmed with Beauty's kind and generous offer, but I cannot yield to it; I am old, and have not long to live, so can only lose a few years, which I regret for your sakes alone, my dear children."

"Indeed, father," said Beauty, "you shall not go to the palace without me, you cannot hinder me from following you."

It was to no purpose all they could say, Beauty still insisted on setting out for the fine palace; and her sisters were delighted at it, for her virtue and amiable qualities made them envious and jealous.

The merchant was so afflicted at the thoughts of losing his daughter, that he had quite forgot the chest full of gold; but at night, when he retired to rest, no sooner had he shut his chamber-door, than, to his great astonishment, he found it by his bedside; he was determined, however, not to tell his children that he was grown rich, because they would have wanted to return to town, and he was resolved not to leave the country; but he trusted Beauty with the secret; who informed him, that two gentlemen came in his absence, and courted her sisters; she begged her father to consent to their marriage, and give them fortunes; for she was so good, that she loved them, and forgave them heartily all their ill-usage. These wicked creatures rubbed their eyes with an onion, to force some tears when they parted with their sister; but her brothers were really concerned. Beauty was the only one who did not shed tears at parting, because she would not increase their uneasiness.

The horse took the direct road to the palace; and towards evening they perceived it illuminated as at first: the horse went of himself into the stable, and the good man and his daughter came into the great hall, where they found a table splendidly served up, and two covers. The merchant had no heart to eat; but Beauty endeavored to appear cheerful, sat down to table, and helped him. Afterwards, thought she to herself:

"Beast surely has a mind to fatten me before he eats me, since he provides such a plentiful entertainment."

When they had supped, they heard a great noise, and the merchant, all in tears, bid his poor child farewell, for he thought Beast was coming. Beauty was sadly terrified at his horrid form, but she took courage as well as she could, and the monster having asked her if she came willingly; "y--e--s," said she, trembling.

"You are very good, and I am greatly obliged to you; honest man, go your ways tomorrow morning, but never think of returning here again. Farewell, Beauty."

"Farewell, Beast," answered she; and immediately the monster withdrew.

"Oh, daughter," said the merchant, embracing Beauty, "I am almost frightened to death; believe me, you had better go back, and let me stay here."

"No, father," said Beauty, in a resolute tone, "you shall set out tomorrow morning, and leave me to the care and protection of Providence."

They went to bed, and thought they should not close their eyes all night; but scarce were they laid down, than they fell fast asleep; and Beauty dreamed, a fine lady came, and said to her, "I am content, Beauty, with your good will; this good action of yours, in giving up your own life to save your father's, shall not go unrewarded."

Beauty waked, and told her father her dream, and though it helped to comfort him a little, yet he could not help crying bitterly, when he took leave of his dear child.

As soon as he was gone, Beauty sat down in the great hall, and fell a crying likewise; but as she was mistress of a great deal of resolution, she recommended herself to God, and resolved not to be uneasy the little time she had to live; for she firmly believed Beast would eat her up that night.

However, she thought she might as well walk about till then, and view this fine castle, which she could not help admiring; it was a delightful pleasant place, and she was extremely surprised at seeing a door, over which was wrote, "*Beauty's Apartment*."

She opened it hastily, and was quite dazzled with the magnificence that reigned throughout; but what chiefly took up her attention, was a large library, a harpsichord, and several music books.

"Well," said she to herself, "I see they will not let my time hang heavy on my hands for want of amusement." Then she reflected, "Were I but to stay here a day, there would not have been all these preparations."

This consideration inspired her with fresh courage; and opening the library, she took a book, and read these words in letters of gold:

Welcome, Beauty, banish fear; you are queen and mistress here; Speak your wishes, speak your will, Swift obedience meets them still.

"Alas," said she, with a sigh, "there is nothing I desire so much as to see my poor father, and to know what he is doing."

She had no sooner said this, when casting her eyes on a great looking-glass, to her great amazement she saw her own home, where her father arrived with a very dejected countenance; her sisters went to meet him, and, notwithstanding their endeavors to appear sorrowful, their joy, felt for having got rid of their sister, was visible in every feature: a moment after, everything disappeared, and Beauty's apprehensions at this proof of Beast's complaisance.

At noon, she found dinner ready, and while at table, was entertained with an excellent concert of music, though without seeing any body; but at night, as she was going to sit down to supper, she heard the noise Beast made; and could not help being sadly terrified.

"Beauty," said the monster, "will you give me leave to see you sup?"

"That is as you please," answered Beauty, trembling.

"No," replied the Beast, "you alone are mistress here; you need only bid me be gone, if my presence is troublesome, and I will immediately withdraw: but tell me, do not you think me very ugly?"

"That is true," said Beauty, "for I cannot tell a lie; but I believe you are very good-natured."

"So I am," said the monster, "but then, besides my ugliness, I have no sense; I know very well that I am a poor, silly, stupid creature."

"'Tis no sign of folly to think so," replied Beauty, "for never did fool know this, or had so humble a conceit of his own understanding."

"Eat then, Beauty," said the monster, "and endeavor to amuse yourself in your palace; for everything here is yours, and I should be very uneasy if you were not happy."

"You are very obliging," answered Beauty. "I own I am pleased with your kindness, and when I consider that, your deformity scarce appears."

"Yes, yes," said the Beast, "my heart is good, but still I am a monster."

"Among mankind," says Beauty, "there are many that deserve that name more than you, and I prefer you, just as you are, to those, who, under a human form, hide a treacherous, corrupt, and ungrateful heart."

"If I had sense enough," replied the Beast, "I would make a fine compliment to thank you, but I am so dull, that I can only say, I am greatly obliged to you."

Beauty ate a hearty supper, and had almost conquered her dread of the monster; but she had liked to have fainted away, when he said to her:

"Beauty, will you be my wife?"

She was some time before she durst answer; for she was afraid of making him angry, if she refused. At last, however, she said, trembling:

"No, Beast."

Immediately the poor monster began to sigh, and hissed so frightfully, that the whole palace echoed. But Beauty soon recovered her fright, for Beast having said, in a mournful voice, "Then farewell, Beauty," left the room; and only turned back, now and then, to look at her as he went out.

When Beauty was alone, she felt a great deal of compassion for poor Beast.

"Alas," said she, "'tis a thousand pities anything so good-natured should be so ugly."

Beauty spent three months very contentedly in the palace; every evening Beast paid her a visit, and talked to her during supper, very rationally, with plain good common sense, but never with what the world calls wit; and Beauty daily discovered some valuable qualifications in the monster; and seeing him often, had so accustomed her to his deformity, that, far from dreading the time of his visit, she would often look on her watch to see when it would be nine; for the Beast never missed coming at that hour. There was but one thing that gave Beauty any concern, which was, that every night, before she went to bed, the monster always asked her, if she would be his wife. One day she said to him:

"Beast, you make me very uneasy, I wish I could consent to marry you, but I am too sincere to make you believe that will ever happen; I shall always esteem you as a friend; endeavor to be satisfied with this."

"I must," said the Beast, "for, alas! I know too well my own misfortune; but then I love you with the tenderest affection: however, I ought to think myself happy that you will stay here; promise me never to leave me."

Beauty blushed at these words; she had seen in her glass, that her father had pined himself sick for the loss of her, and she longed to see him again.

"I could," answered she, "indeed promise never to leave you entirely, but I have so great a desire to see my father, that I shall fret to death, if you refuse me that satisfaction."

"I had rather die myself," said the monster, "than give you the least uneasiness; I will send you to your father, you shall remain with him, and poor Beast will die with grief."

"No," said Beauty, weeping, "I love you too well to be the cause of your death: I give you my promise to return in a week; you have shown me that my sisters are married, and my brothers gone to the army; only let me stay a week with my father, as he is alone."

"You shall be there tomorrow morning," said the Beast, "but remember your promise: you need only lay your ring on the table before you go to bed, when you have a mind to come back; farewell, Beauty."

Beast sighed as usual, bidding her good night; and Beauty went to bed very sad at seeing him so afflicted. When she waked the next morning, she found herself at her father's, and having rang a little bell, that was by her bed-side, she saw the maid come; who, the moment she saw her, gave a loud shriek; at which the good man ran up stairs, and thought he should have died with joy to see his dear daughter again. He held her fast locked in his arms above a quarter of an hour. As soon as the first transports were over, Beauty began to think of rising, and was afraid she had no clothes to put on; but the maid told her, that she had just found, in the next room, a large trunk full of gowns, covered with gold and diamonds. Beauty thanked good Beast for his kind care, and taking one of the plainest of them, she intended to make a present of the others to her sisters. She scarce had said so, when the trunk disappeared. Her father told her, that Beast insisted on her keeping them herself; and immediately both gowns and trunk came back again.

Beauty dressed herself; and in the meantime, they sent to her sisters, who hasted thither with their husbands. They were both of them very unhappy. The eldest had married a gentleman, extremely handsome indeed, but so fond of his own person, that he was full of nothing but his own dear self, and neglected his wife. The second had married a man of wit, but he only made use of it to plague and torment everybody, and his wife most of all. Beauty's sisters sickened with envy, when they saw her dressed like a Princess, and more beautiful than ever; nor could all her obliging affectionate behavior stifle their jealousy, which was ready to burst when she told them how happy she was. They went down into the garden to vent it in tears; and said one to the other

"In what is this little creature better than us, that she should be so much happier?"

"Sister," said the eldest, "a thought just strikes my mind; let us endeavor to detain her above a week, and perhaps the silly monster will be so enraged at her for breaking her word, that he will devour her."

"Right, sister," answered the other, "therefore we must show her as much kindness as possible."

After they had taken this resolution, they went up, and behaved so affectionately to their sister, that poor Beauty wept for joy. When the week was expired, they cried and tore their hair, and seemed so sorry to part with her, that she promised to stay a week longer.

In the meantime, Beauty could not help reflecting on herself for the uneasiness she was likely to cause poor Beast, whom she sincerely loved, and really longed to see again. The tenth night she spent at her father's, she dreamed she was in the palace garden, and that she saw Beast extended on the grass-plot, who seemed just expiring, and, in a dying voice, reproached her with her ingratitude. Beauty started out of her sleep and bursting into tears:

"Am not I very wicked," said she, "to act so unkindly to Beast, that has studied so much to please me in everything? Is it his fault that he is so ugly, and has so little sense? He is kind and good, and that is sufficient. Why did I refuse to marry him? I should be happier with the monster than my sisters are with their husbands; it is neither wit nor a fine person in a husband, that makes a woman happy; but virtue, sweetness of temper, and complaisance; and Beast has all these valuable qualifications. It is true, I do not feel the tenderness of affection for him, but I find I have the highest gratitude, esteem, and friendship; and I will not make him miserable; were I to be so ungrateful, I should never forgive myself."

Beauty having said this, rose, put her ring on the table, and then laid down again; scarce was she in bed before she fell asleep; and when she waked the next morning, she was over-joyed to find herself in the Beast's palace. She put on one of her richest suits to please him, and waited for evening with the utmost impatience; at last the wished-for hour came, the clock struck nine, yet no Beast appeared.

Beauty then feared she had been the cause of his death; she ran crying and wringing her hands all about the palace, like one in despair; after having sought for him everywhere, she recollected her dream, and flew to the canal in the garden, where she dreamed she saw him. There she found poor Beast stretched out, quite senseless, and, as she imagined, dead. She threw herself upon him without any dread, and finding his heart beat still, she fetched some water from the canal, and poured it on his head. Beast opened his eyes, and said to Beauty:

"You forgot your promise, and I was so afflicted for having lost you, that I resolved to starve myself; but since I have the happiness of seeing you once more, I die satisfied."

"No, dear Beast," said Beauty, "you must not die; live to be my husband; from this moment I give you my hand, and swear to be none but yours. Alas! I thought I had only a friendship for you, but, the grief I now feel convinces me, that I cannot live without you."

Beauty scarcely had pronounced these words, when she saw the palace sparkle with light; and fireworks, instruments of music, everything, seemed to give notice of some great event: but nothing could fix her attention; she turned to her dear Beast, for whom she trembled with fear; but how great was her surprise! Beast had disappeared, and she saw, at her feet, one of the loveliest Princes that eye ever beheld, who returned her thanks for having put an end to the charm, under which he had so long resembled a Beast. Though this Prince was worthy of all her attention, she could not forbear asking where Beast was.

"You see him at your feet," said the Prince. "A wicked fairy had condemned me to remain under that shape till a beautiful virgin should consent to marry me; the fairy likewise enjoined me to conceal my understanding; there was only you in the world generous enough to be won by the goodness of my temper; and in offering you my crown, I can't discharge the obligations I have to you."

Beauty, agreeably surprised, gave the charming Prince her hand to rise; they went together into the castle, and Beauty was overjoyed to find, in the great hall, her father and his whole family, whom the beautiful lady, that appeared to her in her dream, had conveyed thither.

"Beauty," said this lady, "come and receive the reward of your judicious choice; you have preferred virtue before either wit or beauty, and deserve to find a person in whom all these qualifications are united: you are going to be a great Queen; I hope the throne will not lessen your virtue, or make you forget yourself. As to you, ladies," said the Fairy to Beauty's two sisters, "I know your hearts, and all the malice they contain: become two statues; but, under this transformation, still retain your reason. You shall stand before your sister's palace gate, and be it your punishment to behold her happiness; and it will not be in your power to return to your former state till you own your faults; but I am very much afraid that you will always remain statues. Pride, anger, gluttony, and idleness, are sometimes conquered, but the conversion of a malicious and envious mind is a kind of miracle."

Immediately the fairy gave a stroke with her wand, and in a moment all that were in the hall were transported into the Prince's palace. His subjects received him with joy; he married Beauty, and lived with her many years; and their happiness, as it was founded on virtue, was complete.

Because the genre was adapted, somewhat controversially, to a primary role in children's literature, which it still holds, and many of the particular tales continually reprocessed,[102] it is sometimes forgotten that the production of such tales in the French salons was intended for the amusement of adults, and that the versions circulated orally were probably a good deal more cynical, satirical and erotic than those eventually adapted for the civilization of children. It also tends to be forgotten that the literary battleground into which those stories were first rebelliously introduced was one tyrannically dominated by the theory of Classicism, which held that French literature ought to take its models—and hence, to a large extent, its themes and methods—from the masterworks of Greek and Roman literature.

Regarded contemptuously as a form fit for women, Perrault being granted an honorable exception, the salon *Contes* of the latter half of the 17th century frequently failed to reach print, but they could nevertheless get their authors into trouble, as demonstrated by the fate of Henriette-Julie de Castelnau, Comtesse de Murat, author of *Les Contes de Fées* [The Fairy Tales] and *Les Nouveaux Contes des Fées* [The New Fairy Tales], one of whose tales was allegedly recognized as a satirical dig at one of the king's mistresses, and who was then renounced by her husband, exiled from the court and forced to

---

[102] Although some of the stories composed by the salon writers were based on pre-existing tales, most were original compositions. Many of them, however, fed back into oral tradition, becoming archetypal examples of "fakelore." For example, Catherine Bernard's *Riquet à la Houpe* [Ricky of the Tuft] was plagiarized by Perrault, while Mademoiselle de La Force's *Persinette* was later collected by the Brothers Grimm as an ostensible German folktale, under the title *Rapunzel*. Perrault added one story to his collection that he made up himself, *Le Petit chaperon rouge* [Little Red Riding Hood], which subsequently became one of the most prolifically reprocessed tales ever written.

spend the rest of her life under effective house arrest—which did not, of course, stop her writing. Charlotte-Rose de Caumont de La Force, author of *Les Fées: Contes des Contes* [The Fairies: Tales of Tales], suffered a similar expulsion, being banished to a convent.

Between 1697 and 1702, some of the best authors of Fairy Tales included: The Chevalier de Mailly, with *Les Illustres Fées* [The Illustrious Fairies]; The Marquise d'Aulneuil, with *La Tyrannie des Fées Détruites* [The Tyranny of Destroyed Fairies]; and Jean de Préchac, with *Contes moins Contes que les Autres, Sans Paragon et la Reine des Fées* [Tales Less Tales Than Others, Without Paragon, And The Fairy Queen].

Marie-Anne de Roumier-Robert: *The Water Sprites* (1766) [103]

PART ONE

I. Introduction: The Birth of Tramarine

Lydia, which contains a part of Africa,[104] was once governed by Ophtes, a bellicose prince. Several wars were fought against him by various petty sovereigns jealous of the extent of his estates. The monarch battled them all, successively winning complete victories, and finally rendering them tributaries to his kingdom.

After having pacified the troubles that those princes excited over a number of years, the monarch no longer thought about anything but enabling his people to enjoy a peace that ought to bring back abundance and tranquility to his kingdom. In order to cement it further, however, his minister proposed that he make an alliance with the king of Galata by marrying Cliceria, the daughter of that monarch.

Ophtes lent himself readily to that view; he was charmed by the beauty of Cliceria, whose portrait he was shown. Ambassadors were sent to the King of Galata; they were charged with proposing the marriage of the Princes with the king of

---

[103] *Les Ondins* by Marie-Anne de Roumier-Robert, included in *The Voyages of Lord Seaton to the Seven Planets*, translated into English in 2015, introduced and annotated by Brian Stableford, also available from Black Coat Press, q.v.

[104] This Lydie [Lydia] is evidently not the actual Iron Age kingdom in Asia Minor, nor a misspelling of the African kingdom of Lybie [Libya], but an entirely hypothetical realm.

Lydia. A proposition so advantageous was accepted joyfully; both parties hastened to sign the articles and the marriage was only deferred for the time required to make the preparations with the pomp and magnificence that it was appropriate to employ in those kinds of celebrations.

Princess Cliceria had scarcely entered her fifteenth year; she was endowed with an intelligence superior to all women, and a ravishing beauty; she was received by the King, her spouse, with all the sumptuousness and gallantry that can be expected of a great monarch, especially when amour is combined with reasons of state. For more than a month, the days were marked with further celebrations. The King, although already of a certain age, took great pleasure in the diversions of his court; in addition, he wanted by that complaisance to make known to the Queen, as well as to the princes and princesses who had accompanied her, the satisfaction he had in seeing her embellish his court. The courtiers, in their turn, in order to mark their zeal and their attachment to the King and their Queen, strove to imagine new diversions that might amuse and please her.

Several years passed thus in pleasures, without them being troubled by any anxiety, except that the King appeared to have no successor. The desire to obtain one eventually caused prayers and sacrifices to succeed laughter and games; the King and the Queen went to offer them in all the temples, where they both did so with a piety worthy of example.

The prayers that the heart had formed could not fail to soften the gods; they were eventually granted; the Queen declared that she was pregnant. The joy that the news spread through all hearts is indescribable; the King ordered prayers in actions of grace; the people flocked to the temples in order to ask the gods to grant them a prince who would govern them with a much sagacity, reason, justice and mildness as the one who presently reigned over them; that he should be the inheritor of all his virtues, his clemency and all his talents as well as his estates.

The gods were deaf to their prayers; the Queen gave birth to a princess. There was, nevertheless, much rejoicing at the birth of the princess, who was named Tramarine.

Ophtes, curious to know the destiny of a child so long desired, ordered his prime minister to go to consult the oracle of Venus. He charged him at the same time with rich presents that were to serve to ornament the temple of the goddess.

When the pythoness had set herself on the tripod, she seemed to be immediately agitated by the divine spirit, which filled her; her hair stood on end; the entire lair resounded with a noise like thunder. Then a voice was heard, which appeared to emerge from the depths of her bosom; it pronounced that the child, in taking on a divine form, would not see her father again until after his ruin.

That response, which a second oracle would have been required in order to explain, afflicted the minister sensibly. He returned to the court with a consternated visage, not daring to announce to the King the response that the goddess had pronounced by means of the mouth of the pythoness. To begin with, he searched for some phrase that might clarify the oracle's response by giving it a more favorable meaning; but the king, judging by his sad expression that the prediction was not favorable to the princess, ordered him firmly not conceal anything, under pain of death—which the minister saw that it was necessary to obey.

"It is with great dolor, Sire," he said to him, "that I am constrained to announce to Your Majesty the baleful decrees that the oracle has pronounced regarding the destiny of Princess Tramarine. I wanted to spare Your Majesty the distress of hearing them. Here it is: 'The child, in taking on a divine form, will not see her father again until after his ruin.'

"However, Sire," the minister added, "Your Majesty is not unaware that the gods only ever express themselves with a great deal of obscurity; doubtless that is only to deceive the curiosity of feeble mortals who want to penetrate too far into the future, of which they alone are the depositories. It is prudent and wise to summit to their decrees, without seeking to

301

penetrate the meaning, which they always hide by means of ambiguous responses to which it is easy to give several interpretations. Forgive my zeal, Sire, and the boldness of my reflections, but I am obeying Your Majesty's orders in not hiding any of my thoughts."

It is true that the reflections in question were those of a wise and prudent man. His soul was deployed therein and the interest he had in the tranquility and repose of his master were legible. But what can opinion and prejudice not produce? Neither the King nor the Queen wanted to take their minister's sage advice. The oracle's response was examined in full Council; several sinister consequences were drawn from it, which increased the King's distress in not being able to divine the meaning of the prediction.

It took a long time to decide the course of action that ought to be taken, but a second pregnancy on the Queen's part decided the fate of the Princess. She was sent to the kingdom of Castora, then governed by Queen Pentaphile, the sister of the King of Lydia. That Princess was an Amazon, who devoted her realm entirely to her valor, and had banished all men therefrom.

It was said that the hatred the Princess in question had conceived for men came from the bitter memory of having been deceived by a Prince in whom she had put all her confidence. It is true that the choice one makes of a favorite in youth is hardly ever enlightened by reason. It is neither the most zealous nor the most estimable who obtains preference, because one does not reflect on the price of virtue; glamour seduces, a scatterbrain presents himself with the brilliance and vivacity of his quips; one yields to him without reserve and without taking the time to examine him; one does not distinguish in him the reality from the appearance; one is almost always the dupe of an imposing exterior; and unfortunately, men only make use of the gift they have to please in order that their indiscretion and perfidy might triumph. It is to be presumed that it was very similar reasons that determined the Queen of Castora to banish all men from her estates.

As she was the best Princess in the world, the love that she had for her subjects and the desire to render them perfectly happy caused her to convene a general assembly of all the nobility—I mean all the noblewomen, for the men had been excluded from it. It was in that assembly that several questions were raised regarding the advantages that female society might obtain, by comparing them to all the evils that resulted every day for that same society. After many sessions in which everyone offered her opinion—which I shall not describe, because I was not summoned to that Council, and besides which, I dread attracting the censure of both sexes by composing a discourse that would doubtless be too simple for the importance of the matters that must have been proposed there—it was finally decided, by a majority vote, that the Queen should establish an explicit law by which it would be forbidden for any man, no matter what his quality or condition might be, to remain for more than twenty-four hours within the entire extent of the State, under pain of being sacrificed to the goddess Pallas, the protectress of the realm.

One has some difficulty in being persuaded that young women had the liberty of expressing their opinion in that assembly, into which a great deal of partiality appears to have entered; it is quite probable that the old dowagers had taken sole possession of the deliberative voices—which appeared to the men to be glaringly obvious. "For after all," they said, "ought one not fear that, by the observation of such a rigorous law, the realm might find itself depopulated in a very short time?"

At any rate, the entire Amazon people submitted to it without putting up any resistance—and the goddess Pallas, content with the sacrifice that had been made to her, wanted to recompense them by giving them a striking mark of her powerful protection. In order to perpetuate that population of heroines by procuring them the means of multiplication, the goddess suddenly caused a spring to appear in the middle of the realm, which a few scholarly mythologists took at first for the one into which the handsome Narcissus plunged when he fell

303

in love with his own face. That spring was, for a while, the subject of much reflection, and it became the source of several disputes; everyone wanted to discover its origin, although they were entirely ignorant of its property. That discovery was only due to hazard; this is how it happened.

Several young women attached to the Queen's service fell ill with a kind of languor; the art of medicine was entirely exhausted in the attempt to procure them relief, but the malady, about which nothing was known, seemed to get worse every day. That determined the doctors, doubtless inspired by the goddess, to prescribe the waters of the new spring, hoping that the dissipation of a long journey might contribute to the reestablishment of their health.

The voyage succeeded as perfectly as they had wished; the young woman, on their return to the court, recovered their plumpness and their natural gaiety, and even something more, which immediately gave the spring a great reputation. All the Amazons, those of the highest rank along with the others, made daily journeys in order to bathe there and render their complexion fresher. Imagine the Queen's surprise, however, when, nine months later, each of the young women gave birth to a daughter. An event so singular made the virtue of the spring known, and such a prodigy augmented the respect and admiration of the noblewomen and the people for the goddess.

In order to mark her gratitude to the goddess Pallas for the new favor that she had granted her, the Queen ordered that a temple should be built on the site of the miraculous spring.

A few critics might perhaps think it ridiculous that women should set out to build a temple; my response to that is that a woman who receives an education similar to that given to men can undertake anything. Do not swallows match us in the art of building?

At any rate, the temple was finished in a short time. It is supported by twenty-four columns of white marble; in the middle is a pedestal twelve cubits high and eight square, representing the attributes of the goddess, whose golden statue enriched with the most beautiful diamonds is placed in the center. Around the temple is a cloister, which distributes several apartments designed to lodge the young women consecrated to the worship of the goddess Pallas. To begin with, the Queen named fifty young women, who were chosen from the noblest families, who would be solely occupied for ten years in singing the praises of the goddess. At the end of that time they were permitted to emerge, in order to join the army. All the children born to those priestesses would be brought up in the temple, their birth giving all of them the rights and privileges of their mothers.

Pentaphile, whose vast vision extended into the most remote times, felt obliged by that new establishment to make another law that tended to increase the population, and ordered all her subjects to visit the temple of the goddess at least once a year and to take salutary baths there, in order to contribute, to the extent that they could, in multiplying the number of the Amazons, which ought always to be the wealth of a state, by virtue of the competition in which everyone engages to procure the necessities and even the luxuries of life, and to contain the people in their duty. It is necessary to add that all those who contravened the law, either by neglecting the worship that they owed to the goddess or by seeking the company of the sex long banished by law, were condemned to be imprisoned for the rest of their lives in the Tower of Regrets, without regard to their youth, birth or dignities.

It was more than twenty years after that great event that the ambassadors of the King of Lydia arrived at Queen Pentaphile's court, where they were received with a magnificence worthy of that Princess. As, in accordance with the laws of the realm, they could not stay long in her estates, they were granted an immediate audience. After having granted their request, the Queen sent them away with rich presents, charging them with letters full of tenderness for her brother the King and Queen Cliceria.

Charmed by the proposition that the King of Lydia had made her to permit that Princess Tramarine should be brought up in her court, Pentaphile appointed the foremost ladies in the

305

palace to go to meet the young princess at the frontier, in order to bring her with the women of her retinue. A numerous cortege of Amazons was ordered to accompany them. During their journey the apartment that the young process was to occupy was prepared, which was next to the Queen's, Her Majesty wanting to supervise personally the conduct of the women charged with the education of the princess.

A few critics might perhaps think that there ought to be no danger of seduction in a court, and even in a realm, where no man dared to appear, and that it can be compared to a republic of bees whose drones have been driven away with darts. Although the Queen had liberated her people from dependence on men, however, while making them envisage the domination to which they had been subjected as a tyrannical yoke, and in spite of the despotism that she had established, she nevertheless reflected maturely on the abuses that might be introduced, either by means of disguises or other intrigues on the part of the women of the court. She was not unaware that their society sometimes becomes as dangerous as that of men, especially when ambition, interest or jealousy takes possession of their mind. Those different passions act with so much empire over a heart that is wilted that they often cause the most essential duties to be neglected. It is true that where there are men, those passions are felt with much more force; they are fomented and animated of their own accord; but the habit that men form of profound dissimulation ensures that they are infinitely more able to hide their faults, especially when it is a matter of deceiving a sex that is too weak and too credulous. At any rate, new sects had been introduced into her estates that augmented her fears; she could not, therefore, take too many precautions to protect the young princess.

When Tramarine had arrived at Pentaphile's court, Her Majesty took charge personally of her instruction in the religion and laws of the State, destining her for the throne that she occupied and forming the project of resigning the crown to her as soon as she was of an age to reign. That could only happen, however, one the young princess had given proof of her fecundity by taking salutary baths in the spring of Pallas.

Tramarine had scarcely reached her twelfth year when she seemed a prodigy of beauty and intelligence; all the graces and talents were united in her person, it seemed that her prudence was in advance of her age and nothing escaped her penetration. Her intelligence and enlightenment, however, only served to make her aware of the fact that she was not made to spend her life with those who surrounded her, and, without having a determined objective, she was already experiencing the melancholy that one could place in the rank of pleasures, although it often serves only to sharpen desire. Already Tramarine was sighing, already she was taking pleasure in solitude, in order to have time to sort out her ideas. Her reflections, dictated by ennui, gave her an air of melancholy that worried the Queen and the rest of the court; Celiane, a young princess related to Tramarine, who had accompanied her, was the most alarmed of all.

Amour, however, the passion whose driving force is the most extensive and causes the most trouble, ought to have been banished forever from a realm inhabited by a single sex. One no longer saw there those temporarily agreeable individuals who amuse a court by their continual persiflage, an occupation well worthy of the frivolity of their minds: those gallant fops with their honeyed tones, whose different inflections of the voice appear to be in accord with their gestures, and who, charged with a thousand baubles, often ornamented with beauty-spots, rouge and bouquets, mount an assault of charms on the most coquettish of women; all those Adonises were proscribed in Pentaphile's estates. What a pity! I doubt, however, that it was much of a loss. But let us leave those reflections and pass on to more interesting things.

II. Princess Tramarine's Journey to the Spring of Pallas

As soon as Tramarine reached the age of fifteen, her household was organized. Celiane was appointed her chief lady in waiting. She was a woman of keen and brilliant intelligence and, as I have said, a relative of the princess on Queen Cliceria's side. Tramarine loved her dearly; she had accorded her all her confidence; it is true that no one was more worthy of it, by virtue of her merit, her zeal and her attachment.

Judging that the Princess was now ready for the novena prescribed by law, the Queen assembled her Council to order the baths that Tramarine could not dispense with taking in the miraculous spring. She wanted the journey to be made with all the pomp and magnificence appropriate to a princess destined to occupy the throne of Castora. Four thousand Amazons were commanded to escort the young princess, and the most qualified ladies competed artfully for the honor of accompanying her; each of them hastened to pay court to her, not unaware of the fact that she was to reign as soon as she had given proof of her fecundity—a favor that they did not doubt that the goddess would grant her.

When the Princess arrived at the temple, the priestesses and young women dedicated to the cult of the goddess came to meet her, and, after having received her from the hands of her ladies in waiting, they introduced her into the enclosure of the temple to the sound of a thousand instruments. Tramarine then presented to the goddess Pallas offerings worthy of the rank that awaited her; she said prayers in accordance with the accustomed ritual, to which the daughters of Pallas added their delightful chorus.

When all the ceremonies observed for the reception of the Princess had concluded, she was conducted to the spring in order to take the salutary baths therein, which continued for nine days, without it being permitted to the princess to speak to any of the women of her retinue, who had retired to tents set up in the environs of the temple; the priestesses served the Princess themselves and never quit her by day or by night.

During the Princess' novena, it was forbidden for anyone to approach the spring, in order to avoid her mixing with the vulgar, and also with a view to observing the favors that the goddess would grant her. In consequence, all the Amazons who came to present themselves, in the hope of participating in the benefits of the goddess, were obliged to wait for Tramarine's departure, and none of her women could take advantage of the opportunities of the journey.

When the novena had finished, the high priestess returned the Princess to the hands of Celiane, who was the first to express the pleasure she felt in advance of her accession to the throne. Her other women surrounded her and took their places in her carriage for the return journey to the court, where they arrived at nightfall. The princess was greeted in the city by the acclamations of the entire Amazon people; the Queen's guards were all under arms, and the palace so brightly illuminated that it might have been mistaken for a globe of fire. The Queen welcomed Tramarine with a joy and magnificence that is indescribable; celebrations of every sort were invented to amuse the princess.

When there was no longer any doubt of the favor she had received from the goddess, the joy was redoubled; odes, epistles, elegies and songs were composed, all of which were addressed to the Princess, in order to predict the gifts that the gods ought to lavish upon those who gave birth to the favors of Pallas.

In all of Tramarine's actions, meanwhile, a languor and depths of sadness were observed, which she could not vanquish, in spite of the endlessly varied celebrations that were incessantly held in her honor. The melancholy in question was, however, attributed to her condition. When she entered into the ninth month, the Queen invited several sorceresses, who were particular friends of hers, to be present at the princess' delivery.

The realm of Castora is full of enchantresses and sorceresses, because of the lairs and mountains that surround it. Besides which, the terrain produces an abundance of all the plants that are necessary to the composition of their potions; it is even claimed that it is to this region that Medea sent all the women most adept at her enchantments.

Bagatelle, Petulante, Minutia and Légère, whom the Queen had not invited, fearful of their science, and even more so of their malevolence, were nevertheless the first to arrive. Each of them was in the most brilliant cabriolet, drawn by swallows. Folly, dressed as a runner, came on ahead of them. The Queen, who feared some malice on their part, went to meet them, in order to offer her apologies for not having invited them; Her Majesty blamed her Chancelleress.[105]

The others having arrived, they were taken into the princess' apartment. Légère, Petulante, Minutia and Bagatelle began by taking possession of the four bed-posts, although that honor was due to the enchantress Bonina and the principal ladies of the court; but it was not a moment to argue about rights.

Lucina, having approached the young princess, had no sooner received the child than Petulante and Légère both cried out at the same time that Tramarine had infringed the laws of the State. Camagnole and Bonina, who could not believe it, each put on their large spectacles to examine the matter; but, unable to dissimulate the sex of the child, the enchantress Camagnole assured the Queen that she would take charge of the education of the Prince, and that she ought not to worry about it. Fortunately, Bonina, although annoyed at being anticipated by Camagnole, began by endowing the Prince with wisdom, science, valor and prudence. The other sorceresses endowed him in their turn in accordance with their genius, but they could not destroy the good qualities with which Bonina had endowed him. That enchantress was the best and most prudent of all magicians, and she only ever employed her art to enable happiness.

Bonina remarked the dolor of the Queen, who seemed to be in despair that such an accident had happened to Tramarine,

---

[105] In 1768 English did not have a feminine equivalent of chancellor into which the French *chancelière* could be readily translated, but thanks to Angela Merkel, we have now been forced to invent this one, which I have gladly appropriated.

regarding it as the worst possible insult that could be offered to her authority. Her Majesty could not imagine that the young princess could have contrived such a crime on her own, and took Bonina into her study in order to try to discover its authors. The enchantress was of the opinion that they should first approach the sorceresses, the sole witnesses to the misfortune, in order to engage them to keep a secret that it might be very useful to conceal from the whole court, by simply declaring that the Princess had only delivered a tumor.

Petulante, however, who was Bonina's enemy, had only brought Bagatelle, Minutia and Légère, who were utterly devoted to her, with the design of blocking all her designs. They therefore declared that they were formally opposed to Bonina's ideas; that Pentaphile, having established the new laws herself, would be attacking the foundations of the State by tolerating such abuses; that a striking example was required; and that it ought to fall heavily upon the Princess, who, although better educated than others, had perhaps counted a little too much, for the impunity of her crime, on the grandeur of her birth, which rendered her even more culpable. The sentiments of the others were divided, but the majority opined in favor of exile.

Bonina, however, who was of the most savant, and the one in whom the Queen had the most confidence, employed her eloquence to combat the sorceresses' arguments, and finally succeeded in putting off the judgment of Tramarine until she was fully recovered, since they could not, without glaring injustice, condemn her without being heard. The Queen appreciated her reasoning, and granted a delay of two months.

Bonina then went into Tramarine's apartment, where she found her in a lethargic torpor. Lucina was occupied in preparing remedies for the Princess' relief. The enchantress talked to Celiane, and informed her of the misfortune that had just overtaken Tramarine, the news having not yet spread through the court.

Celiane, surprised and desperate, could not comprehend by what fatality the baths had produced an effect on her so

311

contrary to the wishes of the entire nation. Her first impulse was to think that the goddess, by means of that alteration, wanted to punish the pride of the women who had taken possession of the government in order to cause it to pass into the hands of the Prince who had just been born. She communicated that idea to Bonina, who thought it very sound, and promised to make use of it herself when it was a matter of pleading the princess' cause, but that she dared not voice it while she was in danger, which might last for six weeks.

While Bonina was fully occupied in appeasing minds in favor of Tramarine, the evil magicians took a malign pleasure in publishing her adventure. The Queen, overwhelmed by dolor, was very embarrassed as to the decision she ought to make. She assembled an extraordinary Council, but could not prevent the sorceresses from presiding over it. Bonina continued to support Tramarine's interests there ardently, and it was finally decided to have all the women who had accompanied the princess to the temple arrested, without distinction of rank or quality. Four Council members were appointed for that examination. The order troubled the court and the city, and everyone argued about it according to the range of their intellect.

The report of the arbiters, however, exonerated the princess; everything was found to have been in conformity with the laws of the State. There was then a visit to the temple and the priestesses, in an attempt to discover whether some abuse might not have been introduced there. In order that no one could escape the examination, Amazons were commanded to surround all the avenues of the temple, with a precise order that in case of contravention, the guilty party should immediately be sacrificed to the goddess.

During that research, Tramarine, gradually recovering her strength, often complained to Bonina and her dear Celiane about the indifference of the Queen, who had not visited her. As everyone avoids those whose disgrace is almost certain, for fear of being dragged down in their fall, the entire court had also abandoned Tramarine.

"Alas, I can perceive only too well what is being done to me," said the unfortunate Princess, "Although I don't know what can have occasioned that coldness. I believe, at least, that no one is unjust enough to impute to me anything that might be contrary to my glory. Why am I refused the feeble satisfaction of embracing my daughter? Must that young princess also share my disgrace?"

Celiane groaned internally at Tramarine's error, but she dared not tell her yet what had occasioned the troubles by which the court was agitated. She was therefore constrained to repress her dolor, in order to soothe the bitterness of Tramarine's heart, but without giving her too much hope.

When the two months expired, the enchantress Bonina came to see Tramarine to inform her of the fate that was destined for her, unless the arguments she could put forward in her defense were strong enough to obtain suffrage in her favor.

"It is with much grief," said Bonina, "that I am forced to inform you of the greatest of misfortunes, but my dear Tramarine, it would doom you completely if it were hidden from you any longer. It is in vain that you ask every day to see the child to whom you gave birth; the child is no longer in my power, the enchantress Camagnole having taken possession of him. Nevertheless, you have nothing to fear for his life; that enchantress would employ all the force of her art in vain; I have anticipated her in preventing her from being able to do him any harm.

"But my dear, it would have been much better for your repose and that of the State had the child died before having seen the light of day. How, with the intelligence and reason that have always been remarked in you, after having infringed the laws of the empire, have you had the temerity to expose yourself to all its rigor? Was it necessary for you, my dear, who ought to have been an example to the entire realm, to become its scandal by your imprudence? A little more confidence in me might have saved you; you're not unaware of the influence I have over the Queen's mind. I would have prevented her from convening the assembly of sorceresses; left alone with you, with Lucina, it would have been easy for us to disguise the sex of your child."

"What do you mean?" said Tramarine, interrupting the enchantress. "What is your injurious discourse implying? Have you forgotten who I am, and what my rank is owed? Me, infringe the laws! What reason is there to accuse me of it?"

"Princess," the enchantress continued, in a severe tone, "is it to me that speech is addressed? You're doubtless unaware of how far my power extends; but to punish you for your temerity, I shall withdraw and abandon you. Others will instruct you as to your fate."

It was lucky for Tramarine that Celiane was present at that conversation. "What, my Lady," she said to Bonina. "Would you, who are goodness itself, be so cruel as to abandon the Princess? Far from being annoyed by her vivacity, you ought rather to draw conclusions therefrom favorable to her innocence. Agree, at least, that it is very humiliating for a young Princess, whose conduct has always been stainless in the eyes of the entire court, to find herself unjustly accused."

Upset to have irritated the enchantress against her, and judging by Celiane's speech that the accusations made against her were very grave, and that she might perhaps need the enchantress' help more than ever, Tramarine apologized for her vivacity and begged her to explain the crime with which someone had dared to blacken her name. Bonina, judging, by virtue of the princess' ignorance, that she could not be guilty, softened in her favor, and promised to help her, after having informed her of what had happened and the resolution that had been taken to banish her from the court.

The Princess, whose heart was pure, assured Bonina that she had nothing for which to reproach herself. "Undoubtedly," she said, "the goddess wanted to test my constancy; I should have suspected as much because of the dreams by which I was agitated in her temple. It is also true that the face of which I formed the image has been present in my mind ever since."

"In truth, my dear Tramarine," said the enchantress, "you surprise me infinitely. It's necessary to assure you that you have a very vivid imagination; are there no other arguments to put forward in your defense?"

"No," said Tramarine, suffocated by her dolor. "I have nothing else to add. It is not the exile that will cause me pain, since it will liberate me from an unjust court, but the shame of the unworthy suspicions that have spread through all minds. I can no longer count on anyone but you, my dear Bonina, and the attachment of Celiane; your amity will take the place of all the grandeurs I am losing."

Celiane could only reply with tears. What could she have said that would have soothed Tramarine's distress? Only time can efface the memory of great dolors; all advice and consolations weaken against the blows of fate when they have recently struck. Nature has rights that she does not care to lose, until chagrin has exhausted its strength; then, by virtue of a wise dispensation, reason regains the upper hand, to reanimate within us the faculties of the soul.

III. The Judgment of Tramarine

The following day, Tramarine was taken to the Council Hall to be interrogated. The enchantress Bonina, who no longer left her, spoke first on her behalf, and told the assembly of sorceresses that the process had no other defense to offer for her justification than the power of the imagination; that she protested that she had never seen any of the mortals proscribed by the law since her entry into the realm, except in a dream during the novena at the spring of the goddess Pallas.

Such a declaration surprised the Queen and her Council infinitely; it caused them to postpone the decision of the affair until the return of the council members charged with the visit to the temple.

Meanwhile, Tramarine was in an unbearable perplexity. Death appeared to her to be a thousand times preferable to living under the accusation of a crime of which she could not prove her innocence. In order to remedy to some extent such cruel woes, Celiane advised her to write to her father the King

315

to inform him of the insult that she was on the point of suffering, by virtue of an exile that could only be injurious to her glory.

Following Celiane's advice, Tramarine wrote to the King of Lydia, but because all her women were entirely devoted to the Chancelleress, her letters were intercepted, and that enemy of the princess had sufficient skill to spread a venom of which she alone was capable.

When the council members had returned from the temple, the Queen assembled a Great Council, in order to be able to examine the princess' case. All the noblewomen of the State who had been delegated to examine the priestesses, after having made their report in favor of Tramarine, declared that they had found nothing that was not exactly in conformity with the law. The princess' defense was then exposed.

Conspiracies had been formed within the Council. Tramarine had few friends there; the vivacity of her intelligence made her feared. The Queen, enfeebled by age, did not involve herself much in government, and those who held the most important positions feared, with reason, the solid and penetrating intellect of the Princess. In sum, the cruelest envy of the Eumenides took possession of all hearts, determined to pursue Tramarine all the way to her exile.

Several Amazons, however, still offered opinions in her favor; they even insisted that a new law ought to be made that admitted the force of the imagination. It is easy to imagine that they were young women who offered that opinion, of which the Queen approved, being naturally inclined toward clemency.

The monarch would have been delighted if it had furnished a means of saving Tramarine; but the old Chancelleress and all the old dowagers of the court, who had a greater share in the government, rose up with a common voice against such a law, which was, they claimed, capable of overturning the order of the State. Besides which, it would tend to abolish entirely the virtue of the spring of the goddess Pallas and encourage the young to neglect the worship that was owed to the goddess, from whom new favors were received every day. Anything that might irritate the goddess against the realm, of which he had declared herself the protectress, had to be avoided, in the fear that she might avenge herself with calamities that would ruin the State entirely, robbing the Amazons of the strength to defend themselves against their enemies.

I shall only offer that abridged account of the Chancelleress' speech, which was found worthy of the eloquence of Demosthenes or Cicero; she finally rallied all the voices to her sentiment.

As the means the princess had employed for her defense had leaked out, the Amazons who loved Tramarine dearly were ready to rise up. They were already assembling in the squares; they even came in a tumult to the palace to demand the release of the princess and also that the power of the imagination should be established in law. But the Chancelleress, always firm in her resolutions, opposed yielding anything to the mutinous people; she advised the Queen to make the full weight of her indignation felt by punishing severely those who had contributed, by their seditious discourse, to spreading trouble in the city.

The sorceresses, devoted to the Chancelleress, supported her opinion, and the Queen, dragged away, so to speak, by the torrent, felt obliged to issue a decree by which she declared that her supreme will was that the laws must have their entire accomplishment, and that all her subjects were bound, under the penalties previously announced, to visit the temple of the goddess Pallas once a year, in order to take the baths salutary to population, and also forbidding anyone to employ, in any fashion whatsoever, the power of the imagination. In consequence, Princess Tramarine was condemned to imprisonment in the Tower of Regrets, although her exile, by way of clemency, would be limited to twenty years.

A judgment as rigorous, pronounced against a Princess of Pentaphile's blood, made the Amazon people tremble, but could not prevent them murmuring against such a severe sentence. The Tower of Regrets was known to be a frightful place, filled with terrible monsters that forbade entry thereto.

Thus in spite of the influence that the enchantress Bonina had over the mind of the Queen, the Chancelleress employed so many intrigues that she triumphed over her on this occasion, and under the vain pretext of the good of the State, she contrived to remove from the court a young Princess whose rank summoned her to the throne, in the fear that, had she mounted it, she would not have given her any part in the government. To suppress sedition, she assembled hardened troops and distributed them through all the quarters of the city in order to keep the people in check.

Bonina took responsibility for informing the Princess of the sad news; the latter received it with a great deal of confidence, and showed, on that occasion, that the grandeur of her soul was above adversity. Her heart, like a rock on to which the waves come to break during a tempest, was not broken; she heard the devastating sentence that her enemies had passed against her tranquilly.

IV. Tramarine's Departure for the Tower of Regrets

Of all the women in Tramarine's service, only Celiane remained faithful, which made the Princess see that the demonstrations of attachment and devotion that had always been shown to her by her servants could not hold up against her disgrace. In that encounter she experienced the ingratitude of individuals who are attached to highly placed individuals by interest alone. Always ready to follow the fortunate, they forget you as soon as fortune turns against you; that is why one ought not to carry the torch of truth into the depths of the cavern in order to learn to discern the subtle motives that lurk and hide between those of candor and blow away, so to speak, the sublime phantom of appearances in order to reveal beneath it the frightful monster that mortals often mask.

Tramarine sent Celiane to the Queen to ask her for a private audience, but she had the cruelty of refusing it.

Tramarine, seeing herself deprived of the hope she had conceived of softening the Queen, asked Celiane to go back again,
to beg her not to impute to her a fault of which she could not
admit herself to be guilty; to remember that she had never
failed in the submission she owed to Her Majesty's order; and
to say that she flattered herself that she would at least be permitted, in order to make her exile more bearable, to take with
her the child whose birth had caused her misfortune, whose
destiny, given that he could not be brought up in Her Majesty's court, ought to be indifferent to her; that it would be the
greatest consolation that she could receive to be able to inspire
in her son the respect and veneration that she had never ceased
to have for the virtues and eminent qualities that shone in Her
Majesty; that she dared to hope of her clemency that she might
be accorded that last grace, as a favor for which she would be
grateful as long as she lived.

The Queen replied to Celiane that Tramarine ought not to
be unaware that her son the Prince was in the power of the
sorceress Camagnole, and that it was impossible to remove
him from her until he had fulfilled his destiny; that she could
nevertheless assure the Princess that it was only with regret
that she saw herself constrained to cede to the force of the law,
and that she ordered her to be ready to depart at dawn the following day.

Tramarine was sensibly afflicted in enduring so much rigor on the part of the Queen, to whom she was veritably attached, not only by ties of blood, but also by those of tender
amity. But what can seduction not achieve? Can one not say
that it covers with a thick veil the brightest lights of reason,
and that, closing the eyes that might be enlightened thereby,
all movements become like those of a blind horse that one sets
to turn the wheel of a press, turning in a narrow circle while it
believes that it is traveling the world entire.

The enchantress Bonina came the next day, in accordance with the promise that she had given the princess, to take
her to her place of exile. Her chariot was harnessed to eight
turtle-doves. Tramarine and Celiane climbed into it with the

enchantress, and the birds immediately cleaved the sir with such rapidity that the Chancelleress, who was on a balcony with a few Amazons of her party taking a malign pleasure in watching them depart, lost sight of them in an instant. We shall leave them to rejoice in their triumph in order to follow Tramarine.

As they approached the tower, the enchantress, who wanted to hide the horror of the view from the princesses, caused her chariot to rise above the clouds, which came down thereafter in a vast courtyard, where twelve damsels dressed in green appeared, who, after helping the princesses to get down, took them into a superb drawing room, in which there was a rich dais destined for Princess Tramarine. Then music was heard, whose chords were delightful.

Tramarine, surprised by such a reception, felt herself penetrated by new obligations that she had to Bonina. When the concert had finished she descended from her throne into another room, where she was served the most delicate dishes. The enchantress, sitting down at the table between Tramarine and Celiane, asked them whether they thought that the abode that had been prepared for them was capable of softening the rigors of the Princess' exile.

"I have been unable to oppose your destiny," Bonina added, "but what I can tell you is that you are under the sway of a great genius, to whom my power must cede. I will protect you to the extent that I can; destiny has condemned you to sleep in the tower, but to reduce the rigor of your fate I have raised this palace alongside it; the gardens you see are attached to it, and although you must sleep in the tower every day, it will be easy for you to get out by means of a secret door that I shall open for you, in order that you can enjoy, without constraint, all the amusements that will be carefully procured for you. I hope that they can banish from your mind the somber sadness that I have observed there for a long time. I would have told you in the Queen of Castora's palace about the favorable intentions that I shall never cease to have to contribute to your wellbeing, if I had not feared that Turbulente, who is your cruelest enemy, might have countered them by means of some dark plot, which, in spite of my help, would have heaped a thousand more misfortunes upon you."

Tramarine thanked the enchantress, assuring her of a boundless gratitude

"I recognize," the princess continued, "the full extent of your power, and I perceive already that you have expelled ennui from this abode, for I can scarcely persuade myself that I am in the terrible fortress of which the mere idea filled me with horror. I see, on the contrary, that I shall be treated here as a sovereign, and far from regarding my exile as a punishment, I shall be glad to forget, in your presence, the woes that preceded it."

"I would like that," the enchantress said, "and will devote all my cares to it; follow me now, without any fear, into my park, to which I shall guide you."

Tramarine and Celiane followed the enchantress, who first took them into the tower, and then down a hidden stairway, at the bottom of which was an iron door. She opened it, and gave the key to Tramarine, recommending that she keep it on her person at all times. They traversed the enchantress' gardens, which were the most beautiful in the world, where they admired, above all, the statues of gods and goddesses, distributed in an admirable order.

Bonina led them into a pathway bordered by lemon-trees and orange-trees, which filled the air with a delicious perfume. Tramarine found the place so agreeable that she proposed to the enchantress that she rest under an arbor that terminated the pathway, where there was a spring whose gentle murmur, combined with the chirping of birds, inspired a mild reverie.

They sat down on the bank of a stream formed by the waters of the spring, which broadened out as it drew away from its source. Celiane, naturally cheerful and playful, who was always on the lookout for opportunities to amuse the princess—who had appeared for some time to be overwhelmed by a languor that was beginning to take root in her temperament—proposed to Bonina that they spend the rest of the day in that delightful spot, and even have supper there, if possible.

A thousand zephyrs immediately appeared to agitate the trees surrounding the stream, whose silvery waters formed rippling waves, which seemed to be mocking the joy that had been expressed in the beautiful Tramarine's tender sighs. Dusk had scarcely covered the sky with a somber veil than, in response to a signal from the enchantress, the twelve damsels appeared, and set down a table laden with the most rare and delicate dishes. They remained at table for a long time, and Celiane amused the princess greatly with the remarks full of wit that enjoyment always inspires in people of intelligence.

More than six weeks had already passed, during which the enchantress had taken care to provide new entertainments for the princess every day, without their being able to dissipate her melancholy. Celiane never ceased to make her tender reproaches, but Tramarine, embarrassed by the presence of her women, who had been ordered not to leave her, only responded with sighs.

A matter requiring the attention of the enchantress obliged her to absent herself for some time. She informed Tramarine about the journey that she would have to make, which she could not avoid. Tramarine was disappointed, and because of a presentiment of the misfortune that might overtake her, did what she could to prevent the journey and to engage Bonina not to abandon her.

"I absolutely cannot dispense with attending the assembly of enchantresses," Bonia told her, "which is being hosted by the redoubtable Demogorgon, one of the greatest magicians in the world; your interests too require me to do so. I shall keep my absence as short as I can; have no fear of the enchantress Turbulente. Here is the means of shielding yourself from her malevolence; so long as you carry this protection it will keep you safe for the traps that Turbulente might set for you, provided that you are careful not leave the tower without having it on your person. You will lack nothing during my absence; I have given the orders necessary for your safety, and in addition to the dozen women that are at your service, I shall give you two others, in whom I have every confidence and who are sufficiently instructed in the art of magic to be able to protect you from unexpected dangers that the negligence of the others might occasion. Only suffer, beautiful Tramarine, that they are never far away from you."

Bonina then embraced the Princess and Celiane, who escorted her to her chariot, which disappeared momentarily.

V. The Abduction of Tramarine

In order to dissipate the chagrin caused to them by the departure of the enchantress, Celiane proposed to the princess that they go down to the garden, and Tramarine, not wanting any other company than Celiane's, forbade her women to follow them. The two that the enchantress had left to watch over her safety, however, told her respectfully that, having received precise orders from Bonina not to lose sight of her, they could not, without contravening them, dispense with accompanying her everywhere, but in order not to inconvenience her, they would remain at a distance. Tramarine, obliged to consent to that, went alone the path of the orange-trees to the covered arbor, and at down on a grassy bank perfumed by a thousand little flowers, where, yielding completely to her melancholy, sad reflections plunged her into a profound reverie.

Celiane, wanting to distract her from that somber sadness, sat down at her feet.

"Princess, she said to her, "I flattered myself that you had only come away from your women in order to relieve your troubles by confiding the reasons for them to me, but since my Princess does not hold me in high enough esteem to honor me with her confidence. I beg you at least to listen to the concerts that the nightingales are performing for her."

Tramarine, her eyes fixed on the stream, was paying very little attention to what Celiane was saying. The latter continued: "Don't you admire the happiness of those birds, whose only law is pleasure? For myself, I find that nature, in only according instinct to them, seemed to favor them much more than us. What use is the reason that the gods have reserved for us, which only serves to trouble our pleasures? In truth, the condition of those little animals enchants me, and the state of depression in which I see my princess almost makes me desire to resemble them. What if we were nightingales? How happy they are! No anxiety or regret ever troubles their felicity, they never have any desires that they cannot satisfy, and their joys never costs them any remorse. Why does the enchantress Bonina, who has so much power, not have that of allowing us that metamorphosis? At least I could amuse my Princess with my songs and the vivacity of my caresses, and perhaps please her."

Perceiving that nothing could distract Tramarine, Celiane finally adopted a more serious tone. She had the eloquence of rhetoric; she resumed that of sentiment, and succeeded in touching the heart of the Princess, who decided to confide her secret to her.

"Alas, Celiane," she said to her, sighing, "all your talk, far from easing my pains, only serves to renew them. Is it necessary that we should pass the most beautiful of our days like this? It's high time that I opened my heart to you; always harassed by my women, I have not been able to find the moment.

"I shall not remind you of my childhood; you remember well enough the honors for which it seemed that Heaven had destined me. You see, however, my Celiane, that everything has been reduced to spending my life in solitude, and in spite of your amity and the attentions of the enchantress Bonina, I cannot resist the ennui that is oppressing me. These gardens, whose beauty delights and enchants you, the waters of this stream whose crystalline quality you admire, redouble my distress at every moment, and, by a fatality that I cannot vanquish, and I can no longer distance myself from it. That doubtless appears to you to be a small problem, but when you are informed of my woes, you will no longer be surprised.

"Do you remember, my dear, the journey I made to the spring of Pallas? You know that during my novena, I remained within the enclosure of the temple, where I was served by the priestesses consecrated to the cult of the goddess, a grace only accorded to women of my rank; but the entire court is ignorant of what happened to me there. It is only to your zeal and your amity that I am going to confide a secret that has trouble the repose of my days for such a long time.

"Know, then, that when I had said my prayers to the goddess and had presented my offerings to her, the priestesses took me to the spring, where, after having undressed me and put me in the bath, they went away respectfully, leaving me at liberty. When I was alone, a felt the waters rise up; a slight movement agitated them, and a young man, such as Amour is depicted for us, appeared to my eyes. Timid at the sight of him, I shivered in dread, but, approaching me with a majestic and tender gaze, he took me by the hand and put his arms around me.

"Alas, how seductive it was! I cannot describe to you, my Celiane, the disturbance that was born in my soul. His first glance engraved forever the keenest passion; I know no crime except that of having been able to displease him, and all my misfortunes stem from that of having lost him; it is in vain that I search for him every day in the depths of thee waters.

"But what am I saying, my Celiane? My passion is leading me astray; I cannot think about it without disturbance. I mentioned that which he had spread through all my senses, which prevented me from fleeing; my gaze, attached to such a seductive object, seemed to have taken away all my strength to defend myself from his caresses when the priestesses, coming back, caused him to disappear, and I noticed that as he drew away he placed a finger over his mouth, doubtless to make me understand that I must not reveal what had just happened to me.

"The next day, scarcely had I entered the bath then the same movement that made itself felt the previous day announced the arrival of my vanquisher to me. He approached

325

me, and spoke to me tenderly and passionately. Animated by his presence, my dear, I do not know what I replied, which appeared to transport him with pleasure, because he suddenly took me in his arms and the gleam emerging from his eyes was communicated to my veins, and I felt that I had been set ablaze by a devouring fire. I wanted to flee; my strength abandoned me, but in the midst of my disturbance I thought I perceived that he wanted to take me with him.

"The waters were already swelling, and I felt that I was about to perish. Gripped by fear, a piercing scream escaped me, which attracted the priestesses; but in spite of the shock that was afflicting me, I could not help looking again to see what had become of my vanquisher. I saw him plunged beneath the water, and I distinctly heard a voice that told me that my life and my honor depended on my conduct, and that the felicity of the Prince with whom I had just united myself was attached to the silence that I must maintain. I understood then the sin that I had committed.

"Alas, my dear, it was no longer in my power to repair it. Trembling and desperate, I fell unconscious into the arms of a priestess who had advanced to help me and to discover what had alarmed me. I refrained from confiding the reason to her; I only told her that the rapidity of the waters had frightened me—which caused her to make the resolution to have one of the young women destined to the cult of the goddess enter the bath with me thereafter.

"I confess that I was annoyed by that resolution, foreseeing that it would deprive me of the sight of my dear Prince. I was not mistaken; the rest of my novena passed without me seeing him. Since that day he has been ever present in my mind, but it is in vain that I have searched for him. In spite of my lack of hope, however, I cannot be content except on the edge of waters, which nevertheless only nourish my distress, without the ingrate who is its cause, and perhaps is witness to it, ever deigning to take pity on me."

"In truth, my Lady," said Celiane, "your adventure is one of the most surprising. You will permit me to criticize you for having neglected to employ those reasons, which are more than sufficient to justify you. It's quite certain that Queen Pentaphile could not have refuted their evidence, for it is doubtless some marine god who took on the form of a young man and united with you in the spring. Perhaps it was Neptune himself; and I have no doubt that if the Queen had known all these circumstances, far from ordering your exile, she would unfailingly have placed you on the throne she occupies. You should at least have consulted the enchantress Bonina about such a delicate affair, one which the repose of your days depends."

"What are you saying, my Celiane?" said the princess. "Are you forgetting the silence that was imposed on me? Perhaps at this very moment I'm offending my spouse in daring to confide my secret to you, although he ought to pardon me for that feeble relief. In any case, even if I had not made a vow to sacrifice my repose to him, what proof could I have given of the verity of my adventure? I would have risked my life, and lost all hope of seeing my Prince again. Besides which, you're not unaware of the ennui that afflicted me at Pentaphile's court, and that ennui has been greatly increased since my union with the Prince of the Waters.

"What could I have done in Castora's court, incessantly carrying the image of a Prince who doubtless does not approve of any of its laws? I assure you that I would always have lived in dolor and bitterness; you know how constrained one is there even in one's way of thinking, incessantly harassed by women whose bigotry and falsity renders their commerce unbearable; those women would rather renounce life than their opinions; they only take pleasure in excavating the sentiments of people they want to blacken. Nothing is lacking in their portraits; their scrupulous detail easily reveals the hand that held the brush. At least in this retreat I enjoy the relief of complaining, without fear of the criticism of my enemies."

"I agree, my Lady," said Celiane, "but it is the sole liberty that remains to you, and my princess cannot deny that, dissipation not being the surest remedy against chagrin, yours is

327

nourishing itself and maintaining itself by solitude. I don't know anything as cruel as being incessantly prey to dolor, but permit me, my Lady, to add one more reflection regarding your divine spouse. If it were permitted to criticize the conduct of the gods, I would accuse the one who is the author of your troubles of injustice, for, after all, why has he abandoned you? Such conduct would surprise me less on the part of a mortal; it is so rare to find a sincere attachment among them that I had thought until now that constancy was a virtue that the gods had reserved to themselves, but your adventure has changed my sentiment; it has made me see that, like humans, they lose their appetite for the one they have loved the most as soon as they have satisfied their desires."

"Let us not criticize the gods," said Tramarine. "They doubtless have their reasons when they make us feel the effects of their wrath. It is not for feeble mortals to penetrate the causes, and we ought to submit without a murmur to all that it pleases them to order in our destinies, which are in their hands."

"My Lady," said Celiane, "I can only admire the piety of your sentiments."

"Alas," said the princess, smiling, "How far I still am from the blind submission that they demand from us!"

Lightning and the sound of thunder was heard then, interrupting the conversation, and they made their way back to the tower.

Tramarine, still tormented by the desire to see her spouse the Prince, found herself very agitated during the night. Unable to enjoy the sweetness of slumber, she proposed to Celiane that they go down into the gardens, in order to respire the coolness of a delightful early morning. Dawn was beginning to break, to announce the return of the sun.

Celiane had difficulty putting on a dress in order to follow Tramarine, who was already in the gardens when she traversed them in long strides in order to reach the path of the orange-trees. Perceiving that the Princess had neglected to bring her protective charm, she was about to beg her to go back to the tower when she heard her utter a piercing scream as she turned around.

Celiane, who could not see anyone, could not imagine what had caused her fright; she precipitated her course toward the princess, and fell backwards on perceiving the enchantress Turbulente, who, after having seized Tramarine, forced her to climb into her carriage, and disappeared instantly.

The tender and faithful Celiane reproached herself for her complaisance in following the princess without having alerted her women, or at least the two whom the enchantress Bonina had commissioned to guard her. The tender friend uttered cries that attracted the enchantresses, but while they are running to help her and to share her dolor, we shall follow the unfortunate princess.

VI. Tramarine's Entry to the Empire of the Waters

Although distressed by the latest cruel blow of fortune, the princess did not appear any less firm in her adversity. Indignant at the evil methods of the perfidious sorceress, she demanded to know, with a great deal of firmness, what could have made her bold enough to dare to come into Bonina's gardens to abduct her, since she could not be unaware of the protection that the enchantress had accorded her.

"It's that protection that offends me," Turbulente replied, "and it's in order to punish both of you that I intend to subject you to the punishment your disobedience merits. Bonina was greatly mistaken if she thought she could impose on me, but in order that she won't seek to surprise us in future, you'll remain under my guard."

At that impertinent speech, Tramarine was content to look at the sorceress with a sovereign scorn, without even deigning to respond. Having arrived at a lair adjacent to the tower, the sorceress ordered the princess to take off the dress she was wearing in order to put on a kind of brown canvas sack, but she pretended not to have heard her, which obliged Turbulente to serve as her chambermaid. Then she made her descend into a dungeon full of venomous beasts, leaving her nothing but a little poor flour steeped in water.

Left alone, Tramarine yielded to all the bitterness of dolor. Several days passed without her being able to close her eyes, but finally, overwhelmed by trouble and anguish, and no longer waiting for anything but death, she fell asleep.

A pleasant dream came to charm her mind, and made her see the Prince, her spouse, as tender and passionate as he had seemed in the spring of Pallas, showing her a door by which she could emerge from slavery.

Calmed by a little repose, Tramarine reflected on the vision she had just had, and, by the light of a lantern that spread a feeble glow, she explored the whole cellar. She did indeed discover a door, which she approached with a disturbance that soon changed into a frightful anguish, on finding it closed by several padlocks.

All her firmness crumbled before that last blow of her misfortune; seeing herself frustrated of the hope she had formed, she could not help bursting into tears, on reflecting on the sequence of disasters that had succeeded one another without interruption.

As everything in life dries up, however, and often gives way to more useful reflections, the Princess, after having exhausted her tears, remembered that she still had the key to Bonina's gardens, the sorceress having neglected to take away everything that she had on her person. She approached the door then, in order to try to open it.

She had no sooner put the key into a padlock than the door collapsed of its own accord, and the dungeon disappeared, by virtue of the power that the enchantress had attached to the key.

Tramarine, surprised to find herself alone on the shore of the sea, racked by pains, fatigue and needs, advanced toward the edge with the design of hurling herself into it. But Prince Verdoyant, who was watching all of Tramarine's movements from the bottom of the sea, saw her gazing at the waves and uttering profound sighs; he feared then the effects of a despair that overlong suffering might have excited. He instructed several undines[106] to stay close to the shore and to keep their eyes incessantly on the princess, ready to receive her in their arms and carry her to a grotto hollowed out under a rocky point, where no mortal had yet dared to take refuge.

The undines obeyed Prince Verdoyant and rendered in considerable numbers to the place where the beautiful Princess was, without attempting to guess their Prince's designs.

Tramarine, believing herself to be alone, and not perceiving in the distance any trace that could suggest to her that the place was inhabited, surrendered to the horror of her situation.

"Alas," she said, sighing, "I perceive only too well that this is the place that my husband has chosen to put an end to my woes; it is, therefore, in the waters that I must end my life; and the last wish that I shall form in dying is that that torture will at least be agreeable to you.

"O Neptune," the Princess added, "if it is true that I have been able to offend you, you ought to pardon my ignorance; do you not have proof enough of my constancy, and have you not avenged yourself by the woes that you have made me suffer for such a long time?"

---

[106] Undines, the water elementals of the document apocryphally attributed to Paracelsus annotated in *Voyages de Milord Céton*, are usually imagined as being invariably female, like the nereids and oceanids of Greek mythology, but the French term has both a male form, *ondins*, and a female one, *ondines*, much as the usually-male *gnomes* are provides with a female equivalent in *gnomides*. English also permits "mermaid" to be supplemented with "merman," and when entire undersea realms are imagined in any language, the presiding figure is usually imagined to be male. As there is no English "undin," however, I have been obliged to make use of the more generic term "water-sprite" in the title of the story and to describe Verdoyant.

Then she cast herself into the sea—but the undines, attentive to all her movements, received her in their arms and transported her to the grotto.

Such is the folly of the human mind: the individuals who misfortune overwhelms often prefer death to the services that can be rendered to them. Tramarine, believing herself to be surrounded by naiads, allowed her head to fall languidly, sometimes on one of them and sometimes another, warming their bosom with her tears.

The beautiful undines did everything consoling that they could to calm her dolor; finally, they took away the wretched canvas smock with which the evil sorceress had covered her, in order to dress her in a sea-green gauzy robe decorated with silver, pressing her hair between their hands, which they allowed to fall back in waves on to her bosom; then, perceiving by the rising of the waters the arrival of Prince Verdoyant, they withdrew respectfully.

Tramarine, surprised to see them return to the sea, perceived an extraordinary agitation in the waves, and saw a superb chariot rising out of them, made in the form of a seashell, drawn by eight dolphins that appeared to be bounding over the waves. That chariot stopped outside the grotto; then Tramarine saw the young Prince who had been the object of her desires for such a long time, who descended from it, came into the grotto, and lifted her to her feet.

Seizing one of her hands, which he kissed delightedly, he said: "I have finally found you again, beautiful Tramarine, and I swear that I will never abandon you again. The time has come to tell you that I am the Prince of the Water-Sprites; my father's estates are at the bottom of the sea. As I can only live in the waters, I could not rejoin you sooner. Be certain, divine Tramarine, that it has not depended on me to enable you to avoid the woes that you have suffered since our union in the spring of Palas. Forced to abandon you then, I have shared your anguish without being able to abridge it.

"As it is not permitted to us to unite ourselves with a mortal, I have endured many contradictions before being able to determine our people to consent to accord you immortality; and it is only by proving your constancy and discretion that the favor has finally been granted to me. My father the King has demanded that you must pass through the most humiliating ordeals; he is satisfied with the firmness that you have shown on the various occasions when the jealousy of the Amazons has exercised them against you. Will you forgive me, my adorable Princess, for the woes that my love has caused you to suffer?

"But you're lowering your eyes, and making no response. Is it dread or amour that is making you sigh thus? Are you distressed by the idea of uniting yourself with a genius?

"Perhaps," Prince Verdoyant added, "The abode of my empire frightens you. It's true that until now, no mortal had descended into it without losing their life, but Princess, be reassured; I've obtained from my father the King, whose power extends over all the water-sprites, that in favor of a passion that I have been unable to vanquish, you will be admitted to immortality, and receive in his empire the quality of Princess of the Water-Sprites."

Tramarine was still overwhelmed by the emotion of the latest adventure that had happened to her; joy, dread and shame were all agitating her soul in turn, and robbing her of the strength to reply to the Prince, who continued thus:

"However, beautiful Tramarine, even though everything is ready to receive you, and I am sure of the favorable sentiments that you conserved for me, at least until the moment when you confided them to Celiane—don't blush, my princess, to have made that confession of a legitimate ardor; I was present to your eyes at that moment, and from the depths of that stream, formed expressly to renew the memory of the knots that amour ought to tighten, I admired your candor, the piety of your sentiments, and was ready to show myself twenty times, but in addition to the obstacle presented by Celiane's presence, I had not yet obtained from my father the place that I propose you enable you to occupy—I cannot be absolutely happy if you continue to show reluctance to unite yourself forever with my fate."

Tramarine, simultaneously surprised and flattered by the speech of the genius, but unable to convince herself that she could live under water, finally replied to the prince, while gazing at him with an expression that expressed both love and dread: "Forgive me, my Lord, if I have difficulty believing you; I don't doubt the extent of your power, and that is what makes me doubt that such a great Prince would want to lower himself to the extent of uniting himself with a feeble mortal, and that he would prefer her to the beautiful undines with which his empire is full. I do not know the laws of the genii, but I know that when they have chosen a companion, it is no longer permissible for them to change her, unless that law has an exception for women of my species; that would render me the most unfortunate of all creatures, since I would lose by immortality the only resource that the unhappy have in the excess of their woes, and I would be obliged to drag out a life that would become unbearable to me if you cease to love me, no longer being able to die of the dolor of having lost the heart of a prince who could alone attach me to life."

Prince Verdoyant, transported by such a tender confession, employed the most convincing arguments to reassure the Princess, giving her a thousand praises and taking as many kisses.

"Have no fear, divine Tramarine," the genius said. "I swear to you by this heart, which has never loved anyone but you, and by the vast extent of the waters, that no undine will ever share my tenderness henceforth; I also swear to avenge you for the insults that Pentaphile has made you endure by her injurious suspicions; I shall bring down her pride by submitting her realm to the Prince to whom you have given birth, and I shall punish the King of Lydia for the injustice he did you in expelling you from his court."

"Stop, dear prince," said Tramarine. "Remember that it is my father the King that you have just sworn to ruin. Far from complaining of his injustice, ought I not, on the contrary, to bless the day when he banished me from his presence? Is it not to that exile that I owe the joy of being united with you forever? In any case, deceived by the oracle, he doubtless believed my exile necessary to the repose of his people. How many reasons for daring to ask for grace on his behalf! I flatter myself that I might obtain it in the name of the love that you have just sworn to me."

"I can refuse you nothing," said Verdoyant, "and I see with pleasure that the generosity of your heart is manifest in all your actions; I cannot revoke what I have pronounced against the King of Lydia, but I shall soften, in your favor, the rigor of his fate.

"Let us go, dear Tramarine," the genius added. "It is time to descend to the realm of the water-sprites, in order to introduce them to a Princess as worthy of reigning in all hearts by her virtues as by the purity of her sentiments."

In response those words, Tramarine was not able to conceal her fear at the sight of an element that she had always regarded as very dangerous, and although, two hours earlier, despair had driven her to cast herself into it, what had happened to her since had renewed the appetite that one has for life when one can flatter oneself with entering into an eternally durable happiness.

The young princess, at the sight of the danger that she thought she was running, fainted in the arms of the genius, who, without being astonished by her weakness—the final mark of her humanity—made her take a few drops of elementary elixir, which had the virtue not only of recalling her to her senses and fortifying her, but also of taking away the puerile dreads attached to the fate of mortals. Then Tramarine recovered her spirits, and, like a rose struck by the brilliant rays of the sun, reborn from the coolness of a beautiful night, which, extending its petals to a vivifying dew, stands up on its stem and seems to salute the beneficent dawn that has resuscitated it, the heart of the Princess opened to the sweet transports of joy; that joy reanimated her enfeebled senses, and her extinct eyes reopened to the light, shining with the flame of pleasure.

"How ashamed I am of my weakness," she said to the genius, with a tender and animated gaze. "But what has so suddenly dissipated my fears? Dear prince, henceforth, you may command me; I'm ready to go with you." Then she offered him her hand, with the smile of amour.

Verdoyant took her to his chariot, and the dolphins, which seemed charmed to be carrying away such a beautiful Princess, pranced over the waters, dived as they accelerated their course, and arrived a few hours later in the capital city of the water-sprites, where the King made his usual abode. To enter into the palace they traversed several large courtyards paved with emeralds and passed under an arcade sustained by twenty-four columns of ice. Several officers of the court were lined up there, who made speeches to the princess on behalf of the entire estate. There was no artillery salute; although the water-sprites are perfectly familiar with cannons, they make no use of them.

To begin with, Tramarine, along with a numerous cortege, was taken into a large gallery ornamented with monochrome paintings on the most beautiful glass imaginable; the frames were made of diamonds of different colors, whose assortment made an admirable view. At the end of the gallery was a throne made from a single diamond, which might have been taken for the chariot of the sun when it appears with its full brightness; it is certain that if Tramarine had not participated in her husband's divinity, she would never have been able to sustain the glare.

On the throne, the King of the Water-Sprites was sitting, with a trident in his hand, the sole ornament of his grandeur. To his right were the principal officers of the crown, to his left the beautiful undines who were the ornament of the court. The genius Verdoyant, having approached the throne with Princess Tramarine, introduced her to His Majesty, asking him to accord her all the favors that she had acquired by her virtues, her merit and her suffering.

The young Princess, educated in the mythology of the pagans, did not know any other religion or any principles other than those she had received. Convinced that she was in the presence of Neptune, she addressed him as such.

"Great God, sovereign of the waters, whose empire commands the whole universe...."

"Stop, Princess," said the king, interrupting her mid-sentence. "I am not a god. It is true that I enjoy immortality, but I obtain all my power from a singular divinity, whom we all worship and who formed everything there is in the universe. It is by courtesy of his omnipotence that we reign over the waters." Then, addressing his son in a voice that made the vaults of his palace tremble and, in swelling the entire ocean, announced a furious tempest, he said: "How, Prince, have you dared to surprise me by choosing a pagan to participate in immortality by a union that can no longer be broken?"

Prince Verdoyant, who perceived that Tramarine, non-plussed and trembling, no longer dared raise her eyes, said to the King of the Water-Sprites, in order to appease his anger: "My Lord, you're not unaware that amour is a sentiment born involuntarily, which is nourished by hope. That passion establishes its domination over everything that breathes in this vast universe, its choice often made at first glance. Amour examines nothing and puts no difference between the heart of a pagan and that of a genius, both burning with the same fire and seeking only to nourish it. It is true that I have not examined the beliefs of Princess Tramarine; her misfortunes have touched me, her virtues, her graces, her talents and her beauty have charmed me, and I have judged her worthy of a happier fate. It is for that reason that I have sought all the means of liberating her from the yoke of death; but my Lord, I can answer to you for her docility in listening to the instruction you want her to be given, and she will submit without a murmur to all your wishes."

After confirming the word that Prince Verdoyant had just given to His Water-Sprite Majesty, Tramarine added that she promised to conform to anything that was demanded of her, convinced that such an enlightened genius would not seek to mislead her.

The King seemed satisfied with that response and ordered that she be taken to the apartment destined for her.

VII. Tramarine is taken to the Hall of Marvels

The genius Verdoyant accompanied Tramarine to a crystal pavilion illuminated by carbuncles that appeared to be as many suns. One of the faces of the pavilion overlooked a flower-bed enameled by a thousand kinds of flowers unknown on land, which spread a delightful perfume through the air. A concert of a new kind was heard; voices were singing the praises of the genius Verdoyant and those of Princess Tramarine. When the concert ended, she was taken into a hall of magic mirrors that had the virtue of representing everything that was happening in the world.

Surprised by that marvel, the Princess told the genius that she would be very glad to know what had happened to Celiane since the malevolent Turbulente had so cruelly separated them.

"Fix your attention on the mirrors," said the Prince, "and all your desires will be fulfilled."

Tramarine looked into one of the mirrors, which first showed her the enchantress Bonina's gardens. Celiane appeared there, fainted, and the women commissioned to guard the princess hastened to help her. Their distress and anxiety were evident in their eyes. Tramarine saw her, after recovering from that weakness, recounting her misfortune; her speech was interrupted by sobs, and tears flowed in abundance; it seemed that her words were traces on the mirror. All the Princess' women present at that narration appeared to be in despair, but the deplorable state that the unfortunate Celiane was in did not permit them to scold her for her negligence.

Then she saw the enchantress Bonina arrive, who, informed of Tramarine's abduction, went into her study to consult the great books there. She spent a long time leafing through them with a singular attention; then, she drew several figures, with the great pentacle of Solomon, in order to oblige

338

one of the genii inhabiting the air to descend in order to inform her of Tramarine's fate.

By means of her conjurations she eventually compelled the genius Jael to inform her that the Princess was united forever with the genius Verdoyant, Prince of the Water-Sprites, and had been admitted to the fate of immortals. The enchantress, content to learn such good news, hastened to make Celiane party to it, and gave her the option of remaining with her or being transported to the realm of her choice. Celiane preferred the society of Bonina to all the other advantages that the enchantress offered to give her.

"Look now," said Verdoyant, "at the despair of Turbulente; it ought to serve you as a comedy."

Tramarine saw the disheveled sorceress running in response to the loud sound that struck her ears when the genius broke and overturned the dungeon that she had built by the force of her enchantments. That Megaera tore out her hair in despair, and uttered howls similar to those of Cerberus, imploring the Furies to support her rage and fury, and uttering a thousand imprecations against Bonina, whom she believed to be responsible for liberating her captive.

Then she was seen mounting her chariot, which was harnessed to six monstrous rats, in order to go consult Pencanaldon, a famous magician.[107] As she was entirely preoccupied with her vengeance, however, she abandoned herself to the conduct of her rats by leaving the bridle around their necks and they tipped her into a precipice where she and her vehicle were smashed, and they saw her serve as pasture for the rats that had been hauling her.

Tramarine, whose heart was excellent, could not see that spectacle without horror, in spite of the evils that Turbulente

---

[107] This sentence appears to be mistaken; Pencanaldon subsequently features in the plot as the king of a realm neighboring Lydia, and it seems likely that the magician Turbulente wanted to consult is actually Philomendragon, to whom Camagnole has taken Tramarine's son.

had made her suffer. She turned to another mirror, which enabled her to see Queen Pentaphile, who, after having been told that she had departed for her exile, appeared to repent of the harsh judgment that she had, so to speak, been forced to pronounce against the daughter of the King of Lydia. The sovereign shut herself away for several days without allowing anyone into her presence.

Finally, no longer able to contain her dolor, she sent for the Chancelleress, made her ardent reproaches for having deprived her forever of the sight of a lovable princess who ought to have been the permanent ornament of the court and to whom she had intended to hand over the government of the state shortly, sensing her own forces fading by the day.

"Would it not have been punishment enough," added Pentaphile, "to be unaware of the fate of her son, without ever being able to hear any news of him? Besides which, the King of Lydia might repent of having deprived her of the rights she has to his crown; might he not also ask me to return her in order to form some alliance useful to his kingdom? It is against my will that her exile has been pronounced, and insufficient regard was paid to her rank and birth."

The Chancelleress, judging by the Queen's regrets that she was in danger of losing her favor, wanted to make one last effort at least to conserve her position; that is why she replied that if Her Majesty desired to see the Princess again, it would be very easy to bring her back to court; that the enchantress Bonina, who had taken her under her protection, would take pleasure in returning her; and that the sentence that Her Majesty had passed would serve all the same to maintain her people in their duty, which was the sole objective that her Council had had in mind in the condemnation that they had been obliged to pronounce in order to subjugate her subjects to the observation of the laws that Her Majesty had established herself.

"It required a striking example," the Chancelleress added, "which could intimidate them; but Your Majesty always has it in her power to grant mercy to persons she thinks worthy of it. I will only dare to observe to Your Majesty that, in recalling the Princess to your court after the fatal sentence that it was necessary to pronounce against her, it is to be feared that she will conserve a bitter memory of it and that when authority is in her hands, she might change the entire form of the government, giving entry into the realm of new customs."

This adroit discourse did not save the Chancelleress from disgrace. Her enemies, jealous of the power she had usurped, did not fail to take advantage of the circumstances to finish blackening her in their sovereign's mind. Several memoirs were presented to her, in which there was evidence that the Chancelleress had animated the sorceresses against the Princess with a view to taking possession of all authority, and of the intrigues that she had long been fomenting among the troops, tending to put the administration of the realm in her hands. All the accusations were proven, and it was also remarked that the principal responsibilities of State were no longer occupied by any but her creatures.

The Queen, surprised to discover that he had been deceived by a woman in whom she had put her full confidence and whom she had every reason to believe to be attached to her by virtue of all the favors she had never ceased to lavish upon her, immediately issued an order for her to be taken to the Island of Ennui, finding her too culpable to deprive her of her life. The order was promptly carried out, and all the treasures she had amassed were confiscated, to the profit of the troops.

Tramarine was curious to learn the location of the Island of Ennui, of which she had never heard mention. The mirror immediately showed her a marshy place, perpetually filled by a dense fog, where the sun's rays never made themselves felt: an arid terrain filled with frightful monsters, which, by virtue of their venom, emitted a pestilential atmosphere; nothing grew on the island except poisonous plants. It was in that horrible place that Tramarine saw her enemy arrive, but what she could not see without shivering with horror was what those monsters did, in seizing the criminal and devouring her entrails, one attaching itself to gnaw her heart and others attacking the various parts of her body. By an unusual prodigy, far from those creatures robbing her of her life, they seemed to renew it by means of her suffering.

"It is thus," said the genius Verdoyant, "that all the criminals of state who have abused the confidence of their master by vexing the people ought to suffer for several centuries."

The Princess, continuing her observation of the realm of Castora, remarked that to replace the Chancelleress, a woman of distinguished merit had been appointed, who was strongly attached to her interests. As soon as she had taken the oath of fidelity, her first concern was to propose to the Council the recall of the Princess, whose virtue and superior merit were a sure guarantee of her good conduct. She added, addressing the Queen, that after having given an example of severity in the person of Princess Tramarine, Her Majesty could not give one of clemency in any object more worthy, and at the same time more agreeable to her people.

The Queen yielded without difficulty to this sage advice, and, in order to favor the person who had given it she appointed her to inform the Princess of the mercy that she was showing her in ordering her recall. A detachment of four thousand Amazons was commanded to honor the princess' triumph.

Tramarine, satisfied to learn that they had finally been forced to render to her birth and virtue the justice that was their due, unembarrassed by the regrets that her loss might occasion, and impatient to know what had become of her son, passed on to another mirror. There she saw the sorceress Camagnole, who, after taking possession of the young prince, climbed back into her cabriolet, which caprice took to the abode of Philomendragon, one of the greatest magicians there was. He was a furious, malevolent, rascally and bloodthirsty man; he had instructed Camagnole in the magic arts, and one could say that she knew almost as much as he did.

As soon as she arrived they examined the little prince together, and Philomendragon, after having traced a few figures on a large ebony table, made such a frightful grimace as he showed them to Camagnole that Tramarine, trembling for her son, turned her eyes away from the mirror with a terrible alarm and looked at the genius.

"Dear Prince," she said to him, agitated by anguish, "Will you suffer that abominable sorceress to dispose of the life of the prince your son?"

"Have no fear, dear Tramarine; it is not in the power of the magician to attempt the life of a child who owes his birth to a genius, and the grimace you have just seen him make is only occasioned by the knowledge he has acquired, by means of his art, that he can never harm him."

"But is it not in your power to take him out of the hands of those two monsters," said Tramarine, "who will henceforth be solely occupied in spoiling the mind of the young Prince by giving him false principles and a very bad education?"

"Your reflections are just," said Verdoyant, "but I have foreseen all the inconveniences that might arise, and I can assure you, in order to tranquilize you completely, that one of my friends, a sylph, has taken responsibility for watching over the conduct of your son."

"I thought that your power was limitless," said Tramarine. "At least tell me his destiny."

"I cannot satisfy you on that point at present; be content with the promise I give you that he will be very fortunate."

Tramarine persisted, and the genius, by refusing to content her, irritated her. Women, like men, are naturally curious; the desire to know seemed to be innate within us, and the great ought not to neglect anything in the care they take for their education; talents, sciences and humanity ought to serve to sustain the dignity of their rank, although birth often does not give intelligence and judgment; one might think that nature sometimes compensates those she has caused to be born in a mediocre estate—but that is enough moralizing.

Tramarine persisted with a great deal of ardor; she employed everything she could imagine to vanquish the resistance of the genius, but, in spite of her insistence, seeing that he would not give in, she took his refusal for pure obstinacy, made him a thousand reproaches, complained of his lack of amity, and that she was very unfortunate to have had so much confidence and sentiments so tender for a Prince who responded so poorly to them. Tears and sighs were combined with these reproaches, which softened the genius to the point that he was ready to yield to her impatience.

"What are you demanding of me?" he replied, in an impassioned manner. "Know that my silence is attached to the happiness of the young Prince; if I speak, his fortunate destiny will be changed to one of frightful misfortunes.

Far from yielding to his arguments, Tramarine, convinced that what the genius had said was simply to avoid satisfying the desire she had to learn her son's fate, redoubled her insistence. "At least give me," the Princess added, "this mark of confidence. What fear do you have of my indiscretion? Are not my son's interests a sufficiently powerful motive to enclose within myself a secret that might harm him? Besides which, since it is no longer permissible for me to live on land, the deposit cannot be contrary to him."

What can Amour not do? His power is manifest in the heavens, in the air, on land and under the sea. The genius was about to yield to the insistence of the Princess when the King of the Water-Sprites suddenly appeared in the hall. His presence surprised the Princess infinitely; her disturbance was manifest in the blush that covered her face. She feared that the King might have overheard the altercation she had just had with Prince Verdoyant; she did not know yet that a genius has the power to read what is happening in the heart of a person by looking at her.

The King of the Water-Sprites, judging, by what had just happened as a result of Tramarine's indiscreet curiosity, that she was not yet sufficiently purged of the terrestrial substance that had enveloped her, and that the dose of the elementary elixir that Verdoyant had given her when he enabled her to descend into the empire of the waters had not been sufficient for her repose, ordered her to take another large glass. That completed the process of rendering her entirely similar to the undines, enabling her to envisage the things that affected her most with a Stoic tranquility; and, without losing sight of everything that interested her on land , she only spoke about them henceforth with the modesty appropriate to a Princess of the Waters.

Several months went by, after which the King, content with the dispositions in which he saw Tramarine, engaged the Prince of the Water-Sprites to take her on a journey throughout the immense extent of his liquid estates, in order to make herself known to al his subjects, and at the same time to instruct her in the religion and the laws of the empire. He accorded fifteen years for her voyage, in order that she could stay for a while in the most curious places.

Perhaps that seems like a long time to people uninstructed in the usages of that world, but let them be informed that in the realm of the waters, that time passes like a single day. The voyage that the King of the Water-Sprites ordered Tramarine to make can be regarded as an aspect of his politics. The Princess was the first person of the land he had admitted into his empire without being subject to the yoke of death, which changed entirely the way of thinking of the inhabitants of our hemisphere. The monarch feared, perhaps with reason, that in spite of the double dose of elementary elixir that Tramarine had been made to take, she might fall back into her former weakness, especially if she found herself within range of admiring every day the singular beauties contained in the Hall of Marvels. It was, therefore, in order to fortify her in their maxims and their laws that the voyage was ordered.

It is to be presumed that, although Tramarine was the most perfect of women, she had not yet acquired the virtues and gifts with which the genii are endowed at birth, and that, in spite of the great dispositions she had for the sciences, it was only after many years that she would be filled with the admirable talents that are only accorded to genii of the first order. The King, occupied with the preparations for the voyage of the Prince and Princess, and wanting it to be made with all the pomp due to aquatic majesty, ordered that their retinue would be composed of ten thousand male water-sprites and three thousand undines.

Perhaps one might think that such a numerous cortege would be a great embarrassment in such a long voyage; that is why I ought to inform my reader that water-sprites do not experience any; as they are genii they have no need of any provisions, air being sufficient for their subsistence. Tramarine, having become immortal and, in consequence, participating in all the virtues of water-sprites, was also dispensed of the needs to which human nature has subjected feeble mortals.

VIII. Voyages in the Empire of the Waters

On the day fixed for the departure of the Prince and Princess, they took their leave of His Aquatic Majesty, after which they mounted their carriage, which their retinue followed in vehicles of mother-of-pearl shape in the form of seashells—which must have been the most beautiful sight in the world for those who had the privilege of witnessing it.

To begin with, the genius headed southwards. He stopped in a place where frequent battles took place, which often only served to populate the empire of the waters.

"I see," said the Prince, "that you are gazing in surprise at that multitude of new inhabitants, who have been unknown to you until now. Know, my dear Tramarine, that these people you see arriving at every instant are individuals who have just been subjected to the fate attached to all mortals, death, and that they have been condemned by the Almighty to live among the water-sprites for a number of years, proportionate to the sins they committed on earth. Although I am already informed of their conduct, I shall nevertheless interrogate a few of them, in order to make you aware of how far the malevolence of the humans who presently inhabit the earth can go."

At the same time, the genius summoned a man who appeared clad in a very singular fashion, and asked him why he had been condemned to drink forty pints of elementary tea every day for a hundred thousand years.[108]

"Prince," said the wretch, "although my penitence will be long, I give thanks to the Almighty for not having given me one more rigorous; the hope I have of a happy future will enable me to support it without murmuring, because nothing is so consoling for an unfortunate as to be persuaded that his pains will one day be changed into pure and real pleasures; for it seems that one anticipates one's happiness in the certainty one has of arriving there.

"This, then, is my history in brief, in order not to weary the attention of the Princess who is accompanying you.

"Elevated to the foremost dignities of the state by the bounty of a great monarch who had accorded me all his confidence, far from employing my talents to merit his generosity by my gratitude and a sincere attachment to my master's interests, the sudden elevation of my fortune only augmented my pride. Having become insolent after the success of a few enterprises, I thought I could risk anything. I began by dissipating the finances, and was then obliged to overburden the realm with onerous state debts; in order to hide the bad employment I was making of the immense sums levied on the people every day, I provoked unjust wars in which the bravest officers and the best soldiers perished, and which spread desolation in all spirits. Then I engaged the Prince in false steps capable of

---

[108] "*Thé elementaire*" [elementary tea] can be found in two works by the offbeat moral philosopher Jean-Baptiste de Boyer d'Argens in the context of posthumous rewards and punishments. In *Lettres juives, ou Correspondance philosophique* (1737), however, it is not a punishment but a solace given to mild and virtuous women who join the company of water-nymphs, in contrast to the fate of proud and arrogant ones, who go to dwell in fire with the salamanders. In *Lettres cabalistiques* (1754), by contrast—which is presumably Madame Robert's source—drinking sixty pints of it per day is the punishment inflicted on a bad cardinal.

347

diminishing his power, because they would increase mine. Conduct so opposed to the justice of government eventually attracted the hatred of the public to me; my actions were revealed and the disabused monarch had my subjected to the penalty due to my crimes."

Tramarine, surprised by the ingratitude and bad faith of that favorite, asked the Prince whether one could put any trust in the speech of a man accustomed for so long to lies and intrigue, and whether he was not still trying to impose on them.

"No, my dear Tramarine," said the genius. "when humans have quit the bodies that envelope them and bind them to the earth—as those you can see are only fantastic—it is no longer in their power to disguise the truth or to seek to deceive us. Sent here, in order to execute the sentence of their condemnation, nothing can diminish the rigor of their fate."

"Tell me, I pray you, whether all these people I see arriving in a crowd, and who are said to have died for the defense of their liberty, are condemned to the same punishment; those people seem to me to be full of candor and good faith."

"It's true," said Verdoyant, "that they are simple and devoid of malice; but here punishments are proportionate to the sins one has committed, and all those you see are only descending into the waters in order to be purified there. Less culpable than the others, their punishments will be much lighter and shorter, and they will not be obliged to drink the tea."

Tramarine demanded a much more extensive explanation from the genius, to which he lent himself gladly, for the sake of the Princess' instruction; but as that conversation was very long and perhaps a trifle tedious, we shall pass on to other matters that are perhaps of greater interest.

PART TWO

IX. The History of the Great Ogress

After Verdoyant had instructed Tramarine on the principal articles that ought to interest her, they continued on their way, and paused on the edge of a river that served as the boundary between two nations subject to great revolutions. The Princess was surprised to see a host of people camped as if in battalions, whose various garments formed a rather singular tableau.

"What do those disguises signify?" Tramarine asked. "Doubtless they're preparing to play some comedy and have chosen this location to serve as their theater."

The genius, smiling at Tramarine's error, told her that the different costumes she could see only served to distinguish the regiments composing the army of a sovereign very respectable for his virtues, whom they had served for a long time with much zeal and attachment.

"One of these peoples is guided by a liking for novelty, the other by that for riches. Ambition dominates some, others permit themselves to be carried away by weakness; the largest number have joined forces in order to shake the authority that ought to hold them in respect—but to explain their dispute to you it's necessary to begin by telling you how it originated.

"In one of the republics of this empire, a daughter was born of discord and lies, whose seductive intelligence was able to win over the principal officers of the reigning Princess, who, seduced herself by deceptive appearances, had her come to her court. At first no one thought of opposing the progress that the young woman made in the heart of their sovereign, but as she gradually grew up she became an ogress who was so well fortified in the mind of the Princess that she invaded a part of her authority, and in spite of the obscurity of her birth she nevertheless procured a quantity of admirers who, in order to captivate her good graces and obtain her favors, hastened every day to compose elegies, eclogues and epistles, which were presented to her with great ceremony; it was by that means that she was able to discover those who were most attached to her.

"As she is vain, ambitious, proud and arrogant, and has completely captivated the mind of the Princess, she has had the skill, in order to augment her authority, to change the entire form of the previous government in order to establish new laws; in sum. nothing is any longer done except on her orders; no one is as audacious as those who execute her wishes; they are set to attempt the most extraordinary things every day, without anyone being able to oppose their designs. By virtue of a species of consideration that is believed to be owed to the eminent titles with which they are adorned, they are emboldened to undertake anything—but what is even more singular is that they carry out with assurance what other people would never have dared to imagine.

"The faithful subjects of the Princess, repelled by all these actions, and even more so by the blind submission that the ogress wants to demand of them, have revolted. The boldest have attacked the ogress personally, saying that she is a daughter whose name and birth are unknown; some claim that she is a bastard. That has formed different parties in the estates of the Princess, and many of her subjects are seeking to shake off the yoke of the adoptive daughter, especially since she has attempted to invade all governments and attribute to herself graces that previously ought only to be accorded to the Princess. It is even claimed that she wants to distance the subjects from the obedience that they owe to their sovereigns, by means of new constitutions that seem contradictory and entirely opposed to the old morality. Many corybants have refused to submit to it, and the majority have rallied to the standard of rebellion, giving rise to perpetual wars. The different nations that you can see have assembled here in order to demand the head of the ogress."

"Tell me," asked Tramarine, "what reasons the Princess can have for wanting obstinately to compromise her authority, by leaving it in the hands of a daughter who might set all her estates ablaze? Ought she not rather relegate her to some distant island, in order to reestablish the peace that every sovereign ought to desire in order to ensure the wellbeing of her people? Could she not marry her to some foreign prince powerful enough and firm enough to reduce her to obedience? The Great Turk or the great Khan of Tartary appear to be sufficiently capable of it."

"That's true," said Verdoyant, "but they have refused. However, plenipotentiaries have just been appointed to negotiate a peace; they have orders to propose the marriage of the ogress to Philomendragon, who, as you know, is a great magician and one of the most monstrous ogres ever to have appeared. It is hoped that the Princess will be able to yield to the wishes of her people and that the marriage will deliver them from the tyranny of the young woman, all the more so as the magician's estates are at the antipodes of those of the Princess, which should ensure that there is no reason to dread such a union."

"For myself," said Tramarine, "I fear it, since our son the Prince is in the power of that magician, and I regard his union with this evil ogress as a superabundance of misfortune for the dear child."

"I've already told you, Princess," the genius went on, "that he cannot attempt anything against my son; but to set your mind completely at rest, know that the sylph who is charged with his education presently has him in his power."

The Prince and Princess were interrupted then by noises of conflict that became audible. All the soldiers were running to arrange themselves beneath their standards, and a black swarm of auxiliary troops, advancing in a disorderly fashion, came together and formed into a huge square battalion.

Then the ogress appeared; she resembled one of the pyramids of Egypt. Her head, which was triangular, had three faces; in one she seemed mild and modest; that was the one she showed when she wanted to subjugate new peoples; she showed the second, painted with arrogance and pride, when she had achieved her objectives, and the third face as marked

351

with a furious and menacing expression. Her arms and legs were as many serpents that enabled her to move.

Tramarine, frightened by the sight of such a hideous monster, did not want to stay any longer by the bank of the river; that is why she never knew the outcome of the battle that took place there.

X. *The Accomplishment of the Oracle*

The genius, yielding to Tramarine's desire to go away, took her to the shores of Lydia. The princess, catching sight of an old man whose majestic air seemed to inspire respect, felt very emotional.

"My dear Prince," she said to the genius, "I can't resist the tender emotions I feel for that venerable old man. Grant me, I beg you, the satisfaction of conversing with him."

The Prince of the Water-Sprites complaisant, as all amorous genii are, told Tramarine that she was free to interrogate him, and simultaneously beckoned the old man to approach; although he was not unaware that it was the King of Lydia, he wanted to give the Princess the pleasure of discovering that for herself.

Tramarine, sensing an increase in the interest she was taking in the monarch—for she had no doubt that he was one—asked him, very gently, and in the tone that tenderness and pure amity inspire, who he was and what country of the land he had inhabited before descending to the realm of the water-sprites.

"I am Ophtes," the King replied. "I reigned for more than sixty years in Lydia."

At those words, if Tramarine had not enjoyed the prerogatives attached to great genii, which never permit the experience of any weakness, she would surely have fainted, but she got away with a slight shock.

"Oh, my Father!" cried the Princess. "I can therefore enjoy the happiness of seeing you again; but have you nothing to regret in what destiny has procured for me?"

"My daughter," said the King of Lydia, observing in her the tender emotion that one feels at the sight of an unexpected pleasure, "you will learn, by the story of my adventures, the fatality of my destiny and the accomplishment of an oracle that, until now, has always appeared to me to be impenetrable.

"I know," the King went on, "that you have been instructed in the home of the Queen of Castora of the principal events that had happened in Lydia before the time of your exile. I shall therefore pass over rapidly the first years that went by thereafter, since nothing remarkable happened to me.

"I was enjoying a perfect security; my crown having been ensured in my family by the birth of two princes that the gods had granted me, when I learned that Pencanaldon, whose estates are adjacent to mine, had made an irruption into one of my provinces. I learned at the same time that he had taken possession of one of the strongest places in Lydia. Surprised by such a move, sure that he had no complaint to make to me about anything whatsoever, having never had any quarrel with him, I hastened to have my troops assembled, with a view to opposing the rapidity of his further progress. I departed at the head of fifty thousand men, all hardened soldiers, in the hope of expelling the perfidious Pencanaldon and punishing him for his audacity, but Fortune, who had until then always been favorable to me, made me sense keenly, in that encounter, the scant trust that one ought to place in that inconstant goddess.

"As disorders were increasing by the day, I was constrained to force my march in order to halt my enemy's progress, I finally arrived a short distance from the army of the treacherous Pencanaldon, who was waiting for me in good order in order to do battle. I had resolved to try to avoid combat, in order to give my troops time to rest, but my soldiers were incensed themselves by the bravado of the enemy; I was no longer able to arrest their impetuous courage; the battle was gradually engaged; it was one of the bloodiest. I maintained the advantage for a long time, but just when I was about to render myself master of the battlefield, by a fatality that I cannot comprehend, fear suddenly gripped my entire army; my troops broke up, the greater number taking flight, and in spite of my efforts, I was never able to rally them. In the end, what can I tell you? My defeat was complete and I also had the misfortune of being taken prisoner, with the Queen, who had followed me in the expedition.

"Pencanaldon, glorious with the success of his victory, took us to his capital city, attaching us to his triumphal chariot like miserable slaves. Then he imprisoned us in a tower built on a rocky point that seemed to project far out to sea. What augmented my despair further was that he had the cruelty of separating me from Cliceria.

"I learned a few days later, from two officers commissioned to guard me, who were chatting familiarly together, believing me to be asleep, that the cause of all the disorders that had just occurred was simply the love that the perfidious Pencanaldon had for the Queen, because he flattered himself that, having vanquished me, he would have no difficulty in seducing Cliceria, by proposing to share his kingdom with her and allowing her to dispose entirely of my estates, which he wanted to unite with his crown, having no doubt that, being his prisoner, he could force me to repudiate it when I thought that I could only obtain my liberty at that price.

"Thus, blinded by his passion, he thought that he would find no obstacle to his evil designs, and even dared to declare them to the queen without any hesitation. Cliceria, indignant at the proposition that he had the audacity to make of marrying her once he had succeeded in making me sign the document that would return her freedom of action, marked the scorn that she had for such sentiments as his with so much pride that, far from wanting to hear him out, she went to shut herself in her cabinet, forbidding him to reappear in her presence unless the honor, virtue and probity that he had banished from his court returned to animate his soul and inspire in him new sentiments and procedures worthy of being adopted by Ophtes and Cliceria.

"For a long time, the unworthy Pencanaldon employed the most tender pleas and supplications in trying to seduce the

Queen, but, perceiving that they were only augmenting the scorn that she had for him, he changed his conduct, substituting the most terrible threats if she would not yield to his desires. All those different assaults were in vain; Cliceria, fortified by glory and virtue, sustained them with a firmness worthy of her rank.

"I was informed of some of her troubles by one of the Queen's women, who, enjoying a little more liberty, had found a means of winning over one of my guards, who introduced her into my apartment by night. Although the woman strove to diminish somewhat the frightful situation in which Cliceria found herself, my mind, always industrious in tormenting me, enabled me to see it as it was.

"Overwhelmed by dolor and, unable to do anything to help in her distress a princess who was all the more dear to me because I was convinced that she owed all her woes to the affection she had always had for me, I might at least be able to reduce them. It was difficult to imagine that subjects I had treated more as a father than a king would be so little interested in my fate as not to form the design of delivering me from my captivity; in consequence, I could only exhort the Queen to suffer constantly tribulations that she could not avoid.

Pencanaldon, who did not want to leave the Queen, gave his generals orders to take possession of all of Lydia, which they succeeded in doing in two campaigns, no one opposing their rapid conquests. I learned the sad news that my people had surrendered, without any resistance to the perfidious tyrant, and what completed my despair was the loss of the two young princes that I had left in my palace, under the guidance of their tutor, a man whose probity was known to me. I had feared, rightly, the cruelties of that enemy of humanity, but that was the final blow of his perfidy.

"The Queen, who was pregnant when we were taken prisoner, had hidden her condition with extreme care, Celinde, the maidservant in whom she had the most confidence, offered to deliver her of a princess that she was disposed to conceal from the sight of the cruel Pencanaldon, when he came into the Queen's apartment unexpectedly, and, seizing that innocent victim, took her away himself to give her to his daughter, named Argiliane, with orders to have her exposed in the forest to the voracity of wild beasts.

"Far from obeying her father's orders, Argiliane, shivering at such an inhuman sentence, took the little princess to the Craintive Island. That island had been given to her as her privilege, with the power of command there. After having endowed the child with all imaginable perfections she gave her the name Brillante, and, to protect her from Pencanaldon's research, in case he discovered her disobedience, she placed her in the hands of the wife of a shepherd to be nursed, instructing her not to let anyone see her on any pretext whatsoever.

"The Queen learned that Princess Argiliane had taken charge of her daughter. She knew that the princess was a great sorceress, but she did not know that she only applied herself to the sciences, and especially that of Chiromancy, in order to do good, and with a view to impeding her father's cruelties. Cliceria, whose woes were increasing every day, ordered Celinde, a woman of great intelligence, to employ all her means to reach the princess. Celinde, full of zeal for the service of her mistress, insinuated herself into Argiliane's presence with great ingenuity; she had the art of gaining confidence, and depicted the misfortunes of the Queen in such a touching fashion that she was softened in her favor, and eventually promised to take a keen interest in the unfortunate Cliceria.

"Argiliane, whose heart was excellent, groaned every day, without daring to make her complaints known, over her father's barbaric conduct; that is why she was easily determined to do everything in her power to help the oppressed queen, by procuring her a thousand assistances to sustain her against Pencanaldon's pursuits and help her to support her woes—but without daring to declare herself overtly for fear of irritating her father.

"For a long time, Pencanaldon had been planning to marry his daughter to Prince Corydon, his nephew, who paid court to her assiduously. Although Argiliane recognized qualities in him superior to the other princes of the blood, however, the aversion that she had for dependency always made her distance herself from that union. In the fear that her father would one day constrain her, she made the resolution to propose to the princes that he should marry the Princess of Lydia, who had the reputation of being one of the most beautiful princesses in the world.

"'I know that your sentiments are too delicate,' Argiliane added, 'for you to make use of the influence that you have acquired over my father's mind. I can never be yours, in spite of the preference that I admit I have always given you over your rivals. If I could determine myself to make a choice, you alone would be capable of fixing it, but the resolution I have made to spend my life in independence determines me to beg you no longer to think about our union.'

"Prince Corydon seemed devastated by those words; he could only respond with a sigh, and although he had never felt any great passion for Argiliane, the habit he had formed of seeing her and conversing with her frequently about science and the interests of the State, and perhaps also the hope of acquiring by the marriage one of the most beautiful kingdoms in the world, caused him to suffer the Princess' speech impatiently. He complained bitterly of her indifference and employed all the eloquence that could be formed by an ambition founded on hopes that the King had nourished for a long time. Eventually perceiving that he could not touch Argiliane's heart, however, he limited himself to getting her to conserve her esteem for him, adding that he would always put his happiness and his glory into meriting it.

"It was after that conversation that the Princess advised Celinde to see Prince Corydon, in order to praise the charms of the Princess of Lydia, who ought to be at the court of Pentaphile, Queen of Castora. 'I know,' said Argiliane, 'that she is ravishingly beautiful, that she had all the virtues worthy of a throne, and that Pentaphile has destined her own for her. You ought then to ask him to liberate the Queen of Lydia, and tell him that Tramarine will be the price of the services he will render to that princess. Add, on my part, the assurances of reigning in Lydia after the death of Ophtes, and that I promise to do everything in my power to assist him.'

"The Queen informed me of that negotiation via Celinde, whom I ordered to follow Argiliane's advice exactly. That clever woman had no difficulty persuading Prince Corydon, who had already heard mention on numerous occasions of the advantages that Tramarine had acquired over other women; he was charmed by the prospect that Celinde offered him of an alliance that might satisfy both his desires and his ambition, since he saw himself forced to renounce that of Argiliane. Those advantages, combined with the promises she had made, completed his determination.

"The Queen, delighted to learn that Celinde had succeeded so well in her negotiation, sent her to give me the great news. Celinde therefore came one night to tell me that Corydon had promised to liberate the Queen and then take her to Pentaphile's estates, on condition that I ratified the agreement that the Prince had made with Queen Cliceria. I had, therefore, to engage myself by that treaty to accord to Prince Corydon Princess Tramarine, who, by virtue of her birth and the death of her brothers, had become the heir presumptive of the Kingdom of Lydia. By the same treaty, I had to declare him my successor to the crown in the case that Tramarine had disposed of her hand in favor of some other prince. On those conditions, the Prince promised to return with a powerful army to deliver me from my captivity, and then help me to reconquer my throne.

"As you can imagine, I accepted, without hesitation, propositions that, in the circumstances in which I found myself, appeared to me to be very advantageous. Deprived of all help and languishing for ten years in the most cruel captivity, I consented without difficulty to everything that was demanded of me, and had the Queen told that I gave her *carte blanche* and left her free to act according to the opportunities that presented themselves, trusting myself entirely to her prudence in the various negotiations that she would be obliged to make in order to engage our allies to furnish the necessary resources for me to be able to return to my estates and expel Pencanaldon's troops.

"When the articles of our negotiation were signed, Celinde took them to Princess Argiliane, who was so content that, in order to facilitate their entire execution, she sent the Queen a talisman composed of seven metals that had the virtue of rendering invisible the individuals who wore it around their neck. It was by means of that talisman that the Queen escaped from Pencanaldon's palace, where she had been kept prisoner for such a long time.

"In spite of the natural urgency one has to enjoy liberty, especially after such a long captivity, however, the Queen did not want to leave the castle without expressing to Princess Argiliane how sensible she was to all her evidences of generosity and all the services she had rendered to her, especially what she had just done to facilitate her escape, the first use of which she made was to beg her to extend her benefits to her husband the King and everything belonging to us.

Argiliane promised her that with a very good grace, and the two Princesses, after having given one another a thousand reciprocal assurances of sincere amity, separated full of esteem for one another,

Cliceria then came to surprise me with Celinde, who said to me as she entered my cabinet 'I've finally come, my Lord, to inform you of the deliverance of the Queen. She left the castle without any of the guards seeing her, and that miracle only occurred with the help of Argiliane, who wanted to help the Princess by removing her from her father's power.'

"'I render thanks to the gods,' I cried, 'and ardently wish that they will favor the justice of our rights, in order that I can enjoy the satisfaction of soon being reunited with her.'

"'A part of your wish is granted this instant,' said Cliceria, throwing herself into my arms.'

"Seized by joy at the sight of a Princess that I had always loved passionately, I could not understand how she had initially been hidden from my eyes, but the talisman that she showed me, turning it over several times, caused me to admire the virtue of that masterpiece of the art.

"Celinde left to tell Prince Corydon that the Queen would not be long in coming to him. I took advantage of her absence to express to Cliceria how sensible I was to this last proof of her tenderness, since she was, so to speak, risking her life, or at least the liberty she had only just recovered by a kind of miracle. Finally, after we had given one another a thousand testimonies of our mutual tenderness, I communicated to her all the information I thought necessary for her to make representations o the Queen of Castora and to engage our other allies to aid us with their help. Celinde came back in to tell us that it was time to separate. It was necessary for us to yield to circumstances, but it was not without shedding many tears.

"Accompanied by Celinde, Cliceria went to Prince Corydon, who was waiting for her, and, everything being prepared for the voyage, they left at daybreak. The Prince, in order to avoid the suspicions to which his absence might give rise, had adopted the pretext of visiting the fortifications of Strong Island, belonging to Princess Argiliane. Meanwhile, Pencanaldon, resentful for a long time of the scorn that the Queen never ceased to show her, after having employed the secrets of magic in vain to make her condescend to his infamous projects, finally took the decision of absent himself, on Argiliane's advice. That was what gave the fugitives time to get away, and with Argiliane's help, they arrived in a matter of days in the realm of Castora.

"During the journey, the Queen informed the Prince of the laws that Pentaphile had imposed on all foreigners. Corydon seemed charmed at first, flattering himself that, if he did not have the good fortune to please, at least he would not have any rivals to fear. His joy was soon turned to a profound sadness, however, when he realized that he would not be able to stay in the realm without exposing himself to a thousand dangers.

"Cliceria, who perceived his chagrin and did not want to be deprived of his advice in the various negotiations that she anticipated having to make in the circumstances in which she found herself, and who was no longer forced to conceal herself from the eyes of the curious, offered the Prince the talisman that rendered invisibility. Corydon accepted it with such abundant expressions of gratitude that the Queen was convinced of his attachment to her interests.

"Equipped with the talisman, which enabled him to go anywhere without fear of being discovered—and, in consequence, to see Princess Tramarine, with regard to whom he had formed the most charming ideas, at any hour—the Prince hastened his march, scarcely giving the Queen time to get any rest. When they arrived at the court of Castora, the Prince did not think it wise to appear there, although he accompanied Queen Cliceria in all the visits that she made to Queen Pentaphile.

In the first meeting of the two princesses, Pentaphile seemed at first to be slightly disconcerted when Queen Cliceria asked for news of Princess Tramarine and the reasons that might have prevented her from seeing her. The Queen of Castora could not help manifesting a good deal of disturbance at that question, but, being unable to avoid answering it, she told her the story of Tramarine's adventures, and ended up by expressing an authentic dolor and finding herself unable to give her any news of her.

"Cliceria could not understand any of the story she had just heard, being unable to convince herself that the power of the imagination could produce such surprising effects. She believed, therefore, that everything she had been told was a fable invented to seduce her, and that Pentaphile had perhaps made some secret treaty with her enemy, of which her daughter had been the price. She did not want to make her doubts known, however, and withdrew to the apartment that had been set aside for her in order to confer with Prince Corydon there,

361

whom she seriously feared might have been put off by that first hitch, and, annoyed by the delay, might abandon her enterprise.

"That is why, after having talked to him for a long time about Tramarine's adventures, presuming that it would never be possible to obtain any news of her, she told him that a young princess still remained, whom she offered him in order to fulfill her engagements. 'It's true,' the Queen added, 'that I don't know exactly what has become of her, but as she is in the hands of Princess Argiliane, I flatter myself that it will not be difficult for me to find out.'

"Corydon, who had only attached himself to Tramarine because of the reputation she had acquired of being one of the most accomplished Princesses in the world, had a great deal of difficulty reconciling himself to the exchange that was being offered to him. However, he persisted in the advice that he had given the Queen to employ all means imaginable to discover the place that Tramarine might have chosen for her retreat.

"Although the Queen was very annoyed by Pentaphile's conduct, not only in the matter of Tramarine but that of her own unfortunate captivity, of which I was still experiencing the deplorable fate, she nevertheless told the Prince that she did not think it would be prudent, in the present circumstances, to risk irritating the Queen of Castora by conducting searches that would doubtless be fruitless. The need she had for her help in assisting her to reconquer Lydia caused her to think that it would be more appropriate to dissimulate their subjects of complaint until I had recovered my throne. Those arguments were too good for the Prince not to yield to them.

"As it would take too long to report all the negotiations that it was necessary to make in order to engage my allies to furnish the necessary troops, however, suffice it for you to know that, in spite of the efforts of Pencanaldon, who had made himself hated by all my people because of his cruelties, the Queen returned to Lydia, and I was finally delivered from my captivity.

"It was only after that great event that I learned about your adventures. As little inclined to believe them as the Queen, I was, nevertheless, in despair are having contributed to the disaster by my foolish credulity—or, to put it better, my stupid vanity in wishing to penetrate the secrets of the gods, and banishing you from my court by virtue of an injustice for which I had long been punished by my remorse. I wanted to repair my fault, by doing everything that was in my power to discover your fate, but what I was able to learn completed my despair when I was told that it was not possible to obtain any news of the princess, and that it was presumed that she had thrown herself into the sea. That frightful suspicion caused me such a furious upset that, after having sworn the doom of Queen Pentaphile, I fell victim to an apoplexy, which immediately brought me here.

"I do not regret a life that would only have prolonged my inevitable woes, by incessantly retracing for me the memory of my faults. I flatter myself, on the contrary, that the honors you enjoy in their empire, by virtue of your happy union with the Prince of the Water-Sprites, might have made you forget all the tribulations that preceded them, and that you do not conserve any resentment on their account."

Tramarine assured her father that he was just in his estimation; that, although she had missed his presence for a long time, she had no reason to complain about the rigorous sentence that he had pronounced on her; and that, in order to show him that she did not conserve any memory of it, she would henceforth do everything she could to have him rendered the honors due to his rank and procure him all the satisfactions he might desire.

No one is unaware that when one has quit one's mortal body, all ranks are confounded, and that there is no longer any distinction between souls, especially in the empire of the water-sprites. However, Princess Tramarine obtained from General Verdoyant, by a singular grace, that her father the King would be admitted to the Court, and that he would enjoy the same privileges there as the water-sprites. She also asked that he be dispensed of drinking the elementary tea, but she could not obtain that last favor, for reasons that I have not been able to determine, but which are doubtless unanswerable.

They continued their route thereafter with King Ophtes, with the design of visiting all the parts of the world. Reflecting on her father's adventures, the story of which had informed her that she had a young sister who must still be on the Craintive Isle, Tramarine wanted to know more about her, and made the request of Prince Verdoyant that he should direct his march toward that isle in order to procure her, if possible, the satisfaction of seeing her without it having to cost the life of the young princess.

"I can easily satisfy you," said Verdoyant, "and to dissipate the tedium of a long journey, I shall relate to you, and to your father the King, the adventures of the Princess, which will surely interest you both."

XI. The Story of Brillante and Amour

"Princess Argiliane, still not daring to declare herself in favor of the Queen of Lydia, thought that she could serve her most usefully by affecting to submit to her father's orders. She knew his cruelty, and fearing, with reason, that in one of those moments when the Queen's scorn drive him to despair he might give orders contrary to the desire she had to save the little princess, being accustomed to avenge himself by means of such cruelties, when she had taken her to Craintive Isle she returned to the court and told the cruel Pencanaldon that the child had been exposed, and devoured almost immediately.

"Brillante was, therefore, brought up as the daughter of a shepherd. I shall pass over her childhood rapidly, which was of no interest, because she was not known to be a Princess, the least actions of whom are ordinarily admired. When Brillante had attained her sixteenth year, however, Argiliane thought that it was time to begin informing her of the advantages of her birth, and as she came to the island quite often, in order to give lessons to the little girl—who, by her docility and gentleness, had entirely acquired Argiliane's heart—the Princess remarked with pleasure the beauty and touching graces of her young pupil. She saw germinating within her the talents that nature produces and education perfects; she admired most of all her charming modesty, a true sign of innocence and purity of heart.

"Argiliane, for particular reasons, did not dare allow Brillante to appear in her father's court, but she feared that the young Princess, whose heart seemed disposed to tenderness, might form some engagement whose consequences might trouble her repose. That is why she began to talk to her about the disorders that amour causes in al hearts. 'You ought, my dear Brillante,' Argiliane said in the latest conversation, 'always to be on your guard against the attacks of men, who, for the most part, are only seeking to seduce our heart; conserve the modesty that is the most precious attribute of our sex; it ought always to be the faithful guardian of the purity of the soul. Avoid sacrificing to Amour that which is your dearest possession; Amour is a restless, perfidious and tumultuous god, who is only constant in his frivolity; that god make a cruel sport of the misfortunes and despair of those who follow his laws; often, one sees him confusing male and female lovers and exciting the most tender friend against the person he loves the most; the furies that Amour inspires recognize neither rank, nor duty nor nature; there is nothing sacred so far as he is concerned, especially when jealousy or vengeance animates him, and it is only by avoiding him that one can avoid those woes.

"'Never forget, my dear Brillante,' the Princess added, ' the advice I am giving you; the time is approaching when that god will seek to seduce you; there is no form that he will not take in order to succeed; for, when the endeavors to please, he appears charming and full of attractions that only serve to subjugate reason; Desire and Voluptuousness march in his footsteps, Hope almost always accompanies him, and he seems only to make his happiness out of the felicity of mortals. You

365

ought not allow yourself to be surprised by him now, after the portrait I have I painted for you.'

"It was by means of similar instructions that Argiliane strove to make Brillante experience the joys that one experience in a tranquil state, but youth only seeks pleasure, solitude seems tedious to it, and it is only age and reason that can cultivate a taste for the counsels of reason.

"Brillante began to sense ennui, and her heart told her that there were pleasures that she might savor. Already she was forming desire without knowing where to direct them, and sighs that escaped her caused the Princess to fear that she might form some inclination unworthy of the blood that had formed her. That is why she told her, before leaving her, that Heaven had caused her to be born far above the estate in which she had been brought up, and promised to reveal the mystery of her birth at their next meeting.

"Brillante, raised as a simple shepherd's daughter, was nevertheless not very surprised by the overtures that Argiliane had just made to her regarding her birth; the nobility of her soul had doubtless informed her that an illustrious blood must flow in her veins and animate all her actions. The impatience to know to whom she owed her existence caused her to desire to see the Princess again soon, and as if the desire could bring forward her return, she did not fail to go for a walk every day at the entrance to a forest through which Princess Argiliane had the custom of passing in order to go to her palace.

"One day, Brillante, finding herself much more agitated than usual, had not been able to sleep during the night, which caused her to get up before dawn in order to go to the entrance to the forest. Scarcely had she arrived there than she perceived a carriage in the distance, the splendor of which surprised her and fixed al her attention. It was a caleche upholstered in satin, scented with the most agreeable odors. The imperial of the caleche formed an image representing the goddess Venus, lying nonchalantly on a bed of flowers, her head leaning on the knees of the god Mars, watching the Graces, who seemed to be occupied in making crowns of myrtle to ornament the heads of the happy lovers. On the back of the caleche could be seen the shepherd Paris choosing Venus from the three goddesses in order to present the apple to her; the sides represented the different attributes of the goddess.

"Amour, in the depths of that admirable vehicle, seemed distracted and pensive, his head tilted slightly to the right toward Modesty, gazing with indifference at Favor, who was sitting to her left. Enjoyment, with a submissive expression, was sitting next to Amour, and seemed to be asking him whether he deigned to select her. The Graces were in front, one of them holding the god's quiver and golden arrows, the other two teasing him in order to renew his good humor, appearing to be solely occupied in playing pranks. The Shepherd's Hour served as postillion, holding the reins of eight swans whiter than snow. The Games, Laughters and Pleasures surrounded the charming caleche.

"It was Venus' carriage that Amour had taken, with her entire retinue, in order to hold a party in his new little house, but the retinue still did not know who was to be the heroine of a celebration that Amour had been preparing for a long time; because since the burn that Psyche had inflicted upon him by her indiscreet curiosity, no one had heard any mention of the god having had another mistress; it was even said that, in the dolor that he felt, he had sworn wrathfully, if not on the Styx, never to attach himself to anyone again. But perhaps one ought to mistrust the oaths of a god who puts all his glory into rendering them vain.

"Although Amour was then occupied with Brillante, and the god's apparatus, vanquisher of everything that breathes, was prepared solely for her, as he had not expected her to appear before dawn, he could not help blushing, initially mistaking her for his mother. He was soon disabused, however, on looking at her; her modest expression caused him considerable emotion. He had his carriage stop when it drew level with her, descended from it precipitately, and then approached her with a timid expression, almost not daring to raise his eyes to look at the young Princess, who was solely occupied in gazing at

367

the magnificent spectacle offered to her gaze. Because of that, she did not perceive that Amour was at her feet, in the posture of a supplicant.

"A sigh that escaped the god, as he took her hand, extracted Brillante from her ecstasy. She blushed, and tried to withdraw it, but seeing that he kissed it in a tender and submissive manner, her disturbance increased.

"'Get up, my Lord,' she said, emotionally. 'What can you want from a young woman that hazard has caused you to encounter in this forest? Speak—can I be useful to you in some way? What has obliged you to descend from that beautiful carriage, and to quit the beautiful ladies with which it is filled?'

"'It is to offer it to you,' replied Amour, 'and these ladies, if they have the good fortune to please you, are destined to serve you. Suffer, then, divine Princess, that I lay my quiver and my arrows at your feet; I swear to you that I shall only occupy myself henceforth with the care of pleasing you; you alone can make my happiness. Too long have I reigned over the hearts of feeble humans; today I renounce the empire that I have always exercised over the world. Come, my adorable princess; enjoy the triumph that Amour is preparing for your charms.'

"'What!' said the young Princess, in a tremulous voice, her face covered with a rosy red hue. 'Is it possible that you are Amour? No, I can't believe it, given the frightful portrait that has been made of him for me.'

"'Is my name so frightening, then?' said the god. 'Yes, undoubtedly, I'm Amour; I don't seek to hide myself, like a seducer, who has no other objective than to deceive.'

"At these words, the Princess uttered a cry and wanted to flee, but she did not have the strength, and fell weakly into the arms of Amour. That god was temeritous; he made a sign to Favor, who ran nimbly to help Brillante—but Modesty, who got there ahead of her, caused her to step back, and that goddess, aided by the Graces, put all her efforts into helping the Princess recover from her weakness.

"Amour, who had remained at her feet, asked her, passionately, what could have caused such a great alarm. 'What do you have to fear from me?' the god said. 'Regard me as a child who adores you and will always be submissive to you; my intention will never be to do you any harm. Listen to Favor, yield to her advice; it is only by following it that you will enjoy perfect happiness.'

"Brillante, attentive to Amour's discourse, had not even dared to rest her timid gaze upon him, and, recalling to memory the sage lessons that she had received from Argiliane, anxious and pensive, she looked at Modesty with eyes that the tenderness and ardor of Amour appeared to animate, and sighed without daring to say anything.

"Amour, who was examining her, perceived her disturbance; he ordered Modesty to withdraw, believing that she alone was opposing his happiness. That order redoubled Brillante's dread; she threw herself into the arms of the goddess. 'In the name of the gods,' said the Princess, fearfully, 'stay and help me. What will become of me, alas, if you abandon me? Amour is nothing but a deceiver who is doubtless seeking to seduce me; for pity's sake, help me to flee.'

"'Who, then, has inspired such a bad idea of Amour in you?' said the god, angrily. 'But I can use my power, in order to convince you that I am not seeking to deceive you.'

"'Stop' said the young princess—and seizing the arrow that he was about to shoot, she threw it with so much skill that the god was pierced by it. Far from causing Amour any distress, however, the blow that he received one served to increase his ardor. Withdrawing it from his bosom, still burning with his own substance, he plunged it into Brillante's, without the young princess perceiving immediately the dart that had just been hurled at her.

"Modesty, who saw the trick that Amour had just played on Brillante, wanted at least to favor her with all her power, in order to render their union eternal; she took advantage of that favorable moment to engage Amour to recall Constancy, whom he had long since banished from his presence.

"The god, satisfied with his choice, consented to that without difficulty, and in order to cure entirely the suspicions that might remain in the mind of the Princess, he also permitted the Graces and Modesty to accompany her permanently, on condition that those goddesses were joined by Favor. 'I cannot live without her,' Amour added. 'Her conversation amuses me; she is the one who must always entertain me with a thousand little sallies; but it is time, my adorable mistress, to enjoy the pleasures that have been prepared for you.'

"At the same time, the god signaled to the Shepherd's Hour to approach. Modesty, who was still sustaining Brillante, opposed Amour's designs. The god seemed a trifle annoyed, but he dared not let his chagrin show, in order that he might gain the confidence of the princess by his complaisance; he presented his hand to her with an enchanting smile.

"Brillante, without being fully aware of what the disturbance agitating her was, finally allowed herself to be guided by the god, who had her climb into his carriage and sit down beside him, with the Graces, Modesty and Constancy. Favor sat down behind them, accompanied by a tall woman that Brillante had not perceived before. She asked Amour who she was and why she seemed so pensive. 'That is Enjoyment,' said the god, 'who is waiting anxiously for a favorable moment to make your acquaintance, in order to resume her usual cheerfulness and gaiety.'

"Amour ordered that she be taken to his little house, which might have been mistaken for one of the Sun's, by virtue of the riches that shone there in every part. A troop of Pleasures were detached to announce the arrival of Amour and the princess, who were received in the palace by the Laughters, the Games and the Pleasures. Amour conducted Brillante to a room of mirrors, and ordered the Graces to put her on a bed of roses, which Voluptuousness and Delicacy had prepared for them. Those two favorites of Amour never left that room; they were both charged with the responsibility of ornamenting it, maintaining a temperate air within it and spreading the most exquisite perfumes therein. The Games,

Laughters, Pleasures, Favor and Enjoyment followed the princess into the room.

"Favor and Enjoyment lavished a thousand tender caresses on Constancy to congratulate her on her return; gaiety ornamented all the actions of Enjoyment, who flattered herself, with reason, that the reunion of her companion with Amour would finally allow her to triumph over her cruelest enemy. For, before the god had become sensible to the charms of Brillante, although Enjoyment had always been in his retinue, it had often happened, by a fatality that drove her to despair, that in spite of the orders of Amour, Repugnance, that enemy of her repose, had drawn him toward another object. She flattered herself that he had now been vanquished; the mild and complaisant character and the perpetually even humor of the young Princess would contribute a great deal to her winning the most complete victory over her enemy.

"Brillante, occupied with everything that surrounded her, was not devoting herself to reflection; she forgot Modesty, who had not come in with her, Amour having excluded her from that room, thinking to avoid, by her absence, a thousand petty quibbles to which she was strongly subject. That is why he had appointed the Shepherd's Hour to be the usher of the cabinet.

"In spite of his precautions, however, the god was not expecting to find Decency, a faithful companion of Brillante, who, in order not to abandon her, had hidden under the young princess' dress; when he tried to approach her, that imperious goddess declared to him that she would only cede her place to the god Hymen.

"Amour, inflamed by that further resistance, consented that his brother Hymen could come to light the nuptial torch, in order to illuminate his union with Brillante, which he swore to be eternal.

"Amour, having become constant by virtue of his union with Brillante, presently enjoys a perfect happiness, and his ardor, far from diminishing because of the continuous presence of Favor and Enjoyment, seems to increase; the pleasures that he experiences with their aid appear to him to be always new. It is easy to presume that Brillante has fixed him forever; it is therefore in vain that one will search for him at present in the world, since he has only left his shadow there.

"That, dear Tramarine," the genius Verdoyant added, "is the fortunate fate that your sister the Princess is presently enjoying on Craintive Isle, which the veritable Amour has chosen for his residence, because a perpetual spring reigns there."

When they arrived off the shore of that island, Verdoyant perceived Amour frolicking with Brillante and the Graces, who were out for a stroll accompanied with their entire court. The genius pointed them out to Tramarine, taking his chariot closer to the shore. After helping the princess to descend, he advanced with her toward Amour, who, recognizing Verdoyant at the Prince of the Water-Sprites, came to meet him.

"What brings you to this shore?" asked the god. "You have no more need of me to make you love the charming Tramarine; Esteem and Amity, who are accompanying you, leave me in no doubt of the happiness you are enjoying."

"It's true," said the genius, "that with your help those two divinities have joined us, in order to tighten the knots of a union that ought to be eternal. My primary object, in visiting you, is to express my gratitude to you, and to congratulate you, at the same time, on the fortunate choice you have made of the charming person who is accompanying you. It is so rare to see a sincere attachment on the part of Amour that, if it were known in the world, it would presently be considered as one of those phenomena that only appear very rarely, to announce the happiness of humans. That great victory was only reserved to Princess Brillante, who, by all appearances, ought not to fear your inconstancy."

"I confess," said Amour, "that I had banished Constancy from my retinue for a long time, but, finding her inseparable from Brillante, I recognized that it is only with her that one can experience true happiness, and I can no longer detach myself from her."

"What!" replied Verdoyant. "Have you abandoned mortals forever?"

"They haven't even perceived that I've quit them," said Amour. "Content with the shadow that I've left them, they can't distinguish it from me. Why? It's because the majority have neither morality, nor virtue, nor sentiment; delivered to brutality, changeability and repugnance, what use do they have for a god they cannot recognize? I agree, however, that there are some who merit being distinguished from the vulgar, so those are under my protection, and it is only to them that I distribute my most cherished favors."

"Since when has Amour learned to moralize?" said the genius, laughing.

"Since I took off my blindfold," said the god.

"It's easy to see that," said the Prince, "by the choice you've made of the amiable Brillante, and the greatest eulogy that can be given to her is that of having been able to fix Amour by her charms. But tell me, have you renounced Olympus forever?"

"I don't have any great desire for it," said Amour, "for nothing is more tedious at present than that abode. You can't be unaware that company is only amusing as long as one encounters amiable women there, and that's very rare to find there. Old Cybele no longer does anything but talk nonsense; as for Juno, her jealousy always puts her in a bad mood; Ceres is too sensible of her provincial divinity, and doesn't have the elegant air that the court provides. Minerva is incessantly armed as a Don Quixote, always ready for combat, and Diana only enjoys hunting, and ripping our ears with her horn; it's true that one can amuse oneself making occasional excursions with those two goddesses, but they're so grim that one daren't say a single gallant word to them. Hebe has become a trifle sugary since she had ceded her employment to Ganymede; the occupations of Pomona render her hands too rough, in spite of all the ointments she uses to soften them. I agree that Flora is very amiable, but she's too fond of gardening; besides which, she only enjoys herself with that little fool Zephyr. Aurora gets up so early that one can never catch her, and no one knows what becomes of her for the rest of the day. Venus is charming, but she's my mother; we're not always in accord on many points, which causes us to quarrel often; besides which, she never stays in residence long in one place, sometimes in Paphos, at other times in Cythera, Amathante or elsewhere, and the Graces are often with her. Thetis is only occupied in pleasing the god of day; the Muses are precious and overfond of philosophy; the Fates are spinners who show no mercy to anyone; the Hours run incessantly; and Folly only inhabits the earth nowadays. What can one do at present in Olympus? One dies there of boredom—for I can't amuse myself with Momus since he's giving himself airs and criticizing all the gods."

During this conversation Tramarine, after giving Brillante a thousand tender caresses, told her about the adventures of the King of Lydia, and the two amiable princesses, charmed by one another, would dearly have liked not to be separated again.

"You've troubled my repose," said Brillante, tenderly, to Princess Tramarine. "Since I've been united with Amour, I thought I'd never desire anything again; I was entirely ignorant of what blood and amity might do. In spite of the pleasure I feel in seeing you, though, and that I'd have in spending my life with you, I don't have either the strength to quit Amour or the courage to go with you. If you could live among us, my pleasure would be complete; at least, Tramarine, grant me a few more days, in order to engage Prince Verdoyant to let me talk to our father."

"I'm in despair," said Tramarine, "at being obliged to refuse you, but I can't yield to your desires without breaking our laws. King Ophtes, after having lost the life that attached him to the earth, is veritably welcome among the water-sprites, but he doesn't enjoy the privileges of genii, who can reveal themselves to mortals when they please. I promise, you, nevertheless to come to see you as often as I can."

The genius approached the two princesses then, and told them that it was time to part. After tender farewells, Amour

escorted the genius and Tramarine to their chariot, and promised always to be faithfully attached to them.

That separation was the first chagrin that Brillante experienced. It rendered her pensive for some time, but without
putting her in a bad mood; she never had one of those, and
when she experience dolor her plaints were always tender and
touching. Amour, to dissipate her sadness, gave birth to new
pleasures. It is even claimed that it was of his union with Brillante that the multitude of little frolicsome amours was born,
and I am inclined to believe it.

The genius Verdoyant and Tramarine continued their
voyage, informed the King of Lydia about the happy marriage
of Amour and the princess, and painted him a vivid picture of
the pleasures they enjoyed incessantly in their union—
pleasures all the more desirable and sensible because time
could never diminish them.

XII. The Story of Prince Nubecula, the Son of
the Genius Verdoyant and Princess Tramarine

Verdoyant, wanting to procure the princess Tramarine
one of those surprises that always agitate our senses impetu-
ously, took her to a country where the majority of the citizens
were only occupied with the future. Those people, although
incessantly in dispute, seemed nevertheless to be trying to
enjoy an eternal peace; in the midst of that pretended peace,
however, they were almost all unhappy; they were suffering
ennui and languishing, because they did not want to recognize
amour, which alone is capable of enlivening the mind and
occupying the imagination agreeably. For without amour, is
one not deprived of the pleasure that gives splendor to grandeur, and sumptuousness to wealth? The charms of glory
count for nothing and the attractions of the most touching
beauty become insipid. How I pity them!

It was to the land of those people that the genius
Verdoyant took Princess Tramarine and the King of Lydia.
They arrived at a time when they were preparing a spectacle

customary in that nation when it is a matter of the marriage of the eldest daughter of their king, because it is neither rank nor quality that can obtain her; it is to valor and the intrepidity of courage that she is accorded. That spectacle had been announced for a long time in favor of Princess Amasis. The princess in question was not endowed with graces or beauty, and the deformity of her body seemed to render her union less precious.

It was customary to submit to terrible proofs in order to obtain the alliance from the King. No one had yet asked for the hand of Amasis. Her repulsive portrait, which was not permitted to flatter her, had not tempted any sovereign prince to submit himself to the inevitable dangers. However, the King had so great an affection for Amasis that it often degenerated into weakness, and her sisters, although endowed with all imaginable perfections, were unable to obtain any favors if Amasis did not join with them to ask for them.

The Princess who was intensely annoyed at being deprived of life at court, fell into a languor that caused anxiety for her life; that was what determined the King to permit any foreigner to present himself to the proofs to which it was necessary to submit in order to render himself worthy of the princess.

All the King's daughters were brought up in a temple dedicated to the Sun, from which they only emerged in order to marry. The temple is built on top of a rock, its dome rising into the clouds, and the sea serves as a channel to the gardens that surround it. Before arriving at the temple, one has to pass through seven doors, which are as many proofs, which it is necessary to endure without interruption; they are knows as the Portals of Favor, because those who have the courage to pass through them are regarded as the favorites of the Sun, are worshiped and placed among the number of the gods. It is true that without a particular grace it is almost impossible to be able to get through all the difficulties that one encounters. It is, however, only in overcoming them that they can acquire the glory that immortalizes them.

Those seven doors are made of seven different metals, which correspond to the seven planets, and the last, which opens to the enclosure of the temple is made of gold, as the metal over which the Sun presides. No one has the right to enter the temple except the King, and that is only by a secret door to which he alone has the key, but all the princes and gentlemen of his retinue are obliged to camp in a wood behind the temple.

Scaffolding was erected in the form of an amphitheater facing the first door, which led to all the others. Magnificent lodges were also built in order to house the King and the entire court. It is as well to inform the reader that in those climes, the days are much longer than ours.

The genius Verdoyant, Tramarine and their retinue reached the foot of the rock at the moment when the King and all his court arrived to see the ordeals commence. The Prince of the Water-Sprites had his wife's carriage placed in a gulf near the temple, in order to enable her to see the marvels, which appear to many people to be incredible.

Scarcely were they in position when the King appeared, preceded by his elite troops. Thousands of ensigns standards and deployed flags were fluttering in the air, which served to distinguish the orders and ranks. The troops arranged themselves in order around the King's lodge; he then appeared, with a majestic expression. As soon as the king was in the lodge, the signal was given, which the drums, fifes and trumpets announced with strident sounds.

Then, several champions presented themselves to be admitted to the proofs; but some were unable to get through the first door, and the most determined were checked by the second. They were beginning to despair when a tall young knight appeared; the knight was clad in green armor and on his escutcheon was the figure of Pallas, which seemed to have been engraved by a masterly hand. The death of those who had preceded him did not intimidate him.

Tramarine shivered at the sight of that knight; her heart palpitated with the dread that he might meet the same fate as the others.

"What a pity it would be," said the Princess to the genius, "if foolish ambition were to cause that young knight to perish! That is what vain honors can produce; one runs after a chimera of which death can rob you in an instant; for it cannot be love that makes him desire the possession of a princess who, in spite of her deformity, would perhaps only have the utmost arrogance and scorn for him. Alas, what will his destiny be?"

"Have no fear for him," said Verdoyant. "He will be victorious; his weapons are invulnerable and a superior genius protects him."

The knight advanced immediately, in a proud and intrepid manner, to the first door, entrance to which was defended by a dragon of enormous size. The monster had three heads, which it was necessary to sever, and their combat lasted nearly four hours. Although the monster had lost two of its heads, it still had the strength to lift itself up on its feet in order to devour the knight—who, far from recoiling, thrust his spear into its side. That was the only spot where it could be killed, because of the thick scales that covered it. The furious animal fell, uttering howls that made the rocks and mountains tremble, and the first door opened noisily. Then the knight went into a large courtyard, where he rested for a while.

Not far from there was a mount whose frightful summit was vomiting swirls of flame and smoke, and where the ground shone with a yellow crust, indubitable evidence of the sulfur that formed in its entrails. Above that mount was the second door, guarded by fiery horsemen.

When the knight had rested momentarily, he fought them, and was able to drive them away and pass through the second door.

A giant defended the third, but he severed both his legs with a single sweep.

That victory cost him little; he then marched toward the fourth door, where there was a winged serpent. The animal ejected a venom through its nostrils that infected the air; the monster was twenty cubits long.

The knight could not help shivering at that sight; his heart quivered with dread and horror, stirred like waters agitated by a violent fire, and the decisive moment caused him to recoil momentarily. Blushing at his weakness, however, he reanimated his courage, took firmer hold of his sword and advanced toward the monster, which, hissing in a terrible fashion, caused Tramarine to tremble for the life of the knight—who, having shown his valor and the intrepidity of his great heart, was beginning to despair of his ability to vanquish the furious animal. With a desperate movement, he threw his sword at the moment when the monster, opening an enormous maw, launched itself forward to devour him. The sword opened its throat, and such a great abundance of venom emerged therefrom that the air, which was infected by it, caused the knight to fall unconscious.

Tramarine, penetrated by anguish at that accident, begged Prince Verdoyant to help him, which he did without rendering himself visible.

First, the genius took off his helmet, in order to make him take a marvelous elixir, which reanimated his vigor and simultaneously fortified his courage. The knight, recovering consciousness, was extremely surprised not to see anyone.

"To whom do I owe," he said, "the fortunate aid that I've just received? Undoubtedly a genius is protecting me, and perhaps it's only to him that I owe my victories. I can only attribute such marked favors to the protection of Pallas."

The fortunate conqueror advanced toward the fifth gate, surrounded by a broad ditch that, by virtue of its depth, presented a frightful abyss, into which he was seen to leap with an intrepid courage.

He was soon seen, however, taking the route to the sixth gate, guarded by sirens, who employed their most flattering sounds to charm him with their agreeable music. At first, the knight could not resist such touching accents; he stopped to listen to them; his head was already yielding to the pleasure of hearing them, his strength was weakening and his tremulous legs could hardly support him. It was visible that he was on the brink of losing the fruit of all his labors. That proof is the most difficult to overcome—but, perceiving his weakness, he suddenly armed himself with a new courage, and by means of a singular inspiration, he took his sword in his hand and fled with an extreme speed.

He finally arrived at the seventh door, defended by a bird of monstrous size, which was said to be the phoenix.

Tramarine, attentive to all the knight's actions, thought she would never see the end of such a singular combat. The bird did nothing but flutter incessantly before the knight; it seemed that it was only seeking to blind him with its wings. A hundred times he was seen to strike it down; a hundred times it was seen to reproduce itself.

The knight, not understanding the singular creature at all, realized that he would never be able to vanquish it with his weapons, and that it was necessary to employ cunning in order to try to take it by surprise. After the bird had circled around him thousands of times, doubtless fatigued, it finally came of its own accord to perch upon him, and he immediately seized it.

It was then that the vaults of the temple shook; the seventh door opened with a frightful din, and cries of joy were heard everywhere.

The victorious knight, holding his bird, traversed a great courtyard, at the far side of which was an exceedingly deep lake, which it was necessary to swim across in order to purify himself, but without letting go of the bird, which would have made it necessary for him to engage in a new combat.

The agitated waves of the waters of the lake were making a noise similar to a torrent precipitated from the top of a steep mountain.

After the victor had been subjected to that final proof, he advanced toward the Temple of the Sun. The temple is surrounded by a double row of columns of jasper-lined marble. In the middle of the temple, on a pedestal, is a statue of the god, whose head is ornamented with a crown in the form of rays, garnished with carbuncles.

Under the vast portico formed by the double row of columns surrounding the temple, young girls were lined up to either side. Those children, all chosen for the most agreeable faces, had long curly hair that floated over their shoulders. Their heads were crowned with flowers and they were all dressed in celestial blue. Several were incensing the altar with admirable perfumes; others were singing the praises of the Sun. Their perfect notes were heard everywhere, along with the melodious sounds of several instruments, moved by delicate and light fingers, until the moment when the star of Venus, favorable to lovers, appeared over their hemisphere. Then the Chorus, followed with ardor and delight, lit the nuptial torches, invoking the god Hymen, to whom Amour furnishes gilded features; it was with the torch of the latter god that he lit the durable lamp, and, sustaining him on his crimson wings, he was glad to share his reign with him. It is only by means of that accord between Amour and his brother Hymen that one finds reason, fidelity, justice and purity; and it is only by means of Hymen that the ties of blood, the gentle liaisons of father, son and brother, can be formed, he alone preserving them from sources corrupted by crime.

The sound of trumpets was heard when the high priest appeared, followed by Amasis and her priestesses. That venerable old man, throughout the time of the sacrifices, always had his head covered by a crimson veil. He finally advanced to consult the entrails of the victims that were still palpitating, and whose blood was fuming everywhere.

"O gods!" he cried. "Who, then, is the hero that the heavens have sent to performs such great marvels here?"

As he spoke those words his expression became grim, his eyes sparkled and he seemed to see other objects than those appearing before him. He was troubled; his hair bristled; his face was inflamed; and, raising his arms, he held them immobile. His voice halted; he was hardly breathing any longer, and he appeared no longer to be able to contain within himself the divine spirit that was agitating him.

"O fortunate Princess!" he said, in his enthusiasm. "What do I see, and what is your happiness? Gods, crown your work!" He turned to the knight. "And you, noble stranger," he continued, "whose labors have surpassed those of all mortals, may the God you implore lavish you with the most precious favors!"

The high priest gave them a sign to approach the altar simultaneously. The knight, who was disarmed, presented his hand to Princess Amasis. The princess was still covered by a thick veil. They both advanced to the statue of the Sun, at the base of which the high priest was standing, his hands bearing the nuptial cup. The priestesses were lined up to either side of the high priest, who, after he had made the two spouses drink what was in the cup, took their hands and joined them together, making the knight pronounce the following words:

I swear by the Sun, the father of nature.
Who gives life and fecundity;
And by you, lovely Moon, sole divinity
Who delights in the obscure night;
You, who give birth beneath your paces
To voluptuous and delicate pleasures,
Inflame the heart of the princess forever;
Enable her to respond to my tenderness;
Let her not fear that my flame
Will ever relent one day,
Since the same amour, incessantly
Will reign for her in my soul.

The priestesses and the daughters of the Sun repeated in chorus: "Inflame the heart of the princess forever."

That was repeated several times, with the accompaniment of delightful chords.

Princess Amasis then added, in a silvery and sonorous voice:

> *May the gods expand in our hearts*
> *The torrents of pleasure that are sweetness;*
> *May my spouse, always covered in glory;*
> *Be incessantly accompanied by Victory,*
> *And may his courage be celebrated forever*
> *Beyond time and throughout the ages;*
> *And may a union so fine be engraved in history*
> *In golden letters in the Temple of Memory.*

That was repeated several times by the choirs. The two spouses were then conducted, to the sounds of a thousand instruments, to the door of the temple, where the knight climbed with the princess into a magnificent carriage, which was immediately lifted up by eagles, and transported to the palace of the King.

The Prince of the Water-Sprites, wanting to procure Tramarine the satisfaction of seeing the end of that ceremony, took her with the King of Lydia along a broad channel, whose waters, artfully distributed, spread out through various small channels in a great gallery to form delightful cascades at both ends, into which care had been taken also to make waters distilled with the most exquisite odors flow. It was in one of those cascades that the genius Verdoyant placed Tramarine and her father the King.

In the middle of the gallery was an elevated throne, on which were seated the King and the Princess, the mother of Amasis. That day was a day of triumph for them. The two sides were occupied by the King's other wives and the princes of the blood.

Then the two young spouses appeared, who advanced in a noble manner and came to kneel at the King's feet. After they had kissed them, the monarch, all of whose actions were guided by wisdom, prudence and reason, embraced them both, and took a crown from the Queen's hands, which he placed on the knight's head, in order to render him by that mark of distinction the equal of the princess. She then took off her veil, showing herself for the first time to her illustrious spouse and the entire court.

As soon as Amasis had removed the thick veil that covered her, a murmur of confused voices was heard. All of them went up at the same time, the princes in particular complaining loudly that a considerable wrong had been done to the Princess Amasis by distributing portraits so dissimilar to her, since no one could refuse her admiration and a thousand other sentiments that her virtues, her beauty and the majesty of her figure inspired.

It is true that Amasis appeared in that court like a new star; it seemed that Amour and the Graces had taken pleasure in forming her; a slender and lithe figure, an admirable profile, fine and delicate features in which goodness, candor and modesty were painted, which rendered her even more beautiful. She did not have the grim expression that causes love to flee and tarnishes beauty, but the gentle, innocent and childlike decency that inspires respect at the same time as it inflames desires.

When Princess Amasis saw all gazes fixed upon her face was covered by a divine blush. She looked tenderly at her spouse, her eyes expressing the sentiment that animated her, seeming to say that it was him alone that suffrage ought to flatter, because her heart, obedient to the laws of the kingdom, had immediately attached itself to the young hero, whom it seemed that only some divinity could have formed.

Meanwhile, the King's surprise appeared to be extreme; he was nevertheless unable to dispense with replying to the princes, who begged him to explain the reasons he had had for not giving an accurate portrait of the charms of the princess. The King replied, with the expression of candor that so well befits the majesty of a sovereign, that unless the gods had performed a miracle in favor of Amasis, he agreed that he could only recognize, in the person that was presented to his eyes, the voice of his daughter the princess.

That confession by the monarch only increased the confusion, and as entry to the temples was only permitted to His Majesty, the monarch was humbly begged to transport himself there with the Queen, in order to visit the interior and interrogate the other princesses, to ascertain whether one of them had had the audacity to substitute for Princess Amasis some daughter of the Sun.

The Princess, however, surprised that anyone should seek to cast suspicion on her birth, begged her father the King to permit her to justify herself. "It is not," the Princess added, "that I want to prevent Your Majesty from making the journey that has been proposed; on the contrary, my glory is interested in that visit, in order to dispel all suspicions that might tarnish my birth and leave doubts in minds injurious to my husband; but if Your Majesty cares to recall the various conversations with which he has honored me in the course of my life, perhaps I can convince him that only Princess Amasis is able reveal to him secrets confided to her alone.

"In order to assure him of that," she continued, falling to her knees, "I dare to beg my father to accord me a private audience."

The King, moved by the princess' speech, got up immediately, and they went into his cabinet, where they remained enclosed for a long time.

The entire court waited impatiently for the result of such an extraordinary event. Only the prince, Amasis' husband, seemed tranquil; in the midst of so much disturbance. But the King, who emerged from his cabinet followed by Amasis, calmed all minds when he spoke.

"I am now convinced," the monarch said, addressing is entire court, "that this is Princess Amasis; I recognize her as my daughter, and you should regard her henceforth as your sovereign, since no one else in the world can have had knowledge of the secrets that she has just revealed to me. Although the journey to the temple I have to make has become unnecessary for the justification of Amasis, however, I cannot dispense with fulfilling the promise I have made. I shall therefore go there with the Princess, to thank the gods for the graces they have just accorded to the person of Amasis. I shall offer further sacrifices, and order at the same time that in recognition of the miracle that has just been accomplished in favor of my daughter, on the same day every year, a celebratory fête will be held in honor of the Sun, in order to eternalize the memory of such a great day.

"As for you, Prince," the King added, addressing Amasis' husband, "I associate you with my royalty; you will henceforth share my crown; I believe you to be all the more worthy of it because the gods seem only to have performed such a great miracle in favor of your labors. I recognize now that truth, reason, wisdom and moderation will always be your rules, so our sentiments can never be opposed."

The Prince could only respond to that eulogy with a profound bow.

The King was then escorted to his carriage with Princess Amasis in order to go to renew their offerings and sacrifices in honor of the Sun, to which the magnificent carriage that had conveyed Amasis and her illustrious spouse was dedicated. The King had all the details of the story engraved on tablets of bronze, in order to conserve the memory of it until the remotest centuries.

During the absence of the King and Princess Amasis, it was noticeable that all the courtiers who, before the Prince had been associated with the throne, had hardly deigned to look at him, hastened to pay their court to him. But the Prince, whose intellect was superior to all those mercenary flatterers delicately made them aware of the scorn he felt for their insipid praise, and, advancing toward the Queen, expressed to her, with a great deal of dignity, how sensible he was of the honor he was about to enjoy—a happiness all the greater because it procured him the advantage of dividing his cares between two princesses so worthy of one another, and of obtaining for both a liberty that he was convinced that they would only use to enhance the delights of the union formed by the gods themselves.

When he returned from the temple, the King returned Princess Amasis to her illustrious spouse, heaping him with a thousand marks of esteem and amity, to which the Prince responded with a great deal of respect. With amour painted in his eyes as he gazed at Amasis, who offered him her hand, they prepared to leave the gallery in order to return to their apartments. The pages were already preceding them in order to accompany them when they were stopped again by a venerable old man who suddenly appeared in the middle of the gallery.

The old man advanced in a grave and majestic fashion, but, perceiving the disturbance that his sudden appearance had excited in all minds, he fixed his eyes on the young spouses for a few moments, doubtless to give them time to recover from their agitation. Then he turned to the King.

"Calm the disturbance that I can see you are experiencing, my Lord," he said. "I only have agreeable news to announce to you. I am the genius Carabiel, sent on behalf of the Sun to inform you that the spouse of Princess Amasis owes his birth to the genius Verdoyant, Prince of the Water-Sprites, and Princess Tramarine, the daughter of the King of Lydia, presently associated by her union with the Empire of the Waters, by the protection that her virtues have been able to obtain from the goddess Pallas, daughter of Jupiter, who personally named that young prince Nubecula. You ought to have known, by the striking labors that he has just performed, that the Prince could only owe his origins to a favorite of the gods, and it is only in his favor that the Sun has consented to perform the miracle that has transformed Princess Amasis. That god is content with the election you have made of that young hero to reign with you over all the peoples dependent on our empire. He has charged me with announcing to you that he will extend its limits by joining to it the realm of Castora, and that he will extend his most precious influences over all your posterity. The flourishing land will render your fields always fertile and abundant; peace and concord will reign among the citizens, and the descendants of Prince Nubecula will enjoy his favors for innumerable centuries."

Then the genius turned to the Princess. "Prepare yourself, charming Amasis," he added, "for the departure of your illustrious spouse. Do not attempt to delay the glory that he must still acquire in the conquest of the estates of the Queen of Castora. Pentaphile has offended the gods by establishing unjust laws there, and it is to punish her that they have ordered that the kingdom will pass into the power of Prince Nubecula."

"Respectable Carabiel," said the Princess, "do not refuse me the grace that I dare to ask of the Sun's envoy, and at least permit me to accompany the Prince, my husband, on his new expedition."

The genius consented to that, and disappeared immediately, leaving the King and all his court in a surprise mingled with admiration at all the marvels they had witnessed. It is true that it seemed that had not had time to collect themselves, because the prodigious events had succeeded one another so rapidly; the courtiers, above all, seemed relieved by the declaration of the envoy of the Sun; their self-esteem, which had been under pressure for some time, suddenly recovered all its plenitude; their humiliation disappeared when they learned that it had required nothing less than a demigod to have carried off such great victories in such a short time. Thus, all the marvels that the Prince had accomplished increased his value in their eyes, and the stranger, whom they had found it humiliating to obey at first, could only cover them in honor and glory in future, as soon as the recognized him as the grandson of the King of the Waters.

Then the joy and satisfaction that an unexpected happiness had produced in Amaris' soul were seen shining in her eyes, and that happiness excited in her heart sentiments of the most perfect gratitude toward the gods. Her heart, already disposed to amour, caused her to say to the prince her husband the most tender and witty things in the world—but I shall not attempt to report that conversation, which was doubtless one of the most animated that love can inspire between two young hearts.

Although the King was extremely fatigued by all the events that had just succeeded one another, he was unable to defer for long hearing the adventures of Prince Nubecula; that is why he dismissed a part of his court and went back to his cabinet, followed by the Queen, the young spouses and the corybants most elevated in dignity.

"You ought not to find extraordinary," the monarch said to Prince Nubecula, "The haste I am in to learn the slightest circumstances of the life of a Prince like you; don't delay informing me for a moment."

At that order the Prince could not help sighing. He gazed at Amasis with impassioned eyes, and she knew by that gaze how sorry he was to be obliged to delay the moment of his happiness by yielding to His Majesty's urgency; but a smile from Amasis, similar to that of Amour, appeared to console him and simultaneously to invite him to satisfy her father's desire promptly. He therefore began his story, which he told very briefly.

"At the moment of my birth I was put into the hands of a famous magician, who, constrained by a superior power not to abuse his authority over me, abandoned me to a faun, who cared for me in my infancy. The faun lived in a cavern near the Temple of Ceres, and at the age of four he consecrated me to the goddess, in order to serve her cult at her altars. I had scarcely reached the age of fifteen when I felt penetrated by a poetic fury. Animated by the spirit of the god who protected me, I pronounced several oracles, and spent a few years in that occupation; but the priestess summoned me to her lair one day. "Young man," she said to me, in one of those enthusiasms that the goddess had the custom of exciting in her, "learn that you are to be the most valiant of mortals; it is time to quit this abode in order to go forth and signal your courage; a thousand various exploits are offered to your glory. Go; the god who protects you will take care of your glory, and your triumph will be admired throughout the Universe.

"Those words, dictated by the goddess, gave birth within me to the noble audacity that must always accompany heroes. I went out tremulously and found, under one of the porticos, the armor that has just served me to carry out the exploits of which Your Majesty has been the witness."

Although Their Majesties and those who had been admitted to the conversation would have liked to know the Prince's adventures in much greater detail, no one could complain about his complaisance, and the King postponed demanding those details until another occasion, perceiving that the Prince was burning with impatience to retire with Princess Amasis.

Tramarine and her father, both charmed to have been witnesses of the triumph and glory of Prince Nubecula, expressed their gratitude to the genius Verdoyant, and thanked him at the same time for the agreeable surprise they had experienced at the appearance of the envoy of the Sun, and learning by virtue of that favorite's discourse that the young prince was her son.,

"Undoubtedly," Princess Tramarine added, "it was to the genius Carabiel that you confided his education. I was unjust, alas, when I was able to doubt his fate! He is your son; you love him; you have secured his glory and his happiness."

"His destiny is now known to you," said Verdoyant, "and I believe that no doubt ought any longer to remain regarding the honors that he will enjoy. That is why, as we are very narrowly lodged here, I think it would be appropriate to rejoin the fleet, in order to continue our journey."

Tramarine, whose curiosity was replete with all the objects that might have excited it, perhaps feeling the ennui of such a long journey, and keenly impatient to introduce her father to the King of the Waters, begged the genius to take the fleet back in the direction of the capital, which they reached in a short time.

I shall not attempt to describe the celebrations that were held on their return; suffice it for my readers to now that His Aquatic Majesty, after having examined Princess Tramarine, seemed quite content with the change that had taken place in her. King Ophtes was introduced to him, and he was quite willing, in favor of his son's spouse to confirm the honors of the court that Prince Verdoyant had granted him. His Majesty added to that grace that he be given lodgings in the palace, adjacent to those of Princess Tramarine in the Pavilion of Mirrors.

By virtue of that new favor it was permitted to Ophtes to visit the Cabinet of Marvels frequently. Tramarine judged for herself the urgency that the King might have to learn what had happened in Lydia since his entry to the world of the Water-Sprites, and especially to have news of Queen Cliceria, the fashion in which she was governing his kingdom, and a thousand other matters of interest. That is why, after having given the King a detailed account of the attributes of the marvelous cabinet, she took him there to admire its singular beauties.

Ophtes, remembering his indiscreet curiosity when he had attempted to interrogate the gods regarding Tramarine's destiny, hardly dared raise his eyes to the mirrors. Doubtless he feared irritating the monarch of the Waters against him; but the Princess reassured him, telling him that when one did not form any desire the mirrors did not display anything.

Ophtes thought that he no longer desired anything, but thought is so prompt that one cannot stop it, and desire follows it closely. Ophtes thought, he desired; and the mirrors showed him what, in the depths of his heart, he desired ardently to learn.

He saw, therefore, the Queen of Lydia, who, after having mourned his loss for a long time and having tendered to his memory the honors and respects that could not be refused to a monarch who had only been occupied throughout his life in making the happiness of his people. He saw the amiable Cliceria, who, finding herself overburdened by the weight of guiding his vast estates, and fearing new irruptions on the part of Pencanaldon, sharing that burden with Corydon, the only one she thought worthy of filling the place that Ophtes had occupied for so long and with so much glory.

Without jealousy, Tramarine's father witnessed the union of the Queen with Prince Corydon; he contemplated their happiness in their posterity; and there were further subjects of satisfaction for him and for Tramarine, which they were to enjoy eternally.

ARABIAN NIGHTS

The first European version of the storties that later what became known as *The Arabian Nights* were translated into French between 1704-17 by diplomat Antoine Galland (1646-1715) reportedly from an Arabic text of the Syrian recension and other sources. This 12-volume work entitled *Les Mille et une nuits, contes arabes traduits en français* [The Thousand and One nights, Arab stories translated into French] included stories that were not in the original Arabic manuscript, such as *Aladdin's Lamp* and *Ali Baba and the Forty Thieves*, as well as several other, lesser known tales, and which cannot be found in any of the original manuscripts. Galland wrote that he heard them from a Syrian Christian storyteller from Aleppo, a Maronite scholar whom he called Hanna Diab that the traveler Paul Lucas had brought with him to Paris to meet Galland.

Galland's version of the *Nights* was immensely popular throughout Europe, and later versions were issued by his publisher using his name without his consent. As with the *Féeries*, the Oriental Fantasy tradition created by Galland was continued with much success by a number of imitators, who all claimed to have "translated" a number of "Oriental"" collections, such as: François Petis de la Croix (1653-1713), with *Les Mille et Un Jours* [The Thousand and One Days] (5 vols., 1710-12); Thomas-Simon Gueulette (1683-1766), with *Les Mille et Un Quarts d'Heures* [The Thousand and One Quarters of an Hour] (1723); the Abbé Jean-Paul Bignon (1662-1743), with *Les Aventures d'Abdalla, Fils d'Hanif* [The Adventures of Abdallah, Son of Hanif] (1712-14); and the Chevalier Louis de Mailly (1657-1724), with *Voyage et les Aventures de Trois Princes de Serendib* [Voyage & Adventures of Three Princes from Serendib] (1719).

The story of Prince Ahmed and Pari-Banu is one of the most famous tales of the *Arabian Nights*; however, it, too, is not part of the classical Arabic corpus. As with *Ali Baba* and *Aladdin*, it would appear that it was introduced by Galland into the book. His "translation" has since been republished many times and served as the basis for translations into other languages. The exact origin of the story is unknown; it has appeared in some Arabic versions, such as the Calcutta edition of 1830 and the Bulak Egyptian edition of 1835, but it is possible that these versions were subsequent retranslations into Arabic of Galland's version.

Antoine Galland: *The Story of Prince Ahmed and the Fairy Paribanou*
(1710)[109]

There was a sultan, who had three sons and a niece. The eldest of the Princes was called Houssain, the second Ali, the youngest Ahmed, and the Princess, his niece, Nouronnihar.

The Princess Nouronnihar was the daughter of the younger brother of the Sultan, who died, and left the Princess very young. The Sultan took upon himself the care of his daughter's education, and brought her up in his palace with the three Princes, proposing to marry her when she arrived at a proper age, and to contract an alliance with some neighboring prince by that means. But when he perceived that the three Princes, his sons, loved her passionately, he thought more seriously on that affair. He was very much concerned; the difficulty he foresaw was to make them agree, and that the two youngest should consent to yield her up to their elder brother. As he found them positively obstinate, he sent for them all together, and said to them: "Children, since for your good and quiet I have not been able to persuade you no longer to aspire to the Princess, your cousin, I think it would not be amiss if every one traveled separately into different countries, so that you might not meet each other. And, as you know I am very curious, and delight in everything that's singular, I promise my niece in marriage to him that shall bring me the most extraordinary rarity; and for the purchase of the rarity you shall go in search after, and the expense of traveling, I will give you every one a sum of money."

[109] *L'histoire du Prince Ahmed et de la fée Pari-Banou* by Antoine Galland, translated into English in 1889 by Andrew Lang, introduced and annotated by Jean-Marc Lofficier.

As the three Princes were always submissive and obedient to the Sultan's will, and each flattered himself fortune might prove favorable to him, they all consented to it. The Sultan paid them the money he promised them; and that very day they gave orders for the preparations for their travels, and took their leave of the Sultan, that they might be the more ready to go the next morning. Accordingly they all set out at the same gate of the city, each dressed like a merchant, attended by an officer of confidence dressed like a slave, and all well mounted and equipped. They went the first day's journey together, and lay all at an inn, where the road was divided into three different tracts. At night, when they were at supper together, they all agreed to travel for a year, and to meet at that inn; and that the first that came should wait for the rest; that, as they had all three taken their leave together of the Sultan, they might all return together. The next morning by break of day, after they had embraced and wished each other good success, they mounted their horses and took each a different road.

Prince Houssain, the eldest brother, arrived at Bisnagar, the capital of the kingdom of that name, and the residence of its king. He went and lodged at a khan appointed for foreign merchants; and, having learned that there were four principal divisions where merchants of all sorts sold their commodities, and kept shops, and in the midst of which stood the castle, or rather the King's palace, he went to one of these divisions the next day.

Prince Houssain could not view this division without admiration. It was large, and divided into several streets, all vaulted and shaded from the sun, and yet very light too. The shops were all of a size, and all that dealt in the same sort of goods lived in one street; as also the handicrafts-men, who kept their shops in the smaller streets.

The multitude of shops, stocked with all sorts of merchandise, as the finest linens from several parts of India, some painted in the most lively colors, and representing beasts, trees, and flowers; silks and brocades from Persia, China, and other places, porcelain both from Japan and China, and tapestries, surprised him so much that he knew not how to believe his own eyes; but when he came to the goldsmiths and jewelers he was in a kind of ecstacy to behold such prodigious quantities of wrought gold and silver, and was dazzled by the lustre of the pearls, diamonds, rubies, emeralds, and other jewels exposed to sale.

Another thing Prince Houssain particularly admired was the great number of rose-sellers who crowded the streets; for the Indians are so great lovers of that flower that no one will stir without a nosegay in his hand or a garland on his head; and the merchants keep them in pots in their shops, that the air is perfectly perfumed.

After Prince Houssain had run through that division, street by street, his thoughts fully employed on the riches he had seen, he was very much tired, which a merchant perceiving, civilly invited him to sit down in his shop, and he accepted; but had not been sat down long before he saw a crier pass by with a piece of tapestry on his arm, about six feet square, and cried at thirty purses. The Prince called to the crier, and asked to see the tapestry, which seemed to him to be valued at an exorbitant price, not only for the size of it, but the meanness of the stuff; when he had examined it well, he told the crier that he could not comprehend how so small a piece of tapestry, and of so indifferent appearance, could be set at so high a price.

The crier, who took him for a merchant, replied: "If this price seems so extravagant to you, your amazement will be greater when I tell you I have orders to raise it to forty purses, and not to part with it under." "Certainly," answered Prince Houssain, "it must have something very extraordinary in it, which I know nothing of." "You have guessed it, sir," replied the crier, "and will own it when you come to know that whoever sits on this piece of tapestry may be transported in an instant wherever he desires to be, without being stopped by any obstacle."

At this discourse of the crier the Prince of the Indies, considering that the principal motive of his travel was to carry the Sultan, his father, home some singular rarity, thought that he could not meet with any which could give him more satisfaction. "If the tapestry," said he to the crier, "has the virtue you assign it, I shall not think forty purses too much, but shall make you a present besides." "Sir," replied the crier, "I have told you the truth; and it is an easy matter to convince you of it, as soon as you have made the bargain for forty purses, on condition I show you the experiment. But, as I suppose you have not so much about you, and to receive them I must go with you to your khan, where you lodge, with the leave of the master of the shop, we will go into the back shop, and I will spread the tapestry; and when we have both sat down, and you have formed the wish to be transported into your apartment of the khan, if we are not transported thither it shall be no bargain, and you shall be at your liberty. As to your present, though I am paid for my trouble by the seller, I shall receive it as a favor, and be very much obliged to you, and thankful."

On the credit of the crier, the Prince accepted the conditions, and concluded the bargain; and, having got the master's leave, they went into his back shop; they both sat down on it, and as soon as the Prince formed his wish to be transported into his apartment at the khan he presently found himself and the crier there; and, as he wanted not a more sufficient proof of the virtue of the tapestry, he counted the crier out forty pieces of gold, and gave him twenty pieces for himself.

In this manner Prince Houssain became the possessor of the tapestry, and was overjoyed that at his arrival at Bisnagar he had found so rare a piece, which he never disputed would gain him the hand of Nouronnihar. In short, he looked upon it as an impossible thing for the Princes his younger brothers to meet with anything to be compared with it. It was in his power, by sitting on his tapestry, to be at the place of meeting that very day; but, as he was obliged to stay there for his brothers, as they had agreed, and as he was curious to see the King of Bisnagar and his Court, and to inform himself of the strength, laws, customs, and religion of the kingdom, he chose to make a longer abode there, and to spend some months in satisfying his curiosity.

Prince Houssain might have made a longer abode in the kingdom and Court of Bisnagar, but he was so eager to be nearer the Princess that, spreading the tapestry, he and the officer he had brought with him sat down, and as soon as he had formed his wish were transported to the inn at which he and his brothers were to meet, and where he passed for a merchant till they came.

Prince Ali, Prince Houssain's second brother, who designed to travel into Persia, took the road, having three days after he parted with his brothers joined a caravan, and after four days' travel arrived at Schiraz, which was the capital of the kingdom of Persia. Here he passed for a jeweler.

The next morning Prince Ali, who traveled only for his pleasure, and had brought nothing but just necessaries along with him, after he had dressed himself, took a walk into that part of the town which they at Schiraz called the bezestein.

Among all the criers who passed backward and forward with several sorts of goods, offering to sell them, he was not a little surprised to see one who held an ivory telescope in his hand of about a foot in length and the thickness of a man's thumb, and cried it at thirty purses. At first he thought the crier mad, and to inform himself went to a shop, and said to the merchant, who stood at the door: "Pray, sir, is not that man" (pointing to the crier who cried the ivory perspective glass at thirty purses) "mad? If he is not, I am very much deceived."

"Indeed, sir," answered the merchant, "he was in his right senses yesterday; I can assure you he is one of the ablest criers we have, and the most employed of any when anything valuable is to be sold. And if he cries the ivory perspective glass at thirty purses it must be worth as much or more, on some account or other. He will come by presently, and we will call him, and you shall be satisfied; in the meantime sit down on my sofa, and rest yourself."

Prince Ali accepted the merchant's obliging offer, and presently afterward the crier passed by. The merchant called him by his name, and, pointing to the Prince, said to him: "Tell that gentleman, who asked me if you were in your right senses, what you mean by crying that ivory perspective glass, which seems not to be worth much, at thirty purses. I should be very much amazed myself if I did not know you." The crier, addressing himself to Prince Ali, said: "Sir, you are not the only person that takes me for a madman on account of this perspective glass. You shall judge yourself whether I am or no, when I have told you its property and I hope you will value it at as high a price as those I have showed it to already, who had as bad an opinion of me as you.

"First, sir," pursued the crier, presenting the ivory pipe to the Prince, "observe that this pipe is furnished with a glass at both ends; and consider that by looking through one of them you see whatever object you wish to behold." "I am," said the Prince, "ready to make you all imaginable reparation for the scandal I have thrown on you if you will make the truth of what you advance appear," and as he had the ivory pipe in his hand, after he had looked at the two glasses he said: "Show me at which of these ends I must look that I may be satisfied." The crier presently showed him, and he looked through, wishing at the same time to see the Sultan his father, whom he immediately beheld in perfect health, set on his throne, in the midst of his council. Afterward, as there was nothing in the world so dear to him, after the Sultan, as the Princess Nouronnihar, he wished to see her; and saw her at her toilet laughing, and in a pleasant humor, with her women about her.

Prince Ali wanted no other proof to be persuaded that this perspective glass was the most valuable thing in the world, and believed that if he should neglect to purchase it he should never meet again with such another rarity. He therefore took the crier with him to the khan where he lodged, and counted him out the money, and received the perspective glass.

Prince Ali was overjoyed at his bargain, and persuaded himself that, as his brothers would not be able to meet with anything so rare and admirable, the Princess Nouronnihar would be the recompense of his fatigue and trouble; that he thought of nothing but visiting the Court of Persia incognito, and seeing whatever was curious in Schiraz and thereabouts, till the caravan with which he came returned back to the Indies. As soon as the caravan was ready to set out, the Prince joined them, and arrived happily without any accident or trouble, otherwise than the length of the journey and fatigue of traveling, at the place of rendezvous, where he found Prince Houssain, and both waited for Prince Ahmed.

Prince Ahmed, who took the road of Samarcand, the next day after his arrival there went, as his brothers had done, into the bezestein, where he had not walked long but heard a crier, who had an artificial apple in his hand, cry it at five and thirty purses; upon which he stopped the crier, and said to him: "Let me see that apple, and tell me what virtue and extraordinary properties it has, to be valued at so high a rate." "Sir," said the crier, giving it into his hand, "if you look at the outside of this apple, it is very worthless, but if you consider its properties, virtues, and the great use and benefit it is to mankind, you will say it is no price for it, and that he who possesses it is master of a great treasure. In short, it cures all sick persons of the most mortal diseases; and if the patient is dying it will recover him immediately and restore him to perfect health; and this is done after the easiest manner in the world, which is by the patient's smelling the apple."

"If I may believe you," replied Prince Ahmed, "the virtues of this apple are wonderful, and it is invaluable; but what ground have I, for all you tell me, to be persuaded of the truth of this matter?" "Sir," replied the crier, "the thing is known and averred by the whole city of Samarcand; but, without going any further, ask all these merchants you see here, and hear what they say. You will find several of them will tell you they had not been alive this day if they had not made use of this excellent remedy. And, that you may better comprehend what it is, I must tell you it is the fruit of the study and experiments of a celebrated philosopher of this city, who applied himself all his lifetime to the study and knowledge of the virtues of

401

plants and minerals, and at last attained to this composition, by which he performed such surprising cures in this town as will never be forgot, but died suddenly himself, before he could apply his sovereign remedy, and left his wife and a great many young children behind him, in very indifferent circumstances, who, to support her family and provide for her children, is resolved to sell it."

While the crier informed Prince Ahmed of the virtues of the artificial apple, a great many persons came about them and confirmed what he said; and one among the rest said he had a friend dangerously ill, whose life was despaired of; and that was a favorable opportunity to show Prince Ahmed the experiment. Upon which Prince Ahmed told the crier he would give him forty purses if he cured the sick person.

The crier, who had orders to sell it at that price, said to Prince Ahmed: "Come, sir, let us go and make the experiment, and the apple shall be yours; and I can assure you that it will always have the desired effect." In short, the experiment succeeded, and the Prince, after he had counted out to the crier forty purses, and he had delivered the apple to him, waited patiently for the first caravan that should return to the Indies, and arrived in perfect health at the inn where the Princes Houssain and Ali waited for him.

When the Princes met they showed each other their treasures, and immediately saw through the glass that the Princess was dying. They then sat down on the carpet, wished themselves with her, and were there in a moment.

Prince Ahmed no sooner perceived himself in Nouronnihar's chamber than he rose off the tapestry, as did also the other two Princes, and went to the bedside, and put the apple under her nose; some moments after the Princess opened her eyes, and turned her head from one side to another, looking at the persons who stood about her; and then rose up in the bed, and asked to be dressed, just as if she had waked out of a sound sleep. Her women having presently informed her, in a manner that showed their joy, that she was obliged to the three Princes for the sudden recovery of her health, and particularly to Prince Ahmed, she immediately expressed her joy to see them, and thanked them all together, and afterward Prince Ahmed in particular.

While the Princess was dressing the Princes went to throw themselves at the Sultan their father's feet, and pay their respects to him. But when they came before him they found he had been informed of their arrival by the chief of the Princess's eunuchs, and by what means the Princess had been perfectly cured. The Sultan received and embraced them with the greatest joy, both for their return and the recovery of the Princess his niece, whom he loved as well as if she had been his own daughter, and who had been given over by the physicians. After the usual ceremonies and compliments the Princes presented each his rarity: Prince Houssain his tapestry, which he had taken care not to leave behind him in the Princess's chamber; Prince Ali his ivory perspective glass, and Prince Ahmed his artificial apple; and after each had commended their present, when they put it into the Sultan's hands, they begged of him to pronounce their fate, and declare to which of them he would give the Princess Nouronnihar for a wife, according to his promise.

The Sultan of the Indies, having heard, without interrupting them, all that the Princes could represent further about their rarities, and being well informed of what had happened in relation to the Princess Nouronnihar's cure, remained some time silent, as if he were thinking on what answer he should make. At last he broke the silence, and said to them: "I would declare for one of you children with a great deal of pleasure if I could do it with justice; but consider whether I can do it or no. 'Tis true, Prince Ahmed, the Princess my niece is obliged to your artificial apple for her cure; but I must ask you whether or no you could have been so serviceable to her if you had not known by Prince Ali's perspective glass the danger she was in, and if Prince Houssain's tapestry had not brought you so soon. Your perspective glass, Prince Ali, informed you and your brothers that you were like to lose the Princess your cousin, and there you must own a great obligation.

"You must also grant that that knowledge would have been of no service without the artificial apple and the tapestry. And lastly, Prince Houssain, the Princess would be very ungrateful if she should not show her acknowledgment of the service of your tapestry, which was so necessary a means toward her cure. But consider, it would have been of little use if you had not been acquainted with the Princess's illness by Prince Ali's glass, and Prince Ahmed had not applied his artificial apple. Therefore, as neither tapestry, ivory perspective glass, nor artificial apple have the least preference one before the other, but, on the contrary, there's a perfect equality, I cannot grant the Princess to any one of you; and the only fruit you have reaped from your travels is the glory of having equally contributed to restore her health.

"If all this be true," added the Sultan, "you see that I must have recourse to other means to determine certainly in the choice I ought to make among you; and that, as there is time enough between this and night, I'll do it to-day. Go and get each of you a bow and arrow, and repair to the great plain, where they exercise horses. I'll soon come to you, and declare I will give the Princess Nouronnihar to him that shoots the farthest."

The three Princes had nothing to say against the decision of the Sultan. When they were out of his presence they each provided themselves with a bow and arrow, which they delivered to one of their officers, and went to the plain appointed, followed by a great concourse of people.

The Sultan did not make them wait long for him, and as soon as he arrived Prince Houssain, as the eldest, took his bow and arrow and shot first; Prince Ali shot next, and much beyond him; and Prince Ahmed last of all, but it so happened that nobody could see where his arrow fell; and, notwithstanding all the diligence that was used by himself and everybody else, it was not to be found far or near. And though it was believed that he shot the farthest, and that he therefore deserved the Princess Nouronnihar, it was, however, necessary that his arrow should be found to make the matter more evident and certain; and, notwithstanding his remonstrance, the Sultan judged in favor of Prince Ali, and gave orders for preparations to be made for the wedding, which was celebrated a few days after with great magnificence.

Prince Houssain would not honor the feast with his presence. In short, his grief was so violent and insupportable that he left the Court, and renounced all right of succession to the crown, to turn hermit.

Prince Ahmed, too, did not come to Prince Ali's and the Princess Nouronnihar's wedding any more than his brother Houssain, but did not renounce the world as he had done. But, as he could not imagine what had become of his arrow, he stole away from his attendants and resolved to search after it, that he might not have anything to reproach himself with. With this intent he went to the place where the Princes Houssain's and Ali's were gathered up, and, going straight forward from there, looking carefully on both sides of him, he went so far that at last he began to think his labor was all in vain; but yet he could not help going forward till he came to some steep craggy rocks, which were bounds to his journey, and were situated in a barren country, about four leagues distant from where he set out.

II

When Prince Ahmed came pretty nigh to these rocks he perceived an arrow, which he gathered up, looked earnestly at it, and was in the greatest astonishment to find it was the same he shot away. "Certainly," said he to himself, "neither I nor any man living could shoot an arrow so far," and, finding it laid flat, not sticking into the ground, he judged that it rebounded against the rock. "There must be some mystery in this," said he to himself again, "and it may be advantageous to me. Perhaps fortune, to make me amends for depriving me of what I thought the greatest happiness, may have reserved a greater blessing for my comfort."

As these rocks were full of caves and some of those caves were deep, the Prince entered into one, and, looking about, cast his eyes on an iron door, which seemed to have no

405

lock, but he feared it was fastened. However, thrusting against it, it opened, and discovered an easy descent, but no steps, which he walked down with his arrow in his hand. At first he thought he was going into a dark, obscure place, but presently a quite different light succeeded that which he came out of, and, entering into a large, spacious place, at about fifty or sixty paces distant, he perceived a magnificent palace, which he had not then time enough to look at. At the same time a lady of majestic port and air advanced as far as the porch, attended by a large troop of ladies, so finely dressed and beautiful that it was difficult to distinguish which was the mistress.

As soon as Prince Ahmed perceived the lady, he made all imaginable haste to go and pay his respects; and the lady, on her part, seeing him coming, prevented him from addressing his discourse to her first, but said to him: "Come nearer, Prince Ahmed, you are welcome."

It was no small surprise to the Prince to hear himself named in a place he had never heard of, though so nigh to his father's capital, and he could not comprehend how he should be known to a lady who was a stranger to him. At last he returned the lady's compliment by throwing himself at her feet, and, rising up again, said to her:

"Madam, I return you a thousand thanks for the assurance you give me of a welcome to a place where I believed my imprudent curiosity had made me penetrate too far. But, madam, may I, without being guilty of ill manners, dare to ask you by what adventure you know me? and how you, who live in the same neighborhood with me, should be so great a stranger to me?"

"Prince," said the lady, "let us go into the hall, there I will gratify you in your request."

After these words the lady led Prince Ahmed into the hall. Then she sat down on a sofa, and when the Prince by her entreaty had done the same she said: "You are surprised, you say, that I should know you and not be known by you, but you will be no longer surprised when I inform you who I am. You are undoubtedly sensible that your religion teaches you to believe that the world is inhabited by genies as well as men. I am the daughter of one of the most powerful and distinguished genies, and my name is Paribanou. The only thing that I have to add is, that you seemed to me worthy of a more happy fate than that of possessing the Princess Nouronnihar; and, that you might attain to it, I was present when you drew your arrow, and foresaw it would not go beyond Prince Houssain's. I took it in the air, and gave it the necessary motion to strike against the rocks near which you found it, and I tell you that it lies in your power to make use of the favorable opportunity which presents itself to make you happy."

As the Fairy Paribanou pronounced these last words with a different tone, and looked, at the same time, tenderly upon Prince Ahmed, with a modest blush on her cheeks, it was no hard matter for the Prince to comprehend what happiness she meant. He presently considered that the Princess Nouronnihar could never be his and that the Fairy Paribanou excelled her infinitely in beauty, agreeableness, wit, and, as much as he could conjecture by the magnificence of the palace, in immense riches. He blessed the moment that he thought of seeking after his arrow a second time, and, yielding to his love, "Madam," replied he, "should I all my life have the happiness of being your slave, and the admirer of the many charms which ravish my soul, I should think myself the most blessed of men. Pardon in me the boldness which inspires me to ask this favor, and don't refuse to admit me into your Court, a prince who is entirely devoted to you."

"Prince," answered the Fairy, "will you not pledge your faith to me, as well as I give mine to you?" "Yes, madam," replied the Prince, in an ecstacy of joy; "what can I do better, and with greater pleasure? Yes, my sultaness, my queen, I'll give you my heart without the least reserve." "Then," answered the Fairy, "you are my husband, and I am your wife. But, as I suppose," pursued she, "that you have eaten nothing to-day, a slight repast shall be served up for you, while preparations are making for our wedding feast at night, and then I will show you the apartments of my palace, and you shall judge if this hall is not the meanest part of it."

Some of the Fairy's women, who came into the hall with them, and guessed her intentions, went immediately out, and returned presently with some excellent meats and wines.

When Prince Ahmed had ate and drunk as much as he cared for, the Fairy Paribanou carried him through all the apartments, where he saw diamonds, rubies, emeralds and all sorts of fine jewels, intermixed with pearls, agate, jasper, porphyry, and all sorts of the most precious marbles. But, not to mention the richness of the furniture, which was inestimable, there was such a profuseness throughout that the Prince, instead of ever having seen anything like it, owned that he could not have imagined that there was anything in the world that could come up to it. "Prince," said the Fairy, "if you admire my palace so much, which, indeed, is very beautiful, what would you say to the palaces of the chief of our genies, which are much more beautiful, spacious, and magnificent? I could also charm you with my gardens, but we will let that alone till another time. Night draws near, and it will be time to go to supper."

The next hall which the Fairy led the Prince into, and where the cloth was laid for the feast, was the last apartment the Prince had not seen, and not in the least inferior to the others. At his entrance into it he admired the infinite number of sconces of wax candles perfumed with amber, the multitude of which, instead of being confused, were placed with so just a symmetry as formed an agreeable and pleasant sight. A large side table was set out with all sorts of gold plate, so finely wrought that the workmanship was much more valuable than the weight of the gold. Several choruses of beautiful women richly dressed, and whose voices were ravishing, began a concert, accompanied with all sorts of the most harmonious instruments; and when they were set down at table the Fairy Paribanou took care to help Prince Ahmed to the most delicate meats, which she named as she invited him to eat of them, and which the Prince found to be so exquisitely nice that he commended them with exaggeration, and said that the entertainment far surpassed those of man. He found also the same excellence in the wines, which neither he nor the Fairy tasted of till the dessert was served up, which consisted of the choicest sweetmeats and fruits.

The wedding feast was continued the next day, or, rather, the days following the celebration were a continual feast.

At the end of six months Prince Ahmed, who always loved and honored the Sultan his father, conceived a great desire to know how he was, and that desire could not be satisfied without his going to see; he told the Fairy of it, and desired she would give him leave.

"Prince," said she, "go when you please. But first, don't take it amiss that I give you some advice how you shall behave yourself where you are going. First, I don't think it proper for you to tell the Sultan your father of our marriage, nor of my quality, nor the place where you have been. Beg of him to be satisfied in knowing you are happy, and desire no more; and let him know that the sole end of your visit is to make him easy, and inform him of your fate."

She appointed twenty gentlemen, well mounted and equipped, to attend him. When all was ready Prince Ahmed took his leave of the Fairy, embraced her, and renewed his promise to return soon. Then his horse, which was most finely caparisoned, and was as beautiful a creature as any in the Sultan of Indies' stables, was led to him, and he mounted him with an extraordinary grace; and, after he had bid her a last adieu, set forward on his journey.

As it was not a great way to his father's capital, Prince Ahmed soon arrived there. The people, glad to see him again, received him with acclamations of joy, and followed him in crowds to the Sultan's apartment. The Sultan received and embraced him with great joy, complaining at the same time, with a fatherly tenderness, of the affliction his long absence had been to him, which he said was the more grievous for that, fortune having decided in favor of Prince Ali his brother, he was afraid he might have committed some rash action.

The Prince told a story of his adventures without speaking of the Fairy, whom he said that he must not mention, and ended: "The only favor I ask of your Majesty is to give me leave to come often and pay you my respects, and to know how you do."

"Son," answered the Sultan of the Indies, "I cannot refuse you the leave you ask me; but I should much rather you would resolve to stay with me; at least tell me where I may send to you if you should fail to come, or when I may think your presence necessary." "Sir," replied Prince Ahmed, "what your Majesty asks of me is part of the mystery I spoke to your Majesty of. I beg of you to give me leave to remain silent on this head, for I shall come so frequently that I am afraid that I shall sooner be thought troublesome than be accused of negligence in my duty."

The Sultan of the Indies pressed Prince Ahmed no more, but said to him: "Son, I penetrate no farther into your secrets, but leave you at your liberty; but can tell you that you could not do me a greater pleasure than to come, and by your presence restore to me the joy I have not felt this long time, and that you shall always be welcome when you come, without interrupting your business or pleasure."

Prince Ahmed stayed but three days at the Sultan his father's Court, and the fourth returned to the Fairy Paribanou, who did not expect him so soon.

A month after Prince Ahmed's return from paying a visit to his father, as the Fairy Paribanou had observed that the Prince, since the time that he gave her an account of his journey, his discourse with his father, and the leave he asked to go and see him often, had never talked of the Sultan, as if there had been no such person in the world, whereas before he was always speaking of him, she thought he forebore on her account; therefore she took an opportunity to say to him one day: "Prince, tell me, have you forgot the Sultan your father? Don't you remember the promise you made to go and see him often? For my part I have not forgot what you told me at your return, and so put you in mind of it, that you may not be long before you acquit yourself of your promise."

So Prince Ahmed went the next morning with the same attendance as before, but much finer, and himself more magnificently mounted, equipped, and dressed, and was received by the Sultan with the same joy and satisfaction. For several months he constantly paid his visits, always in a richer and finer equipage.

At last some viziers, the Sultan's favorites, who judged of Prince Ahmed's grandeur and power by the figure he cut, made the Sultan jealous of his son, saying it was to be feared he might inveigle himself into the people's favor and dethrone him.

The Sultan of the Indies was so far from thinking that Prince Ahmed could be capable of so pernicious a design as his favorites would make him believe that he said to them: "You are mistaken; my son loves me, and I am certain of his tenderness and fidelity, as I have given him no reason to be disgusted."

But the favorites went on abusing Prince Ahmed till the Sultan said: "Be it as it will, I don't believe my son Ahmed is so wicked as you would persuade me he is; how ever, I am obliged to you for your good advice, and don't dispute but that it proceeds from your good intentions."

The Sultan of the Indies said this that his favorites might not know the impressions their discourse had made on his mind; which had so alarmed him that he resolved to have Prince Ahmed watched unknown to his grand vizier. So he sent for a female magician, who was introduced by a back door into his apartment. "Go immediately," he said, "and follow my son, and watch him so well as to find out where he retires, and bring me word."

The magician left the Sultan, and, knowing the place where Prince Ahmed found his arrow, went immediately thither, and hid herself near the rocks, so that nobody could see her.

The next morning Prince Ahmed set out by daybreak, without taking leave either of the Sultan or any of his Court, according to custom. The magician, seeing him coming, followed him with her eyes, till on a sudden she lost sight of him and his attendants.

As the rocks were very steep and craggy, they were an insurmountable barrier, so that the magician judged that there were but two things for it: either that the Prince retired into some cavern, or an abode of genies or fairies. Thereupon she came out of the place where she was hid and went directly to the hollow way, which she traced till she came to the farther end, looking carefully about on all sides; but, notwithstanding all her diligence, could perceive no opening, not so much as the iron gate which Prince Ahmed discovered, which was to be seen and opened to none but men, and only to such whose presence was agreeable to the Fairy Paribanou.

The magician, who saw it was in vain for her to search any farther, was obliged to be satisfied with the discovery she had made, and returned to give the Sultan an account.

The Sultan was very well pleased with the magician's conduct, and said to her: "Do you as you think fit; I'll wait patiently the event of your promises," and to encourage her made her a present of a diamond of great value.

As Prince Ahmed had obtained the Fairy Paribanou's leave to go to the Sultan of the Indies' Court once a month, he never failed, and the magician, knowing the time, went a day or two before to the foot of the rock where she lost sight of the Prince and his attendants, and waited there.

The next morning Prince Ahmed went out, as usual, at the iron gate, with the same attendants as before, and passed by the magician, whom he knew not to be such, and, seeing her lie with her head against the rock, and complaining as if she were in great pain, he pitied her, turned his horse about, went to her, and asked her what was the matter with her, and what he could do to ease her.

The artful sorceress looked at the Prince in a pitiful manner, without ever lifting up her head, and answered in broken

412

words and sighs, as if she could hardly fetch her breath, that she was going to the capital city, but on the way thither she was taken with so violent a fever that her strength failed her, and she was forced to lie down where he saw her, far from any habitation, and without any hopes of assistance.

"Good woman," replied Prince Ahmed, "you are not so far from help as you imagine. I am ready to assist you, and convey you where you will meet with a speedy cure; only get up, and let one of my people take you behind him."

At these words the magician, who pretended sickness only to know where the Prince lived and what he did, refused not the charitable offer he made her, and that her actions might correspond with her words she made many pretended vain endeavors to get up. At the same time two of the Prince's attendants, alighting off their horses, helped her up, and set her behind another, and mounted their horses again, and followed the Prince, who turned back to the iron gate, which was opened by one of his retinue who rode before. And when he came into the outward court of the Fairy, without dismounting himself, he sent to tell her he wanted to speak with her.

The Fairy Paribanou came with all imaginable haste, not knowing what made Prince Ahmed return so soon, who, not giving her time to ask him the reason, said: "Princess, I desire you would have compassion on this good woman," pointing to the magician, who was held up by two of his retinue. "I found her in the condition you see her in, and promised her the assistance she stands in need of, and am persuaded that you, out of your own goodness, as well as upon my entreaty, will not abandon her."

The Fairy Paribanou, who had her eyes fixed upon the pretended sick woman all the time that the Prince was talking to her, ordered two of her women who followed her to take her from the two men that held her, and carry her into an apartment of the palace, and take as much care of her as she would herself.

While the two women executed the Fairy's commands, she went up to Prince Ahmed, and, whispering in his ear, said:

"Prince, this woman is not so sick as she pretends to be; and I am very much mistaken if she is not an impostor, who will be the cause of a great trouble to you. But don't be concerned, let what will be devised against you; be persuaded that I will deliver you out of all the snares that shall be laid for you. Go and pursue your journey."

This discourse of the Fairy's did not in the least frighten Prince Ahmed. "My Princess," said he, "as I do not remember I ever did or designed anybody an injury, I cannot believe anybody can have a thought of doing me one, but if they have I shall not, nevertheless, forbear doing good whenever I have an opportunity." Then he went back to his father's palace.

In the meantime the two women carried the magician into a very fine apartment, richly furnished. First they sat her down upon a sofa, with her back supported with a cushion of gold brocade, while they made a bed on the same sofa before her, the quilt of which was finely embroidered with silk, the sheets of the finest linen, and the coverlet cloth-of-gold. When they had put her into bed (for the old sorceress pretended that her fever was so violent she could not help herself in the least) one of the women went out, and returned soon again with a china dish in her hand, full of a certain liquor, which she presented to the magician, while the other helped her to sit up. "Drink this liquor," said she; "it is the Water of the Fountain of Lions, and a sovereign remedy against all fevers whatsoever. You will find the effect of it in less than an hour's time."

The magician, to dissemble the better, took it after a great deal of entreaty; but at last she took the china dish, and, holding back her head, swallowed down the liquor. When she was laid down again the two women covered her up. "Lie quiet," said she who brought her the china cup, "and get a little sleep if you can. We'll leave you, and hope to find you perfectly cured when we come again an hour hence."

The two women came again at the time they said they should, and found the magician up and dressed, and sitting upon the sofa. "Oh, admirable potion!" she said: "it has wrought its cure much sooner than you told me it would, and I shall be able to prosecute my journey."

The two women, who were fairies as well as their mistress, after they had told the magician how glad they were that she was cured so soon, walked before her, and conducted her through several apartments, all more noble than that wherein she lay, into a large hall, the most richly and magnificently furnished of all the palace.

Fairy Paribanou sat in this hall on a throne of massive gold, enriched with diamonds, rubies, and pearls of an extraordinary size, and attended on each hand by a great number of beautiful fairies, all richly clothed. At the sight of so much majesty, the magician was not only dazzled, but was so amazed that, after she had prostrated herself before the throne, she could not open her lips to thank the Fairy as she proposed. However, Paribanou saved her the trouble, and said to her: "Good woman, I am glad I had an opportunity to oblige you, and to see you are able to pursue your journey. I won't detain you, but perhaps you may not be displeased to see my palace; follow my women, and they will show it you."

Then the magician went back and related to the Sultan of the Indies all that had happened, and how very rich Prince Ahmed was since his marriage with the Fairy, richer than all the kings in the world, and how there was danger that he should come and take the throne from his father.

Though the Sultan of the Indies was very well persuaded that Prince Ahmed's natural disposition was good, yet he could not help being concerned at the discourse of the old sorceress, to whom, when she was taking her leave, he said: "I thank thee for the pains thou hast taken, and thy wholesome advice. I am so sensible of the great importance it is to me that I shall deliberate upon it in council."

Now the favorites advised that the Prince should be killed, but the magician advised differently: "Make him give you all kinds of wonderful things, by the Fairy's help, till she tires of him and sends him away. As, for example, every time your Majesty goes into the field, you are obliged to be at a great expense, not only in pavilions and tents for your army, but likewise in mules and camels to carry their baggage. Now, might not you engage him to use his interest with the Fairy to procure you a tent which might be carried in a man's hand, and which should be so large as to shelter your whole army against bad weather?"

When the magician had finished her speech, the Sultan asked his favorites if they had anything better to propose; and, finding them all silent, determined to follow the magician's advice, as the most reasonable and most agreeable to his mild government.

Next day the Sultan did as the magician had advised him, and asked for the pavilion.

Prince Ahmed never expected that the Sultan his father would have asked such a thing, which at first appeared so difficult, not to say impossible. Though he knew not absolutely how great the power of genies and fairies was, he doubted whether it extended so far as to compass such a tent as his father desired. At last he replied: "Though it is with the greatest reluctance imaginable, I will not fail to ask the favor of my wife your Majesty desires, but will not promise you to obtain it; and if I should not have the honor to come again to pay you my respects that shall be the sign that I have not had success. But beforehand, I desire you to forgive me, and consider that you yourself have reduced me to this extremity."

"Son," replied the Sultan of the Indies, "I should be very sorry if what I ask of you should cause me the displeasure of never seeing you more. I find you don't know the power a husband has over a wife; and yours would show that her love to you was very indifferent if she, with the power she has of a fairy, should refuse you so trifling a request as this I desire you to ask of her for my sake." The Prince went back, and was very sad for fear of offending the Fairy. She kept pressing him to tell her what was the matter, and at last he said: "Madam, you may have observed that hitherto I have been content with your love, and have never asked you any other favor. Consider then, I conjure you, that it is not I, but the Sultan my father, who indiscreetly, or at least I think so, begs of you a pavilion large enough to shelter him, his Court, and army from the violence of the weather, and which a man may carry in his hand. But remember it is the Sultan my father asks this favor."

"Prince," replied the Fairy, smiling, "I am sorry that so small a matter should disturb you, and make you so uneasy as you appeared to me."

Then the Fairy sent for her treasurer, to whom, when she came, she said: "Nourgihan"--which was her name--"bring me the largest pavilion in my treasury." Nourgiham returned presently with the pavilion, which she could not only hold in her hand, but in the palm of her hand when she shut her fingers, and presented it to her mistress, who gave it to Prince Ahmed to look at.

When Prince Ahmed saw the pavilion which the Fairy called the largest in her treasury, he fancied she had a mind to jest with him, and thereupon the marks of his surprise appeared presently in his countenance; which Paribanou perceiving burst out laughing. "What! Prince," cried she, "do you think I jest with you? You'll see presently that I am in earnest. Nourgihan," said she to her treasurer, taking the tent out of Prince Ahmed's hands, "go and set it up, that the Prince may judge whether it may be large enough for the Sultan his father."

The treasurer went immediately with it out of the palace, and carried it a great way off; and when she had set it up one end reached to the very palace; at which time the Prince, thinking it small, found it large enough to shelter two greater armies than that of the Sultan his father's, and then said to Paribanou: "I ask my Princess a thousand pardons for my incredulity; after what I have seen I believe there is nothing impossible to you." "You see," said the Fairy, "that the pavilion is larger than what your father may have occasion for; for you must know that it has one property--that it is larger or smaller according to the army it is to cover."

The treasurer took down the tent again, and brought it to the Prince, who took it, and, without staying any longer than till the next day, mounted his horse, and went with the same attendants to the Sultan his father.

The Sultan, who was persuaded that there could not be any such thing as such a tent as he asked for, was in a great surprise at the Prince's diligence. He took the tent and after he had admired its smallness his amazement was so great that he could not recover himself. When the tent was set up in the great plain, which we have before mentioned, he found it large enough to shelter an army twice as large as he could bring into the field.

But the Sultan was not yet satisfied. "Son," said he, "I have already expressed to you how much I am obliged to you for the present of the tent you have procured me; that I look upon it as the most valuable thing in all my treasury. But you must do one thing more for me, which will be every whit as agreeable to me. I am informed that the Fairy, your spouse, makes use of a certain water, called the Water of the Fountain of Lions, which cures all sorts of fevers, even the most dangerous, and, as I am perfectly well persuaded my health is dear to you, I don't doubt but you will ask her for a bottle of that water for me, and bring it me as a sovereign medicine, which I may make use of when I have occasion. Do me this other important piece of service, and thereby complete the duty of a good son toward a tender father."

The Prince returned and told the Fairy what his father had said; "There's a great deal of wickedness in this demand?" she answered, "as you will understand by what I am going to tell you. The Fountain of Lions is situated in the middle of a court of a great castle, the entrance into which is guarded by four fierce lions, two of which sleep alternately, while the other two are awake. But don't let that frighten you: I'll give you means to pass by them without any danger."

The Fairy Paribanou was at that time very hard at work, and, as she had several clews of thread by her, she took up one, and, presenting it to Prince Ahmed, said: "First take this clew of thread. I'll tell you presently the use of it. In the second place, you must have two horses; one you must ride yourself, and the other you must lead, which must be loaded with a sheep cut into four quarters, that must be killed to-day. In the third place, you must be provided with a bottle, which I will give you, to bring the water in. Set out early to-morrow morning, and when you have passed the iron gate throw the clew of thread before you, which will roll till it comes to the gates of the castle. Follow it, and when it stops, as the gates will be open, you will see the four lions: the two that are awake will, by their roaring, wake the other two, but don't be frightened, but throw each of them a quarter of mutton, and then clap spurs to your horse and ride to the fountain; fill your bottle without alighting, and then return with the same expedition. The lions will be so busy eating they will let you pass by them."

Prince Ahmed set out the next morning at the time appointed by the Fairy, and followed her directions exactly. When he arrived at the gates of the castle he distributed the quarters of mutton among the four lions, and, passing through the midst of them bravely, got to the fountain, filled his bottle, and returned back as safe and sound as he went. When he had gone a little distance from the castle gates he turned him about, and, perceiving two of the lions coming after him, he drew his sabre and prepared himself for defense. But as he went forward he saw one of them turned out of the road at some distance, and showed by his head and tail that he did not come to do him any harm, but only to go before him, and that the other stayed behind to follow, he put his sword up again in its scabbard. Guarded in this manner, he arrived at the capital of the Indies, but the lions never left him till they had conducted him to the gates of the Sultan's palace; after which they returned the same way they came, though not without frightening all that saw them, for all they went in a very gentle manner and showed no fierceness.

A great many officers came to attend the Prince while he dismounted his horse, and afterward conducted him into the Sultan's apartment, who was at that time surrounded with his favorites. He approached toward the throne, laid the bottle at the Sultan's feet, and kissed the rich tapestry which covered his footstool, and then said:

"I have brought you, sir, the healthful water which your Majesty desired so much to keep among your other rarities in your treasury, but at the same time wish you such extraordinary health as never to have occasion to make use of it."

After the Prince had made an end of his compliment the Sultan placed him on his right hand, and then said to him: "Son, I am very much obliged to you for this valuable present, as also for the great danger you have exposed yourself to upon my account (which I have been informed of by a magician who knows the Fountain of Lions); but do me the pleasure," continued he, "to inform me by what address, or, rather, by what incredible power, you have been secured."

"Sir," replied Prince Ahmed, "I have no share in the compliment your Majesty is pleased to make me; all the honor is due to the Fairy my spouse, whose good advice I followed." Then he informed the Sultan what those directions were, and by the relation of this his expedition let him know how well he had behaved himself. When he had done the Sultan, who showed outwardly all the demonstrations of great joy, but secretly became more jealous, retired into an inward apartment, where he sent for the magician.

The magician, at her arrival, saved the Sultan the trouble to tell her of the success of Prince Ahmed's journey, which she had heard of before she came, and therefore was prepared with an infallible means, as she pretended. This means she communicated to the Sultan who declared it the next day to the Prince, in the midst of all his courtiers, in these words: "Son," said he, "I have one thing more to ask of you, after which I shall expect nothing more from your obedience, nor your interest with your wife. This request is, to bring me a man not above a foot and a half high, and whose beard is thirty feet long who carries a bar of iron upon his shoulders of five hundredweight, which he uses as a quarterstaff."

Prince Ahmed, who did not believe that there was such a man in the world as his father described, would gladly have excused himself; but the Sultan persisted in his demand, and told him the Fairy could do more incredible things.

The next day the Prince returned to his dear Paribanou, to whom he told his father's new demand, which, he said, he looked upon to be a thing more impossible than the two first; "for," added he, "I cannot imagine there can be such a man in the world; without doubt, he has a mind to try whether or no I am so silly as to go about it, or he has a design on my ruin. In short, how can he suppose that I should lay hold of a man so well armed, though he is but little? What arms can I make use of to reduce him to my will? If there are any means, I beg you will tell them, and let me come off with honor this time."

"Don't affright yourself, Prince," replied the Fairy; "you ran a risk in fetching the Water of the Fountain of Lions for your father, but there's no danger in finding out this man, who is my brother Schaibar, but is so far from being like me, though we both had the same father, that he is of so violent a nature that nothing can prevent his giving cruel marks of his resentment for a slight offense; yet, on the other hand, is so good as to oblige anyone in whatever they desire. He is made exactly as the Sultan your father has described him, and has no other arms than a bar of iron of five hundred pounds weight, without which he never stirs, and which makes him respected. I'll send for him, and you shall judge of the truth of what I tell you; but be sure to prepare yourself against being frightened at his extraordinary figure when you see him." "What! my Queen," replied Prince Ahmed, "do you say Schaibar is your brother? Let him be never so ugly or deformed I shall be so far from being frightened at the sight of him that, as our brother, I shall honor and love him."

The Fairy ordered a gold chafing-dish to be set with a fire in it under the porch of her palace, with a box of the same metal, which was a present to her, out of which taking a perfume, and throwing it into the fire, there arose a thick cloud of smoke.

Some moments after the Fairy said to Prince Ahmed: "See, there comes my brother." The Prince immediately perceived Schaibar coming gravely with his heavy bar on his shoulder, his long beard, which he held up before him, and a pair of thick mustachios, which he tucked behind his ears and almost covered his face; his eyes were very small and deep-set in his head, which was far from being of the smallest size, and on his head he wore a grenadier's cap; besides all this, he was very much hump-backed.

If Prince Ahmed had not known that Schaibar was Paribanou's brother, he would not have been able to have looked at him without fear, but, knowing first who he was, he stood by the Fairy without the least concern.

Schaibar, as he came forward, looked at the Prince earnestly enough to have chilled his blood in his veins, and asked Paribanou, when he first accosted her, who that man was. To which she replied: "He is my husband, brother. His name is Ahmed; he is son to the Sultan of the Indies. The reason why I did not invite you to my wedding was I was unwilling to divert you from an expedition you were engaged in, and from which I heard with pleasure you returned victorious, and so took the liberty now to call for you."

At these words, Schaibar, looking on Prince Ahmed favorably, said: "Is there anything else, sister, wherein I can serve him? It is enough for me that he is your husband to engage me to do for him whatever he desires." "The Sultan, his father," replied Paribanou, "has a curiosity to see you, and I desire he may be your guide to the Sultan's Court." "He needs but lead me the way I'll follow him." "Brother," replied Paribanou, "it is too late to go to-day, therefore stay till to-morrow morning; and in the meantime I'll inform you of all that has passed between the Sultan of the Indies and Prince Ahmed since our marriage."

The next morning, after Schaibar had been informed of the affair, he and Prince Ahmed set out for the Sultan's Court. When they arrived at the gates of the capital the people no sooner saw Schaibar but they ran and hid themselves; and some shut up their shops and locked themselves up in their houses, while others, flying, communicated their fear to all they met, who stayed not to look behind them, but ran too; insomuch that Schaibar and Prince Ahmed, as they went along, found the streets all desolate till they came to the palaces where the porters, instead of keeping the gates, ran away too, so that the Prince and Schaibar advanced without any obstacle to the council-hall, where the Sultan was seated on his throne, and giving audience. Here likewise the ushers, at the approach of Schaibar, abandoned their posts, and gave them free admittance.

Schaibar went boldly and fiercely up to the throne, without waiting to be presented by Prince Ahmed, and accosted the Sultan of the Indies in these words: "Thou hast asked for me," said he; "see, here I am; what wouldst thou have with me?"

The Sultan, instead of answering him, clapped his hands before his eyes to avoid the sight of so terrible an object; at which uncivil and rude reception Schaibar was so much provoked, after he had given him the trouble to come so far, that he instantly lifted up his iron bar and killed him before Prince Ahmed could intercede in his behalf. All that he could do was to prevent his killing the grand vizier, who sat not far from him, representing to him that he had always given the Sultan his father good advice. "These are they, then," said Schaibar, "who gave him bad," and as he pronounced these words he killed all the other viziers and flattering favorites of the Sultan who were Prince Ahmed's enemies. Every time he struck he killed some one or other, and none escaped but they who were not so frightened as to stand staring and gaping, and who saved themselves by flight.

When this terrible execution was over Schaibar came out of the council-hall into the midst of the courtyard with the iron bar upon his shoulder, and, looking hard at the grand vizier, who owed his life to Prince Ahmed, he said: "I know here is a certain magician, who is a greater enemy of my brother-in-law than all these base favorites I have chastised. Let the magician be brought to me presently." The grand vizier immediately sent for her, and as soon as she was brought Schaibar said, at the time he fetched a stroke at her with his iron bar: "Take the

423

reward of thy pernicious counsel, and learn to feign sickness again."

After this he said: "This is not yet enough; I will use the whole town after the same manner if they do not immediately acknowledge Prince Ahmed, my brother-in-law, for their Sultan and the Sultan of the Indies." Then all that were there present made the air echo again with the repeated acclamations of: "Long life to Sultan Ahmed"; and immediately after he was proclaimed through the whole town. Schaibar made him be clothed in the royal vestments, installed him on the throne, and after he had caused all to swear homage and fidelity to him went and fetched his sister Paribanou, whom he brought with all the pomp and grandeur imaginable, and made her to be owned Sultaness of the Indies.

As for Prince Ali and Princess Nouronnihar, as they had no hand in the conspiracy against Prince Ahmed and knew nothing of any, Prince Ahmed assigned them a considerable province, with its capital, where they spent the rest of their lives. Afterwards he sent an officer to Prince Houssain to acquaint him with the change and make him an offer of which province he liked best; but that Prince thought himself so happy in his solitude that he bade the officer return the Sultan his brother thanks for the kindness he designed him, assuring him of his submission; and that the only favor he desired of him was to give him leave to live retired in the place he had made choice of for his retreat.

This abundance of material eventually led an enterprising publisher, the Chevalier Charles-Joseph de Mayer(1751-1825), to gather the best fairy tales of the times in a prodigious, forty-one volume anthology, entitled *Le Cabinet des Fées* [The Fairies' Cabinet], published in Amsterdam and Geneva between 1785 and 1789. *Le Cabinet* has the honor of being the first specialized fantasy imprint ever published.

But the writing was on the wall. Jacques Cazotte (1719-1792), who had started as a writer of *Féeries*, such as *La Patte du Chat* [The Cat's Paw] (1741) and *Les Mille et Une Fadaises* [A Thousand and One Silly Stories] (1742), soon tired of the increasingly precious and effete *Féeries* of later years, and eventually ended up writing much darker tales such as *Le Diable Amoureux* [The Devil In Love] (1772), in which a young nobleman conjured up a demon who assumed the shape of a beautiful woman.

In this fashion, the literary evolution of the *Féeries* paralleled that of French Royalty, with the decadence and corruption of Louis XV replacing the aristocratic grandeur of Louis XIV. Cazotte well embodied the transition between the *Contes de Fées* and a darker and grimmer *fantastique*.

Eventually, the French Revolution came and, in an act tantamount to a literary execution, guillotined the heads of, if not the fairies and the little people, but many of the people who had become so much associated with this *Ancien Régime* genre per excellence.